T0182519

MR. GARCIA

T L SWAN

 Arndell

Arndell

Keeperton Australia acknowledges that Aboriginal and Torres Strait Islander people are the Traditional Custodians and the first storytellers on the lands of which we live and work. We pay our respects to Elders past, present and emerging. We recognise their continuous connection to Country, water, skies and communities and honour more than 60,000 years of storytelling, culture and art.

Paperback ISBN: 9781923232020

Library of Congress Control Number: 2024936531

Printed in the United States of America

Sydney | Washington D.C. | London
www.keeperton.com

ALSO BY T L SWAN

SUGGESTED READING ORDER

The Mr. Series books can all be read as standalone books. However, for the best reading experience, we suggest the following reading order:

Mr. Masters
Mr. Spencer
Mr. Garcia
Mr. Prescott (Coming 2025)

ACKNOWLEDGMENTS

There are not enough words to express my
gratitude for this life that I get to live.
To be able to write books for a living is a dream come true.
But not just any books, I get to write exactly
what I want to, the stories that I love.

To my wonderful team,
Kellie, Christine, Alina, Keeley and Abbey.
Thank you for everything that you do for me,
you are so talented and so appreciated.
You keep me sane.

To my fabulous beta readers, you make me so much better. Vicki,
Am, Rachel, Nicole, Lisa K, Lisa D and Nadia.

To my home girls in the Swan Squad, I feel like I can do anything
with you girls in my corner.
Thanks for making me laugh every day.

My beautiful Mum who reads everything I write and gives me
never-ending support. I love you Mum, thank you xo

My beloved husband and three beautiful kids, thanks for putting
up with my workaholic ways.

And to you, the best most supportive reader family
in the entire world.

Thank you for everything, you have changed my life.

All my love,
Tee xoxo

GRATITUDE

The quality of being thankful; readiness to show appreciation for, and to return kindness.

DEDICATION

I would like to dedicate this book to the alphabet.
For those twenty-six letters have changed my life.

Within those twenty-six letters, I found myself
and live my dream.

Next time you say the alphabet
remember its power.

I do every day.

MR. GARCIA

DISCLAIMER

Sebastian Garcia is not the "sweet kind of guy".
If you are not into strong willed men, you will be
by the end of this book.
Enjoy!
XO

1

April

THE WHIRL of the traffic spins past at a deafening speed.

People, like ants, conform as they rush along the congested sidewalk.

Morning rush hour in London is always hectic. A fast-paced mecca filled with the busiest of the busy people, and I'm no different, rushing to get to my job at a coffee house.

I'm late, as usual, after studying into the early hours of this morning.

I really need to get a High Distinction on my test this afternoon. Getting a full scholarship for my law degree was amazing, but living on the other side of the world from my family and friends now is not.

If I get enough HDs, I'm hoping to transfer back to the United States and study there. At least then I'll have my family, and being a broke student won't be so fucking lonely.

I stride up to a busy four-way intersection. It's packed, and a lot of people are waiting for the lights to change to cross the street. I stand up against the row of shops, waiting, only to glance over and see a man on his knees, dishevelled and shoeless. He sits on his knees, holding a cup out, asking for spare change from those around him. I take out my purse. Damn it, I don't have any cash on me.

My heart constricts as everyone pretends not to see him, like he doesn't exist or matter—a stain on society.

How did we become so numb to the homeless and poor? It's just assumed he's an addict. That's how these people justify ignoring him. They think that if they react, then they will be feeding his addiction. They think you have to be cruel to be kind.

I don't get it, I really don't.

I exhale at the thought of our depressing reality. One filled with brand names and social media. Everything this poor man is not.

From the corner of my eye, I see a man stop in front of him.

He's tall, wearing an expensive suit. He looks cultured and wealthy, with black hair and a handsome face.

He stands and looks down at the man.

Oh no, what's he going to do? Is he going to kick him off the street for begging?

Is he going to call the police? Or worse...

He drops to one knee in front of the homeless man, and my heart constricts.

The lights change, but I'm too worried to walk across the street. I need to see what this guy is going to do. He'd better not drag him to his feet, or I'll lose my shit.

He's harmless. Leave him alone.

I get a vision of me kicking the handsome man in the balls in the beggar's defence.

Stupid rich twat.

The man in the suit says something, and the homeless man nods. I watch as he reaches into the inside pocket of his suit jacket to retrieve his wallet, pulls out a fifty-pound note, and hands it over.

What?

He asks the homeless man a question, and the beggar smiles

up at him as though God himself has just bestowed a sacred gift. The homeless man puts his hand out to shake the handsome man's hand, and he shakes it with no hesitation.

With a kind nod, the rich guy stands, completely oblivious to anyone around him, and he bids him goodbye before he turns and crosses the street.

I watch him walking away, and I smile to myself, my faith in the human race restored.

Wow, that was unexpected. I continue on my way with a spring in my step. I finally cross the street and make my journey via two streets before I walk two blocks, and I catch sight of the man in the suit up ahead again. I crane my neck to look ahead to see him. He disinfects his hands with a small bottle of hand sanitizer that he has pulled out from his pocket.

My heart swells. He waited until he was out of the homeless man's sight to clean his hands.

Thoughtful, too.

I stop still and watch him; he's handsome and possibly in his midthirties.

I wonder who his wife is, the lucky bitch. I bet his kids are kind, too.

He disappears around the corner, and I turn and walk into my coffee shop, listening to the bell over the door ringing out.

Monica looks up from her place on the register. "Hey."

"Hi." I smile and walk past her, out the back to put my bag in a locker.

The café is packed, with every seat occupied. Damn it, I was hoping for a slow morning. I need to save my energy for my exam this afternoon.

"Hey, chick," Lance says as he carries a box of cups out the back door.

"I thought you were working tonight." I frown.

"I got called in." He sighs. "*So* not in the mood for this fucking shithole today."

"Join the club." I put my black and white apron on and tie it at

3

the back before I walk to my place at the cash register. "I'll take over."

I bump Monica out of the way with my hip, and she stumbles to the side.

"Good," she mumbles, "I'm dying of Bourbon-itis."

"Bourbon is bad. That shit will kill you," I whisper.

The next person in line steps forward.

"Hello. How can I help you?"

"Do you have goat's milk?" the trendy-looking woman asks.

"Umm." I glance behind me to ask Monica, but she's disappeared. I've never heard of goat's milk before.

"I want a goat's milk turmeric latte, thank you," the customer says.

"Let me go check." I quickly dart out the back to find someone to ask. Lance is cutting up boxes. "Do we serve goat's milk turmeric lattes?"

Lance screws up his face. "Who the fuck would want to drink that shit?"

"This nut out there."

"Fuck's sake," he mutters dryly. "People are trying too hard to be trendy. Goat's milk turmeric. Now I've heard it all."

"So that's a no?"

"Hard no." He smashes a box up. "This is a goat-free milking zone."

I giggle. Monica walks past us, out the back door and into the ally. "Going to the bathroom. I feel sick."

"You okay?" I call, watching as she runs for the door.

"What's wrong with her?" Lance asks.

"Hungover. Bourbon."

Lance winces. "Nasty."

"Cover the coffee machine for me, will you?" Monica says as the door bangs shut behind her.

I go back to the front of the shop to see I now have a huge line waiting. Great. "I'm sorry, we don't have any goat's milk turmeric."

"Why not?" the customer asks.

"Because we don't stock it. I'm sorry." I fake a smile. "This is a goat-milk-free coffee house."

"That's not good enough. I want to see the manager."

Oh, fuck off, bitch. I'm not in the mood for you today. There isn't even a manager on duty.

"Now!" she demands.

I fake another smile. "I'll just go get him." I march out the back to Lance. "She wants to see the manager."

"Who does?"

"The goat chick."

"What about?"

"I don't know. Fucking goats! Get out there." I march back out to the register. "He won't be a moment." I smile. "Can you please step aside so I can serve the next person?"

She glares at me and crosses her arms, then steps to the side and waits.

"Can I help you?" I ask the next man.

"Hi." He grins. Oh God...*not you*. "It's me, Michael."

"Yes." I cringe. "I remember. Hi, Michael. What can I get you?"

"I'll have the usual." He winks.

I take his order and the bell rings over the door to tell me someone else has entered. "That will be four pounds ninety-five," I say coldly.

I take Michael's card and swipe it through the card machine. I can't make casual conversation with Michael because he's way too flirty.

"I want goat's milk," I hear the woman demanding.

"Well, we don't have any," Lance replies. I can tell by the tone of his voice that he isn't in the mood for this crap today, either.

"I want you to put it on the menu immediately."

I glance over to Lance. His face is murderous, and I bite my lip to hide my smile.

"Look, lady, if you want goat's milk, you're going to have to go somewhere else. We are not into milking goats."

"You'd rather milk a cow?"

5

"Or kick them out of my coffee shop," Lance mutters dryly. "Either, or."

Jeez... I drop my head to hide my smile.

"Did you just call me a cow?" the woman gasps.

Shit, buzz off, bitch. Enough with the dramatics. Just leave already.

"Can I help you?" I ask the next customer, and look up at the queue.

Big brown eyes stare back at me, and I step back in surprise.

It's him.

The guy from the street.

"Hi." I smile bashfully and tuck a piece of hair behind my ear.

He's wearing a perfectly fitted dark navy suit and a crisp white shirt. He looks like he might be European or something.

"Hello." His voice is deep and husky.

I feel my cheeks blush, and I smile nervously. "Hi."

We stare at each other. *Fuck me.* This guy is completely gorgeous.

A trace of a smile crosses his face, as if he's reading my mind.

I smile goofily over at him and hunch my shoulders.

He raises his brows. "Do you want to know my order?"

"Oh." I pause. "I was waiting for you," I lie. Fuck, I'm acting like a starstruck teenager. *Get it together, stupid.* "What would you like?"

"I'll have a double macchiato, please."

I twist my lips to hide my smile. Even his coffee is hot.

"Would you like anything else?" I ask.

He raises his eyebrow. "Such as?"

I open my mouth to say something, but no words come out.

He smirks, realizing he has me completely flustered.

Oh, hell, act fucking cool, will you?

"A muffin?" I reply. "They're delicious."

"All right." His eyes hold mine. "Why don't you surprise me, April?"

I stare at him as my brain misfires. "How do you know my name?"

"It's on your apron."

6

I scrunch my eyes shut. "Oh...right." *Please, Mother Earth, swallow me whole. Way to bimbo it out.* "Ah, excuse me. I'm not with it today," I stammer.

"You look completely with it to me." He gives me his first genuine smile, and I feel it to my toes.

It's official: *this man is delicious.*

"And your name?" I ask, holding my pen to his cup.

"Sebastian."

"Mr. Sebastian?"

"Mr. Garcia."

Sebastian Garcia. Even his name is hot. "Would you like another coffee for your wife?"

"There's no wife."

"Girlfriend?"

"No girlfriend." A smile crosses his face once more. He knows I'm fishing for information.

Our eyes are locked, and the air crackles between us.

The man behind him in the line sighs heavily. "I'm in a rush, you know."

Oh, get lost. I'm trying to flirt here.

Dickhead.

Mr. Garcia steps to the side, and I bring my attention to the man behind him. "Can I help you?"

"I want a toasted ham and cheese sandwich, and you'd better make it quick," he barks.

"Of course, sir." Fuck, why is every asshole in London in my café today?

"Excuse me," I hear from the side.

The man and I look up to see Mr. Garcia has taken a step towards us.

"What?" the asshole snaps.

"What did you just say?" Mr. Garcia raises an eyebrow, clearly annoyed.

The man shrivels, taken aback. "I'm in a rush."

"No need to be rude." Mr. Garcia's eyes hold his. "Apologize."

7

The man rolls his eyes.

"Now."

"Sorry," the man mumbles to me.

I press my lips together to hide my smile.

Mr. Garcia steps back to his place by the wall.

I feel my cheeks flush with excitement.

Saw-oon.

"That won't be a minute," I say, and the man nods, not saying another word.

I glance around, wondering who is making the coffees.

Oh, shit, I'm supposed to be.

Wait, how do you make a double macchiato again?

I have never done this before, although I have watched the others do it a million times. I concentrate and do what I think they do. I turn back to the customers.

"Mr. Garcia," I call, and he steps forward. "Here you go."

His eyes hold mine as he takes it from me. "Thank you." He nods and then turns, and I watch him walk towards the door. Shit...that's it?

Turn around and ask me out, damn it.

He stops on the spot and I hold my breath. He turns back. "April, I'll see you tomorrow."

I smile. "I hope so."

He dips his head, and with one more breathtaking smile, he turns and walks out onto the street. Like a little kid, I pick up a cloth and practically run to the front of the café so I can watch which direction he takes.

I pretend to wipe a table near the window so I can spy.

Sebastian walks past a few shops, and I see him take a sip of his coffee and wince. He screws up his face, and with a shake of his head, he throws it in a trash can.

What? After all that, he didn't even drink it!

My mouth falls open.

"Am I going to get served here or what?" the rude man calls from the counter.

"Yes, of course, sir." I fake another smile and make my way back to the coffee machine.

You're going to get the worst fucking coffee I've ever made, asshole.

And judging by Mr. Garcia's reaction, that's pretty bad.

I walk down the corridor of Holmes Court, my dormitory accommodation at university.

I think I flunked my exam, damn it.

The sound of laughter echoes through the hall, and a faint techno beat can be heard in the distance. Coming home to this place is a living hell.

I have never hated living somewhere as much as I hate it here. I mean, everyone is nice enough, but I feel like their grandmother. At the age of twenty-five, I'm considered a mature student, yet for some unknown reason, my scholarship houses me with the freshmen, all of which are eighteen and on their first leave of absence from home.

Everyone is either blind drunk or having sex, and I don't really care what they do, but do they have to make so much fucking noise when they do it?

This place is like a twenty-four-seven nightclub. They party all night and sleep all day.

How they are actually passing any of their subjects is beyond me.

I exhale heavily as I trudge up the stairs. The music is getting louder now. Of course it is.

Penelope Wittcom: my neighbour and archenemy. We share a common wall, and on my side of it, I try to study, sleep, and be a respectable student. On her side, it's party and orgy central. Her bedroom is known around campus as the 'Rave Cave'.

Open all fucking night.

She even has a disco ball in there.

People come and go at all hours, slamming doors, partying,

and yahooing. To be honest, I think she might be dealing drugs. She has to be. Nobody can be that popular and have so many visitors.

And that's not the worst of it by far.

I've never heard so much screaming during sex in my life!

I've lost count of how many men she has gone through. I mean, good for her—at least one of us is getting it—but does she have to howl every time she comes?

I've put in complaints. I've requested to move buildings. I've done everything possible. But it's pretty hard to be heard when Penelope is sleeping with the floor manager.

And besides, I'm on a scholarship. I'm not paying to live here, so I have to suck it up.

I just have to get through the rest of this year, and hopefully my grades will be good enough to get a scholarship to return to the States.

When I left my cheating, douchebag ex-husband Roy, I walked out with nothing. Every cent I had earned is in the house that he still lives in, and until he agrees to sell it, I have to live with the fallout.

I'm in my second year of law school, which I'm so proud of, but I also need to live while I study. I've applied for every job under the sun, but my course hours are intense, and nothing ever seems to fit in with my schedule. I'm grateful for my job at the café, but with only three shifts a week, it just doesn't pay enough for me to get an apartment of my own. So, for now, this is my life.

The music is really pumping when I walk past Penelope's room. Her door is propped open. Four or five guys are sitting on her floor, and the distinct smell of cigarette smoke invades the corridor.

I walk past them without so much as a smile and close my door behind me. The loud music only softens a little, so I put my headphones on. Who knew I would need noise-cancelling headphones just to get through my day?

I flick the television on, which is connected by Bluetooth to my headphones. I grab a mineral water from the fridge, flop onto the couch, and I begin to scroll through my phone. I open an email.

Subject: Application
From: Club Exotic
To: April Bennet

Congratulations, April.
You have been successful in securing an interview with Club Exotic.
We look forward to meeting you at 290 High Street, London East, at 11:00 a.m. on the 22nd of next month.
We pay above National Minimum Wage, have an excellent career development pathway plan, and we are recruiting ten team members to join our beloved crew.
Please RSVP within seven days of receiving your invitation.

Club Exotic.

I sit up instantly.

I applied for this job *months* ago. A girl who used to work at the café worked at Club Exotic one night a week at the bar, and it covered her entire rent.

I jump off the couch in excitement.

I mean, I know it's not ideal. It's a gentlemen's club, but it *is* only behind the bar.

How hard can it be to pour drinks?

Plus, I've had to listen to Penelope having sex every night for free, anyway. I'm pretty sure my pure eyes and ears can handle anything these days.

If I don't find something beforehand, this could work out okay. I speed-read the email again. Gosh, that's five weeks away, though.

Damn it, five weeks is a long time.

My phone begins to vibrate.

"Hello."

"Hello, April?"

"Yes." I don't recognize the voice.

"This is Anika from Club Exotic."

"Oh." I frown. "I actually just opened an email from you."

"Yes, that's why I'm calling. We've just had somebody leave without notice, and you were the first person on our interview list who has answered."

"Okay..."

"Do you want to come in tomorrow for an interview? I know it's last-minute, but otherwise your interview isn't until next month."

I quickly run through my schedule for tomorrow. I guess I can skip my lecture. "Yeah, sure. That would be great. What time?"

"Can you be here at eleven?"

I don't finish my shift at the café till 10.30 a.m., though I could get ready before my shift. "Okay, that sounds great, thank you." I smile, excited. "I'll see you then."

"Can I help you, sir?"

"I'll have a toasted cheese on rye and a flat white, please."

"Sure." I smile as I tap his order into the computer. It's another day at the café, another few pounds. "That will be nine pounds ninety-five, thanks."

He hands over his money, and I hear the distant bell over the door as someone new enters the building.

This is the longest shift I've ever done at the café. I'm nervous about my interview this morning. After thinking on it all night, I've decided that I really want that job.

If I could just work two shifts a week, then I could move out of the dorm and into my own studio apartment.

Imagine that!

Don't get excited. You haven't gotten it yet, I remind myself.

"Can I help you?" I ask as I glance up and stare straight into the eyes of Mr. Garcia.

He came back.

"Hello," he says in his deep voice.

The air between us is doing that thing again...electricity and butterflies all rolled into one.

"You back for more of my great coffee?" I smirk.

He gives me a slow, sexy smile. "I am."

2

April

"Well…" I drop my shoulders and stand tall as I try to act cool. "How can I help you?"

Amusement flashes across his face. "I'll have a double macchiato, please."

"Of course." I type it into the computer then glance up at him. "Will that be all?"

His eyes hold mine. "For now."

I roll my lips as I try to hide my smile. Why does everything that comes out of his mouth sound sexy?

For now isn't theoretically a hot sentence.

Lance looks over my shoulder to see the screen. "It's okay, Lance, Mr. Garcia likes it when I make his coffee," I say as I try to stay straight-faced.

Sebastian's forehead wrinkles, and I know he's inwardly cringing inside. Ha-ha, this is classic. Oh well. That will teach him for throwing away my coffee yesterday.

"Okay, okay," Lance says, taking over from me at the register.

I turn to the coffee machine, and I really want to burst out laughing. I'm so shit at this, it isn't funny. Right. What do I do again? This coffee machine is so confusing.

I glance over my shoulder to see Mr. Garcia waiting patiently as he watches me. His hands are tucked into the pants pockets of his grey suit. He's wearing a cream shirt today, and it really makes his dark hair pop.

He gives me a soft smile, and I smile back.

He really is dreamy.

I make his coffee and turn back to him. "Here you go."

"Thank you." He takes it and dips his head. "Have a nice day."

I will, now that I've seen you.

"You too." I beam.

He turns and walks out of the store. I pick up a cleaning cloth and practically run to the front of the café to spy on him through the window. He walks out into the street and crosses the road. I watch on as he takes a sip, winces, and screws his face up.

He hates it.

I giggle.

He takes another sip, and then, with a shake of his head, he throws it in the bin.

I burst out laughing and return to the cashiers' desk.

"What's so funny?" Lance asks.

"That guy."

"Who, the Italian dude?"

"Yeah, the gorgeous one. I don't think he's Italian, though."

"He's a bit old for you, isn't he? What about him?"

"He is not too old for me, and he hates my coffee."

"And?"

"He hates my coffee, and yet he came back."

Lance frowns. "I don't get it."

I widen my eyes. Lance can't be this clueless. "Well, if he doesn't like my coffee and he came back, it means he's coming to see me, doesn't it?"

"Perhaps he just works close, and this place is convenient."

"Maybe." I smile as I wipe the counter. "We'll see tomorrow, won't we?" I smile as I reorganize the menus. "If he comes back tomorrow, it's definite confirmation that he's coming to see me."

"You women and your mind fucks." Lance rolls his eyes. "If you like him, why don't you just ask him out? You don't have to make the poor bastard drink your petrol coffee."

I giggle as I remember the disgust on his face.

I really am a funny bitch.

I exhale heavily and look up at the sign over the door.

CLUB EXOTIC

I can't believe I'm actually doing this. I've never even been to a gentlemen's club before, let alone considered working in one.

It's fine. It's totally fucking fine.

It's not—not by a long shot—but I can't live where I am for much longer. Penelope and her Rave Cave have me going insane. I push on the large brass knob on the heavy black door and walk in.

Instantly, my senses are overloaded with luxury: dark charcoal walls, huge chandeliers, and incredible gilded mirrors that are hanging as artwork.

"Hello," a pretty blonde girl says with a smile. "I'm Anne-Marie."

"Hi." I grip my résumé folder with white-knuckle force.

Run. Run the fuck away, right now.

Oh, hell, what am I doing here? I think I'm going to throw up.

I swallow the lump in my throat to try and push some sort of sentence past my lips. "H-hi. I'm April. I'm here for an interview."

Anne-Marie looks down at her clipboard and ticks off my name. "Great. Just this way, please, April."

She turns and walks off across the club. I follow, looking her up and down.

She's gorgeous and looks so glamorous in her tight black

knitted turtleneck dress. Like a sexy, smart businesswoman or something. How does she walk in shoes that high?

She opens a door to a waiting room of some kind. There's a girl sitting alone in the corner, and she looks up at us with a timid smile.

"Just take a seat here. Porsha will be with you shortly." Anne-Marie smiles.

"Thank you."

I sit down on the closest seat, and Anne-Marie disappears, the door clicking closed behind her. The room falls silent, and I drag my eyes up to the other girl who is waiting. She gives me a lopsided smile.

"Hi," I say softly.

"Hi."

We fall silent again, and finally she whispers, "What the hell am I doing here?"

"I know. Me too."

She moves to sit beside me so that nobody can hear us. "You need to tell me to leave. This shit is crazy."

"If you tell me first," I whisper back. "Are you here for the bar job?"

"Yeah."

"Me too. I'm broke."

"Same. I'm studying. I'm Kayla, by the way."

"Same." I smile. "I'm April."

"What are you studying?"

"Law." I look around nervously. "Is this place even legal?"

"Who knows?" Kayla shrugs. "I'm studying medicine. In my third year."

I smile, feeling a little at ease. Kayla is attractive and obviously intelligent. "Apparently, they pay seventy pounds an hour, and you work ten-hour shifts," she whispers.

"Shit, really? God, I could do with that."

"Me too. I'm living in the biggest dump on Earth."

"Well, I'm on campus, and it is literally hell."

"I did that my first year. Never again. Let's hope we both get the job so that we at least know one person."

The door opens, and a beautiful woman with a black bob comes into view. "Hello." She smiles and looks between us. She's gorgeous, made up to the nines with a full face of makeup and red lipstick. "My name is Porsha. I'm the manager here."

"Hello." We both smile.

Porsha looks between us with calculating eyes. This woman is no pushover. I can tell already.

"Who was first here?" she asks.

"Me," Kayla says nervously, standing. "I'm Kayla."

"Hello, Kayla." Porsha smiles. "This way." She turns and walks into the office, and Kayla gives me a nervous shake of her head.

"Good luck," I mouth.

"Thanks," she mouths back before disappearing into the office and closing the door behind her.

I tip my head back and stare at the ceiling. There are old-fashioned paintings on it, as if it's the Sistine Chapel.

Wow... Weird.

This place really is something. I wonder what used to be in this building.

I wait for fifteen minutes, and then the door opens. I watch as Kayla shakes Porsha's hand. "Thank you for the opportunity, I'm really excited," she says.

Oh, she must have gotten the job.

"Take a seat, Kayla. I will be with you after I interview April."

"Okay, thanks." Kayla hunches her shoulders together and sits down. "Good luck," she mouths to me.

"Hello, April, nice to meet you." Porsha smiles at me and holds out her hand to mine. She then holds the door open for me. "Please take a seat."

After shaking her hand, I sit down at the huge black desk.

Porsha sits down opposite me, and she studies me intently. "Welcome."

"Thanks."

She has an air about her that's powerful and confident. She waits for me to speak, as if assessing everything that I do and say.

"So, tell me...why are you here?"

"I—" I pause. "I'm applying for the bar position."

"And what do you know about Club Exotic?"

"Not much, I'm afraid. I'm hoping you can shed some light on the position."

She sits back with a knowing smile and crosses her legs. "Tell me about yourself."

I shrug. "What do you want to know?"

She raises an eyebrow. "All of it."

"I'm twenty-five. American."

"I can hear that."

"I'm studying law here in London on a scholarship."

"Are you currently working?"

"Yes, in a coffee house in Kensington."

"And you aren't happy there?"

"I am, but it doesn't pay enough, and I need to find a new apartment."

"Okay," she replies. "Tell me about your financial situation."

Fuck, that's a bit personal.

"April, don't waste my time. Why do you need this job, darling?"

Something inside me snaps. "Because all of my money is tied up in my house at home in the States, and my bastard ex-husband won't get out of it so I can sell it."

She smiles as if happy with my answer. "So you're starting again?"

I nod, slightly embarrassed. I bet her ex-husband wouldn't get away with this shit. "Yes, I am."

"Can you stand up for me?" I frown as she stands and comes around to my side of the desk. "Stand."

Huh?

I do as she asks anyway, and she circles me, looking me up and down. She holds my hair up and studies my face. She runs her hand down over my hip, and then she tilts her head.

"What are you doing?" I ask.

"I think I have another role for you."

I frown.

"Please, take a seat." She sits back down and links her fingers together in front of her. "Let me tell you about Club Exotic."

I grip my résumé on my lap. Does she even want to see it? I worked on this for hours last night.

"We're the most exclusive gentlemen's club in London," she goes on. "And we have franchises all over the world."

Exclusive? *Please, give me a break.*

I fake a smile and act interested.

"Our members pay a premium membership fee to ensure confidentiality."

"How much is premium?"

"That depends on the level of membership they have. A bronze membership, for example, is fifty thousand pounds."

"A year?" I gasp.

Porsha smiles. "Yes, a year. A silver membership is seventy-five thousand, and a gold membership is around one hundred and ten."

What the fuck?

"What's the difference between the memberships?" I ask.

"Bronze has access to the facilities, an open bar, an award-winning restaurant, a gym…"

I frown. A gym? Wait, I'm confused.

"April." She pauses, as if trying to articulate herself properly. "Our members come here to be able to mix with their friends in the comfort of privacy. The calibre of men here is exceptionally high, including celebrities, politicians, professional athletes, those types. They don't want or need photos turning up on social media about their private lives, so we make it possible for them to escape their public status."

I try hard not to roll my eyes. It's a brothel. Say it like it is, lady.

"I see." My eyes hold hers. "And what do the other memberships get?"

"They get access to all the facilities, but they also get unlimited lap dances, as well as a few vouchers a year."

"Vouchers?"

"We'll get to that later."

"What do gold members get?"

"All of the above benefits, as well as time in the Escape Lounge."

"Escape Lounge?"

"Do you have any idea what it would be like to be a man of stature and have women throw themselves at you when you go to a public bar?"

I stare at her flatly. No, and I don't care.

"And do you know how many women try to take advantage of powerful men by blackmailing them with images?"

I shrug. "I haven't really thought about it before."

"Celebrities need to unwind without the fear of being photographed. Our members don't come here for the women. They pay big money to protect their reputations, and they come here to be anonymous."

I nod. "Okay."

"Of course, they can get a lap dance if they wish, or they can spend time in the Escape Lounge, but our girls are more guarded than our members. NDA legal documents are signed on employment and on memberships."

"What does that mean?"

"We protect our women's reputations as much as our clients'. We only have high-calibre women working here. Intelligent, beautiful women who are putting themselves through university or striving to give their children a better life. Ninety-nine percent of our applicants won't be successful in securing a position."

Shit, I'm not going to get it, and this is her way of letting me down nicely.

She sits back in her chair and raises her chin. "I take it your ex-husband did a number on you?"

I grip my résumé tightly. "He did."

"And what are you going to do about it?"

"Get a law degree." I shrug.

"I think it's about time you started making decisions that are going to set you up for life, don't you?" I frown, but she goes on. "I think you're above bar work."

"What does that mean?"

"Every night, in the Escape Lounge, we hold a fashion parade with twenty-four of the most beautiful women we have."

Huh? Fashion parade.

"Every night, twenty-four men reserve an Escape Night, and at the end of the fashion parade, we have a private cocktail party."

I listen intently as I imagine the scenario she is setting.

"During the cocktail party, our Escape Girls will choose their partner for the night."

"I'm sorry, I'm lost."

"Being an Escape Girl doesn't mean you sleep with anyone, April. What it does mean is that you will spend the night with the man that you choose."

"Spend the night?"

What the hell?

"We have a five-star hotel above us, and we own a floor of apartments."

"The men pick you and then you have to sleep with them?" I frown in horror.

"No, nothing like that," she replies calmly, and I wonder just how many times she's given this spiel. "The woman picks the man and she decides if she kisses him or if she lets him touch her." She pauses. "*Or if she chooses to sleep with him.*"

"So..." I raise my eyebrows. "This *is* a high-class brothel?"

Porsha laughs. "Not at all, darling. Trust me. The men we have here don't have to pay for sex."

"Why are you telling me this?"

"You're something special." Her eyes hold mine. "You have that X factor, April."

"Meaning?"

"I want you to be an Escape Girl."

I sit up in my chair. "Oh, I'm sorry if I gave you the impression that I'm—"

"Five thousand pounds a night."

I freeze. "What?"

"The payment to be an Escape Girl is five thousand pounds a night. That's nearly seven thousand dollars in American currency. You don't have to sleep with anyone. You don't even have to touch them. You do have to spend the night in a suite with them, but there are two bedrooms in the apartments if you choose not to go there. We have twenty-four-hour security, and your safety and identity are always protected."

"I'm... I don't... I mean... *What?*" I sit up in a fluster. "Five thousand pounds a night?"

Porsha smiles, knowing she's piqued my interest. "That's right, April. You could earn twenty thousand pounds a month by simply working one shift a week."

I could pay my rent for an entire year in just one month.

What the fuck?

"Think about it."

I stay silent.

"Kayla just signed up."

"Kayla from the waiting room?"

"Yes, she's out there waiting for the backstage tour now."

"Oh." I have no words.

She stands. "Come and look around. You can think on it." She stands and opens the door while I sit still, in shock. What the hell?

"Kayla." Porsha smiles. "Are you ready for the tour?"

"Sure am," Kayla replies. She seems as sure as day about this. Did she know what position she was applying for?

Porsha turns her attention to me. "Are you coming, April?"

I stand. "I don't think..." My voice trails off.

Five thousand pounds a night.

"Come on." Kayla widens her eyes at me. "A look around won't hurt."

I look between them, feeling like the ultimate party pooper. "Umm, okay, I guess."

I follow Porsha and Kayla out of the office and down the stairs. The club seems like it was an old theatre at one stage. It has a gradual drop to the stage at the front, and there are small sections above, clearly once alcoves. Porsha takes a card, swipes a scanner, and a big, black security door opens. We walk through what looks like the back of a Victoria's Secret show. Small dressing tables line the space, filled with makeup, wigs, and all kinds of glamorous things.

We walk through to another room, and I see a huge rack lined with designer dresses, all of sequins, lace, and feathers.

Jeez.

"All your laser and beauty treatments are on the house while you work here," Porsha says as she walks us around. "And there is a cap on your shifts. Escape Girls can only work four times a month."

Kayla does a jig on the spot, as if this is the most exciting thing that has ever happened to her. "Can you believe this?" she whispers.

"Are you crazy?" I mouth.

"Shh." She links her arm through mine. "Just look around."

We follow Porsha around the club. She introduces us to the security team and then takes us into the elevator. "On a normal shift, you would come in and have your hair and makeup done professionally, and then you would pick your dress."

My stomach flutters with nerves as we ride up in the elevator. I imagine the scenario she is setting.

"You would be introduced to the Escape members during the fashion parade, and then after the cocktail party." The elevator doors open, and we follow her down the swanky corridor. "You would pick your partner and come up to your suite with them."

She uses her security card and swipes the door open and then holds it back for us to pass through.

We walk in, and as I look around the luxurious apartment, my stomach begins to flutter with even more nerves.

Porsha's phone rings. She glances down at it in her hand. "I have to take this. Excuse me for a moment. Look around, girls." She walks out into the corridor, and Kayla begins to jump around in excitement. "Oh my fucking God." She grabs my hands in hers. "Can you believe this?"

"I can't fuck a rich guy for money," I whisper.

"Sure you can. I've fucked dead shits for free before."

I giggle. This is true.

"Five thousand pounds, April, and you don't even have to sleep with them."

"I can't do it. My morals won't let me."

"I need a new apartment and a month in Spain more than I need morals. Where does being a nice girl get you?"

I shrug.

"Living in a dump. That's where."

"Kayla," I whisper. "This is *full-on*."

"Come on. We can help each other through it. When will we ever get the opportunity to make this kind of money again?" She smiles, her face full of hope. "And besides, if it's crap, we just leave."

"It's prostitution," I whisper.

"It's just an offer, that's all. We don't have to sleep with them. Porsha said so herself."

"But you know we probably will."

"I can think of worse things than sleeping with a pro athlete."

I giggle.

"And besides, nobody will ever know. It's the perfect fucking job, April."

"God," I whisper. I can't believe I'm even considering this.

Porsha comes back into the apartment. "So?" She smiles as she looks between us. "What do you girls think?"

"I'm in!" Kayla announces.

Porsha smiles. "Great." She turns her attention to me. "What about you, April?"

"Oh." I pause. I really want the money, but... God. "I don't think I—"

"Why don't you just try it for one night?" she cuts me off.

I stare at her, my mind a clusterfuck of confusion.

"Five thousand pounds for one night. It's worth a try." She smiles.

My eyes flicker between the two of them, and Kayla nods in excitement.

Five thousand would get me out of the dorm, if even for a few months.

Oh, fuck it.

"Okay, one night," I agree.

Porsha's grin widens. "Fantastic. We start your training tomorrow."

I close my eyes.

What the fuck did I just agree to?

Sebastian

I walk into the restaurant at exactly 7:00 a.m. Spencer and Masters are already seated at our usual table in the back. These breakfast meet-ups are all we seem to be able to squeeze in these days.

Time with my two best friends is precious.

Julian Masters and Spencer Jones.

We've been close since childhood. They're the brothers I never had.

Julian has children, and now a wife, so all his spare time is taken up, and Spencer is newly married to his wife, Charlotte, who is pregnant. He needs these breakfasts with us to survive. She's busting his balls, and it's hilarious.

"Hey." I smile as I fall into my seat.

"Hmm," Julian grunts while reading the paper.

"Can you stop being so fucking grumpy?" Spencer asks him as he butters his toast. "I'm sick of fucking grumpy people. They piss me off."

"What's grumpy about that?" Julian asks. "I said hi."

"Oh my fuck. Can you even hear yourself? It's your tone." Spencer rolls his eyes.

Julian fakes a smile. "Feeling a bit precious this morning, are we, Spence?"

"I am, actually. Good morning, Seb. How are you, my dear friend?" he asks sweetly.

I chuckle as I lay the serviette out on my lap. "Morning, boys."

The waitress appears. "Can I take your order?"

"I'll have the omelette and a fresh juice," I say.

"Same."

"Make that three," says Julian.

She smiles and disappears.

"So, what's new?" Spence asks, taking a sip of his coffee.

"Nothing." I yawn and stretch. "I'm tired."

"Not sleeping well?" Spencer asks.

"No, I'm fucking good to go."

"Yeah, well, enjoy the peace." Spencer blows into his coffee. "I have no doubt that Charlotte is trying to fuck me to death. By the time this baby is born, I won't have a dick left. There will be two mothers in our family."

Julian smiles as he reads his paper. "Ah, pregnant sex. Is there anything better?"

"Sleep, Masters. I would like some fucking sleep once in a while." Spencer sighs. "I'm running on fucking empty here."

"What a hardship. A hot and horny wife." I roll my eyes. "Give me a fucking break, will you?"

"More coffee?" the waitress asks, holding the coffee pot up.

"Please."

"Thank you."

The waitress pours us our coffees and leaves us alone.

"Oh." I smile. "Buddy has a girlfriend."

"He does?" Spence sits up. "This is his first, right?"

"He called me last night, he's that excited." Buddy is my sister's son. His father left when he was two, and I've been his stand-in dad ever since. We catch up a couple of times a week. I couldn't love that kid more if I tried.

"He's bringing her over on the weekend," I say.

"What do fathers say when they meet their child's first partner?" Spence frowns.

"'Fuck off'," Masters says flatly, never taking his eyes off the paper. "Plain and simple. 'Fuck you' and 'fuck right off'."

We chuckle.

Julian hasn't had it easy. His daughter Willow puts him through his paces with her bad partner choices.

"Well, I'm excited for him." I smile wistfully. "Apparently, she's the best thing since sliced bread."

"Aren't they all when you're at that age?" Masters asks.

"What are you guys doing today?" Spence asks.

"Same shit, different day." Julian shrugs.

"Well." I pause and rearrange the napkin on my lap. "After I leave here, I'll be driving across the city, through peak-hour traffic, to go to a café to be served by the hottest woman I've seen in a very long time. Who," I add, "makes *the* worst coffee I have ever fucking tasted."

They both laugh at me.

"You drive all the way across the city for bad coffee?" Julian frowns.

"You couldn't even call it coffee. I could literally die from this shit, it's that bad."

Spencer raises a brow. "Jesus, she must be hot."

"She is. Way too wholesome and young for me, though."

"Why? How old is she?"

"I don't know." I twist my lips as I run my hand over my stubble. "She would be in her midtwenties, at a guess."

"That's not too young," Spencer replies.

"It is." I frown. "I'm in my late thirties. If I asked her out, she'd probably think I am a creep."

"That's because you're fucking creepy," Masters mutters dryly.

"My point exactly." I hold my coffee cup up towards him. "Anyway, I have a plan."

"Such as?"

"I'm going to keep going back there until *she* asks *me* out."

"Attaboy." Spencer pats me on the back. "Persistence pays."

"That's if you live through the coffee," Masters says as he turns the page of his newspaper.

We finish our breakfast, and before long, I find myself driving to Kensington to the café. I'm not quite sure what it is about this girl, only that I've thought about her constantly, which is weird in itself. I don't think about women...ever.

I park the car and push open the heavy door of the café, not missing the way the bell overhead jingles.

April looks up, our eyes meet, and she smiles softly. I feel it in my gut.

She and the guy she works with exchange looks, and he gives a subtle shake of his head.

What does that mean? Has she said something about me?

I walk to the counter.

"Hello, Mr. Garcia." She smiles sexily.

I twist my lips to hide my delight at the fact that she remembers my name. "Hello, April."

"Double macchiato, sir?"

Death in a cup.

I raise my eyebrow. Actually, that's the last thing I want. "Yes, please."

"I'll make it," she says to the guy she's working with. With a nod, he disappears out the back. She turns to the coffee machine, and my eyes drop down her body and linger on her behind. She's wearing tight blue jeans that hug her in all the right places.

Seriously...*hot as fuck.*

She's tall, with an athletic body. Her hair is cut into a short, blonde bob. It's thick and has a bit of a curl to it. Her eyes are big and brown, and her skin has a beautiful honey hue to it.

Just looking at her makes me hard.

"What are you up to today?" she asks me over her shoulder.

Jerking my cock off to the thought of you. "Just working."

"Oh. What do you do?"

What do you want me to do? "I'm an architect."

She turns and grins. "Wow, that's impressive."

Our eyes lock, and I get an image of her on her knees in front of me, sucking my cock. I bite my lip to try and hide my reaction to her. It's been a long time since a woman affected me this way.

She smiles, as if reading my mind, and we stare at each other while the air crackles between us.

Ask her out.

"Here's your coffee." She passes it to me.

Ask her out.

"Thank you."

Ask her out.

"Have a nice day, Sebastian." She offers me a playful smile.

My cock clenches at the sound of her saying my name. "You too."

I begrudgingly turn towards the door.

Shit.

I exhale with frustration and push through the doors. Damn it.

I take a sip of the coffee and wince.

Christ almighty, that's fucked-up coffee. I immediately throw it in the trash.

It looks like I'm coming back tomorrow.

April

"Wow." Porsha looks me up and down. "You look incredible."

I put my hand over my stomach. "This is crazy."

"Crazy good." Porsha smiles.

The chatter of the girls around us fills the room. They all seem so excited to be here. For the last three hours, I've been primped, preened, and I've had every damn beauty treatment known to man. My hair and makeup are done, and I'm wearing the most beautiful sequined dress I've ever seen.

It's my first shift in the Escape Club, and I'm just about to walk out onto the catwalk. Kayla isn't here. Apparently, two new girls can't start on the same night because of something to do with an announcement.

I think I'm going to throw up. I've never been so nervous.

What was I thinking?

"You ready?" Porsha asks.

"N-no," I stammer.

"You'll be fine." She holds my shoulders in her hands. "Follow my lead and do just as we taught you in training."

I nod. "Okay."

I can hear the music playing. One by one, the girls go out and do their thing. I can also hear the chatter of the men in the cocktail bar as they watch the fashion parade.

I pick up a cocktail from a table and down it in one.

God help me.

Then I hear the announcement. "And tonight, we introduce a brand-new Escape Girl. This is her first shift, so please welcome the beautiful Cartier."

I walk out onto the stage and look around at the men gathered around the catwalk. Immediately, my eyes lock with a man who is standing at the end of the runway.

His face falls when he sees me.

Oh no...

It's him.

Mr. Garcia is here.

3

April

I FREEZE ON THE SPOT, and we stare at each other.

What the hell?

Damn it, no. I don't want him to see me here.

Wait a minute... What the fuck is he doing here?

Are you freaking kidding me?

Oh my God, and I thought he was nice. What a joke.

Typical. Another man of my dreams who turns out to be a walking, fucking sperm bank. Ugh.

I'm so done with men.

He narrows his eyes at me, and I narrow mine right back.

Don't look at me like that, asshole. I see you for what you really are now.

Sleazebag.

"May I introduce you all to our newest Escape Girl," Porsha says into the microphone. "This is her very first shift. She's completely untouched."

The hushed whisper of awe falls over the room, and I feel the heat of everyone's eyes on me.

"I'm sure you'll all agree Cartier is as intelligent as she is beautiful, gentlemen."

I glance around at all of the men who are standing, captivated, around the catwalk. The scent of money hangs in the air. So many expensive suits on well-groomed, handsome men. Each in their thirties or forties.

I wonder if any of them are married.

Hell.

What the fuck am I doing here?

Damn Kayla and her contagious excitement. Where is she now, huh?

This is a living nightmare.

Just go to a room and go to sleep. I don't have to do anything with anyone, I remind myself.

"Gentlemen, who's it going to be?" Porsha asks the room.

The men all smile darkly, drinking me in.

I can almost feel their hunger.

My breath quivers on the intake, and I drop my shoulders and force a smile.

If I'm going to hell, I may as well go hard.

"Gentlemen," Porsha says, as if this is some kind of stage show. Well, I guess it is, really. "State your intentions. Who wants to be the very first man Cartier spends the night with?"

The men all begin to move around, and they come and stand in front of me, just like Porsha said they would.

I glance up at the one man that doesn't: Mr. Garcia.

"Hello, I'm Jonathan," a blonde man says as he picks up my hand and kisses the back of it. His eyes hold mine, and he kisses my hand again. "Lovely to meet you."

"Hello." My stomach flutters with nerves, and I force a smile. "Likewise."

"Bennet." A dark-haired man smiles. "It's a pleasure."

I shake his hand and smile. "Nice to meet you."

One by one, the men introduce themselves, and Porsha is right:

the majority of them are gorgeous. And even if they haven't been genetically blessed, they all have the 'It Factor'.

I glance over to Sebastian, who is standing alone and sipping his scotch. His eyes stare straight ahead, as if preoccupied.

Why isn't he lined up to meet me? I know he likes me. At least, I thought he did. I glance over at the line of beautiful girls beside me, and the penny drops.

He's here for someone else. One of them.

Fuck.

"I'll start the bidding!" a man from the back calls. "Thirty thousand pounds."

A few of the men chuckle. "Fifty thousand."

Huh? What's going on?

"Seventy-five-thousand tip to spend the night with me!" one man calls in an assertive voice.

I glance around. There seems to be some kind of auction happening.

Oh crap, they told me about this. I get 25% of the auction price on top of my wage if I accept one of them.

"Eighty-five."

"One hundred!" another man calls.

From my peripheral vision, I see Sebastian place his scotch down on the table and turns towards the exit door.

What, he's leaving?

I look around nervously. *He's just leaving?*

"Him!" I call.

Sebastian keeps walking, and I point towards him. "That man there. The one walking towards the door."

"Mr. Smith!" Porsha calls.

Sebastian stops on the spot, still facing the exit.

"Cartier has chosen you," she calls.

Sebastian turns, and his eyes hold Porsha's before he says, "She doesn't have what I want," his voice flat and lifeless.

I glare at him. *Asshole.*

"That isn't how this works, and you know it, Mr. Smith," Porsha says. "Our girls call the shots. If Cartier wants you, Cartier gets you."

Sebastian's eyes meet mine, and then his chin rises in defiance. "I'm not interested."

I feel my face flush with embarrassment. This is possibly the most degrading thing that has ever happened to me. *Fuck you.*

"Mr. Smith, you play by the rules or you hand in your membership." Porsha sneers.

He runs his tongue over his teeth, clearly angered, and he walks back towards me. "One hundred and thirty!" another man calls from the back.

Sebastian stands in front of me, inches away from my face, and we glare at each other.

Anger bounces between us. What, exactly, we are angry about, I don't know. Actually, that's a lie. I do know.

It's the fact that he's fucking here, that's what. And here I was thinking he was someone special. I don't know if I've ever been so pissed off with someone I don't even know.

I raise my eyebrow.

He stares at me, and then, without a word, he takes my hand.

"This way," he mutters under his breath.

Porsha smiles at him. "That's more like it."

I feel the other men in the room staring at us as we walk towards the door and then get into the elevator. As soon as the doors close, Sebastian drops my hand like a hot potato. We stare forward in total silence as we travel upwards.

She doesn't have what I want.

Like fucking hell, I don't. I could make you beg for me if I wanted to, you self-absorbed prick.

The elevator door opens, and he marches down the hallway with the key to the apartment in his hand. I follow him. I don't even want him now, but I'll be damned if I'm letting him embarrass me like that or take one of the other girls in front of me. Who the hell does this jerk think he is?

She doesn't have what I want.

My blood begins to boil as he opens the apartment door and walks in. The door nearly slams shut in my face. *Nice manners, asshole.*

I storm in behind him.

He walks straight to the bar and pours himself a scotch. He holds the bottle up in question.

"No, thanks," I snap.

I place my purse down on the table and see a silver bucket filled with ice and a bottle of champagne in it. That's more like it.

Sebastian follows my line of sight.

"Do you want one of those?" he asks.

"Please."

He opens the bottle and pours me a glass of champagne, eventually passing it to me.

We glare at each other as we take a sip of our drinks, animosity bouncing between us.

"I thought your job was making shit coffee?" He sips his scotch.

A sarcastic smile crosses my face. "You sound quick to judge for a man that pays for sex."

He fakes a smile as if I'm stupid. "I'd rather pay than sell myself."

"Same fucking thing." I sip my champagne and then smile sweetly. "But I've been paid now. So run along, *Mr. Garcia,*" I mouth.

Contempt drips from his every pore as his eyes hold mine. "What the fuck are you playing at?" he whispers.

I step forward so that I'm only inches from his face. "I was hoping to get some sexual satisfaction," I say quietly. "But you don't have what I want."

His jaw clenches as he glares at me, and he slowly takes his suit jacket off. "I have more than you fucking want."

"I doubt—"

He cuts me off by grabbing my hand and putting it over his crotch. His dick is rock-hard beneath the material of his suit pants.

My blood begins to heat, and, unable to help it, my hand closes around the shape of his hard penis.

"Do your job!" He sneers, and it's obvious that he's furious that I'm here.

"You wish."

His eyes are fixed on mine. "Get on your knees and suck my dick, you dirty whore."

Excitement screams through my body. This is fucked up...but holy hell, it's hot.

"I wouldn't suck your dick if it were the last cock on Earth," I whisper. "I'm broke, not desperate."

A trace of a smile crosses his face. He likes this game too.

He steps forward and takes my face in one hand, his grip almost painful as he licks up the side of my face and drops his mouth to my ear. "You want to be a whore, Cartier?"

My heart begins to thump hard in my chest at the dominance of him.

"You want to be used?" he growls against my ear, squeezing my face harder. "You want me to blow my load on your face?" He grabs a handful of my hair and pulls my head back so that my face is to his. "Because I've got a really full cock that's looking to be emptied."

Christ almighty, *he's fucking filthy.*

Goose bumps scatter over my body. His grip is almost painful.

He pulls my head back again and bites my neck hard. My body betrays me and pumps with arousal.

Yes.

He licks my open lips, and I feel it in my sex. He takes my bottom lip between his teeth and stretches it out. I flutter all over and whimper.

He licks my face again, and I'm pinned by the grip of his hand. All I can do is close my eyes.

"Answer the question, Cartier. Do you want my cock, or will I have to go and find someone else who does?" he whispers darkly. "Any wet pussy will do."

His grip on my face is painful when he licks up my face once more, and then he bites my earlobe.

Holy mother of fuck.

This is not how respectable men speak or behave.

Some kind of moral rubber band snaps, and suddenly, I want to be who he thinks I am.

I want to be his whore.

"You wouldn't survive my pussy," I whisper. "I'll ruin you for fucking life, little boy."

His mouth breaks into a slow, sexy smile, and he steps back from me as he pulls at his tie hard and undoes it. "You wish."

I pick up my champagne and take a sip.

Our eyes are locked, and button by button, he slowly undoes his shirt. His chest is broad and olive with a scattering of dark hair, and blow me down, if he isn't the most perfect male specimen I've ever seen.

All man.

My sex begins to throb. God, he *does* turn me into a whore—a filthy whore who wants him badly.

He pulls his shirt completely open, untucking it from his pants.

My eyes drop down his body, and I swallow the lump in my throat. I don't know if I've ever been this turned on.

This is wrong and messed up and so damn primal.

He undoes the button on his pants and rearranges himself in his pants. The tip of his hard cock sits over his waistband, and my eyes linger on the thick, purple head.

He's hung.

Okay, this little fantasy just keeps on giving.

Thump, thump, thump goes my pulse.

He steps closer and takes my champagne glass to take a sip of my drink. Then, with his eyes on mine, he slowly tips the glass and lets the champagne drizzle down my cleavage. It's cold, and my nipples harden.

He kisses my neck and bites and sucks his way down to the

champagne. There, he licks it up with strong strokes of his thick tongue.

My insides flutter.

Fuck!

Who's ruining who here?

"Get that fucking dress off," he growls.

I laugh out loud because this is insane, and who the hell am I?

"You want it off, you take it off," I tell him. "I undress for nobody, least of all entitled assholes."

He jerks me forward. "You'll do more than un-fucking-dress for me."

He spins me around and unzips my dress in one sharp movement. He slides it over my shoulders, and it pools on the floor around my feet.

He slaps me on the behind. "Knees," he growls.

I turn and stand still, now eye to eye with him.

"I said, get on your fucking knees," he says.

This is too hot to handle.

Unable to disobey, I fall to the floor and watch as he slides his pants down until his thick cock springs free.

This was not part of the plan, April.

His cock is engorged, with thick veins running down the length of it. He bounces it on my cheek, watching me. "Tongue out."

I stick my tongue out and look up at him in wonder.

Finally, a man who knows what he wants.

"Farther," he growls.

I do as I'm told, and he stands to the side, sliding the underside of his cock over the top of my tongue.

"*Yes*," he hisses. "Just. Like. That." He repeats the movement, and pre-ejaculate beads on his end.

The idea of him coming undone because of me fries my brain, and I clench hard to stop my own orgasm.

He's got me, and he's got me good. This is next level fucking hot.

I want to taste it. I want him in my mouth.

I turn my head towards him. He grabs a handful of my hair and pulls my face back to his with his dark eyes holding mine.

"Stop." He bends and slowly licks my lips. "I'll tell you when to suck." He licks me again, but this time it turns into a kiss, his tongue dancing seductively against mine. My eyes close.

Oh God.

With his hands still in my hair, his tongue rides the top of mine, back and forth, back and forth.

Everything about this setting is wrong, hot—and damn, I feel bad to the bone. Like a porn star or something. This is unchartered territory for me. My sex life has always been average at best.

He grabs the base of his cock and stands upright, breaking the kiss. He rubs the tip of his cock through my open lips, and his eyes darken with delight. A dark and dangerous smile flashes across his face. "I like this look on you."

I smirk around him. "Shut up or I'll bite it off."

He chuckles before he slides his dick down my throat, and I gag.

"Take it." His hands tighten in my hair. "Fucking take it all."

Good God, he's a big man.

I close my eyes and try to deal with the sheer size of him. The taste of his pre-ejaculate warms my taste buds.

Our eyes lock, and then, as if he's unable to hold off any longer, he pulls me to my feet and slides my panties down my legs. He slides his fingers through my dripping lips, and his eyes flutter shut as he lets out a sharp hiss.

He turns quickly and shuffles through his jacket pocket. Before I know it, he's rolling a condom on and dragging me over to the sofa, where he falls into a seated position. He pulls me over the top of him and then holds the base of his cock up, his eyes locked on mine. "Get on it."

I laugh as I lose all control and straddle him.

His fingers find that spot between my legs, and he slowly slides two fingers deep inside.

"Tight and wet," he says. "Just how I like it."

His fingers move inside me, almost violently as I kneel above him, and I grip his broad shoulders for balance. The sound of my arousal echoes in the room, and I shudder.

"Don't even fucking think about coming." He bites my nipple through my bra. My head tips back, and I whimper out loud.

Holy shit. What the hell is going on here?

He's a god.

And I'm not supposed to be doing this.

He grabs my ass cheek, and with one hand holding himself up, and the other pulling me down onto him, he slides in deep. I feel the sharp sting of his possession stretching my body completely open.

Oh... Fuck.

We stare at each other, and it feels like something shifts between us.

"Fuck..." I whimper before I bend to kiss him. "So...good."

He smiles against my lips, and he grabs my hip bones, grinding me down onto him, circling himself deep within me.

A deep, guttural moan escapes me, and I begin to see stars.

No... Hold it!

He repeats the delicious movement once more, and I almost lose control.

"I'm going to come," I whimper. "I can't hold it." Nobody could be fucked like this and not come.

"That's okay." He looks up at me and brushes the hair back from my forehead. "You come hard for me, baby. Milk my cock."

He slams me down hard as he takes my lips in his, and I cry into his mouth, my body convulsing. Then the weirdest thing happens. His grip on my face softens, and our kiss turns tender. We stop moving, and we kiss as if we have all the time in the world, like it's the only thing that matters. It's sweet and wonderful, and I forget where I am.

He smiles against my lips and then lifts me to lay me back on the couch, where he spreads my legs open.

His eyes stay fixed on my sex as he slowly spreads my lips apart with his fingers.

I hold my breath.

What's he doing?

Is he stopping?

Doesn't he want to come?

He spreads my thighs and drops to his knees beside the couch, and he licks me. "I need to taste you."

His thick tongue swipes through my flesh, and his eyes close in pleasure. "So fucking good," he moans against my sex.

Goose bumps scatter up my spine as I watch the most sexual creature I have ever encountered lick me up.

I reach down and run my fingers through his black hair. He looks up and our eyes lock.

Holy hell.

Then he's all in, moving almost violently against me, his lips, whiskers, and face glistening with the evidence of my orgasm.

He closes his eyes in a state of absolute bliss. His thick tongue thrashes and, oh God, my back arches off the couch.

"Ahh!" I cry.

He flips me over and drags me to the end of the couch, positioning me on my knees before he slams in hard from behind.

The air is knocked from my lungs, and I push my face into the cushions.

Ouch, fuck!

He fucks me, and it's hard, deep, and powerful strokes. His thick cock is moving at a piston pace, and somewhere in my daze, I come to the realization that I've never been fucked like this before.

So thoroughly.

So completely.

He begins to moan, and I smile against the cushions. What a fucking hot sound that is. He slams into me and then holds himself deep. I feel the telling jerk of his cock as he comes hard. He lets out a low, guttural moan, and he continues to slowly slide in and out, releasing his body of the last of his orgasm.

I'm gasping for breath, my body wet with perspiration. I glance over my shoulder to see Sebastian's satisfied smile.

I pant and drop my head, my body still shuddering with waves of pleasure deep inside.

Just wow.

He pulls out, panting for breath as he tips his head back to look up at the ceiling. His hands rest on his hips.

"Fucking hell," he gasps.

I'm speechless. There's not a coherent thought in my empty head.

He was meant to be sweet and simple, not hot and devious.

That was so random.

"Shower," he says, and he grabs my hand to pull me up. He leads me down the hall and into the bathroom. After he turns the hot water of the shower on, he removes his condom and throws it in the waste bin.

Without another word, he spins me away from him and unfastens my bra.

I glance over at our reflection in the mirror. My hair is all over the place, and he's completely naked.

I think we've been in the apartment for all of fifteen minutes. So much for me not sleeping with anyone. I guess I really am an Escape Girl.

Whorebag extraordinaire.

Sebastian throws my bra to the floor, and then he moves my hair to one side of my neck and tenderly kisses me on the sensitive skin there.

"You were incredible," he breathes against my ear.

My hand instinctively rises to his face, and we stand cheek to cheek for a moment. Our eyes lock in the mirror, and his forehead creases. I turn towards him to take his face in both hands, and I kiss him softly. I don't want anything hard anymore.

I want sweet. I want gentle. I want tenderness.

We kiss for a few moments, and his big, strong arms fold around me. He holds me tightly, and oh... *This man.*

Our kiss turns desperate, and he pins me to the wall, letting our tongues explore each other's. Taking our time. His hard erection is up against my stomach. I open my eyes to see that his are firmly shut. He's right here with me.

He lifts me, and I wrap my legs around his waist. Wasting no time, he slides in deep, right where he's supposed to be. It feels so natural between us that I can't help but smile against his lips.

We move in sync.

"Fuck," he whispers before he pulls out in a rush and puts me down.

"What's wrong?"

He drags his hand down his face. "I've got to..."

"What?" He looks around the room like a scared animal. "Sebastian?"

He tears a towel from the hanger and wraps it around his waist. "Condom," he says before he rushes from the room.

Huh? I turn the shower off, and my eyes widen. Oh shit, we forgot a condom.

Oh...he's getting a condom. I turn the shower back on and get in under the hot water, waiting for him to get back in. I put my head under the water and smile up at the ceiling as the steaming hot water runs over my face. I can't believe this night.

Sebastian comes back into the bathroom, now fully dressed.

"I've got to go," he says.

"What?"

His eyes hold mine, but he says nothing.

"What are you doing?" I frown. "We have all night together."

He opens his mouth to say something and then stops himself. "I'll see you later." Without another word, he rushes out of the room.

I turn off the shower and run after him, grabbing a towel from the rack.

"What? Why?" I call out.

"I have to go." He storms towards the front door.

"Where?"

"Home."

My face falls as I connect the dots. "Are you kidding me?" I snap.

He stops.

"Are you fucking married?"

He stops and spins back towards me. "What?"

"You're married!" I cry. "You do have a wife and family, don't you? That's why you come here. That's why you have to leave?"

He screws his face up, clearly disgusted. "What?"

I get a vision of a wife at home, waiting for him, and three little kids tucked up safely in their beds, waiting for Daddy.

I get a lump in my throat because, hell, I do feel like a whore now. The lowest form of low.

"Are you married?" I whisper.

"No."

"Is there someone waiting for you at home?"

"That's none of your business."

My eyes well with tears.

He drags his hand through his hair. "I'm single," he finally says. "Not that it matters."

He turns, and without another word, he leaves.

Regret swims around in my stomach.

I walk to the door and rest my forehead on the back of it.

What the hell just happened?

4

April

I TURN and look around the now silent apartment, taking in all its luxurious splendour. My eyes drift to the two half-empty glasses of alcohol on the counter.

"Fuck," I whisper. "What the hell was that?"

I drag my hand down my face and trudge back up the hall. I look back towards the front door.

Maybe he'll come back?

I roll my eyes at myself.

Yeah, sure he will.

I get back in the shower and put my head under the steaming hot water.

My body is still thumping. I can feel a pulse in my sex. I wash myself, and it stings from the stretch of having him inside me. His body worked mine over well—too well.

How did that all go so wrong?

I finish up in the shower and dry myself. I put on the black velvet robe that's hanging on the back of the walk-in wardrobe door, and I walk back out to the living area. A sense of regret sits in my chest.

Damn it... I'm pissed at myself.

Why would I sleep with him when I promised myself I wouldn't? That is not who I am.

Mind you, he was the last person on Earth I thought would come to a place like this.

I pour myself another glass of champagne, and I peer inside the fridge to find a huge serving of chocolate-covered strawberries sitting on a silver platter. I take them out and walk into the living room, placing them on the coffee table in front of me. I pick up the remote and turn the television on.

I drop down and curl my legs up beneath me.

Sipping on my champagne, I stare into space, his words coming back to me.

I'm single. Not that it matters.

I eat a strawberry, and the wonderful flavour bursts through my mouth.

"Answer the question, Cartier. Do you want my cock, or will I have to go and get someone else who does? Any wet pussy will do."

God.

I thought we were role-playing...but were we?

I close my eyes and drain my glass, only to refill it immediately. I want to forget tonight ever happened.

Five thousand pounds never felt so cheap.

"Don't be lazy. Your essay details are in the assignment sheet that was emailed to you last week," the lecturer says from his place on the stage. "Remember, this is thirty percent of your total mark. Switch on, people."

The class gives an audible groan.

The bell rings through the speaker, notifying us of the end of the class, and we begin to pack up our desks.

"If you are having problems," the lecturer calls, "I'm holding a study group after class next Thursday night in the library to help you prepare."

I put my laptop inside my bag. I really should go to that. I have no idea how to navigate this essay. I looked at it briefly last week, and it confused the hell out of me.

Thursday, though. Why do I feel like I have something on Thursday?

I sling my backpack onto my back and walk out of the auditorium.

Shit... I'm working in the Escape Club next Thursday. It's my second shift.

Ugh, I've felt like crap all day today.

Sleeping alone in that Escape Room last night was definitely a low point of my life. When I was leaving this morning, I saw a few of the other girls leaving their apartments with their dates from last night. It rubbed salt into my wounds a little.

They stayed with their date.

I trudge down the crowded corridor now, towards my last lecture of the day.

Why the hell has this upset me? It's not like I went there looking for love. I went there with an agenda. The money. Five thousand pounds, and that's what I got.

I made a plan and I stuck to it.

Stop beating yourself up about this, I remind myself.

Only three more shifts to go. In one month, I'll have twelve months' rent and I can resign. This is not my jam, but I'm sticking to my game plan. I need twenty thousand pounds, and damn it, I'm getting it.

"April!" I hear someone call from behind me.

I turn to see Brandon running to catch up with me.

"Hey." He smiles as he falls into step beside me.

"Hi." I smile. "How are you?"

Brandon is one of my friends on campus. He's studying engineering and is on my football team. He's a freshman and has a girlfriend at home.

"Good. Hey, Harvey asked me to see if you're going to that party on campus tomorrow night."

"Oh God," I frown. "You tell Harvey, for the fifteenth time, even if I am going, I am not into him. He's way too young for me."

Brandon chuckles. "I keep telling him that." He bumps me with his shoulder. "He's hoping you will change your mind. He wants to be your boy toy."

I laugh out loud. "Yeah, well, that's not happening."

"What are you doing for dinner tonight? Do you want to grab something with me and Lara?" Lara is our other friend. She's lovely too.

I feel like shit because I hardly slept a wink in that Escape apartment last night. "No, I've got an assignment to do, but thanks, anyway. You guys have fun."

"Do you want us to bring you something back?"

"Maybe." I frown. "Text me from wherever you go."

"Okay. Oh, and word on the street is that there's an after-party to the party in Penelope's room tomorrow night."

I exhale heavily. "Great." I sigh.

"Do you want to sleep on the floor in my or Lara's room again?"

"No, it's okay. I might be going away for the weekend."

"Really? Where to?"

"A friend of mine is over here. I'm thinking of catching up with her." That's an appalling lie, but I'm thinking of taking a mini break out of London for the weekend. I do have a little extra cash injection now, and maybe I could find somewhere dirt cheap. Anything is better than sleeping next door to the Rave Cave when it's in full swing.

"Okay, I'll text you tonight with the menu of wherever we end up eating," Brandon says before he turns off towards his next tutorial.

A weekend away. That's not actually a bad idea. Yeah, I could go away by myself.

I smile as I walk up the corridor. Hmm.... Where, exactly, could I go?

Sebastian

I bring the club back and hit the ball with force. It whistles through the air.

"Nice shot," Spencer coos.

"Your game is on point today, Garcia," Julian says as he retrieves his golf club from his bag.

I watch the ball bounce and then land on the green. "It's always on point. What are you talking about, Masters?"

Spencer chuckles as he brings the ball towards him on the ground with the back of his club. Golf on a Sunday is one of my favourite pastimes.

We watch Spencer hit the ball with force, and it hooks at the end and bounces over the net, out onto the road.

"Fuck it!" he cries out. "Why the hell am I playing so bad?" He pretends to snap his club over his knee. "I know. I'm overfucked and underpaid, that's why."

We chuckle.

Spencer being overfucked is something we never thought we'd hear. He's a deviant from way back.

We put our clubs into the back of the golf cart and climb in. I get behind the wheel and pull out onto the gravel road to take us to the next hole.

"Hey, I got a very interesting job offer this morning," I tell them.

"Such as?" Julian asks.

You know how I've been helping with the planning of the roads on the eastern distributor for government?"

"Yeah," they both say.

"They've offered me a position on Cabinet."

"You. A politician?" Spencer gasps. "You fucking hate politicians."

"I know." I pull into the next hole and park the buggy. "I'm not taking it, of course."

"What's the position?" Masters asks.

"Minister of Planning and Development."

Masters frowns. "Wouldn't be a bad gig. What's the coin?"

"Decent, although I make more now." I take the club from my bag and line up my shot.

"Could you do both?" he asks.

"I don't know." I slice the ball, and it flies off into the distance. "Fuck, I'm getting good at this game."

"Please," Spencer scoffs. "I can beat you with my hands tied behind my back."

"Okay, let's see it," Masters replies flatly. "You're all fucking talk, Spence."

I chuckle as Masters lines up his shot.

"I'd look into taking both jobs. It could be great for the CV. Town Planner and all that," Masters says as he hits his shot. It bounces low, hits a tree, and flies back towards us.

"You're completely shit," I smirk.

"Get fucked," he snaps as he puts his club back in the bag. "Unlucky."

"Sebastian Garcia, the politician," Spencer teases just as he strikes the ball.

"Has a ring to it." Masters smirks.

I roll my eyes. "I'm not taking it."

We get back into the golf buggy. "Hey, you still drinking shit coffee from that hot chick across town?" Spencer asks.

I grip the steering wheel tightly. "No."

Spencer's eyes fly to me. "Why not?"

I shrug. "Lost interest."

The last thing I need is a lecture from these two. Ever since I found my wife in bed with our gardener, they've become a tad overprotective, and I am not in the mood to talk about the head-fuck of a week I've had.

Least of all *her*.

I pull the cart up to the next hole.

"Bree wants to set you up with her friend," Masters says as he climbs out. "Apparently, she's smoking hot."

"I'm not going on a fucking blind date, Masters."

"Why not?"

"Because I don't want or need a woman. Been there, done that. Not fucking doing it again." I climb out of the buggy.

"You still horny or what?"

"Problem has been eradicated," I say, lining up my ball.

"Tell me you went to the Escape Club?" Spencer sighs dreamily.

Masters and I chuckle. Spencer is living vicariously through me now that he's settled down.

"Fuck, I love that place," he snaps.

"May have." I hit the ball with force, and it slices through the air.

"That's the only thing I miss about being single, you know? The thrill of that Escape Club. Bidding on the girls, waiting for them to choose me." He narrows his eyes as he stares off into the distance. "It's like the ultimate gaming and shopping experience. Those were good times, man."

Masters chuckles. "And then you went and fell in love and ruined it all."

"I mean, I wouldn't change it. Charlotte is it for me, but, you know..." He lines up his shot. "Hot, gorgeous women just waiting to please you. No strings, no demands. It is the ultimate fantasy."

Masters smirks. "I have to agree."

I clench my jaw when I get a vision of April... Cartier... Whatever her fucking name is.

The way she looked at me when she came. I feel my cock twinge in appreciation.

Fuck.

I throw my club into my golf bag with force. I don't want to think about her. I *won't* think about her.

She pisses me off.

April

I wipe the table near the window and peer out into the street.

Why hasn't he come back?

I glance at the clock. It's 8:45 a.m., and Sebastian would have normally been in for his coffee by now. He didn't come on Friday. He didn't come on Monday or Tuesday, either. Now, here we are on Wednesday, and he still hasn't shown.

He's not coming.

Fuck, was our night together so dreadful that he doesn't even want my coffee now?

I've been analysing our night together and overanalysing it to the point that I'm driving myself insane.

Everything was good. I mean, not great, but he was consistently coming back to see me despite being served the worst coffee on Earth. And he was sweet, lovely, handsome, and we would flirt with each other.

My heart swells when I think of him like that.

And then he saw me at the club, and he was angry that I was there.

I chose him, too, even though he didn't want me. But that's the thing: I know he did want me before that.

I wipe the table and let my mind run back over the chain of events.

We went back to the Escape Room and we got into some kind of fucked-up role-playing.

Then we had the best sex of my life.

And he was right there with me. He lost his head too. It wasn't one-sided; I know it wasn't.

I go to the next table and wipe it over, lost in my memories.

Then we had a thing in the shower when we were kissing. We were so completely lost in the moment that we forgot a condom. I scratch my head as I think back. That was definitely the turning point. Things just spiralled downhill from there.

I'm single. Not that it matters.

I wipe all the tables down and peer back out through the window.

I hate that he's the first guy that has interested me since my divorce. I hate that we met at the club. I hate that we had the best sex ever and that he turned out to be an asshole. I hate that he's stopped coming in for my bad coffee.

"Excuse me, miss," someone says from behind me.

"Yes?"

"Do you have a bathroom?"

"It's just outside and down to the left." I point out the door. "I'll show you where it is."

"Thank you."

I walk out the front door of the café and direct the person on where to go. Then I look over the bustling crowd walking past.

I just wish I had told him I was only working four shifts to pay for my rent. I wish I had explained myself. I should have said more...

I sigh heavily and go back into the café.

Oh well. He's gone.

It is what it is.

I sit on my bed and scroll through the places for rent, and I make my list of properties to look at this weekend. It feels great to have options. For the first time in a long time, I have money in the bank, and I forgot how good that feels.

My earnings from Escape Club hit my account today, which means that I now have five thousand pounds to my name. After my shift on Thursday night, I'll have ten thousand, and I can start looking for an apartment. I'll have enough for the bond plus six weeks' rent, and I'll start to actually move on this.

But I am *not* sleeping with anyone else.

No way in fucking hell am I making myself have a shit week like this again.

I stare at my computer, and then I allow myself to do something I shouldn't.

I type into Google

Sebastian Garcia. Architect, London.

The results come up.

Sebastian Garcia
London's Rock Star of Architecture

What the heck? I speed-read through the information.

Age: 37
Estimated worth: 15 million
Marital status: divorced

I frown as I read on. He's divorced?
I click on Wikipedia.

Sebastian Garcia is an architect best known for his cutting-edge designs and high-profile clients. Rarely seen without a beautiful woman on his arm since his divorce two years ago.

I click on the images, and my eyes widen.
Fuck.

There's image after image of him in a black-tie suit with a beautiful woman on his arm. There are also some of him playing golf. That looks like a charity golf thing.

I go through more images of him on nights out, laughing, smoking a cigar. There are two good-looking men with him in a lot of the images. Who are they?

I exhale heavily as reality sinks in. So, he's a player.
I slam my computer shut in disgust.

. . .

After washing my hands in the basin and looking at my reflection in the mirror, I fix my hair and straighten my apron. The thought of my shift tonight at the club has me anxious. I just have this morning at the café to get through, and then I have two lectures, and then...

Then I'm halfway there to my financial goal.

"Focus," I mouth to myself in the mirror. "Ten thousand pounds."

I fix my hair one last time and make my way up the laneway next to my café. I turn the corner and glance up and over at the congested street. It's super busy, like it is every day.

And I see him.

Sebastian is walking on the other side of the street, staring over at the café.

My heart jumps.

I watch as he pushes his hands into his pockets and stops for a moment. What's he doing?

Then he turns around and begins to walk away.

I watch him walk away up the street, and I look around in a panic. What, he's just leaving?

I run across the street. "Sebastian!" I call. He doesn't hear me and keeps walking. "*Sebastian!*"

He turns, and his face falls when he sees me.

"What are you doing?" I throw my hands up in the air. "You're just leaving without coming to see me?"

He presses his lips together, his eyes locked on mine. His hair is dark, his skin tanned against his crisp white shirt.

Damn, I've never seen a man wear a navy suit so well.

For some reason, I feel like I need to defend myself. I can't stand the thought of him thinking I'm a dirty whore...even though he's one.

I don't even understand what I'm feeling, or why.

"I'm only doing four shifts there." I shrug. "At the club, I mean."

His jaw clenches.

"I need the money so I can move out of my university dorm. I'm here on a scholarship, and I can't live there anymore. There are parties every night, and I'm going crazy. You don't know how bad it is," I say in a rush.

We're staring at each other. I'm being open and vulnerable here, and he still has his hands in his pockets, standing there, completely cold and guarded.

"I'm working the next three Thursday nights, and then I'm resigning."

After a while, he replies, "Why would I care?"

"Because I..." I pause because, damn it, what the fuck am I doing right now? "I don't want to do a shift there without you. I can't stand the thought of it."

His brow furrows.

"I'm not who you think I am, Sebastian."

His lips twist as if he's holding his tongue.

"If it hadn't been with you, I wouldn't have had sex that night. It was only because I liked you before I even worked there."

He stays silent.

I throw my hands up in disgust. "Is that it? Is that all you've got to say? I'm begging to see you, and you can't say a single fucking word?"

His eyes hold mine.

"You know what?" I shake my head. "Forget what I said. I beg for nobody. Don't bother coming."

More silence.

"You're not the only one who's disappointed," I snap at him.

He frowns. "Meaning?"

"You're not who I thought you were either."

"Who did you think I was?"

I look around at the people surrounding us, so lost in their routines that they don't even notice us. I turn back to him and shrug. "Someone who was worth it." I smile sadly. "Guess not."

I turn and walk back out onto the street in a daze. A car blares its horn at me when I nearly walk in front of it.

I march back into the café.

That's it. It's done.

I stare at the reflection of the girl in the mirror with her full face of makeup and her strapless black lace dress.

The buzz in the air is electric. The Escape Girls are excited for tonight. It's showtime.

The thought of entertaining a man tonight turns my stomach.

I'm not sleeping with anyone. I don't want to even talk to a man, let alone have sex.

Mr. Garcia well and truly tamed the tiger that was my libido. After taking in the size of him, I was sore for days. But it was my ego that took the biggest hit. I'm still licking my wounds, and to make it worse, I begged this morning when I saw him.

Pathetic.

I hear the excited squeal of one of the girls. She peers around the curtain that hides a one-way window that shows the catwalk area. The girl has long dark hair and is drop-dead gorgeous.

"He's here. He hasn't been here for months." She dances back to her makeup chair. "I'm so excited, I could die."

"Who's here?" someone else asks.

"Mr. Smith."

"Garcia?" someone else asks.

"You aren't supposed to know his real name," another girl says.

He's here.

The girls all break into excited chatter, and my heart drops.

Fuck...he has a fan club.

5

April

THE MAKEUP ARTIST applies my blush, and I feel my face heat with frustration. Or is that excitement, or just sheer terror? I can't even tell anymore.

"Curtain time, girls!" Porsha calls. "Line up in your order." Her eyes glance over to me. "Cartier, darling, you will be choosing third tonight."

I nod.

"You will work your choosing order number backwards to number ten, and then for the next two weeks after that, you will choose last. This is how we keep it fair."

"Okay, sure." I fake a smile. I won't be here then, anyway.

"Can I choose first?" the girl with the long dark hair asks. "I know it's not my turn, but I really want a certain person. I've been waiting for him to come back for months."

Sebastian.

I look her up and down. She's beautiful, with thick, long dark hair and a small tight and toned figure. She has the most attractive face of anyone I've ever seen. She's wearing a short red dress that shows all of her curves. Her large breasts are peeking out of her top, and her legs go on for miles.

Sebastian's slept with her before, I know it. I get a vision of her with him, and my stomach twists with disgust.

"No." Porsha looks through her printed schedule. "You are..."

I hold my breath, waiting for Porsha to finish. I don't know if I want to choose before or after the girl. What if I pick him and he really wants her?

Damn it, I'm now regretting asking him to come at all.

"You are second tonight, Luna," Porsha finishes.

"Yes." Luna smiles and punches the air.

Shit... She's before me.

I drop my head. I just want to get the hell out of here.

"Line up, girls." Porsha smiles. "Game faces on. Our gentlemen pay a lot of money for your company."

The girls laugh and chatter as they line up, while I close my eyes and try to brace myself to be brave.

The first girl makes her way out onto the catwalk. She walks up and back, and then she spins and walks back out to the end. She performs a sexy twirl to the sounds of quiet excitement from the men, before she stands to the side of the catwalk and places her hand on her hip.

Luna is next, and I watch on as she does the same. My heart is literally in my throat.

Fuck this, I'm never coming back here. This is beyond stressful.

The song changes to "Sexual Healing" by Marvin Gaye, and I exhale heavily. This music is slower, sexier...tantric, even. And now it's my turn.

I walk out to the seductive beat. When I make it to the end of the catwalk, I glance around at the gorgeous men before me.

But not the one I'm after.

I walk to the back, twirl, and then I strut back to the front, placing my hand on my hip just in time to look up into the hungry stare of Mr. Garcia.

He's sitting at a table at the back with a glass of amber fluid in one hand and a cigar in the other. His legs are spread wide, his appearance dominant.

Our eyes lock, and he slowly brings the cigar to his lips and sucks hard. He inhales, and a thin stream of smoke disappears into his mouth.

Fuck me, this man is sex on legs.

My insides begin to pulse as I imagine him naked and on top of me.

I remember the way he gripped my face the last time we were together. The way he licked my lips. The way he bit my neck. The way he went down on me midway through sex and licked the mess he'd made.

My nipples harden at the memory. No wonder he has a fucking fan club.

I'm the damn president.

I can pretend all I want that there is something between us, but when I see him here, like this, reality hits home. I want to be dominated by him. I want him to use me, and damn it, I want to be fucked.

His eyes are dark, and I nearly forget what I'm supposed to be doing.

I slowly turn and take my place at the side of the stage.

I watch the rest of the parade, concentrating on not looking up, but I can feel the heat of his gaze.

Is he always this sexual? Or does this club bring something out in him?

The parade ends, and Porsha walks out with the microphone in hand.

"Gentlemen, may I introduce Eleonore."

The men fall into silence.

"State your intentions!" Porsha calls.

The men line up in front of Eleonore and, one by one, they introduce themselves. "Who will you choose, Eleonore?"

"Mr. Parker." She smiles.

A good-looking man steps up and takes her hand. He walks

her from the stage. He looks like an athlete or something. Young and virile.

Good choice.

"Gentlemen, may I introduce Luna," Porsha says, holding Luna's hand up. "State your intentions."

The men line up again. All except one.

Mr. Garcia remains seated as he sips his scotch. He looks every bit like the powerful, walking orgasm that he is.

"Who will you choose, Luna?" Porsha asks.

Luna smiles and points to Garcia. "Mr. Smith."

Shit.

He runs his tongue over his teeth and tilts his jaw to the ceiling.

"Mr. Smith." Porsha smiles. "You are one lucky man tonight."

Sebastian slowly stands and then comes and takes Luna's hand. He leads her from the stage, and I drop my head in dismay. *What?*

Fuck, fuck, fuck.

"May I introduce Cartier!" Porsha calls. "This is only her second shift. Who will be her second date?"

The men move and stand in a line in front of me.

"Fifty thousand!" a man calls.

"Sixty-five!" another man calls.

I glance towards the door to see Sebastian leaving with Luna. He's holding her hand. He says something to her, and she laughs in response as they continue to leave.

He didn't even stay to see who I will choose. I taste the bile of my stomach as it turns.

God, I read this all wrong.

He doesn't care that I work here. He just doesn't give a fuck.

I go through the introductions with the men one by one, and they all seem nice.

But none are who I want.

"Who will it be, Cartier? Who will be your date for tonight?"

I look between them. I want to go for the kindest-looking man —the one I know will handle my sexual rejection.

"Mr. Stevenson," I say softly.

He's blonde and sweet-looking. He walks over and takes my hand to kiss the back of it. "Hello, Cartier."

"Hi." I force a smile.

He leads me down the catwalk, and we walk towards the exit.

Is Sebastian kissing her right now? Is he grabbing her face and licking it?

God, it's one thing to never experience a man like Mr. Garcia, but to know what he's like and not be able to have him—to know that someone else is having it in your place—that's another level of torture.

Mr. Stevenson and I make it into the elevator, and I stare at the back of the doors.

He picks up my hand and kisses the back of it.

"I can't wait to get you alone, Cartier. I bid for you last week too."

I force a smile and, unable to think of a reply, remain silent.

The elevator doors open and we walk down to a room, where he opens the door and lets me inside.

Should I just leave? Fuck, *this is a mess.*

"Champagne?" he asks.

"Please." I cross my arms and walk over to the window to stare out at the city of London below. The heavy flow of traffic lights up the streets.

So, this is what it feels like to hate yourself.

No money is worth this.

Stop it.

Moments later, Mr. Stevenson passes me a glass of champagne.

"Thank you." I take a tentative sip as his eyes hold mine. "Do you come here often?"

"When I need to."

My heart pounds in my chest. "You mean...when you need sex?"

"Among other things."

God.

There's a knock at the door. "Are you expecting someone?" I ask.

"No." He frowns, walks to the door, and opens it.

Mr. Garcia stands in the corridor.

"Can I come in?" he asks.

"What do you want?" Mr. Stevenson responds.

Sebastian walks past him and into the apartment. He closes the door behind him, and his eyes find mine across the room before he turns his attention back to Mr. Stevenson.

"We're swapping partners," Garcia announces.

"Over my dead body."

"Don't fucking test me."

"I said *no*." Mr. Stevenson pushes Sebastian, and then Sebastian pushes him back. "Leave. Your new room is 121. Luna is waiting for you. I've made it worth her while, and she's excited for the swap," Sebastian tells him.

"She didn't pick me first, asshole. I want Cartier." He shoves him again.

"You can't have her," Sebastian growls.

"Stop it!" I snap. "I'm not an object you can just *have*! Neither of you can fucking have me." I walk over to the door and open it in a rush. "Get out. The both of you. I'm not having sex with either of you idiots, so just leave."

Sebastian tilts his chin, clearly happy with my outburst.

"See?" He gestures to me with his hand. "She's not having sex with anybody. You may as well take Luna up on her offer. We both know she's a sure thing."

I stare at Sebastian for a moment as I process his words, and an angry haze begins to cloud my vision. Just how many fucking times has Sebastian been with Luna?

"You know what? Just get out." I'm going to get fired for this, but I don't give a crap. I'm too angry to care anymore.

"Me?" Sebastian scoffs.

"Yes, you! What makes you think I want Luna's sloppy seconds? Anyone's sloppy seconds, actually. This place, as well as you, insults my intelligence." I push him out the door, and then I turn to Mr. Stevenson. "This is your last chance: Luna or the spare room?"

His eyes hold mine. "You're actually serious?"

"Yes. I'm fucking serious." I march up the hallway towards the bedroom. "Having sex with you is the last thing I want to do, so I know what offer I would take if I were you," I call as I slam the bedroom door shut behind me.

My heart is beating hard in my chest, and I take a deep breath to try to calm myself down.

Damn it, I'm going to get fired.

Ten thousand pounds is better than nothing, though. It's a start.

But will I even get paid for tonight?

I needed twenty thousand, but I don't care anymore. No amount of money is worth degrading myself to this level.

I walk into the bathroom and stare at myself in the mirror. All dressed up with nowhere to go. What a joke.

I hear the door slam, and I put my ear to the back of my door and listen carefully.

I think Mr. Stevenson has gone.

I walk back up the hallway, and when I see the key to the apartment on the kitchen counter, I exhale with relief.

Thank God for Luna. I wonder if she will be with both of them now. Is that even a thing?

For fuck's sake... Just yuck.

I can't believe I'm being forced to even think about that.

Champagne. I need all the champagne.

I take the bottle and fill my flute to the top. I take a sip. It's crisp, refreshing, and tastes delicious.

"Are you going to offer me a glass?" a deep voice asks behind me.

I spin to see Sebastian sitting back with his arms stretched out across the back of the couch, his leg crossed at the ankle.

I didn't see him when I came in. Was he there the whole time?

"I told you to leave," I say.

"And I told you that I wanted to spend the night with you," he replies calmly.

"Well, you can't," I snap. I drain my glass and refill it.

"What's wrong with you tonight?"

My eyes widen. "You have to ask? You can't be that stupid."

He gives me a slow, sexy smile. "Try me."

I roll my eyes. "Go away, Sebastian. I'm not interested."

"Why not?"

"Because you're fucking with my head!" I snap. "And I don't even know you."

He stands and comes to me in one movement. He pours himself a glass of champagne and then taps his glass with mine. "I think you have that the wrong way around...Cartier." He takes a slow sip.

"My name is April."

"Is it? Because I was introduced to you as Cartier."

"See?" I bark. "You're doing it again. Fucking with my head."

He chuckles and sips his champagne.

He thinks this is funny.

"Please leave." I turn my back to him. "I wanted to talk to you this morning and you didn't want any of it, so don't show up here now demanding sex."

"Have I mentioned sex?"

I spin back towards him. "I believe your words were *any wet pussy will do*."

Amusement flashes across his face. "I may have been a bit"—he pauses, as if searching for the right word—"aggravated the last time I saw you. My apologies if I ruffled your feathers."

"You were an asshole."

"I didn't expect to see you here."

"But *you* were here."

He sips his champagne as his eyes hold mine. "As a means to an end."

"Oh, you mean my means on your end."

"Don't be crass."

I lean closer. "I'll be whatever I fucking like, Mr. Garcia," I whisper.

We stare at each other as the air crackles between us, and damn it, it's there again...the temptation to have angry sex with this man.

Fucked-up, hot, and toe-curling pleasure. The kind that you only dream about.

"Why did you leave in a rush the other night?" I ask.

He stays silent.

I shake my head. "Go home, Sebastian." I sigh. "I'm not playing your mind games. I'm twenty-five, not twelve."

"Regardless of your age, you're too young for me." He lifts his glass, and I watch his tongue dart out and swipe across his bottom lip.

I feel a throb between my legs.

"I know that."

He raises an eyebrow, as if surprised by my answer.

"Maybe I am too young for you...which is a shame," I add.

"Why?"

"Because you were the first man I ever slept with."

A confused frown creases his brow.

"I'd slept with little boys before, but never a man, and it was pretty fucking perfect...until you ruined it."

His jaw clenches, our eyes locked, and damn, if he isn't the hottest man I've ever seen in my life. Tall, dark, and dangerous, the kind out of romance novels.

He steps towards me and cups my face. "You thought it was perfect." He dusts his thumb over my bottom lip, and his eyes search mine.

"You know it was—"

He cuts me off with a kiss. His lips take mine, and his tongue dances seductively in my mouth.

My toes curl. Damn it, the way he kisses. It's just so...

"We're no good for each other, Sebastian," I murmur against his lips.

He takes my face in both hands. "I know. So let's be bad for each other instead."

Something snaps inside of me.

I bring my hands to the back of his head, and I kiss him back with everything I have. Our kiss turns desperate. We lose control and turn into animals. I've never had a sexual attraction like this to anyone. It's uncontrollable. Kissing this man is the very last thing I should be doing, but hell, I can't stop.

"Naked," he growls. "I need you fucking naked."

I tear his suit jacket off his shoulders and throw it to the side. I get to work on his shirt buttons. I need *him* naked.

His lips find my neck, and he runs his teeth down it. I feel like I'm about to combust and am filled with urgency as I struggle with his pants. The button finally breaks free, and I pull his pants down in one sharp movement.

His hard cock springs free. Pre-ejaculate is already beading on its end, and my insides turn to jelly. He puts me over his shoulder and marches up the hallway, the room passing me by upside down.

When we get to the bedroom, he slowly slides me down his body until I'm standing before him.

His eyes close, and his lips press against mine. "Do you know how fucking beautiful you are?" he whispers.

Taking his face in my hands, I kiss him, our tongues dancing together for a long time.

He reaches around and works the zipper of my dress before he takes it off. I stand before him in pale pink lace underwear. His eyes darken as he drinks me in.

He licks my shoulder with his thick tongue. Goose bumps scatter, and I shudder at the mere sight of him.

"Tell me what you want," he murmurs against my mouth.

"You," I breathe. He lifts my behind, bringing me up against his erection. "All of you," I pant, curling my leg around his hip.

He stops and steps back from me. As his chest rises and falls and he struggles for air, he takes my bra off, and then he takes my erect nipple into his mouth. He bites it, and I cry out. There's just the right amount of pain mixed in with pleasure. His hands slide down my panties, and he lifts one of my legs to the bed. His fingers explore my sex while he continues to suck on my nipple. He slides three large fingers deep inside my sex, and my head tips back.

God, he knows his way around a woman's body.

He pulls back to look at me, and with his dark eyes fixed firmly on mine, he works me. The sound of wet flesh hangs in the air, and the muscles in his shoulders flex as he finger-fucks me with force.

Sebastian Garcia may be wrong for me in every single way, but how could I ever deny myself this pleasure?

His lips curl, and he inhales sharply. "You have no fucking idea how badly I want you."

He bites me hard, as if losing control, and I cry out as my head thrashes back. "Ahh."

He throws me back onto the bed and tears a condom wrapper open with his teeth. He spits out the wrapper, slides the condom on, and crawls over me.

"Open," he mouths.

I do as he asks, and he lifts my legs and places them over my shoulders.

"Careful," I whisper.

His face softens. "Baby." He kisses me tenderly. "I won't hurt you."

My heart constricts. It almost feels safer when he's mean. At least then I have some resistance.

He falls back onto his knees and brushes the tip of his penis back and forth through my swollen, wet sex. I shudder when he rubs it over my clitoris. I'm so close to coming, it's not even funny. Oh, dear God...

Hold it.

He pushes the tip in a little and meets resistance. His jaw hangs slack as he watches where our bodies meet.

"Let me in. Give me some cream and let me in." He pushes in a little farther, and my body sucks at his. It wants this.

Fuck...*we all do.*

He slowly pushes in, and my head falls back.

He holds my legs in the air as he slowly pushes his full length in. He puts his hand on the bottom of my stomach and holds our bodies snug up against each other to try and let me adjust to his size. My insides flutter.

This is too good. *He's* too good, and a fucking heartbreak waiting to happen.

"Sebastian." I reach for him.

His eyelids are hooded as he watches me, lost in his own world of gratification, unable to answer my call to him.

I sit up to grab his body and pull him down on top of me. I need him closer.

He brings my legs higher and circles himself deep inside of me. We both moan in pleasure.

"Fuck, *yes...* April," he whispers against my ear. "Can you feel how deep I am inside of you? Do you know how many times you've made me come this week, thinking about this beautiful, creamy cunt of yours?" He bites my ear hard, and goose bumps scatter down my spine. "I want to blow inside of you so fucking hard...again and again and again."

Oh God.

I glance over to the mirror on the wall to see us together like this. His thick quads are spread wide, and his dark skin is rippled with muscles. The visual is a sensory overload, and I cry out as a freight train of an orgasm rips through me.

He smiles darkly as he pumps me through it, and then he readjusts his stance to hold my ankles and spread my legs wide.

"Squeeze me," he pants, pumping me with force. The bed begins to slam into the wall. "You suck my cock for me, baby."

Our eyes are locked, and I clench around him.

His lip curls in appreciation. "Harder."

I clench harder, and his head tips back. My hands are on his thighs, and the power behind them is doing things to my brain cells, frying every last one.

His hands drop to the mattress, and he holds himself up on straightened arms as he really lets me have it. The sound of our skin slapping together echoes throughout the room, and then he begins to moan. The sound is deep and guttural, almost animalistic. He scrunches his face up and hits me hard. I feel his cock jerk as he comes hard deep inside of me.

We move together slowly to rub out his orgasm, our lips meeting once again.

Our kiss is tender, and an unexpected intimacy runs between us.

And then he falls still. His haunted eyes rise to meet mine.

For some reason, I feel the need to comfort him.

"It's okay, baby," I whisper as I brush the hair back from his face. "I'm here."

He rests his head on my chest and nestles in between my breasts. Our hearts are still racing as he clings to me for dear life.

I hold him tightly and kiss the top of his head, a feeling of uneasiness filling me.

Something is wrong. He clings to me tighter, and I hold him right back.

Something tells me that Mr. Garcia is damaged goods.

It's pitch-black as I dream a heavenly scene.

Arousal swims throughout my body, and I lie back to enjoy it.

It feels good.

I like this dream. I like it a lot.

My legs spread farther apart, and I smile to myself.

I feel a kiss on my inner thigh, and my sleepy eyes flutter open. My hand goes down to the covers, and I feel movement beneath them.

Wait, what?

A thick tongue swipes through my sex, and a thrill runs through me.

This is real.

I'm still in the Escape Room with Sebastian.

This man is insatiable. We had sex three times last night before we fell asleep, and now I wake up to this.

I pull the covers back, and in the twinkle of the moonlight pouring through the window, I see Sebastian licking me up like his life depends on it.

I smile with a sharp inhale, and I cup his face in my hand.

His eyes hold mine, and he kisses my sex with an open mouth.

"Nightcap," he whispers.

I spread my legs wider. "Please...be my guest."

He licks me deeper and deeper, and with every stroke, my arousal grows.

My back begins to arch off the bed, chasing a deeper connection.

"Get up here, Garcia."

He chuckles as he crawls up over my body with my arousal glistening on his skin. When he kisses me, I taste myself on him.

"You're quite the tomcat," I whisper.

He smiles against my lips as he rolls a condom on. "The temptation with you is just too great." I wrap my legs around his waist, and he slides in deep.

My body ripples around him.

"You're perfect," I whisper up at him in awe.

He smiles softly. "And you're deluded."

I smile as he kisses me deeper. I'm not even joking—Sebastian Garcia is male perfection.

I don't ever want this night to end.

"I have to go, babe."

I roll over and squint against the light, trying to regain my focus.

Sebastian is dressed in his suit, doing up his tie.

I sit up on my elbows. "Where are you going?"

"I have a meeting." He bends and kisses me softly, brushing my hair back from my forehead. "I'm already late."

"Well..." I pause and flop back down onto my pillow. "When will I see you?"

He moves to the mirror and readjusts his tie. "I'm not sure."

I stare at his back. He makes eye contact with me in the mirror and then looks away.

"Will you come to the café and see me?" I ask.

I know I sound whiny, but last night was special, and I know he felt it too.

"No." He adjusts his cuff links without making eye contact.

"No?" I frown. "Just like that? No?"

"I'm not seeing you out of here until..." His voice trails off.

"Until what?"

"Until you resign."

I give him a stifled smile. Well, that's better than never, I guess. "Two more shifts to go."

He raises an eyebrow as he walks into the bathroom. "We'll see." I hear him mutter under his breath. I hear him brushing his teeth, and then he reappears again. He moves to the bottom of the bed and pulls the blankets back to grab my foot. He drags me to the end of the bed, and I laugh out loud. He bends and kisses my sex.

"Last night was amazing," he whispers before kissing me on the inner thigh.

My heart swells as I watch him. "It was, wasn't it?" I smile.

He kisses my sex again. "I have to go. Stop distracting me."

I giggle and sit up. "I'm not saying anything."

He turns and raises his eyebrows.

I curl my finger. "Come here."

He dives over me on the bed, pinning my hands behind my head as he spreads my legs with his knee.

"Until next time," he whispers as he looks down at me, his face millimetres from mine.

My stomach flutters. "Until next time."

He kisses me softly and then gets up and walks down the hallway with purpose. I hear the front door click closed, and I smile goofily up at the ceiling and scrunch my eyes shut tight in excitement.

Until next time.

I watch my glass of water bouncing across my desk to the beat of the loud music next door.

This is fucking bullshit.

I close my eyes and turn up the volume on my headphones.

It's fine. It's totally fine.

I hear something smash up against our shared wall, and I tear my headphones off.

What was that?

I hear screaming, and laughter follows. She must have at least thirty people in her tiny room. I've called security three times already tonight, and none of them ever come because Penelope is fucking them all.

My phone beeps with a text from Brandon.

> *I can hear Penny's party from here.*
> *Do you want to sleep on my floor?*

I exhale heavily. No, I don't want to sleep on a mattress on someone's floor.

"*Drink it down, down, down, down,*" the chorus of drunk people chant on the other side of the wall.

I text him back.

> *Thank you.*
> *I'll be there soon*

Twenty minutes later, I knock on Brandon's door. He answers wearing his flannel pajamas.

"Hi." He stands back to let me walk past him.

I smile at his cute little getup. He's so young at only eighteen, yet he's already made up a bed on the floor for me.

"Do you want to sleep in my bed?" he asks. "It's way more comfortable."

"No." I drop my bag on the dresser. "The floor is great, thank you."

"Do you want to watch a movie?"

"Yeah, okay." I smile because I already know I won't be watching the movie. I'll be lying on the floor, daydreaming about my Mr. Garcia.

I wish tonight were next time.

I sit in a café and smile as I read through the Saturday-morning paper.

Today's the day.

After my little slumber party last night on the floor, I'm determined to find a new apartment. I don't care where or what it is; as long as it's half decent, I'm taking it.

I circle another one to look at.

"Here you go." The waitress arrives with my pancakes.

"Thank you." I fold my paper in half and put it on the bench seat beside me. I sip my coffee and begin to eat my blueberry pancakes. Yum, these are good. I take a big bite and then glance down at my folded newspaper.

I frown when I see Sebastian.

I quickly open the paper and read the headline on the back. It's the social page.

Highflyers for Charity

There's a picture of him and two men, and they each have a beautiful woman on their arm.

I read the note beside the picture: Julian and Brielle Masters, Spencer and Charlotte Jones, and Sebastian Garcia with partner Gabriella Beckman attending the Governor's Charity Ball in London.

I quickly read the article. The ball took place last night, meaning he spent Thursday night with me, took me a million times, and then he spent Friday night with her.

Did he have her a million times too?

My heart constricts with disappointment.

Asshole.

6

April

I sit back in my chair. *Wow.*

A smile crosses my face. And here I was, thinking that he was damaged in some way.

Sebastian isn't damaged. He was just feeling guilty. I give a subtle shake of my head. I don't know why I'm even surprised.

Actually, who am I kidding? I'm not surprised. I expect men to be a letdown. They always are.

I thought we had a connection, a little voice whispers from deep in my heart.

I fold the paper back in half and put it down with a heavy exhale.

My thoughts drift to the morning when we woke up and how he was with me. At the time, I did feel it was out of character for him to be so sweet, but I liked it, so I didn't let my mind explore why. I can still hear his sexy, deep voice when he told me he was leaving and asked if I was okay. When he told me that he'd had an incredible night.

I roll my eyes. No wonder he was being all wonderful and caring, calling me babe and shit. Did he feel guilty then because he was going home to her? Is that why he was being nice? Or was he being so nice because he knew I was being a fucking idiot for him?

God.

I'm not his babe.

Screw him, and screw the lot of them.

With a shaky hand, I sip my coffee. I have no idea why I thought he was different.

Because he is, that pathetic bitch who lives in my heart argues.

I go over the cold, hard facts—the ones I can't deny.

I met him in a brothel, and deep down, I already knew who he was.

"Can I get you anything?" the waiter asks, interrupting my thoughts.

"No, I'm good. Great, actually." I smile up at him.

"Let me know if you want another coffee." He smiles.

"Sure thing."

I watch him walk away, and I lift the drink to my lips with a sad smile.

You know you're fucked up when you're secretly relieved when a man shows his true colours. Call it what you will—an alarm bell, a sixth sense, or the universe looking out for me—but I know it's just a little reminder of what it feels like to be hurt by someone you love.

And a warning to never go there again.

"Hmm, I'm going to have that too." I smile as I hand over my menu.

"So, anyway," Lara continues. "Now I'm going to get a bad mark, all because this stupid witch couldn't be bothered to do her half of the assignment."

"That sucks." Brandon sighs. "I hate group assignments."

"It's never fair," I add. "One person always ends up doing all the work."

"You need to tell someone," Brandon says.

"You really do." I sip my wine.

It's Saturday night, and as usual, I'm out for dinner with Lara and Brandon.

My phone vibrates across the table, and I turn it over to see the name Porsha lighting up the screen.

Shit, she's found out about Sebastian swapping last week.

She is going to fire me. Oh well...it's not like I want to go back, anyway.

"I've just got to take this," I say as I stand. "Back in a minute." I rush towards the exit door and answer the phone. "Hello."

"Hello, Cartier."

"Hi, Porsha."

"Darling, there has been a change of plans to this week's roster."

"Okay..." I frown.

"Mr. Smith has requested a private night with you, so you will be working tomorrow night instead of Thursday."

"I don't know what you mean."

"We have a platinum service here, and Mr. Smith has decided to option that. Come to the club and we will style you, of course, but you won't be taking place in the auction as usual."

"Is that a thing?"

"It is very rare, I must admit."

"But that's not part of my job description."

"Well—"

"No, thanks," I cut her off. "I'm not interested in doing private nights with any of the clients. Least of all him."

"I thought you liked Mr. Smith."

My eyes bulge as I try to think of a professional reply. "I'm sorry. I'm just not interested."

"Well, what will I tell him?"

"Whatever you want; I really don't care. Tell him I'm washing my hair. Why don't you organize Luna to take my place instead?"

Porsha chuckles. "Are you sure? He's put in a very large bid."

I roll my eyes. "Very sure. Thank you for the opportunity, though."

Porsha exhales. "He won't be happy."

"Not my problem. I'll see you Thursday night."

"Yes, okay. Have a good night."

I smile, feeling a little more of my power return. "Goodbye." I hang up and walk back into the restaurant.

"Who was that?" Brandon asks.

"The café," I lie, taking my seat again. "I got an extra shift."

The morning sun beams through the café window.

"Can I help you?" I ask.

"I'll have an English breakfast tea with milk, please," the customer says.

I type it into the computer. "And would you like a scone today, Mrs. Henderson?"

"Yes." She grins. "You have a good memory."

"How could I forget you? Take a seat and I'll bring it out."

I turn and put the order onto the coffee machine line for Lance, and then I go about getting her scone ready.

I go to the computer and address the next customer. "Can I help you?"

"Double macchiato," a deep voice says.

I look up and into the stare of Sebastian. He's wearing a navy suit and a crisp white shirt. His dark hair hangs over his beautiful face, and his lips are a perfect shade of come-fuck-me. A stupid thrill runs through me before I catch myself.

I look back down at the screen. "Is that everything, sir?"

He stays silent, forcing me to look up.

He raises an eyebrow, and I raise mine back.

"Is. That. Everything. Sir?" I repeat.

He clenches his jaw. "A word? Outside?"

"I'm sorry. I'm very busy. Do you want something with your macchiato or not?"

"Outside, *now*, or I'll drag you out. The choice is yours."

I fake a smile. "I'm not interested in what you have to say, Mr. Garcia."

"April..." He glares at me. "You have three seconds to get your fucking ass outside before I drag you out there."

"Go to hell," I mouth. We glare at each other and that crazy anger bounces between us.

"What is your fucking problem?" he hisses.

I push his order into the computer, becoming a little flustered. "Leave me alone, Sebastian."

Lance turns towards us.

"I'm just going to steal April for a moment." Sebastian fakes a smile at Lance. "It's a matter of urgency. She won't be a minute."

Lance looks between us. "Okay."

For God's sake.

I march out to the street with Sebastian hot on my heels. He drags me around the corner into the alleyway.

"What is your fucking problem?" he snaps.

I cross my arms and roll my eyes. "I don't have a problem."

"I knew you'd fucking carry on."

"Carry on?" I whisper angrily. "I'm not the one carrying on here, Sebastian. Go away."

"It was a blind date that was organized weeks ago."

"Fuck off. It clearly said she was your partner."

"And you believe everything in the tabloids?"

"I don't care, anyway."

"We're not together, April."

"My point exactly." I move to brush past him. He grabs me by the arm and pulls me back. "Stop it," I whisper. "You're too old for me, anyway."

"Obviously, because it feels like I'm dealing with an errant teenager right now."

My cheeks heat with embarrassment. He's right—I am acting like a child, but screw it, I'm angry. I cross my arms in a huff.

"I didn't touch her," he says calmly.

81

I roll my eyes.

"It was a blind date that I didn't organize. Besides, why would I want to go out with another woman when all I can think about is you?" My eyes meet his, and a trace of a smile crosses his face. "Now, are you finished with your tantrum?"

I twist my lips as I try to hold in my snarky tongue. "You made me feel like shit."

He pauses for a moment. "I'm sorry."

He tries to place his hand on my arm but I flick him off.

"You're no good for me, Sebastian."

He smiles his first genuine smile. "No shit."

I tuck my hair behind my ear. "I don't even care what you do."

"Are you sure about that?" He steps forward so he's only inches from my face.

I drop my gaze to the ground, and he places his finger under my chin and brings my face up to his. "I'm not seeing anyone."

"It's none of my business who you see."

"You're wrong." He smiles. "It's all of your business."

His lips take mine, and he kisses me with just the right amount of suction, enough to curl my toes. "Come and stay with me tonight."

My brows furrow. Fuck it, this was not in my game plan.

"I organized this so you don't have to go to the auction on Thursday night. My bathrooms are being remodelled, and I'm staying at the hotel for a few nights. And Porsha owes me a favour."

"What does that mean?"

"I drew up the plans for her renovation. She owes me."

I raise my brow. "*I'm* the favour?"

He smiles as he rearranges my apron.

"You're staying above the club all week?" I frown. "Are you going inside?"

He chuckles, grabs the lapels of my shirt, and drags me to him. "I like this jealousy thing." His lips dust mine.

"I'm not jealous. I'm just not interested in sloppy seconds."

He smirks as his eyes hold mine.

"If you want to go inside the club, that's fine, but..." I look down the alleyway as I try to make this sound less loser-ish.

"But?" He kisses me down my neck.

How am I supposed to think when he's all over me like this? He doesn't play fair.

"I shouldn't like you," I say.

He smiles against my neck. "But you do."

"Will you stop it?" I step back from him to get some distance. "I just..." God, I'm feeling all needy and territorial. Damn this man.

We're just fucking, I try to remind myself.

"I don't like that you go there," I say.

"I don't like that *you* go there."

"I've got two more shifts left."

"One after tonight."

My gaze drops to the pathway beneath us.

He takes me into his arms. "Come and stay at the club with me." He kisses my temple. "I'm only going there for you." He presses his lips to my ear. "Don't make me beg."

I give him a stifled smile, my tantrum on the way out. "I'll think about it."

"I can order in, we can have cocktails," he offers to try and sweeten the deal.

My eyes hold his. "What do you even like about me, Sebastian?"

He hesitates as if searching for the right answer, and eventually he replies, "You make me forget who I am."

What does that mean? "What's wrong with who you are?"

"Everything."

My heart constricts. "Well, apart from you taking other women to balls and making me crazy jealous, *and* the small fact that you're a cranky asshole"—I shrug—"I think you're kind of wonderful."

He gives me a slow, sexy smile and pushes his hands into his pant pockets. "I'll see you tonight, then?"

I nod with a smile, and then I walk back down the alleyway to my café.

"April?" he calls from behind me.

I turn back towards him.

"Where's my kiss goodbye?"

My heart swells. I turn and he takes me into his arms. Then I kiss him softly. His big lips linger over mine, and alarm bells scream all around me.

I have no resistance when it comes to this man. None. He has me completely where he wants me, and I can't even pretend to want to fight it.

"I'll count down the hours till I see you," he whispers.

I nod, already knowing that this train is going straight to hell.

But like the fool that I am, I can't get off.

The makeup artist applies the finishing touches to my face, and I stare at my reflection in the illuminated mirror.

"How's that?" she asks.

"Great." I smile, happy with the result. "Thanks."

I asked for a natural look tonight. My blonde hair is straight in its sharp bob. I had a toner put in it, making it more of a champagne colour now. For the first time since I've been at the Escape Club, I'm wearing a pantsuit. It's black with a gold silk button-up top and a fitted black suit jacket.

I feel sexier than I have felt before in here. I wanted to be more me.

This is something that I would wear in the outside world. Lacy strapless dresses, while nice, are not something I would wear on a night out.

I stand and turn to look at my behind. The pants are fitted, and I unfasten my two top buttons of my shirt, revealing a peek at the cream lacy bra beneath it.

Excitement fills me, knowing that I get to see him soon.

I had an epiphany in the shower earlier: It's okay to enjoy a man and know that there's no future with him. I'm giving myself permission to fall in lust because, let's face it, that's what this is: an intense, out-of-this-world sexual attraction. He feels it too. He's made that very clear.

Our bodies work well together. He's big, strong, dominant—and, well, it turns out that I like being dominated by him.

Who knew?

I'm taking this little thing between us as a break from reality. For however long it lasts—I'm predicting it won't be for much longer—I'm going to enjoy the ride, because men who look and fuck like Sebastian Garcia are a rarity.

He's a precious diamond in the rough. The pinnacle of a woman's sexual experiences.

I'm twenty-five and in my prime. I have no commitments, and I like handing my power over to him. He knows exactly what to do with it. No man has ever satisfied me like he does. The sex we have is out of this world.

So fucking hot.

Andrew walks past with his earpiece in. "Cartier, your key is at the front desk. You are on the other side of the hotel tonight."

I frown. "The civilian side?"

The hotel has two towers. One for the Escape Club, the other for regular hotel visitors.

"Yeah, that's it. The penthouse, Tower One."

The girl standing next to me hisses, "Lucky bitch."

I smile, and with one last look at myself, I make my way to reception to grab the key and make my way to the penthouse of Tower One.

Standing at the door, I let out a deep, shaky breath to brace myself. I'm nervous tonight. For many reasons, I guess. The main one: being close to him.

I swipe my card to open the door, and my senses are instantly overloaded.

"Sexual Healing" by Marvin Gaye is playing through the speakers. It's the song I walked down the catwalk to on that second night.

I walk through the luxurious foyer to see him standing in a black dinner suit by the window. His back is to me as he stares out over the city with a glass of amber liquid in his hand.

I watch him uninterrupted for a moment. Tall, dark, and handsome, but it's his persona that is calling to me. There's a sexuality about him that's deep and ingrained into his psyche. Hell, I'm addicted.

"Hello."

He turns, and his eyes drop down my body and back up to my face. "Hello." He lifts the glass to his lips. "You look beautiful," he says after taking a drink.

I smile bashfully as I walk towards him. "So do you."

He puts his drink down and meets me halfway. As soon as we connect, we kiss. Our eyes close, and he holds my face in the way he always does. The kiss is deep and passionate, as if we haven't seen each other in forever.

Words aren't necessary when we're together; it's like we speak another language, or maybe it's that our bodies do all the talking. "Hi," he mumbles against my mouth.

I smile with him. "Why do you turn me into a sex maniac, Mr. Garcia?"

He chuckles and leads me to the bar. "I'm afraid you have that the wrong way around."

He fills two glasses with champagne and passes me one. He taps the top of his glass against mine.

"I think we've said all of twenty words to each other since we met."

I smile around my glass, knowing that he's completely right.

His hungry eyes drop down my body and, as if unable to help it, he runs his hand down my chest and cups my breast through my shirt. "I like you dressed like this."

"I prefer you naked," I retort.

He raises a brow. "I promised myself that we would at least have a conversation." His eyes drop to my lips, distracted.

"Talking is overrated. I prefer to use my tongue on better things," I tell him.

He inhales sharply. "Please don't let me stand in your way. What do I know?"

I walk up to him and grab his crotch through his trousers. "You've got something I want, Mr. Garcia."

He takes a sip of his champagne.

I put my mouth to his ear. "I want to lick you up and drink you down."

He grabs a handful of my hair. "Then get on your fucking knees."

I whimper, the grip on my hair painful as he pushes me to the floor.

He swiftly has his fly undone and his hard cock at the back of my throat. I gag.

He's too big.

He smiles darkly and eases out a little. Then he places his hands on the back of my head and pumps my throat, pushing himself in deep.

I whimper, and he tips his head back in ecstasy.

His eyes darken as he watches me, and I get the feeling I'm going to get it hard in a minute. Real Hard.

"*Fuck...me,*" he pants.

I pull off him and smile. "Now, isn't that better than pointless conversation?" I run my hands up his thick quads.

"I'd have to agree." He chuckles

We lie naked, facing each other. It's late.

The moonlight filters through the room, casting a magical spell.

I don't know how many times we've had sex now, but with every earth-shattering orgasm, I fall a little harder for Mr. Garcia.

He reaches out to dust his thumb over my bottom lip. "How did you get so beautiful?"

"It's all that come I've been drinking."

He laughs out loud, and it's a wonderful sound.

"So, your bathrooms are getting redone?" I ask.

"They are." He leans in and kisses me, clearly bored with that topic.

"How many nights are you here in the hotel?"

"Seven." His eyes hold mine, as if he's deep in thought, and then he kisses me again. "Stay."

"What?"

"Stay with me for the week."

"Why?"

"Because I want you to."

I smile softly as hope blooms in my chest. I know this is a bad idea. I should be running away, but I can't make myself.

I cup his face in my hand, and my lips take his. "Okay."

7

April

I WAKE to the buzz of an alarm.

I glance over to Sebastian's phone on his side table. He frowns and switches it off before he reaches for me, pulls me close, and kisses my shoulder.

"Morning." I smile, my cheek up against his.

"Good morning." His voice is deep and husky, his eyes remaining closed. "Let's stay in bed today."

"I wish. I have a lecture."

He looks up at me. "What are you studying?"

"Law."

He raises an eyebrow, as if surprised.

"What?" I smile.

"I never pegged you as a lawyer." He sits up in bed. The blankets pool around his waist, and my eyes drop to his dark, broad chest. "What year?"

"End of my second."

"One of my best friends is a lawyer. He's a Supreme Court Judge now."

"Really?" I smirk. That's a new piece of information for me to store away.

He lies back against the headboard and puts his hands behind his head, linking his fingers. I sense that he has something on his mind.

"What?" I ask.

"Why haven't you got a boyfriend?"

I shrug. "Nobody interests me."

"Really?"

I laugh. "Why is that so shocking to you?"

He rolls over me and pins my hands above my head. "Are you saying that I'm uninteresting?" He bites my nipple.

"Well...you're not exactly boyfriend material." I giggle. "Are you?" I struggle to escape his grip.

He bites me again, and the mood changes. "Although..." I smile.

"Although what?" He bites me again.

"Your sexual stamina is definitely résumé-worthy."

He smiles as he spreads my legs with his knee.

"Stop it." I laugh as I try to buck him off. "There is no sex happening this morning."

"Why not?"

"Because you're an animal that's trying to fuck me to death, and I'm sore."

He drops his chin to rest on my chest. I brush his hair back from his forehead.

"Because you're so wholesome and pure, right?" He smirks up at me.

I huff. "I am wholesome and pure, thank you very much. You're just a bad influence on me."

"Little Miss Let-Me-Drink-You-Down." He moves back and gets out of bed.

My eyes drop to his semi-hard penis as it hangs between his legs. "What do you expect with that thing hanging around?"

He holds his hands out to his sides. "Last chance."

"It's a pass." I raise both brows, making my point.

"Your loss." He shrugs casually and saunters to the shower, leaving me to lie in bed.

I like this mood he's in.

I hear the shower turn on, and I put on my robe and walk into the bathroom to find him under the water, washing himself with soap.

I sit on the chair in the corner. "How come you don't have a girlfriend?"

The water runs over his head. "They ask too many personal questions."

I smile. *Smart-ass.* "So you can ask me personal questions but I can't ask you any?"

He pours shampoo into his hand and begins to wash his hair. "That's right."

"We should go out for dinner tonight," I say.

He frowns. "Umm."

"What?" I frown.

"I'm not supposed to date you."

"Why not?"

"Because you work at the club. It's in the membership rules."

"Oh, Heaven forbid you should risk your membership."

"You could always leave." He winks.

I stand up and put my hands on my hips as I act outraged. "Sebastian Garcia, are you trying to bribe me to leave my job with a paltry dinner date?"

He washes the shampoo off. "Maybe." He smiles with his eyes closed. "Maybe I'm trying to bribe you to date me."

I twist my lips to hide my delight. "I'll think about it." As if I don't care either way.

"Well, you have ten minutes to decide. I'm in meetings all day today, and if you want me to book a restaurant for tonight, I need to know now." He steps out of the shower and tears my robe off to pull me under the water. "Anything I can do to swing your decision?" His lips go to my neck with a sharp bite, and I laugh out loud.

"No, sex maniac. You've done enough."

Half an hour later, Sebastian is dressed in his suit, and I'm getting ready for college.

"Do you need a lift?" he asks.

"No, I have my car here."

He has this mischievous smirk on his face.

I smile up at him as I straighten his tie and dust his lapels.

"I probably need your number," he says.

"Probably." I shrug. "Seeing as you spent half of the night inside my body."

He chuckles and grabs me into a bear hug. "And what a beautiful body that is."

When he pulls away, he digs his phone out of his pocket and types something into it.

"What are you typing?"

"Your name." He tilts his phone so I can't read it.

"What did you save me as?"

"Never you mind. Give me the number."

I lean over his shoulder and read the name

Honey Babe

"Don't call me, though. I'm very busy and important," I say casually.

He grabs my behind. "I'll call you whenever I fucking like."

I giggle and take out my phone. I type in a name for him

April's Fool

He reads it over my shoulder. "You got that fucking right."

He reads out his number and I store it swiftly.

"So, dinner tonight?" he asks.

"Uh-huh." I rise up to kiss him, and he wraps his arms around me. "I like you." I smile up at him.

His eyes twinkle with a certain something I haven't seen before. "I like you." His hands drop to my behind, and he gives it a hard squeeze. "I especially like fucking you."

"I noticed." I kiss him. "You have a good day, baby."

"How could I not when it started out like this?"

My stomach flutters. We didn't even have sex this morning.

This could really be something.

"Anyway, stop distracting me," he mutters dryly. Regaining his composure, he steps back from me, which makes me smirk. "I don't have time to be swanning around with you all morning."

I cross my arms as I watch him.

"I've got a million appointments to go to," he says.

That's like waving a red flag to a bull. Stupid move.

Game on.

I take my robe off and throw it on the kitchen counter and put my hands on my hips. "That's a shame. I'm suddenly feeling all tingly, wet, and...*in the mood.*"

He narrows his eyes. "Don't even."

"I guess I can always"—I push my finger into my mouth and suck seductively—"sort myself out."

His tongue sweeps over his bottom lip.

"Actually, I think my vibrator is in my overnight bag." I rub my hands down over my breasts and pull at my nipples until they harden. "Maybe I'll ride that. Do you want me to send you a video of it?"

His eyes darken as he unzips his trousers and falls back onto the couch. "The only thing you have permission to ride is my cock." He drags me over him and spreads my legs. "Get the fuck on it."

I laugh out loud. "But you've got to go. You have a *million* meetings, Mr. Garcia. I couldn't possibly hold you up."

He impales me in one sharp movement, and I'm instantly silenced.

"April's fool," I mouth.

He grabs my hair and drags my face to his. "Shut up or I'm going to fuck that slutty little mouth."

I lick his open lips, and his grip on my hair tightens. "Fill me up, big boy," I whisper against his lips. "Show me what you've got."

Sebastian takes my hand as we get out of the cab. I can hardly wipe the huge smile from my face.

I'm on a date. A real-life bonafide date.

With a god.

He hasn't asked me if I've resigned from the club, but I will. Without question, I will.

We walk into the restaurant.

"Hello, booking under the name of Garcia," he says, I stand and hold his hand like the groupie I am.

I glance around, expecting everyone around us to be looking at him...and me for being with him.

Look how gorgeous he is, people.

I really am smitten. I spent my whole day smiling goofily and staring into space.

The waiter leads us through the restaurant to a table for two in the back.

It's lit by candlelight, all moody and romantic. We take a seat, and the waiter pours us a water each.

"Can I get you something to drink?"

I open the menu. "What's good?"

"The cocktails are amazing."

"Okay." I close my menu. "I'll have a margarita."

Sebastian glances up with a smile and closes his menu. "Make that two."

The waiter leaves us alone to stare at each other.

"Garcia..." I frown. "Is that Italian?" He's darker skinned, so I know his origin is from somewhere European.

"Spanish."

"You're Spanish?"

He chuckles. "My parents are, yes."

"Which part?"

"Valencia."

I grin. "You speak Spanish?"

He takes my hand over the table and kisses my fingertips.

"Sí, hablo español, y pienso que eres la mujer más hermosa que he visto."

"What did you just say?"

"That I do, and that you are the most beautiful woman I have ever seen."

My heart swells, and I rearrange my napkin on my lap. "Just when I think you can't get any hotter."

He chuckles. His hand rests on his temple. "What brought you to London from America?"

I shrug. I don't want to talk about my divorce. It's a stain that I don't want to share. My marriage breakdown makes me feel like a failure.

"I had a bad breakup and wanted a fresh start."

"Who in their right mind would let you go?"

He didn't let me, he just slept with everyone else until I had no choice but to go.

I shrug. "Some things are just not meant to be."

From my little search on Google, I know that Sebastian was once married, too, but I don't want to ask him about it until he offers the information.

"I was studying International Law and was offered this scholarship. It was too good of an opportunity to pass up."

"Here you are, two margaritas." The waiter puts down our drinks.

"Thank you." I instantly pick mine up and take a sip. "Oh, yum. Good choice."

Sebastian sips his drink and nods in approval. "And that's why you are in the dorms?"

I nod. "Uh-huh, and it's so bad. The students are partying every night and day. There are drugs and orgies. I feel at least a hundred years old."

He chuckles. "I must admit, my college days were pretty wild."

"And rent is so expensive in London. That's why I took the job in the club."

He sits back, and I can tell that he doesn't even like talking about it.

"I was only ever doing four shifts," I add. "I worked out a year's rent, and Porsha promised me that I didn't have to have sex with anyone."

His eyes hold mine. "But you did."

"You were different."

"How?"

"I watched you from afar. Before we even met, I saw you give money to a man who was begging on the streets, and I knew you were kind."

He frowns.

"And I told the girls at work about this gorgeous man that I'd seen on the street. And then the universe delivered you to my door." I take his hand over the table and kiss his fingertips. "Some things are meant to be."

He pulls his hand away from my grip, breaking the moment. "So what you're saying is that you're a stalker?"

I smile. "Maybe."

"And you tried to kill me with poisoned coffee."

I chuckle. "Definitely."

"And then you fucked my brains out in the club."

I laugh out loud. "Yes, that too."

"And now you've made me your April's Fool."

I hold my drink up to his. "Golden trifecta."

"That was four things." He chuckles and sips his drink as his eyes hold mine. He falls silent, and after a minute, he says, "You're never going back to that club."

"I wouldn't want to. I want to see where this goes."

His eyes linger on my face, and a frown creases his brow. I know that I just got a bit too heavy, and I need to change the subject.

"So, you're an architect," I say.

"I like what you did there."

"You like that casual change of subject, huh?"

"Very well done." He nods. "Yes, I'm an architect."

"What do you design?"

"Skyscrapers."

"Skyscrapers? Holy wow, that's incredible. You must be super smart."

"That's debatable."

"But there aren't many skyscrapers in London."

"My market is mainly in the US and Dubai."

"Ah, so you travel a lot."

"Usually for four or five months of the year."

I imagine sharing a jetsetter's life with him...sharing anything with him.

Stop it.

I'm getting ahead of myself here. I need to slow the fuck down.

We lie in the darkness. Sebastian is spooning me tightly from behind, his body still deep inside mine. We fell asleep like this last night too.

Three wonderful nights I've spent in Sebastian Garcia's arms.

We're still at the hotel, and I don't want this to end. Everything is perfect as it is.

His big lips kiss my face, our shared body fluids smeared between us.

He's everything I never knew I needed.

I'm falling.

Hard.

"Seb," I whisper.

"Yeah, baby." He holds me tightly, and his lips drop to my shoulder as he covers me in tender kisses.

"What's happening here?"

"I don't know." I feel his lips curl into a smile as he kisses me once more. "But I really like it."

"Me too." I smile when he pulls me closer. "Me too."

Sebastian

"Sebastian, Buddy is here."

"Thanks, Carly, send him in," I say into the intercom.

I stand, and moments later, my door opens to reveal my favourite person.

"Hey, Dad."

"Hey, sweetheart." I smile. "Where do you want to go for lunch?"

Buddy is my sister's son. His father ran out when he was two, and I stepped in to be his father figure.

He began calling me Dad at the age of five when he started school, and he didn't want the other kids to think that he was different.

"Why do you insist on calling me sweetheart? No other fathers call their sons sweetheart. It's so girly."

I smile as I squeeze his shoulder. "That's because no other fathers have a son with a heart as sweet as yours. And let me assure you, having a sweet heart is not girly."

He gives me a lopsided smile. Buddy is the only person who gets to see my unguarded emotions. I save all of them for him. He is the most important person in my life.

"Can we get McDonald's for lunch?"

I wince. "I'm too old for that shit." I grab my jacket from the back of my chair. "We'll get lunch at the pub."

He sighs. "Yeah, okay."

. . .

Fifteen minutes later, we are sitting at the pub with our sodas, waiting for our lunch to arrive. I yawn because I'm tired as fuck. April is wearing me out.

"Don't forget that we have Willow's final football game on Saturday morning, and then in the afternoon, I want to go and look at some cars for you," I tell him.

"What's wrong with my car?"

"It's a heap of junk. I'm constantly worried if its airbags are working."

"Ugh." He rolls his eyes. "I don't want to spend my Saturday watching Willow's football."

"Tough shit. Deal with it. It's one week."

He widens his eyes at me.

I sip my drink. "What's happening with that girl, anyway?"

He gets a big goofy smile on his face. "Oh, Dad." He shakes his head, as if he's lost for words.

"That good, huh?" I smirk.

"She's perfect. I'm so in love."

"Ease up, big guy. *Love* is a very strong word."

"Well... I *do* love her. She's the one for me. I know it."

"I'm happy for you. She better be good enough. When do I get to meet her?"

The waitress puts our lunches down in front of us. "Thank you."

"I'm not good enough for her." He shrugs his shoulders. "I'll bring her over on Friday night."

"Okay."

"Just don't be weird."

I hold my salt shaker midair. "Define weird."

"You know...don't be wearing a stuffy suit. Wear something cool."

"What's wrong with my suits?"

"You look ancient."

99

I shake my head. "This suit pays for all your shit, you know."

"I'm not complaining. I'm just saying that first impressions are everything."

Oh, to be young and unjaded. "Okay."

"I'll come over tomorrow and pick out something for you to wear."

"I am quite capable of picking my own clothes."

"I just want everything to be perfect. She's very important."

I roll my eyes. "I get it."

"Oh, and can you go into my room and take down my posters?"

I frown. "Why?"

"Because I don't want her to think I'm a little kid."

"What will you be doing in your room with her, exactly?"

"I don't know, she's pretty hot for it."

My eyes widen. "Please tell me you're wearing fucking condoms..."

"And don't you dare call me sweetheart in front of her," he says, ignoring my question.

I smirk.

"I mean it."

I hold my hands up in surrender. "Okay, got it. Cool clothes, hard heart, and no posters. With an extra-large box of condoms to go." I raise an eyebrow. "You will not be having sex in your bedroom with me downstairs listening. Do I make myself clear?"

"Whatever." He bites into his burger. "Life is just so great at the moment, you know?"

I smile as my eyes linger on his face. I love seeing him like this.

"You should try it," he says with his mouth full of food. "Love, I mean."

I pick up my burger and get a vision of April and the week we've had together.

Maybe it's time.

. . .

April stands naked in the kitchen with her arms around me, her lips lingering over mine.

"Have a nice day," she breathes.

I smile down at the temptress. She's incredible. I squeeze her behind.

"I will."

"I wish you weren't checking out today," she says. "I've had the best week in this hotel room." She kisses me again.

"Me too." Our lips meet again. We can't stop kissing whenever we're together. "What are you doing this weekend?"

"Nothing much. I'm looking for an apartment all day tomorrow. Do you want to come with me?"

"I can't tomorrow. I'm watching a friend's daughter play football."

"Tonight?" she asks.

I inhale, knowing it's too soon to introduce her to Buddy. "I have a family thing on."

Her face falls.

"Do you want to come over tomorrow night? I'll cook," I offer.

"Really?"

"It's time to get you back for that coffee." I poke her in the ribs.

She giggles. "Okay." She pulls me into a hug, and we stand in each other's arms for a while. I don't like that I'm not going to see her tonight.

"Will you miss me tonight?" she asks.

"Nope." I smirk.

"Good, 'cause I'm not going to miss you either. Glad to get rid of you, actually."

With one last lingering kiss, I make my way to the door. I look back to see April doing a little naked jig.

"Until next time." I smile.

She blows me an exaggerated kiss. "Until next time."

April

"So, what are we going to see?" I ask Brandon as we drive.

"I thought we would see that new sci-fi. The one with Matt Damon."

"Okay." I glance over at him. "Why couldn't Lara come?"

"She had something on."

"I think she's secretly seeing that guy from block two. She seems to have a lot on lately."

His eyes flash to mine. "You think?"

"I saw them talking in the gym the other night, and they seemed very familiar."

He smiles. "Good for her."

I frown as he turns off the road towards the movies. "Where are we going?"

"I have to pick something up. We have plenty of time."

"Okay." I scroll aimlessly through my phone.

"You know I like you, right?" Brandon says.

"Yeah." I scroll through Instagram. He's been a bit clingy lately. Wait, what? "What did you mean by that?"

"Just that. You know that I like you."

I frown over at him. I've always had my suspicions that Brandon has had a secret crush on me, but surely not. I'm way too old for him.

I must have misunderstood what he was saying. I wasn't really listening to the first half of the conversation.

He pulls the car into the driveway of a mansion with beautifully manicured gardens. The building is three stories high.

"Where are we?"

"I just have to pick up the tickets."

"Oh."

"Come in."

I don't want to be rude. "Okay." I get out of the car and follow him to the front door. "Wow, this house is amazing," I say as I look around.

We get to the front steps, and Brandon grabs my hand.

I frown and go to pull my hand from his grip, but he holds me tightly.

"What are you doing?" I ask him.

"I like you, April."

"I beg your pardon?"

"I think it's time."

"For what?" I frown. Huh, what the hell is going on here?

"That we make it official."

"Brandon, what are you talking about? I'm completely lost."

"I love you."

My eyes widen. "What?"

He leans in and kisses me, and the front door opens behind us. I jerk back, shocked at what just happened. What the hell is he doing?

My eyes flick to the person who just opened the door.

Sebastian's eyes hold mine.

My eyes widen. *What the actual fuck?*

"Dad," Brandon announces. "This is April, the love of my life."

8

_____

April

SEBASTIAN STARES at me for a moment, and then, without a word, he turns and walks inside the house.

My eyes widen. Sebastian is Brandon's father?

What the actual fuck? He has a kid?

"Brandon!" I splutter as I march in after Sebastian. "We're just friends."

"April, you know it's more than that," Brandon argues, following us.

Sebastian turns and glares at me with such contempt that I have never seen before.

"I swear to you, Seb, we are just friends." I shake my head in a panic. "There's *nothing* going on."

Brandon looks between us in confusion. "How can you say that? You stay in my room all the time."

"On the floor!" I gasp.

Sebastian's eyes hold mine. His stance is cold and detached.

"I love you, April," Brandon says.

Jesus Christ. What the hell? He chooses now to do this?

How the fuck is he Sebastian's son? They couldn't be more opposite.

"Brandon...*enough!*" I snap in an outrage, my eyes glued to Sebastian. "We are not a thing. Get it through your head!"

Sebastian's eyes flicker red. "Do not speak to my fucking son like that."

"But...he's got it wrong."

"I saw it with my own fucking eyes." Sebastian steps towards me, and I step back, our eyes locked. "You think you can play him...while you're playing me?" he whispers darkly.

I shake my head. "No, Sebastian. I swear to you, I'm telling the truth."

Brandon looks between us. "Wait...what? Do you two know each other?"

I stay silent, scared to speak. Sebastian's chest rises and falls as he struggles for control.

"Do you know my father?" Brandon demands.

Sebastian's eyes are fixed on mine.

I stay silent.

"Answer him!" Sebastian yells.

My eyes fill with tears, and I nod.

Brandon's eyes flick between us. "How?"

My heart begins to race. Sebastian's scaring me. I've never seen him like this. He's mean when he's angry.

"Seb," I whisper. "Brandon and I are just friends. I swear to you."

"You stay in my room. We were just kissing not two minutes ago," Brandon cuts in. "You know we are more than friends. Everybody knows it."

Sebastian's jaw tics with fury.

"How do you know my father, anyway?" Brandon demands again.

Oh, for the love of God, *just shut the fuck up, kid. You're ruining my life here!*

I look between them.

"Answer his question," Sebastian whispers darkly.

"Sebastian." I shake my head. "I swear to you—"

"Dad?" Brandon asks. "What's going on?"

Sebastian's eyes drift to Brandon. "She's not the girl for you."

Brandon frowns.

Yes, tell him I'm your girl.

"Tell him what you do for money, April."

My face falls.

"Sebastian, stop," I snap. If he says this out loud, he can't take it back. *We can't go back.* "I mean it. Do not go there."

Sebastian's chin tilts up, as if my words only throw fuel to the flame. "Cartier works in a strip club."

Brandon's face falls. "Who's Cartier?"

"That's the stage name April uses."

"Stop," I cry.

We stare at each other as the hairs on the back of my neck stand to attention.

Don't say it. *Please don't say it.*

"April's a prostitute who charges men to have sex with her."

Brandon's face falls. "How do you know that?"

No.

Sebastian's eyes don't leave mine. "Because I paid her to have sex with me."

My eyes fill with tears.

"You had sex with April?" Brandon frowns.

"Yes."

I let out an audible gasp of horror.

"She was playing both of us," Sebastian whispers.

I screw up my face in tears. "No, I wasn't."

Betrayal floods my soul.

Sebastian's cold eyes hold mine. "Get out of my house, you lying whore." He steps forward. "Go near my son again and see what fucking happens to you."

What the fuck?

106

Shame fills my every cell, and I sob out loud at his hurtful words.

"Get the hell out of my house!" he shouts at the top of his voice as he loses control.

I turn and stumble. If he hit me with a physical blow, it would have been less painful.

I need to get away from him.

I can hardly see from the tears streaming down my face. I stumble out the front door and look around. It's dark and starting to rain. I have no idea where to go.

I scurry around to the side of the house and stand up against the wall, hiding. I don't want to see them...either of them.

"Get out of my house, you lying whore."

I slap my hand over my mouth to quieten my sobs.

"April." Brandon comes running out of the house, and I press myself further against the wall. "April!" he calls in the rain. "Where are you?"

Sebastian walks out after him onto the front lawn.

"What the fuck have you done?" Brandon turns and cries.

"She's been lying to both of us."

"You don't know what you're saying."

"Yes, I do."

"I can't believe you slept with her!" Brandon cries.

Silence.

Pain lances through my chest.

"Come inside," Sebastian says.

"I love her," Brandon cries.

"I know."

"You've ruined everything!"

"She's not the girl for you. I'm sorry, but I could never lie to you, and I could never keep a secret like that from you. I love you too much."

My head rests back against the bricks. The rain is beginning to fall harder now, and I taste hot, salty tears on my lips.

What about me?

This is it for us... There's no coming back from this.

He told his son that I'm a prostitute.

My chest tightens. I knew it. I knew it was too good to be true.

"I hate you!" Brandon cries.

"Come inside and hate me."

Silence.

"Buddy, come on. Inside."

I'm overcome with shame. I've never felt so abandoned in my life.

"Where did she go?" Brandon asks. "April!" he calls out.

The front door slams shut, and I put my head into my hands, crying in silence.

Sebastian walks out to the street and looks one way and then the other. He drops his head and pushes his hands into his trouser pockets. He stands in the rain for an extended time, and then eventually slowly walks back inside.

The door slams shut, and I sob, my shoulders bouncing as the tears fall.

Get out of my house, you lying whore. The shame.

This hurts.

Is that how he sees me? All the time, while I was falling, he saw me as nothing but a whore?

She's a prostitute who charges men to have sex with her.

My breath quivers as I try to hold in my sobs.

I take out my phone and order an Uber. I have to keep wiping my eyes so I can see the screen.

Because I paid her to have sex with me.

I'm embarrassed. I'm ashamed and so confused.

I'm fucking hurt.

And the worst part is, he's right. What he said is all true. Why the hell did I work there?

Go near my son again and see what fucking happens to you.

With a shaky hand, I stuff my phone back into my bag and slide down the wall to sit on the ground.

And in the rain and dark, I cry...alone.

. . .

The television drones in the background of the hotel room. I've been here for three days. I couldn't stand the thought of returning back to the dorm on Friday night after I left. I still can't stand it today.

I can't risk running into Brandon...or Lara. Anyone. What would I say to them?

And I don't know what to do.

I've never been so low.

And not because of what happened on Friday night, but because of what happened in the two weeks before that.

I let poverty take my morals—something that should never have been for sale.

And I met him...

The permanent lump in my throat is big and it hurts. I can't even think of our time together without crying.

I thought it was special.

Only it wasn't. I was delusional, seeing something in a man that wasn't even there.

He isn't who I thought he was.

That's the worst part: knowing that I let myself down. I was so blinded by his light.

My vision clouds as the tears come once more.

I'm at the precipice of my life. A turning point. But I just don't know which way to go.

I want to go home. I want to pack up and return to America to be with my family.

But then this will just be another failure to add to my life.

My mind drifts back to my worst day. The day I came home sick from work and walked in on my beloved husband having sex in our bed with a girl he worked with.

The way he looked up at me...while he was still inside of her.

My stomach drops. I can still see it so clearly—can still feel the pain of my heart breaking. Still see him running from the room with an erection...*for her.*

I close my eyes and swallow around the lump in my throat, and it hurts the entire way down.

At least then I had my dignity.

I inhale with a deep and shaky breath. "You'll be okay," I say to myself. "It's okay. You're going to be okay." I wipe a lone tear from my face.

But I don't know if I will be okay.

This cut is deep.

The door opens.

"April." The woman smiles.

I grip my handbag and stand. "Hello."

"Come in, dear." She ushers me into her office. "Please, take a seat."

"Thank you." I sit down while she goes behind her desk.

"I understand you are looking to transfer your scholarship to Manchester University?"

"Yes." I force a smile. "That's right."

After a week in a hotel doing some serious soul-searching, I've decided that I'm not letting another man take something from me. This is my dream, and damn it, I'm fucking keeping it alive.

The woman stares at me for a moment. "You do know that Manchester doesn't have the credibility we have here in London."

"I know."

"I just don't see why—"

"I need to get out of London," I cut her off.

Her eyes hold mine. "Are you okay?"

"I need to get out of this campus. I can't be here anymore."

She stares at me. "Have you been assaulted?"

I shake my head, trying to keep it together. "Please, just organize the transfer."

"Are the police involved? Can I get a counsellor to spend some time with you?"

"I'm fine. I just had a really bad breakup, and I need to move."

She sits back in her chair and exhales heavily. "Okay." She types something into her computer. "When would you like to start?"

"Next month." I shrug. "It'll take a few weeks to move and get myself sorted."

"Okay. I'll see what I can do."

"Do you think it will be okay?" I ask. "I mean, do you think I will get in?"

"They're not at capacity, and your scholarship is transferable."

"I also won't be needing dormitory accommodation."

"Where will you live?" She frowns.

"I'm getting an apartment. Rent is a lot cheaper there."

"When are you leaving?"

"Tonight. As soon as I pack up my room."

"Has something happened, April? Can I help you in any way?"

My eyes well with tears. *Please don't be nice to me... I'll lose my shit.* "I'm fine, but I do need to leave now." I stand to finish the conversation.

"Well, don't sign a lease until I get this approved, okay?"

"Thank you." I give her a weak smile.

I walk across the campus to my room. The classes are on at this time, so the hallways are relatively quiet. I want to be packed up and out of here by three o'clock before everyone gets home.

I put the key into my door, and Penelope's door opens, bringing her into view.

"Hi," she says.

"Hello." I struggle with the key, eventually pushing the door open to walk inside.

She stands in my doorway, holding the door open. "Where have you been?"

"I stayed with a friend," I lie.

"Word has it that you're turning tricks."

I swallow the lump in my throat. "Who told you that?"

"Apparently, Brandon is heartbroken. He confided in Lara."

I nod as I get a running picture of events. "And Lara told everyone."

She crosses her arms. "Yep...pretty much."

My eyes fill with tears of shame.

"You all right?"

I press my lips together and shake my head. "I'm leaving."

"Now?"

I nod.

She walks into my room. "I'll help you pack."

She begins to fold my bed linen and take things out of my wardrobe and lay them on the bed.

I stare at her for a moment.

"Well, what are you doing?" she asks. "Don't you want to be out of here before the gossip columns go into meltdown? You know what these fuckers are like."

I give her a lopsided smile and pull my suitcase out of my wardrobe.

It's rare that people surprise me.

"Thanks."

SIX YEARS LATER...

9

─────────

April

MY PHONE VIBRATES on the table as a text comes through.

You up?

I smirk and turn my phone over so that I can't see the screen.

Penelope holds her wineglass midway to her mouth. "Kill me now. Is that Duke?"

I sip my margarita. "Uh-huh."

"Are you fucking crazy?" Anna snaps.

I roll my eyes.

Penelope and Anna exchange an unimpressed look.

"If you two like him so much, you can be his booty call." I smile against the rim of my glass.

"Um, okay." Penelope widens her eyes as she pretends to pick up my phone and answer it.

"I wish a fuckable football player wanted to be my baby daddy." Penny puts her hand up in the air as if she's in class, waiting to be picked. "Hell to the yeah, I'm totally down with that."

I smirk and see my phone vibrate once again. I ignore it a second time and flick it on silent.

"What the hell is wrong with you?" Penelope huffs in disgust.

"I tell him all the time to go find someone else."

"You actually say that to him? 'Go find someone else'?"

"Uh-huh."

"And yet he calls you every night for a booty call, which you conveniently take him up on?"

I shrug. "He's just so hot, and we're friends."

The girls laugh.

"I don't want a relationship." I sip my drink. "But I'm not *completely* stupid."

My phone begins to ring, and I know I have to answer it. He won't stop calling until I do.

"I'm just going to take this. Back in a minute," I say to the girls. "Hi," I answer as I walk towards the front door of the bar.

"Are you ignoring my texts?"

"Of course I am." I push the heavy front door open and walk out onto the footpath. "Fuck, its freezing out here." I pull my jacket closed.

"Where are you?" he asks.

"I told you, I'm out with the girls tonight." I glance at my watch. "Why are you still awake? It's 2:00 a.m."

"Because I'm fucking horny, and I need my girl to come and sort me out."

"Duke." I smile. "There are so many things wrong with that sentence that I don't even know where to start."

"Just get over here, woman."

Hmm...tempting.

Duke Montana is a gorgeous pro-footballer with more groupies than sense.

He has me on speed dial.

He's two years younger than me, six foot four, with a body to die for. He's the golden boy of his sport, with a tall, muscular physique. He has sandy blond hair and big brown eyes, not to mention he is insanely talented. Both in and out of the bedroom.

We met three years ago in Manchester when I was at university, and he was playing for United. We were both new in town, and on a particularly rainy week, we ran into each other in a launderette, of all places. We got chatting while waiting for our washing to dry. We went to dinner, he came back to my place, and we ended up having sex for the entire weekend. He was exactly what I needed at that time, and I think I was the same for him.

We're close friends—the kind with benefits—and I think we know each other better than anyone else. But lately, things have changed.

He's getting clingy.

He plays for Arsenal now. He recently moved to London, and he's ruining everything. He's given me an ultimatum more than once: either be his full-time girlfriend or he won't see me anymore.

I wish I *could* settle down and want what he wants, because he really is a special guy...but I don't know. I can't even put my finger on the problem.

He demands answers, we fight, but he always calls me the next day, and we always end up sleeping together and then not talking about anything too deep.

Until two weeks later when it happens again.

I decided two weeks ago when he had his last meltdown that I'm going to wean him off me.

I really care about him, and my plan is to distance myself enough so that he has to go and meet someone else. Someone who can love him the way he deserves to be loved. I'm not her. I wish I were.

Who knows what the future holds?

"Seriously, April. Just get over here," he says.

My gaze drops to the ground beneath me as I run my toe over a join in the concrete.

"Duke." I smile sadly. "Remember, we talked about this."

"I know, but I need you."

"Sweetie." I sigh, feeling guilty.

God, I need to break it off altogether. This isn't fair to him. But he makes it damn hard when he's so good in bed.

"I don't care, just get over here."

"I'm not finished with the girls. I'm going to be a while."

"That's okay."

I point my toe and trace a line on the concrete. "Why don't you ring one of your groupies? There are a million girls who are totally in love with you." This is the weird thing. I give zero fucks about who he sleeps with besides me, and that's how I know it's wrong.

"I don't want a groupie, I want you."

This is going to end badly, and I really don't want to lose his friendship. "I'll see."

"I won't sleep unless I know you're coming."

"Fine." I widen my eyes in exasperation.

"Okay," he says softly, and I can tell he's smiling.

"Duke..."

"Yes."

"This has to stop."

He stays silent.

"Okay?"

"We have the museum thing on Saturday night, remember?" he reminds me.

"Seriously?"

"You promised me you would come."

"You're going to be signing autographs all night, anyway. You don't need me there."

"April, you promised."

I roll my eyes. "Fine, but I want Chadwick's for dinner afterwards."

"Deal."

Chadwick's is my favourite restaurant. I always make him take me there when he makes me go to football stuff. To be honest, I'm the anti-groupie. I really don't see the appeal in his football. I mean, it's not like it's gridiron or something. It's a cultural thing, I guess. He always asks me to come to his games, and I always decline. It's not real football to me. But I'm an American, and my sporting tastes will never change.

"I'll see you in about an hour," I say.

"Okay." He hangs on the line.

I know that pause. "What?"

"I've been watching porn for about four hours. I'm good to go."

I smirk. "Make that half an hour."

"I've already jerked off twice."

I feel a twinge down below. "See you in fifteen."

I lie in the dark and stare at a swirly pattern on the wallpaper. The moonlight peeks through the crack in the curtains. I don't know how long I've been awake, but it must be hours.

Duke is wrapped around me like a blanket, nestled in close and holding me tightly from behind. He told me that he loved me tonight.

And I feel like shit.

Because I do love him, but...

My stomach twists with sadness.

What is wrong with me?

I don't feel jealousy. I don't feel attachment. I don't feel that rush of closeness. I don't feel anger. I don't feel anything except the physical release of an orgasm.

And it's not just Duke. It's been like this with others too. Up until now, I always thought it was them, not me. This time it's different.

Deep down, I know.

A lone tear rolls down my face and onto my pillow. I'm filled with a sadness I can't comprehend. I'm lonely...but I'm not.

I'm with someone but I'm alone.

It's like the men that I've loved have broken me.

I know they were douchebags, too, and I know that I deserve better, but it's as if my heart no longer believes that I'm worthy of being loved, so it blocks everyone out before they get the chance to hurt me.

Duke always jokes and calls me the Ice Queen. Is it true?

I wish I had met him before. I wish I had met him when I could have loved him.

I would have given him my all.

He stirs and kisses my shoulder. "What's wrong, baby?" he whispers.

I turn and kiss his cheek. "Nothing, sweetie, go back to sleep. Bad dream."

He pulls me closer. "It's okay, I'm here. You're safe with me."

Tears well in my eyes. *I wish you were safe with me.*

Duke deserves better.

"Don't forget, staff meeting in ten," Lewis says, his head peeking around the door.

Damn it, I'm too busy for morale-boosting crap this morning.

I fake a smile anyway. "Sure thing."

I send my emails and print out my to-do list for the day. I'm the newest lawyer at Sterling Law, and I like to keep on top of my workload. It was a huge win, landing this job. I applied for it believing that I had no chance in hell of getting it, and I got the surprise of my life when I got the call.

I've been here ten months now, and I've settled in nicely.

I moved from Manchester for the position. Got myself a nice apartment and a new car to go with my fancy new job. I feel all grown up, and I am loving life.

It's funny how things turn out. I had every intention of returning to the States after I finished my degree. I'd made steps towards doing that. But when I went back to the States for a visit and began looking around for where I was going to resettle, nothing jumped out at me. I was more confused about what I wanted than ever.

I decided that I'd just stay here until the answer to where I'm supposed to be appeared.

I'm happy for the interim, and I never thought I would say this, but England is beginning to feel like home. I mean, I have been here for seven years now, so I guess it makes sense.

I make my way to the conference room and take a seat at the back, watching on as the large room begins to fill. Sterling Law is the biggest law firm in the United Kingdom. We have thirty-four lawyers, and they each have their own personal assistants and secretaries. I don't have a PA yet, but when I do, I'll know that I've made it.

The room is full to capacity when Philip Rogers, the owner, comes into view. I haven't seen him around lately. I think he's been working a lot from our other office across the city. Philip is in his late fifties, a distinguished-looking man with silver hair. His accent sounds all snooty, like the Queen's or something.

He walks to the front of the room and addresses the crowd. "Hello," he says with a huge smile on his face. "Firstly, I would like to thank you for all of your hard work. Your efforts have not gone unnoticed, and I really appreciate it."

Everybody smiles proudly. It really is nice to be acknowledged.

"I guess you're all wondering why I've called this meeting this morning. Well..." He sits on the corner of the desk at the front of the room. "As a few of you know, my wife is unwell. She..." He pauses, as if the next sentence is hard. "She will make a full recovery, but I am stretched. Because of that, I have decided to do something that has been in the back of my mind for a long time now. I'm taking on a partner."

The room falls deadly silent.

He stands and puts his hands into his suit pockets and begins to pace back and forth. "So, the next question is...who? Who will be the right fit for our firm? Who will take our company into the twentieth century with the same passion that we are all accustomed to? I have been looking a long time for the right person."

He's such a kind man. Whenever I hear him speak, I come away motivated.

"Bart McIntyre."

The room releases a collective gasp.

What the fuck?

Philip holds his hands up in a comforting gesture, his smile widening. "Now, I know that Bart's reputation precedes him, and I know that he doesn't represent the kind of clients we are accustomed to."

"Damn right about that," someone mutters.

Bart McIntyre is a legal rock star. He represents high-end clients, models, celebrities, those kinds of people. He's won every case he's ever had and is legendary.

"Our normal workload will carry on, of course. However, we will now have an arm of our organization that will look after Bart's high-end clients."

Holy shit.

Excitement runs through me. This is going to be amazing.

Philip holds his hands out towards us in a welcoming gesture. "So, there you have it, and we're wasting no time. Bart starts here in this office on Monday."

The room breaks out into excited chatter.

"There will be a memo going out to you all this afternoon with all the details, but..." He smiles as he looks around the room. "This is exciting news for our business." He claps his hands. "You can go back to ruling the world now."

Everyone chatters as they stand and make their way back to their offices.

"April!" Philip calls. "Can I see you for a moment, please?"

Oh, shit, am I in trouble? "Sure."

"Down to my office." He gestures to the corridor, and I follow him down. "Please, take a seat," he says once we step inside his room.

I sit down and nervously clutch my clipboard. Oh no, what's this about?

Philip sits down and leans back in his chair. "I wanted to offer you a new position." His eyes hold mine. "How would you like to be Bart's junior?"

I frown. "What?"

"He wants an offsider. Someone he can train up."

"But... What... I mean, what...?" My eyes widen. "Me?"

He chuckles. "He wants someone relatively green so he can mould them how he likes to work. He asked for me to assign someone who is eager and intelligent."

I bite my bottom lip to hide my goofy smile. *He thinks I'm intelligent.*

"Okay," I say, trying to act cool.

"You will be working with Bart on some things, and then on other days you will return to your own cases."

I grin. "The best of both worlds."

"Yes." He smiles. "How does that sound?"

"Amazing."

"Great. I'll let Bart know."

I stand and shake his hand. "Thank you so much for the opportunity. I'm really excited."

"You earned this, April. Your work ethic hasn't gone unnoticed."

I smile proudly. "Thank you."

He turns his computer on. "Go out and celebrate tonight. This is an amazing start to your career."

"I will." I hunch my shoulders together and feel like jumping in the air. "I'll see you later."

"Okay."

I close his door behind me and practically dance back to my desk.

Holy. Fucking. Shit.

Duke pays for the cab while I climb out of the backseat.

It's Saturday night, and we are at the London Arts Museum.

There's a sporting memorabilia auction in aid of the Children's Hospital's Oncology Ward. Duke and a few other sport stars are signing autographs, but I'm here for my reward dinner afterwards. Chadwick's: the most heavenly restaurant of all time.

We walk in through the foyer, and I catch sight of myself in the mirror.

I love this coffee-coloured dress with spaghetti straps. It fits in all the right places.

We walk into the elevator, hand in hand, and we turn to face the doors.

"What are you going to eat?" I ask as the door closes and we begin to make our way to level four, where the auction is being held.

Duke raises an eyebrow. "You."

"Apart from my vagina." I smirk.

"Your ass."

I laugh, and he puts his arm around me and pulls my head into a playful headlock.

The doors open on level one. A man is waiting, talking on his phone. He glances up at us as he goes to walk in, and he stops midstep.

My eyes lock with Sebastian Garcia.

His brow furrows, and he stands dead still.

We stare at each other, and I get a lump in my throat at the sight of him.

I haven't thought of him for so long, and yet seeing him here and now brings back the sting of his betrayal as if it happened only an hour ago.

I can hear my heartbeat in my ears as it thumps hard in my chest.

He hasn't changed.

Sebastian doesn't move as he stares at me, phone still to his ear, and the elevator doors close.

He didn't get in.

I drop my head as a barrage of emotions slams me hard.

"MP looks like he saw a ghost," Duke says.

I frown. "What?"

"The MP, Minister of Parliament."

"The who?" What's he talking about?

"That dude on the phone just then. You recognize him, don't you? He's all over the news lately."

I stare at Duke. I knew Sebastian had gone into politics—I have heard his name in passing over the years—but I don't stay up to date with everything in the UK. I still watch the American news...damn it.

"April, that was Sebastian Garcia."

I know who it was.

My heart races hard in my chest.

"He was just appointed as the Deputy Prime Minister."

"When?" I frown. How do I not know this?

"Like three days ago or something."

I stare at Duke, wide-eyed.

Can't be!

10

April

"He's what?" I gasp.

"Yeah, he's all over the news lately. How haven't you seen him?"

My blood begins to boil. "Just lucky, I guess."

Duke frowns. "Do you know him?"

I raise my brows, realizing how I must sound. "He used to come into a café I worked at years ago." My nostrils flare as I try to hold in my unexpected surge of anger. "He was a real asshole."

Duke chuckles. "That's probably how he got into office."

I fake a smile.

My cheeks begin to heat as my temper soars. How dare he be here? How dare he breathe in the same air that I am?

I get a vision of his face as he held the phone to his ear, and I grit my teeth. I should have smacked him straight in that stupid square jaw. The elevator doors open, and Duke takes my hand and leads me out into the large conservatory.

I try to calm myself, knowing my anger shouldn't be here.

What happened between us was years ago.

I don't care what he does. I don't care at all.

I look around at all the sports memorabilia and the people gathered at their tables.

"Do you want to walk around and see what's for auction before we get a drink at the bar?" Duke asks.

I fake a smile. "Sure."

We begin to walk around to look at stuff, but my mind is anywhere but here.

I should have said something.

I should have told him off. Why didn't I?

In my mind, I've gone over and over what I would say to him if our paths ever crossed again. I hate that, all those years ago, I ran like a coward and never got to say my piece. For so long afterwards, I would have imaginary arguments with him while driving or in the shower, going over all the things I should have said to him.

Hurtful things, like the things he said to me.

My stomach twists as I'm taken back to that fateful night.

I hate that it still gets to me.

I exhale heavily and shake my shoulders, trying to forget that I just saw him.

Let it go, April. Stewing over him is not achieving anything.

It's fine. Totally fucking fine. What do I care, anyway? He's nothing to me.

I glance back towards the door to see Sebastian stepping out of the elevator, and once again, I see red.

Bastard.

I stand at the bar and sip my horrible wine. If you can even call it wine. Who picks the selection for these function things? Obviously, someone who has absolutely no taste.

The auction has been on. Duke paid ten thousand pounds for a signed surfboard that belonged to Kelly Slater. What the heck is he going to do with that? Oh well, it is for a good cause, I suppose.

We have had a few drinks and chatted to a few people, and

now Duke is signing autographs over at a table with six other sportsmen.

He's scheduled on for an hour, and then we can go.

Sebastian is on the other side of the conservatorium with two other men—one blond and handsome, the other one dark and broody-looking.

They look around Sebastian's age and are undeniably gorgeous.

I'm having a hard time not watching him, and I'm beating myself up for not saying something. Although, what would I have said? I have no idea.

Stop it!

I take out my phone and text Penelope.

Who would have ever thought my archenemy from the Rave Cave would now be one of my closest friends?

> *You're not going to believe who's here...*

A reply comes back.

> *Who?*

I glance over at Duke as I type.

> *Sebastian Garcia. We ran into each other in the elevator.*
> *Apparently, he's the Deputy Prime Minister now.*

A response comes quickly.

> *Oh, shit, that's right, I saw that.*
> *He was elected this week, I keep forgetting to mention it.*
> *I hope you spat in his slimy face.*

I giggle.

I wish

"Is this stool taken?" a man asks.

"No, take it." I smile.

"Thanks." He lifts the stool over to his table, and a reply bounces back from Penelope.

> *Fuck him. He's just an asshole.*
> *Be grateful you don't have to see him ever again.*

I type my reply.

> *This is true. Speak tomoz.*
> *xoxo*

I put my phone into my bag and glance over the room to see Sebastian staring at me from across the room.

His face is devoid of emotion, and then, in slow motion, he raises his wineglass in the air to me, as if toasting the occasion.

Our eyes are locked.

I feel adrenaline surge through my system. Are you fucking kidding me?

You have the nerve to address *me?*

His blond friend looks over and then says something to him, and Sebastian chuckles into his wineglass.

What's so funny, asshole?

My heart pounds as the hurt and shame that he caused come flooding back.

His other friend says something to him, and then all three men laugh out loud.

I sip my drink. It feels like the sky has turned red.

I'm never going to see him again. I'm never going to get the chance to tell him what I think of him.

I drain my glass as my mission becomes crystal clear, and I slam it onto the table.

Before I know it, I'm marching over to his table. I catch Sebastian off guard, and he only sees me when I am standing beside him.

"A word," I say.

He raises his eyebrow sarcastically. "I'd rather not."

I glare at him. "Unless you want to be wearing your fucking drink, get outside. Now," I growl, losing all control.

"Um...wow." His blond friend raises his brow too. "Do we know you?"

I turn my attention to him, and he withers under my glare.

The dark friend smirks and holds out his hand to shake mine. "Julian Masters."

"I don't care," I bark.

The blond friend chuckles. "Fuck me, who *is* this?"

"Outside!" I snap before marching into the foyer.

I stomp through the conservatory like I'm The Hulk. I don't remember ever being this angry. I can taste it in my mouth like it's poison.

I make it to the foyer, and I turn to see Sebastian walking behind me. He seems pissed off too.

He puts his hands into his pants pockets. "What do you want?" he snaps.

I see a cloakroom. "Over here." I walk over to it and open the door to find it's empty. "In private."

"I've got nothing to say to you."

"Well, I've got plenty to say to you," I whisper angrily.

He marches past me into the cloakroom. I follow him in and slam the door shut.

"I don't have time for your shit," he barks.

"You'll make time, you entitled fucking asshole," I scream. "How dare you?"

His eyes bulge, and he points to his own chest as if outraged. "How dare *I*?"

"That's what I said."

He opens his mouth to argue.

"Shut up and fucking listen." I push him hard in the chest.

He narrows his eyes and tilts his chin to the ceiling in defiance. "Touch me again and see what fucking happens to you," he growls.

"I will do whatever I want, and you are going to listen to every fucking word I say. First of all," I say, "I never touched your son. Not once," I cry. "If he had a crush on me, it was completely one-sided. I had *no* idea about it until we were on your front porch."

He opens his mouth to argue.

"Shut the fuck up, Sebastian, or so help me God!" My chest rises and falls as I fight to stay in control. "Second of all...you called me a lying whore."

His eyes hold mine. "That's right."

I slap him hard across the face; the sound echoes throughout the small space. His eyes flicker with fury, and he pushes me back up against the wall to get me away from him.

"I'm nobody's whore, least of all yours," I whisper.

He holds me tight, his face so close to mine. "You sure about that?"

I push him off me, and he stumbles back.

"*You* pay for sex, you pathetic piece of shit, and you have the audacity *to judge me*?"

"Go to hell." He clenches his fists by his sides.

"I won't." I smile sarcastically. "You see, Mr. Garcia, my conscience is clear. I'm a good person with a good heart, and I don't have double standards. And you," I whisper. "You are just another *sleazy...entitled...*politician."

His nostrils flare, and I know I hit a nerve.

"Stay the fuck away from me," I sneer. With one last look, I march out into the foyer and straight into the ladies' room. Once in the cubicle, I close the door as tears fill my eyes.

I can feel my heartbeat pounding everywhere. I drop my head into my hands, overcome with anger.

I hate Sebastian Garcia with all of my being. I hate him. I hate that he still affects me.

I hate that I still care.

Sebastian

I run my hands through my hair as I try to calm down. *Fuck!*

What is she doing here?

I thought she went back to America. I pinch the bridge of my nose and stay alone in the cloakroom for a moment. Her words come back to me.

You are just another sleazy...entitled...politician.

Bitch.

That's it. I'm out of here. I open the door and march out with purpose.

She turns up here, tells me that she's going to throw a drink on me if I don't speak to her, slaps me across the face, and then she calls *me* entitled.

What the fuck?

"Sebastian," I hear a woman's voice call from behind me.

I turn and see Gisselle, an old friend I have recently reconnected with. We've been chatting online and over the phone for a few weeks.

Fuck...worst timing ever.

I fake a smile. "Gisselle, hi." I kiss her on the cheek. I glance down at her, and although I'm too angry to even see what she looks like, I pay her a compliment. "You look gorgeous."

"Thanks." She beams, and I remember why I had begun messaging her. She is stunning. "I didn't know you were going to be here. Are you having a good night?"

"I am." I pause. "Unfortunately, though, I'm on my way out. I have another engagement I have to attend for work."

Her face falls.

"I'll call you tomorrow. Maybe we could get a coffee or something?" I offer.

She smiles. "I'd like that."

"Okay." I bend and kiss her on the cheek before I brush past her.

I walk into the conservatorium, straight over to Spence.

"I'm leaving," I tell them.

Spencer frowns. "Why?"

"Because I'm not in the mood for this fucking shithole, that's why. Are you coming or not?"

"Masters!" Spence calls over to Julian, who is talking to someone. "We're heading off. You coming?"

Julian frowns, still focused on the man he's talking to. He holds his finger up to tell Spence to wait a moment. Moments later, he turns back to us. "What?"

"We're leaving," I say, as I head for the door.

"Why?"

"Please tell me it has to do with that smoking hot blonde bitch," Spencer says, following me out.

"*Bitch* being the operative word. What the fuck was her problem?" Masters asks dryly.

"You know, I think it's hot when women are bitches," Spencer says as we walk out through the foyer. "It's a real turn-on, you know. I don't like you, but just fuck me hard anyway."

"Will you shut up?" I roll my eyes. "The shit that comes out of your mouth sometimes, Spencer. Honestly."

"It's a fine line for the bitch level to be worth it," Masters chimes in. "She was fucking hot, though."

"I said, will you two shut the fuck up?" We get into the back of my waiting car.

The driver turns to us after we've climbed inside. "Where to?"

The boys both look to me.

"Do you want to get something to eat?" I ask.

"I guess." They both shrug.

"Hugo's in Kensington, please."

The car zooms through the streets of London, and the boys chatter between themselves, leaving me to stare out the window at the passing traffic, lost in my own thoughts.

You are just another sleazy...entitled...politician.

"Who was that chick?" Masters asks.

"Nobody."

"Shit, she sure seemed like a somebody. She dragged you out to the foyer, and then you come back looking like you saw a ghost."

"Shut. Up," I hiss.

"How do you know her?"

They're going to keep going on about this, so I have to give them something.

"We dated a few years ago. It went badly." I give a subtle shake of my head. "That was the first time I've seen her since, and—"

"And now she wants to cut your dick off," Spencer finishes for me.

"Basically." I stare out the window.

"Well, see if she can do it with her teeth," Masters says.

Spencer laughs. "Right?"

Masters' phone beeps, and he reads a text and rolls his eyes. "Fuck's sake," he mutters under his breath.

"What?" Spence asks.

"Bree is busting my fucking balls over this renovation for Willow."

I get a vision of Bree giving it to my grumpy friend, and I smirk.

"Why?"

He holds his phone up and looks at us deadpan. There are two images of different types of carpet. "Who thinks about carpet on a fucking Saturday night?" He raises his eyebrows. "I mean, seriously."

Spencer and I laugh, and I feel a little of my anger dissipate.

I stare back out the window as normality comes back into focus and I feel my equilibrium return.

I have the best friends in the world, and that's all that matters.

April

"Hi, Mom," I answer my phone.

"I'm sorry to call you at work, darling. I know you're busy, but I couldn't wait until tonight. Have you heard anything about your new position yet?"

I smile. My mom is so excited about my new job, maybe even more than I am. "Not yet. I should find out something this week, I guess."

"Oh, this is so exciting, are you getting a big pay rise? What about a company car?"

I giggle. "I don't know, probably not."

"Eliza thinks you will," she replies.

"Hi, chick," I hear Eliza call in the background.

I smile broadly. "Tell Lize I'll call her tonight." I would say Eliza, my sister, is my best friend. I speak to her daily, sometimes twice.

"She said that she's calling you tonight," my mother tells her.

"April, your next appointment is here. Helena Matheson," sounds through the intercom.

"Thanks, Melissa. I'll be right out."

"I've got to go, Mom," I say. "I'll call you later."

"Bye, darling, love you."

"Love you too."

I click out of the file I'm working on and make my way out into the waiting room in the foyer.

"Helena?" I ask when I see a beautiful woman with long dark hair.

She stands, her smile warm, and we shake hands. "Hi. Yes."

"I'm April." I smile. "This way, please." I lead her to my office and gesture to the chair at my desk. "Take a seat."

She's breathtakingly beautiful and kitted out in designer clothing from head to toe. I glance quickly at her Prada handbag. Damn, I love that bag. I bet it cost ten thousand pounds, or something as equally ridiculous as that.

"How can I help you today?" I ask.

"I would like to go over the terms of my divorce."

"Okay." I try to understand her better. "So, you're looking for someone to represent you in your divorce?"

"No. I've been divorced for seven years."

I frown. "You've already been through the settlement?"

"Yes." She clutches her handbag on her lap. "But I feel that I was wrongly represented."

"I see." I get out my paper and pen to take notes. "Tell me a little about what you would like to achieve."

She straightens her back as if steeling herself. "I want the dog."

My eyes hold hers as I get an off feeling. "Okay..." I say warily, writing my first note. "Are there any children involved?"

"No."

"And did you ask for the dog in the first settlement? What's the dog's name?"

"I didn't at the time, although I have mentioned it over the years. His name is Bentley."

"And what kind of dog is it?"

She shrugs, as if uninterested. "A Labrador."

"And how old is Bentley?"

"No idea, but fucking old."

I'm really trying to understand what I'm dealing with here. "And what were the terms of the initial agreement?"

"Well, my ex-husband completely ripped me off. He paid for the best lawyers money could buy, so I had no chance. He has money." She dusts something invisible off her shirt.

"What did you receive?"

"I got the house."

I make more notes. "And how much was that worth?"

"Six million at the time. I got two of the cars, including a Porsche and a Maserati."

I try to keep a straight face as I take the notes.

"I got the holiday house in Italy too," she says.

I scribble some more. This guy must be loaded.

"What did he request in the settlement?" I ask.

"The dog."

My eyes rise to meet hers. "Bentley," I correct her.

"Yes." She crosses her legs with attitude. "He got nasty."

"How many other..." I pause, trying to get my wording right. "I mean, what else did he own at the time?"

"Nothing."

"You got everything?"

"Yes, but he got nasty."

"How so?"

"I had an affair."

My eyes rise to meet hers. I hate this bitch. "And was it a one-time thing?"

"No, it went on for a few months. It was with our gardener, and it was my ex-husband's fault, anyway. He was always away working, and I had needs."

My stomach twists as my own history rears its ugly head.

I scribble down my thoughts. "And you said he got nasty. Can you tell me how so?"

"In order for me to get any assets, he demanded that I change my surname."

I frown. That's a weird request.

"I wasn't legally allowed to have his surname. Like, who the hell does he think he is?"

I bite my lip to hide my smirk. "I see. So his only requests were that he wanted the removal of his surname and the custody of Bentley."

"Yes."

My eyes rise to meet hers. "What's changed, Helena? Why do you want to rehash this when you clearly did so well from the first settlement?"

"He's doing very well now, and I feel"—she hunches her shoulders—"I deserve more."

"You want the dog?'

"God, no, I don't want the stupid dog. The dog is my only bargaining tool."

Spiteful bitch.

"I see." I want to tell her to get the hell out of my office. "Has your ex-husband remarried?"

"You've got to be joking," she huffs. "He's pathetic."

I run my tongue over my bottom lip as I stare at her. I really don't like this woman. "He doesn't even date. Oh…" She laughs, as if remembering something. "There was that one time about a year after we separated, where he fell in love with a prostitute…but she was also sleeping with his son."

I begin to hear white noise ringing in my ears.

No, it can't be!

"What kind of an idiot would fall in love with a prostitute?" she smirks.

"Who told you that?"

"Told me what?"

"That he fell in love with the prostitute?"

"His sister and my sister are still friends. It was a big family breakup. Apparently, the son and my ex-husband were both in love with her at the same time." She flicks her hair. "The son didn't speak to him for months when he found out. What a joke. At least I was only sleeping with one other man. He should have stuck with me."

I stare at her. "What's his name?"

"Who, the son's?"

"Your ex-husband. What was his name?"

"Sebastian Garcia."

11

April

I stare at her. "Pardon?" I mean, I heard it...but surely not. "His name is Sebastian Garcia?"

"Yes. You know him?"

"No," I say too quickly.

"Of course you do. The politician. He's the new Deputy Prime Minister. Everyone knows him."

Relief fills me as I realize how this looks. I should know him. "Oh, yes, I see. I knew the name sounded familiar."

My thoughts flash back to our fight in the cloakroom the other night, and I have to force it from my mind.

"So, what do you think?" Helena asks.

"About?"

"The dog," she snaps, exasperated.

I sit back, and I hate to admit it, but I really don't like this woman. "Helena...let me ask you something: *why* do you want Bentley?"

"I'm entitled to more of his estate."

"But you already got everything."

"He has much more now."

"But you're not married to him now."

"Are you going to help me or not?"

I begin to lose my patience with her. "Helena, there isn't a judge on Earth that would grant you more of an estate that you have already settled on."

"Yes, well, we'll see about that, won't we?" She stands in a huff and throws her handbag around her shoulder. "Goodbye, Miss Bennet. I wish I could say that you've been helpful." She stomps towards the door. "But that would be a complete lie, wouldn't it? I don't appreciate you wasting my time."

She disappears through the door, and it slams hard on her release.

God.

What a fucking bitch.

I pull up the records she submitted when she booked her appointment. I can't believe he married a witch like her. What the hell was Sebastian thinking?

Actually, who am I to talk?

I married an asshole too.

I go back through the notes and search for the date of the last settlement.

February. Seven years ago.

I work out the dates. That was just over twelve months before he met me. I scan the file until I get their marriage and separation details. They were married for five years, until he discovered that she was having an affair with the gardener. I exhale heavily, knowing too well how that feels.

I wonder if he walked in on them doing the deed like I did.

Poor bastard. He would have been badly burnt, and then he thought that I...

Stop it! Do not dare make excuses for that man.

His wife is a bitch, but that doesn't excuse his behaviour. He's an asshole, and if truth be told, they probably deserve each other. Who knows how many affairs he had on her with his visits to sex clubs, for Christ's sake?

Ugh, why am I even thinking about his side of the story? Who cares, anyway?

I read over the notes and go through Helena's history. She doesn't work. Of course she doesn't. She's too busy living off her ex-husband.

With a heavy exhale, I throw the file into the cabinet. I know she's going to go to another lawyer. I also know that another lawyer won't be able to touch her, but nothing surprises me these days. As long as I'm not the lawyer, I don't care.

The tree casts a shadow on the wall. It's 1:00 a.m., but I haven't slept.

I can't.

I keep going over the argument I had with Sebastian and the way I hit him. I can still hear the crack as my hand connected with his face.

Why *did* I slap him?

That's not who I am—not even close. I'm not violent, and I've never hit a man before.

Imagine if he slapped me and how outraged I would be.

God, it's just another low point that I wish never happened. Sebastian Garcia seems to bring out the best of them—low points, that is.

I stare into the darkness some more as my mind wanders. Deputy Prime Minister.

How the hell did he get that position? Was he a politician when I knew him before? I think back to any sign I may have missed, but I can't think of anything. There were no signs, but I didn't really know anything much about him then. We were too busy fucking like rabbits.

I thought he was just an architect.

Maybe that was all bullshit. Architects don't become Deputy Prime Ministers. I walk out into the living room, turn the light on, and open my laptop. I want answers. I want to know when and how.

I type his name into Google and scroll through to Wikipedia.

Sebastian Garcia

Named the people's politician, Sebastian Garcia is a 42-year-old English architect. Garcia began his political career when consulting for the (then) town planner Thomas Harvey. Since he had been active in the role for several years, on Thomas's retirement, Garcia was voted as the Minister of Town Planning. With a reputation for being ruthless and a clear vision of protecting the common people, Sebastian Garcia does not shy away from being controversial.

He made his first political impression when he publicly called out the Prime Minister in a press release over a reneged promise on the development of the M4 motorway. Garcia demanded that the Prime Minister keep his promise and reroute the motorway to a safer position for the surrounding suburbs that were to be demolished.

With his fuss-free, no-frills approach, he deservedly earned the respect amongst his peers, and over the following three years was voted up throughout the ranks.

In the worst-kept secret of parliament, it has been revealed that Garcia is making most of the planning and budget decisions. Prime Minister Theodore Holsworthy and Garcia clash heads often, having had many public exchanges.

Speculation circulates how long Holsworthy can hold his party votes with Sebastian Garcia tipped to be the next Prime Minister of the United Kingdom.

I sit back in my chair in surprise. Wow.

Well...kudos to him, I suppose.

I stand, fill the kettle, and turn the television on. I flick through the channels, knowing it's going to be another long night. I'm not sleeping well. I haven't been since seeing Sebastian last week. I keep going over and over everything we said to each other... including the way he looked. The feelings.

So many unfinished feelings.

Most of all, I think about the anger he brought out in me.

But, regardless of any of those things, I should have never slapped him.

It was a shitty thing to do. Guilt doesn't feel very nice.

There's a knock at my door, and I look up from my computer.

"Come in."

"Hello, April?" A distinguished-looking man steps forward with a broad smile on his face. "I'm Bart McIntyre."

Oh shit. I stand and shake his hand. "Hello, Bart. Nice to meet you." I smile.

He's tall and blond with a scattering of grey hair. He must be in his late forties, I think. Quite handsome. He's wearing an expensive suit, and he looks every bit of the celebrity lawyer he is.

"Have you got two minutes for a quick chat?" he asks.

"Yes, sure. Please, take a seat." I gesture to my chair.

"Thank you. I'm still finding my way around the offices. I wanted to meet you first, seeing that we will be working so closely together."

"I can't thank you enough for the opportunity, Mr. McIntyre."

"I've been looking over your file. You have a very impressive résumé, Miss Bennet."

"Thank you. Can you tell me a little bit about the position?" I ask. "What would you like me to do, and what are your expectations?"

Bart sits back in his chair. "Well, for a start, you will be accompanying me to all of my appointments. Most of my clients are off-site. They don't like to be seen going into a lawyer's office, hence why I visit them. We'll start those appointments next Monday. I'm in the office this week. I have a lot to sort out and get accustomed to. But I just wanted to pop in and meet you."

"Thank you. I can't wait to get started."

He gives me a warm smile. "Please let me know if there are any problems or issues while we are working together. I like to be professional, and I like my coworkers to be happy."

"Sounds great." Excitement fills me.

He moves towards the door but turns back to me. "Oh, and April, starting the week after next, we will be going away for three days a week over the next month."

"Okay." I frown. "Where would we be going, Mr. McIntyre?"

"Just out to the countryside, not too far from here. It's always within a two-hour radius of London. My client has to travel, and we have to accompany him."

"Sounds good."

"I'll get reception to work on our travel packs. You will need some extra equipment to keep in the car for our visits."

"Perfect."

He gives me a kind nod before leaving, and I smile to myself. Wow, going away a few nights every single week for a month is going to be amazing, I can already tell.

Sebastian

I fill the coffee cups with boiling water, then stir in the milk.

"Marina wants me to set you up with her."

I glance up at my sister. "You have got to be kidding. I have no interest in Marina whatsoever."

"Sebastian." Violet exhales. "You have no interest in anybody anymore."

"Yes, so? I like it that way." I pass her the coffee cup.

"Thanks." She watches me intently.

I roll my eyes. "What?"

"When are you going to let yourself be happy?" she asks.

"I am happy. What are you talking about?"

"I mean really happy, you know...a family of your own, wife and kids."

"That's not in my future."

"Why not?"

142

"I've been there and done the whole marriage thing. It's not somewhere I want to return to."

"Seb," she sighs. "Helena was just a bad egg. It wouldn't have mattered who she married; she would have done the same to them. And that other woman... The—"

"April," I cut her off before she says it.

Her eyes hold mine for a moment. "I'm just saying...you can't spend the rest of your life living in the past."

"I'm not. I just don't have the same expectations that I used to."

"Are you really going to live in this huge house alone?"

"I'm perfectly happy as I am." I glance over at the golden Labrador sprawled out in front of the fire. "And I don't live alone. I live with Bentley." I smirk against my coffee cup.

"Why aren't *you* dating?" I ask, deflecting.

"I have a date on Saturday night, actually."

"You do?"

"Uh-huh." She smiles.

"Who with?"

"You don't know him." Her response comes too quickly.

I stare at her for a moment. "You know, Vi, I've come to understand the patterns of when someone is lying to me."

She rolls her eyes.

"Are you lying to me?"

She smirks.

"So...I do know him."

"I just don't want to jinx it." She smiles.

I frown. "Do I like him?"

"Have you ever liked a boyfriend of mine?"

I smirk, knowing she's got me. "No."

"So, can I set you up with Marina?"

"Definitely not."

We fall silent for a while. I love my sister. She's single like I am, and with Brandon living on the other side of the country with his new wife, she gets lonely sometimes. We eat dinner together a few nights throughout the week. She's become my rock.

143

"I saw her," I find myself admitting.

"Who?"

"April."

She frowns as she listens. "Where?"

"Last week, a charity auction at the Art Museum."

"Did you talk to her?"

"You could say that." I sip my coffee. "We fought in a cloakroom."

"Of course you did." She smirks. "How is she?"

"Still beautiful."

Violet blows into her coffee. "And totally wrong for you, Sebastian. Get that out of your head right now."

"It doesn't matter, anyway." I shrug casually. "She was with someone else. Maybe a boyfriend. She didn't have a wedding ring on, though."

"You looked at her hand?" she asks dryly.

I twist my lips, unwilling to admit to it out loud again, but hating that I did.

"Was he there with her?" she asks. "Her boyfriend or whatever he is?"

"Yes. He's a football player. Pretty good one, from what I hear. He's a Man United player." I think for a moment. "Maybe Arsenal, I don't know which club."

"Good. I hope she marries him tomorrow and stays the hell away from you."

I smile at my overprotective sister, and I let myself sink back into thought— something I've been doing a lot of lately.

The wrath of reflection. I drift back to all those years ago, and how it felt to be in her arms. For a while, it was perfect.

My stomach twists when I remember how badly it ended.

I have many regrets in my life. That week, that night, and the months that followed. They're all up there with the biggest.

April

We ride the elevator to the top floor with my nerves at an all-time high. I glance at my reflection in the mirrored doors. I'm wearing black high heels, a black pencil skirt, and a matching jacket with a cream silk blouse and sheer black stockings. My blonde bob is hanging in loose curls, and my makeup is minimal.

It's my first day on the road with Bart McIntyre, and I have to admit that this shit is scary. We have Jeremy with us, who is Mr. McIntyre's personal assistant who travels everywhere with him.

I glance over at Jeremy standing beside the door. He would have to be in his early thirties. He's a very good-looking man in a perfectly fitting suit. He has chocolate brown hair and big green eyes. He's apparently been Bart's PA for six years. He's very friendly too. I haven't quite worked out the dynamics between the two of them yet. I think they might be together, as they seem very familiar. But maybe that's just what you get from working together for so long, and my mind is just depraved. I mean, just because he's his PA, that doesn't mean that they're fucking.

Or maybe my gut feeling is right and it means they totally are. I guess time will tell whether I'm right or wrong.

There's so much to learn. A little thrill runs through me at the prospect of all the new and exciting things.

The doors open, and Jeremy steps out and walks up to the desk. He immediately takes his laptop out of its bag. There's a metal scanner at the entrance leading into the offices, as well as two security guards.

Huh? Is that a metal detector?

I glance over at Bart in question, wondering who, exactly, we are seeing.

"You'll have to take your laptop out and pass through security," Bart tells me as he begins to unload his laptop bag. He takes his phone and keys out of his pocket and places them on a tray.

"Shoes off," the security guard commands as he runs a metal detector over my body.

I slip out of my shoes and put them on the tray. Bart was supposed to send our schedule to my email last week. It never arrived, and I didn't want to sound pushy by requesting it.

Once we pass through, I slip my shoes back on and gather up my things. Eventually, we walk through the doors and into another large reception area. It's all black marble floors and fancy as fancy can be.

"Good morning, Bart." The receptionist smiles. "Morning, Jeremy." Her eyes come to me in question.

"Rebecca, this is April," Bart introduces. "She's my new associate and will be travelling with me from now on."

"Hello." Rebecca fakes a smile and looks me up and down. I can almost hear her judgement.

"Hello." I smile in return.

Why are women such bitches to other women? She's probably got the hots for Bart or something...or Jeremy. She's around his age.

"Just go up to his office. He's expecting you."

"Thanks." Bart gestures to me. "This way." I follow him up a large corridor.

Jeremy veers off and walks into an office on the left. "See you soon," he says as he takes a seat at a desk.

Bart and I walk over to two large black double doors, and Bart knocks once.

"Come in!" a voice calls.

Bart opens the door. "Hello, my friend." He walks in.

I look at the person sitting behind the large mahogany desk, and my heart stops.

It's Sebastian Garcia.

Oh, fuck.

He sees me and rolls his lips. "Bart," he says dryly, his eyes holding mine.

"Sebastian." Bart smiles as he gestures to me. "Meet April Bennet, my new associate. She will be working closely with me from here on in. April, this is Sebastian Garcia, the man currently helping to run our country."

Sebastian's eyes stay fixed on mine, and he holds out his hand to shake mine. "Hello, April. Nice to meet you." His voice holds no emotion.

Fuck, fuck, double fuck.

This isn't happening.

"Hello." I grimace.

"Please, take a seat." He gestures to the chairs at his desk.

Oh hell...this is bad. Really bad.

I take a seat to stop myself from falling. I couldn't make this shit up if I tried. My heart is beating fast. I wipe my brow, feeling faint.

Sebastian sits back in his chair, his eyes still locked on mine. He raises his chin in defiance.

He's wearing a perfectly fitted navy suit. His dark hair has a wave to it, and his deep olive skin is in stark contrast to his crisp white shirt.

Arrogance personified.

"So, I've been researching our options." Bart slips straight into business mode.

Sebastian's eyes rise to him for the first time since we walked in.

But my gaze stays fixed on Sebastian's face.

He's older than when we met, a little weathered, but still so *beautiful.*

Sebastian Garcia is still the most handsome man I have had the misfortune of meeting.

I feel my heart constrict in my chest as I listen to his deep voice as he speaks to Bart.

I get a vision of him looking up at me with his head between my legs, his lips glistening with my arousal, and I bite my bottom lip to get rid of the memory.

Stop it! He's a complete asshole.

The bastard of all bastards.

I remember the way he used to kiss me, the way he would grab my face in his hands and his eyes would close, making me feel it all the way to my toes.

Fuck, cut it out.

I hate that he still affects me.

Bart and Sebastian keep talking business—something about an overpass on a motorway, and legislation about something else, but I can't focus on a word they are saying, which I really need to because this is fucking important.

For half an hour, I sit, frozen on the spot. Sebastian hasn't looked at me once.

Bart fishes into his pocket and digs out his ringing phone. "Sorry, I have to take this. I'll be back in a moment. You two acquaint yourselves." He stands and rushes from the room, closing the door behind him.

We are left alone.

Sebastian's eyes meet mine, and we stare at each other. There are no words to say to this man.

He stays silent.

I need to say it. I need to get it off my chest. I take out my phone and scroll through my numbers. When I get to his name, I hope this is still his number. I type.

Is this room under surveillance?

A phone beeps from inside his desk's top drawer. He opens it and reads the message and holds up his phone. "Is this you?" he asks.

I nod.

He sits back in his chair and crosses his leg at the ankle. "No, the room is not monitored."

I twist my fingers on my lap as I brace myself. "Sebastian, I'm sorry for slapping you the other night in the cloakroom. I don't know what came over me. That isn't who I am. I regretted it the moment I did it."

He glares at me, and animosity swims between us.

God, this is a nightmare.

"Can we just keep this professional between us?" I ask.

He gives me a sarcastic smirk. "Like you are now?"

"If we have to work together, can we at least be civil?" I whisper angrily as I begin to lose my patience.

He leans forward and places his palms on the desk. "Let me tell you something, April Bennet. You are in my office, and you will work under my rules from here on in. If you dare ever fucking hit me again, expect a return."

I narrow my eyes as I imagine knocking the fucker clean out. "Mr. Garcia, I will not hit you again. Hell, I don't even want to look at you."

He raises an eyebrow. "Are you sure about that, April? Because you haven't taken your eyes off me since you walked in."

Fucking asshole.

I give him a sweet smile. "That was me wondering what I ever saw in you, and for the life of me, I just can't work it out."

His jaw tics, and I know that stung. Well, too bad.

Our eyes are locked when the door opens behind me.

"Sorry about that," Bart says as he interrupts our standoff. "Where were we?"

Sebastian stands in a rush. "We have to leave it here for today, Bart. I've been called to an urgent cabinet meeting."

"Oh, that's fine," Bart replies. "I'll work on that and get back to you."

"Thank you." He nods to Bart, and then at me. "Nice to meet you, April."

I smile sweetly. "The pleasure was all mine, Mr. Garcia."

He looks murderous, like he's about to explode.

Bring it, asshole. You don't scare me.

Seriously, nobody pisses me off more than this man.

"Goodbye." Sebastian rushes from the room.

Bart frowns as he watches him leave. "Hmm, I wonder what's up with him today."

"No idea." I pack our things from the desk.

I'm not taking his shit anymore.

Those days are done.

I'm lying in bed, watching *The Late Show* at 11:00 p.m., about to slip into a carbohydrate coma. I've eaten an entire block of chocolate tonight.

I keep going over my meeting today with Sebastian. What a nightmare situation.

I'm going to lose my job over this, I can feel it.

My phone rings on my nightstand. Who would be calling me this late?

I pick it up and see the name lighting up the screen.

April's fool

12

April

I SIT UP, startled.

Shit.

Oh fuck... I exhale and answer in a rush. "Hello."

"April," his deep voice purrs down the line.

"I was expecting this call. I'll talk to Bart and let him know."

"Let him know what?"

"That you don't want me working in your office. I understand."
I close my eyes in frustration. Trust him to make this personal.
"Thanks for letting me know."

He pauses. "That's not why I called. I have no problem working
with you."

Huh?

"Why do you still have my number?" he asks.

"What do you mean?"

"Why didn't you delete my number?"

"Like you did mine, you mean?"

"Yes."

"Because I don't need to delete numbers to stop myself from

calling people, Sebastian. I have a little bit more self-control than that."

He stays quiet, processing my words. After a while, he replies, "I see."

We both stay silent on the phone, as if waiting for the other person to say something.

I have so much I want to say to him and so much anger inside of me, but if I have to work with him, I need to get this off my chest.

"Sebastian." I pause as I try to get my wording right. "I know that it doesn't matter now, and I know it has no relevance to where we are...and I don't even know why I feel like I really have to say this, but I'm sorry that..."

"What, April?"

"That you thought that I was with your son."

He stays silent.

"Brandon and I were never together, Sebastian. I had no idea that he even had a crush on me until he kissed me on your front doorstep. I was as horrified as you were—"

"You and I weren't together," he cuts me off.

"In my eyes, we were." I feel myself getting emotional. What is it about this fucking man that turns me into a sap? "I couldn't have been with anyone else because I was too wrapped up in you."

Silence again.

I shake my head, annoyed that I just said that out loud.

"Anyway, whatever. I don't care anymore. I moved on years ago, but I just wanted you to know that."

"I'm not proud of the way I handled that night, April," he whispers.

I close my eyes, just listening to his deep voice. It brings back so many memories.

"I lost my temper," he says softly. "I just... I couldn't deal with it, and I needed you gone."

"Is that your apology?"

He stays silent.

"Because calling someone a lying whore deserves an apology," I say. "And I've never lied to you—not once—and you and I both know that I'm not a whore."

"Why did you work there, then?"

I feel my anger rising. "Because I walked in on my husband having sex with another woman, Sebastian!" I bark. "And I left with nothing but the clothes on my back." Angry tears well in my eyes. "And you have no fucking idea how it feels to be so broke that you can't afford food and rent. So don't you *fucking dare* judge me, you entitled asshole. Why don't you ask yourself why it's okay for you to pay for sex? Why do you think girls work at those places, Sebastian? You think they're there for your magical dick alone?"

"Calm down."

"I will not calm down!" I cry. "It's rich bastards like you who make girls like me feel cheap." I shake my head. "Stick your pathetic apology up your ass."

"April."

I hit the end call button and jump out of bed with purpose, pacing back and forth. I'm too angry to lie still.

Fuck him and his judgement. He can go to hell.

Sebastian Garcia is still an asshole.

Sebastian

"We got a problem," Max says as he rushes into my office.

I glance up from my computer. "What now?"

"Theodore is a mess."

I roll my eyes in disgust. I already know what he's going to say before he opens his mouth. The Prime Minister is an asshole. "Why?"

"He's still high from last night. Just spilled his coffee all over his shirt and thinks it's hilarious."

"What the fuck?" I glance at my watch. "He's supposed to be doing a press conference in half an hour."

"I know. The press is setting up outside number 10 as we speak."

"Fuck's sake," I hiss. "I'm sick of his shit. When the hell is he going to get over his midlife crisis and do some fucking work?"

Max drags his hand down his face. "His cocaine problem is seriously out of control." He shrugs. "How much longer can we cover for him?"

I scratch my head in frustration. "I don't know." I shuffle some papers. "He was reporting on the border restrictions, yes?" I ask.

"Yes. You wrote the speech for him last week. Looks like you'll have to deliver it for him too."

"I don't want to deal with the media. This is not what I am assigned to do." I bring up the report on my computer.

"Nobody else can deliver it to the media without it looking suspicious."

"It is fucking suspicious." I stand. "Let's go. Where is he?"

"In the library. Marcela is looking after him in the tearoom."

I march down the corridor and into the elevator. I take the lift up to the library and walk through to the tearoom to find Theodore spinning on his chair. He's laughing like a child, obviously as high as a kite.

"Theo," I say.

"Hey!" He laughs. "Garcia. Get a chair. Spin with me."

"Where is Leona?"

"Who?"

Max and I exchange looks. This isn't fucking good at all. "Leona. Your wife."

"Who fucking cares?" he scoffs. "In Italy, spending my money, I expect."

"Why don't you go and join her? You need a vacation."

"I'm having a holiday without my wife." He tips the chair and falls spectacularly onto the floor.

Max and I scramble to pull him to his feet. "I'm calling Leona," I say.

He dusts himself off. "She left me." He stumbles back and side-steps. "Said she doesn't love me anymore."

I exhale heavily and plant my hands on my hips. Fuck, this explains a lot.

I help him back into his seat, and he tries to spin it again. I stop it with my hand. "Stop."

"Come on." He claps his hands and tries to stand again. "Let's go. It's Tuesday, and we've got a press conference."

I push him back down into his chair. "You're not going anywhere." I crouch down so that we are at eye level. "Theo, listen to me. I'm booking you into a private facility. You need to go to rehab."

"What?" he explodes. "I don't need to go to fucking rehab, Garcia. What the hell are you talking about?"

"If the press get a hold of this, your career is going to come to an abrupt end."

"I'm not going anywhere," he growls. "You don't control everything around here."

"I'm trying to protect you."

"Like fuck you are. You want my job." He snatches his arm from my grip. "I don't need your help." He tilts and tips the chair once again, and goes sprawling onto the floor.

Jesus. I take out my phone and call Warren from security.

"Can I have four security guards to the tearoom in the library, please?"

"Sure thing."

"What do you need security for?" Theo growls.

I exhale heavily. Fuck this, I don't need this shit. "Nothing to worry about, Theo."

Two minutes later, the security guards walk in. "Yes, sir?"

I gesture to Theodore. "Keep him up here until he sobers up. Do not let him downstairs under any circumstances. He needs to sleep it off."

Their eyes go to Theo, who laughs out loud. "I'm not going to bed. I'm going to party."

I watch Theodore. He's off his head. "I'm going to get some intervention. He'll be fine. I'll be back after the press release."

"Yes, sir."

I march out of the tearoom and back into the elevator.

"I'm going to have to book him into rehab before the press find out about this. How are we hitting the campaign trail with a coked-up Prime Minister?"

"He's a train wreck waiting to happen," Max mutters under his breath.

I pinch the bridge of my nose. "Don't I know it."

I return to my office, collect my speech, and then I head down to the press release. I take my place at the podium in front of the reporters.

"Hello," I say as I shuffle through my papers.

"Where is Prime Minister Holsworthy?" someone asks.

"He's unable to make it today. He has a prior engagement."

"He was scheduled to take this meeting," the male voice replies.

I glance over to who asked the question. Fuck, Gerhard. The sniffer dog of all sniffer dogs. Reporter of the fucking year or some shit. If there's a story,

guaranteed, he'll uncover it.

"Theodore sends his apologies. He had an important call from an overseas colleague he had to take," I lie.

Gerhard's eyes hold mine, and I know he doesn't buy my story for one moment.

I fall into my role and address the press, anyway. "Thank you for coming. We are here to talk about the proposed border control changes." I turn the page of my dossier. "As usual, please hold all questions until the end."

My intercom buzzes. "Sebastian?"

"Yes, Rebecca," I reply, typing on my computer.

"Bart is here."

I hit enter. That means *she's* here.

"Send them in." I rearrange my tie and run my fingers through my hair. There's a knock at the door. "Come in."

The door opens and Bart comes into view, smiling broadly. "Hello, Sebastian."

"Hi." I stand, and my eyes drift past him to April. She's wearing a fitted navy dress. Her blonde hair is down in soft curls, tucked behind one ear.

Her eyes find mine, and she gives me a soft smile.

My stomach twists.

"Hi." She smiles awkwardly.

"Hello." I put my hands into my pockets and try to hide the starstruck look on my face.

Dear fucking God, she's beautiful.

I gesture to the chairs in a fluster. "Please take a seat," I tell them.

They both sit down, and April crosses her legs. I glance down and see the muscle in her thighs. I snap my eyes up to her face.

Stop it.

I shuffle the papers on my desk to distract myself. This damn woman turns me into a horny teenager.

"What's the problem?" Bart asks as he unpacks his laptop.

I glance up at him.

You're my problem. Get out so I can fuck April on my desk.

I get a vision of her lying naked on my desk, her legs open. She's all pink and wet and...

My cock throbs, and I hesitate, trying to remember what I am supposed to be talking about.

Focus, fool.

"Theodore is having a few problems, and I need to get him into a private facility," I finally say.

"What kind of problems?"

"Substance abuse."

Bart pinches the bridge of his nose. "Are you kidding me?"

"I wish I were. He's turning up to work high."

Bart closes his eyes. "For how long?"

"A few weeks. It's been escalating, and I don't know how much longer I can cover it up. The staff are beginning to notice."

"For fuck's sake," Bart snaps. "Why haven't I been told about this earlier? Isn't my job here for crisis management?"

"It isn't a crisis." I glare at him. This man pushes my buttons sometimes. "I do not need you to tell me your position, Bart. I'm telling you now."

"I'm just saying—"

"Don't," I bark, cutting him off.

My eyes float over to April, who is watching me from across the desk.

I can't deny that there's an electric current between us.

She moves to the left, and a little hint of her lace bra peeks through the material of her dress. I clench my jaw so that I don't look down.

How the hell could any man not want to look down?

"How bad is it?" Bart asks.

"Bad," I reply. "I don't know what I'm going to do with him. Campaigning starts on Monday, and I have a Prime Minister with a major drug problem."

"Fuck."

April picks up her pen and places the tip in her mouth as she listens. My eyes drop to her lips. I feel the long, deep throb inside my pants as I imagine myself in her mouth, looking up at me.

Fuck this. The woman drives me to distraction. How the hell am I supposed to do any work around here?

You hate her, remember?

I get back to what I'm supposed to be doing: working.

"I'm not sure what we're going to do or how we are going to address his absence, but I need you to find him a facility and get him checked in to get help. Hopefully then, in a week or two, he'll be back to his best, and we can move along." I shuffle the papers on my desk. I don't want to be distracted by April for one more second.

Damn, this woman is fucking driving me mad. I need to get up before I begin to stare at her.

"That'll be all for now. I've got another meeting I have to attend. Sorry." I stand and walk to my door, opening it in a rush. April frowns as she looks at me, and I glare back at her.

That's right, get out of my office, you temptress. I know what you're doing, and it's not going to work.

I got two hours' worth of sleep last night. Images of that damn forbidden fruit, April Bennet, were running naked through my mind.

"What's wrong with you today?" Spencer asks.

"Nothing."

"Then why do you look like someone has stuck something up your ass?"

"Get off my fucking case."

"Listen here, you little bitch," Spencer says. "I've got enough fucking hormonal women busting my balls at home. I don't need to put up with a moody prick like you at breakfast."

"Will you two shut the fuck up?" Julian sighs as he reads his paper.

I roll my eyes at Spencer. "Oh, you've got it so hard. A beautiful woman you love who's pregnant with your fourth baby," I mutter dryly before I sip my coffee.

"I have, actually," Spencer says. "Charlotte is either trying to fuck me to death or she's so hormonal that she wants to kill me. Either way, I'm a dead man walking, Sebastian."

I smile because Spencer's dramatics always cheer me up.

"There is nothing wrong with me, so leave me alone," I tell him.

Masters looks over his paper. "When is your blind date with that friend of your sister?"

"Don't even mention it. I'm not going."

"That's not what I heard," Spencer says. "I saw Marcy this week, and she said that your sister has already set it up."

"Oh, for Christ's sake." I exhale heavily. "I'm not in the mood for fucking blind dates. I don't have time for this shit when everything is going wrong."

"Like what?"

"I'm about to catch on fire. The temperature in my office is rising, and that woman is driving me crazy," I say.

Spencer frowns. "What woman?"

I stare at them for a moment, knowing that I may as well fill them in now.

I exhale heavily. "There's this girl."

Masters chuckles. "I knew it. There *is* a woman involved here. You are never in a bad mood."

"Just shut the fuck up, Masters," I snap. "It's a long story."

"We've got time."

"Remember that bad-coffee woman that I met in the Escape Club that was seeing Buddy at the same time as me?"

"Yeah."

"The woman that I had the fight with at the auction the other night is her."

They exchange looks. "The hot blonde one?"

"Yes, and guess who turned up at my office this week as a member of my new legal team."

Their eyes widen.

I throw my hands up in the air in disgust. "So now I have a woman working in my office who was the best sex of my life, and I can't act on it. Plus, she hates my guts, and here I am walking around with a fucking semi on the whole time."

They both stare at me for a moment before bursting into laughter.

"Not. Funny," I growl.

"In other words, you're fucked," Masters chuckles.

"Completely."

"What are you going to do?" Spencer asks.

"Nothing." I rearrange the napkin on my lap. "I'm going to ignore April Bennet and pretend that she doesn't exist."

April

The bar is bustling, and I take another sip of my margarita.

"How does he look, anyway?" Penelope asks.

"Good," I sigh. I can't think of a man more gorgeous than Sebastian Garcia.

I hate that he is.

"Too bad he's an asshole." Penelope shrugs.

"Don't I know it. You know, it's like I'm being tested. I'm thrown into a job where I have no idea what I'm doing, and it's with the biggest asshole on the planet who is an absolute god in bed." I sip my drink. "And the worst part is that I know he still wants me."

"How?"

"The way he looks at me. The way his eyes drop to my lips when I speak." I stare into space, remembering the heat of his gaze. "Everything about him screams *Have sex with me, April Bennet!* God, do I want to."

My phone beeps with a text from Duke:

Nightcap?

I flick my phone off and turn it over so I can't see the screen. "I'm going to have to deal with this."

"What the hell is wrong with you? Duke is the hottest guy I've ever seen!" Penelope cries. "Are you crazy?"

"I know he's gorgeous. I know he should be everything I want, but it's just..." I pause as I try to articulate my thoughts. I can't because they just don't make sense, not even to me. "I do know that I love him as a friend, but that's it. Duke deserves better."

Penelope watches me for a moment with assessing eyes. "I know what's wrong with Duke," she says.

"What's that?" I sip my drink.

"He's not Sebastian Garcia."

"That has nothing to do with it."

"All I'm saying is that if Garcia still floats your boat after being the biggest asshole on Earth, and you still think about him six years later..." She scoffs. "And, may I add, you have a gorgeous man in front of you right now"—she gestures to my phone—"who you don't even want to message back, then I think we have a problem."

I tip my head back and drain my glass.

We have a fucking problem, all right.

We walk down the corridor towards Sebastian's office, and I run my hands over my hips. Do I look okay?

What the hell is wrong with me? Something ridiculous is going on in my brain.

I even wore new underwear today, as if he is going to see it.

Check yourself, April. You hate this guy. Get it through your thick head.

What part of 'Sebastian Garcia is no good for you' don't you understand?

We walk up to the door. "Come in!" Sebastian calls.

My stomach flutters at the sound of his voice.

Damn you, what's going on with my hormones? *Behave.*

Sebastian stands behind his desk. His eyes drop to my feet and back up before he gives me a slow, sexy smile, as if forgetting that Bart is in the room with us.

"Hello."

"Hello," I reply casually, as if I don't have a care in the world.

Bart's phone rings. "Hello." He frowns as he listens. "Are you okay? Damn it. All right, I'm on my way." He hangs up the call and turns to Sebastian. "My wife has just had a car accident around the corner."

"Oh no," I say.

"It's nothing serious, although I'm going to duck out and see if she's okay. I'll be back in ten minutes. Sorry about this." Bart turns his attention to me. "April can just start running through the progress we've made on the facilities for Theodore."

"That's fine. I hope everything is okay?"

"She's assured me she's fine. April will take over."

"I'm sure she will," Sebastian says, a trace of amusement across his face. He seems happy that we are going to be left alone.

Great.

Bart takes off in a rush, and I sit down nervously. Sebastian drops into his seat and sits back.

I flick through my papers and get my computer out. "What would you like to know?" I ask, faking confidence.

"You really want to know?"

"Yes."

Sebastian's eyes hold mine. "I'd like to know if you've thought about me."

"What?"

"Have you thought about me, April?"

"I don't think that's an appropriate question, Mr. Garcia."

"Call me Sebastian."

I don't know what's going on here, but I do know that this is going to end badly if I'm alone with him.

When I say badly, I mean with me under his desk, sucking his dick, because that seems to be all I can think about lately.

I stand in a rush. "I think I should go outside and wait for Bart to return. I'll see you when he gets back." I turn and walk towards the door.

A hand comes over my shoulder and stops the door from opening. I can feel Sebastian's breath on the back of my neck. Goose bumps scatter up my spine.

"Turn around, April."

Oh fuck... I close my eyes. This isn't good.

"Turn around," he commands.

I turn back towards him, and he steps forward, forcing my back up against the door. His face is only millimetres from mine. "I

163

think about you all day," he whispers. "I dream about you all fucking night."

Our eyes are locked, the air between us electric.

"What do you want, Sebastian?" I whisper.

"I want you to kiss me."

13

April

"WHAT?"

Sebastian gives me a slow, sexy smile, and he leans a little closer. "I want you to kiss me, April."

I stare at him, lost for words. He *cannot* be serious.

His eyes drop to my lips, and I feel myself being pulled towards him. Somehow, I regain my composure.

"Well," I whisper. "This lying whore has better taste."

"Shut up." His lips drop to my neck, and he kisses me softly there. My eyes close as I feel the flutter of arousal running through me.

Oh, that's nice.

Stop it.

"Sebastian." I step back from him, creating some much-needed distance. "Your dick isn't that good." I raise my brows. "Now, if you don't mind..." I gesture to the door. "Get out of my way so I can leave."

Sebastian puts his hands in his pockets, and he tilts his jaw, clearly agitated.

I open the door in a rush, brush past him, and march down the hall.

Why is that feeling still there between us when it's been years? We are finished.

Done.

I walk into the bathroom, slam the door shut behind me, and then I stare at my reflection in the mirror. My heart is racing, and my face is flushed.

Fuck!

I need to get a handle on these hormones. I shouldn't want him. I don't want him.

I stare at my lying face. I hate that I do.

I lie in bed and pretend to watch a rerun of some crap detective show.

I went to bed early to try and catch up on some sleep, and yet here I am, still tuned in to the television.

My mind is on all things Sebastian Garcia.

I know that I'm wrong—I'm under no disillusions—but I have this ridiculous feeling that, underneath all the bullshit, he's a good man. But I know it's not true. How could it be true when he's treated me so appallingly?

My mind keeps going over my meeting with Helena, his ex-wife, and I wonder what he saw in her. She just doesn't seem like the kind of woman that he would like at all. I can't imagine him and her together. It's just... I don't know.

That's the thing: I don't know anything anymore. I guess, once upon a time, I couldn't imagine myself being without my ex-husband either. Yet here I am.

My phone beeps with a text. It's Sebastian.

I'm thinking about you.

Shit.

My heart drops. Why is he thinking about me?

Worse still, why am I thinking about him?

This man is an asshole. He's treated me so badly, it makes me sick. I turn my phone off and throw it on the bedside table.

He doesn't want me. He wants the last say, that's all.

I feel anxious, and worse than that, I feel an attachment for a man that I shouldn't have. I keep defending him to myself in my mind, and I know I shouldn't be.

Get out of my head, Mr. Garcia.

I sit in the backseat of the car as the driver drives us towards the city. We've been out visiting clients all day, and I'm exhausted.

Bart's phone rings. "Hi, Sebastian."

My eyes flick over to him.

"Yes, sure," he replies casually. "We'll be right over. We can swing by now." He hangs up. "Just call into Downing Street, please," he says to the driver.

The driver turns left. "Sure."

"We'll only be there for fifteen minutes. We've got to pick up some programs we need to run through the security settings. I want to work on them over the weekend." Bart looks at me. "We can drop them back on Monday. Don't forget, April, that we leave on Monday afternoon for three nights."

"I'm looking forward to it." I smile. "Where did you say we were going again?"

"We're going on the campaign trail."

"The campaign trail?" I frown.

"Yes, you know, as the acting crisis management team."

I stare at him, deadpan. "We're going away with Sebastian Garcia?"

"That's right. There will be about twenty-five of us in total. Sebastian has press releases that we need to check. Especially now

167

with the Theodore issue. We will be travelling with them over the next six weeks."

I fake a smile.

Great. Just great.

This is a nightmare waiting to happen.

As the car drives into the parking lot, I feel a little bit more of my confidence subside. Sebastian Garcia brings out the weakling in me.

I hate that about him.

Twenty minutes later, we are walking down the corridor, and we make it to Sebastian's floor.

I don't want to see him today, I just don't.

"I've got some emails that I need to get to," I say. "I might just stay out of today's visit, if that's okay?"

"Of course." Bart walks down towards the office. "I won't be long."

I take a seat at a desk in one of the waiting rooms. I open my computer and get to work on my emails. Not five minutes later, I notice someone standing at the door. I look up to see Sebastian.

"What are you doing?" he asks in his deep, sexy voice.

"I'm working." I look back at my computer.

"Why aren't you coming into our meeting?"

"I have other more important things to get to today."

"Like what?"

I try and think of something without sounding pathetic.

"I'm having trouble with my software. It's not working for me." That's not a total lie. I am having trouble with a few things.

He pushes his hands into the pockets of his suit jacket and walks into the office.

He gives me a slow, sexy smile. "I find that hard to believe," he says.

I look up and frown at him. "What do you mean?"

"I happen to know that your software is the best there is."

Our eyes lock, and we stare at each other. The double meaning of his sentence is not lost.

By software, he means my vagina.

Vivid memories of us rolling around in the sheets fill my mind. Dangerous things that shouldn't be in my head.

"Well, your time with my software is well and truly over, Mr. Garcia." I straighten my spine to try and appear in control.

He gives me a smile. "We'll see." He turns towards the door and then turns back. "Oh, and April?"

"Yes."

"Why didn't you reply to my text the other night when I told you I was thinking about you?"

"I was busy."

"Doing what?"

"Ignoring you, Sebastian. Go back to work. You're annoying."

"This conversation isn't over." With one last sexy look, he disappears up the hall.

For some stupid reason, I bite my lip to stop myself from smiling.

He is one hot asshole, I'll give him that.

I happen to know that your software is the best there is.

Idiot.

"Just this way, please." The waiter leads us through the restaurant, up to a mezzanine level at the back. The waiter pulls out my chair, and I take a seat.

I'm here tonight to tell Duke that we can't see each other anymore.

This restaurant has high security and is one of the few places in town that Duke isn't photographed in.

As fun as it's been, and as wonderful as he's been in my life, lately, I just don't want to see him at all, which is weird because all

I do seem to want to do is lie around and think about that bastard Garcia.

Either way, it's unfair to Duke, and I want him to be happy. I want him to find the woman of his dreams, get married, have children, and be happy.

Tonight is the first step in him doing that. I'm going to end it once and for all, and I'm not going to let him talk me out of it. We're good friends, and he's someone that's been a constant in my life for a couple of years now, but we don't want the same things anymore. I don't know if we ever did.

When he was into partying, it was all great, but now he wants to settle down, and I'm not there with him. For the life of me, I don't understand why.

But it is what is it, and I figure if I have to try and analyse this so hard to understand it, something is wrong.

"Can I get you a drink?" the waitress asks.

"I'll have a margarita, please." I smile as I hand the drinks menu back to her.

"And I'll have a whiskey sour," Duke says with a smile.

"Okay. We have some specials on the cocktail list tonight at the bar. I can get the first one for you, but you will have to go to the bar to purchase any you want after that."

"Okay, fantastic."

She disappears through the crowd, and my attention falls back to Duke.

"So," he says. "I haven't seen you much."

I give him a sad smile. "I've just got so much on with work lately." I pause as I try to articulate my feelings. Let's get through dinner before I lay it all out on the table. "What's going on with you?" I ask to change the subject.

"We go into a training camp next week."

"Is that here or are you going away?"

"France for three weeks."

"Fun." I smile.

The waitress arrives with our drinks. We smile and thank her when she puts them in front of us.

I take a sip. "Oh, this is good." I smile, and just as I glance over, I see three security guards walking into the restaurant. Behind them I see Sebastian walking as he follows the waiter. He has a woman with him. She has long dark hair and is wearing a red dress.

Who the fuck is she?

I watch them sit down at the table. Sebastian says something, and the lady in red laughs in response. He gives her that sexy smile I've seen so many times.

I think about you all day, and I dream about you all night.

What a load of fucking shit.

I snap my eyes back to Duke as my blood begins to boil.

"Didn't you say you were away next week?" Duke asks.

"Umm." I sip my drink, completely distracted by the douche on the other side of the restaurant. "Yes, with work for a few days."

"Where are you going?"

"Kent."

My eyes go back to Sebastian. He's wearing blue jeans, a cream linen suit jacket, and a white shirt. It sets off his dark hair and olive skin perfectly. I tear my eyes away angrily. Damn him.

So much for wanting me. Another lie.

Why did I think that anything that comes out of that man's mouth is credible?

Asshole.

"What's in Kent?" Duke asks as my eyes travel back to Sebastian across the room.

The woman in red says something, and he laughs before he says something back.

"April?" says Duke, interrupting my thoughts.

I snap my eyes back to Duke. "I'm sorry." I'm totally distracted. "Yes, I'll be with Bart."

Duke frowns. "Are you okay?"

"Um." I frown and tuck my hair behind my ear. *Oh my God, April, stop it.*

Who cares about Sebastian?

Duke takes my hand over the table. "I've missed you these last few weeks," he says.

I wanted to wait until after dinner, but I need to tell him now.

I give him a sad smile. "Duke," I whisper. "I think we both know where this is going."

I glance up to see Sebastian has now spotted me; he's glaring over here.

Duke is holding my hand.

Oh, fuck me...

This night can't get any worse.

"No, we need to make this better," Duke insists. "How can we see each other more? I know you're so busy with work."

"Sweetie," I whisper. "Remember, we talked about wanting different things?"

Duke's eyes hold mine, and I give his hand a gentle squeeze. "I want you, April."

I smile sadly. "I don't want marriage and babies, Duke, and I know you do. I'm not holding you back anymore."

"Stop it."

"I can't say it more than I already have. It is what it is. You need to believe me this time. We can't keep having this conversation. It's not fair on either of us."

"Ready to order?" the waitress asks, interrupting us.

"Oh." Duke opens his menu as my phone beeps with a text. I put the phone on my lap so I can read it discreetly. It's Sebastian.

Get to the bar, now!

My eyes flick up to see him glaring across the restaurant at me. He has got to be fucking joking.

Go to hell!

A reply bounces back.

Okay, fine. I'll come over to your table to see you.

Fuck!

This man is infuriating. I don't want poor Duke to think that Sebastian is the reason I don't want to see him anymore. I see Sebastian making his way to the bar. He picks up a menu, and then his furious eyes find mine once more.

Christ on a cracker.

"What will it be?" The waitress smiles.

I fake a smile and open the menu. I couldn't care less about this fucking food. First thing on the list, I choose. "Risotto, please." I snap the menu shut. "Thank you." She takes Duke's order and scribbles her notes, then wanders off.

I just want this night over with and to get the hell out of here.

Ugh, men... Who dates these idiots for fun?

My phone vibrates on my lap, and I look over to Sebastian typing.

Oh my God, he cannot be serious?

My phone keeps vibrating on my lap.

Fuck.

"I'm going to look at the cocktail special board." I fake a smile and stand.

"Already?" Duke frowns.

"Yep. What do you want?"

"Surprise me."

I casually walk over to the bar. Sebastian's eyes drop to my toes and back up to my face, and he raises his chin.

Well, bring it, asshole. I'm angrier than you.

I stand beside him at the bar and pick up a menu to pretend to read.

"What?" I whisper.

Sebastian's eyes stay fixed on the menu in front of him. "You're on a fucking date?"

My eyes shoot up to him. "Are you serious?"

"Deadly," he says through gritted teeth.

My eyes go back to my menu. "Listen here, you fucking asshole." I smile sweetly. "I don't know what crack you're snorting, or who the fuck you think that you are—"

"What will it be?" the barman asks.

"Um." Sebastian and I quickly look at the specials choices. "Two dirty martinis, please." I smile.

"Make that four." Sebastian grimaces.

The bartender turns his back to us and gets to work.

"I'm so glad you think about me all day and dream about me all night," I whisper. "So, in your dreams, are we having a three-some with your fucking date?"

"You're one to talk," he fumes. "You're actually dating him?"

"That's none of your business."

"It's all of my fucking business."

I can feel the adrenaline pumping through my body. Nobody pisses me off more than Sebastian Garcia.

I flick my hair over my shoulder. "Go back to your date, Sebastian."

"I'm here because my sister made me come."

"Ha! Don't insult my intelligence. You're here because she's beautiful, and you're going to have sex with her tonight."

"I'm not."

"Oh, yes, you fucking are."

"It was a blind date."

"Sure, it was." I grip the edge of the bar tightly.

"So, he's your boyfriend?" His eyes hold mine.

I look over to see Duke innocently scrolling through his phone. Damn it. Why can't Duke make me feel alive like this asshole does?

"I'm actually here to tell him I can't see him anymore. So thank you for stressing me out before I even get the chance to do it."

"Why can't you see him anymore?"

I stare straight ahead, unwilling to answer.

"Is it because of me?"

"What?" I screw up my face. "You're delusional."

"Why, then?"

"Sebastian." I grit my teeth so I don't have a full temper tantrum. "I am not interested in talking to a man while he is on a date with another woman. Go back to her."

He looks around the restaurant. "Let's go."

"What?"

"Fuck this. Let's just leave. Neither of us want to be here with them. We have things we need to discuss."

I drag my hand down my face. "You would actually do that to her?"

"I would take her home first, of course. Let's do that." He glances at his watch. "Can we meet at, say, eleven?"

"What?"

"I have security with me."

I pretend to look at the menu.

"Near the door."

I look over and see two men in suits standing to the side of the entrance. "I saw them before."

"Once I'm home for the night, they leave me alone," he says. "You could come over to my place if you wanted to."

I stare at him, deadpan.

This man is a fucking idiot. "I have nothing to say to you other than you're a douche, and I feel sorry for your date."

He smiles softly as his eyes hold mine. "It's good to see you."

My heart somersaults in my chest.

Don't look at me like that.

"Don't, Seb," I whisper.

"April, we have things to talk about. You know we do. We need a clean slate before we go away next week."

"You're going to ruin everything. This job is really important to me, and I don't want to fuck it up. If Bart finds out about any of this—"

"He won't."

"Please, Sebastian, stop this. We have a past. That's it."

He stares at me.

"Just leave the past where it belongs, back there. I don't want anything to do with you now. I'm not the same girl you knew back then."

He clenches his jaw as his eyes hold mine.

"Here you go." The bartender puts the four drinks on the counter.

"Thank you," Sebastian says. "Put them on my bill." He picks up his drinks, and with one last lingering look, he says, "Goodbye, Bennet." He turns and walks back to his table, and my heart drops in disappointment.

So that's it? He's just giving up? Of course he is.

I mean, I don't want him, but it would have been nice if he fought a little harder.

Maybe he is into his date?

What the hell is wrong with me? He makes me act and feel like an errant, indecisive teenager.

With a heavy exhale, I make my way back to the table. "What's this?" Duke asks as I put the two cocktails down.

"Dirty martini." I smile.

Duke takes a sip, and I watch him for a moment as guilt rolls around in my heart. "You're a really great guy, Duke."

He smiles sadly. "But..."

"But we both know that this is our last date."

His gaze drops to his glass. "If it's our last date, can we at least make it worth it?"

My eyes hold his. "No, baby." I take his hand over the table. "No more lovemaking. No more dates. No more booty calls. Just fond memories from here on in."

"I'm going to miss you."

"I'm going to miss you too." I squeeze his hand in mine. "Hey, but it was fun, right?"

He smiles sadly and nods. "I don't know what you're looking for, babe, but I hope you find him."

My eyes fill with tears, and it's unexpected.

I don't know what I'm looking for, either, but I don't think I'll ever find him.

Because someone who can make me feel whole again doesn't exist.

Duke begins to chatter on and talk about his day, but my mind is far away.

How did I get like this? So cold and detached?

My ex-husband has a lot to answer for.

It's not that he slept with someone else. It's not about the infidelity.

Far from it.

Something in my DNA changed that day; it altered who I was as a person.

And I miss her.

I'm feeling overemotional and teary-eyed. I need to pull myself together. I just need to get through dinner, and then I can fall apart when I get home.

"I'm just going to the bathroom."

I walk down the corridor at the side of the restaurant and into the bathroom. It's a single cubicle with its own sink and mirror. I wash my hands and stare at my reflection in the mirror. I feel fragile.

My eyes well with tears. God, April, pull yourself together.

What's wrong with me? I'm never teary.

The door handle turns, telling me that someone else is waiting to use the restroom. "Just a minute!" I call.

I wipe the makeup from under my eyes, and I pinch my cheeks and shake my hands before I exhale heavily and open the door.

Sebastian's big brown eyes meet mine.

He steps into the bathroom, forcing me back, and he closes the door behind him.

Without a word, he takes my face in his hands and kisses me.

His lips are soft, his intent is strong, and I screw up my face against his.

His tongue dances against mine.

"I couldn't go home without kissing you," he whispers against my lips.

And I feel it for the first time in forever.

I feel it to my toes.

Please, God, don't let it be him.

14

***

April

HE KISSES me deeper this time, and I melt into him as his tongue dances seductively against mine. We lose control, and he slams me up against the wall. My hands go to his hair while his hands go to my behind, and he grinds me onto his hard, waiting cock.

This is bad.

Real bad.

I'm here with another man.

I step back and pull out of his grip. "Stop it," I pant.

"You want me."

"N-not like this," I stammer.

He grabs me again and kisses me hard. My sex clenches in appreciation. Fuck, I love his dominance. Nobody takes control of my body like Sebastian Garcia.

I had forgotten what he was like.

"Sebastian," I whimper into his mouth as an ache of submission begins to throb between my legs.

"My place," he pants, and I know he's losing it too. He slams me harder against the wall, lifting my leg around his hip. "I fucking need you." His lips go to my neck, and he bites me hard. "You're all I can think about."

My head tips back as goose bumps scatter up my spine.

I'm making out with someone in the bathroom while on a date with someone else. I *am* a dirty whore.

But worse than that, I'm being a dirty whore with a bastard.

"Stop it," I whisper angrily.

I turn and open the door in a rush.

He grabs my arm and pulls me back towards him. "I need to see you. Tonight." He kisses me again. "Don't leave me in this state."

"Sebastian." I pull out of his grip once more. "Get it through your head... I'm not going there with you again."

God... I want to.

In one quick movement, he reaches down and puts his hand up my dress and through the side of my panties. He slides his fingertips through my sex.

He smiles darkly when he finds the evidence he was searching for. "Dripping wet, baby girl."

He rubs his thumb back and forth over my clitoris, and I shudder.

He grabs my face and puts his mouth to my ear. "Don't tell me you don't want me." He slides three thick fingers deep into my sex, and I whimper, his grip on my face near painful. "We will fuck again, April." He licks up the side of my face. "Mark my words." His fingers pump me hard. "You're going to be naked, wet, and full of my fucking come."

He bites my bottom lip and then pushes off me. He opens the door and leaves in a rush.

I fall back against the wall and look up at the ceiling.

Hell.

My heart is racing. I'm gasping for air.

And, oh boy, I need to be fucked.

I close my eyes, feeling my pulse throughout my entire body. Fuck, fuck, fuck, fuck.

I wash my hands and try to pull myself together.

Now I have to go back out there to Duke.

I'm such an asshole.

I rush back to the table and sit down. "I don't feel so well."

Duke's face falls. "You okay?"

"Not really." I just need this night over with. "I'm so sorry. Do you mind if we just go home? I feel like I may throw up," I lie.

"Sure thing," Duke says. "Come on, you'll be okay." He puts his arm around me and leads me up the hall towards the exit. We walk back out into the restaurant and through to the cashier.

While Duke pays the bill, I glance over to see Sebastian's furious eyes holding mine.

Fuck.

I'm still thumping with arousal. Everything inside me is screaming for his body. Duke turns to me. "You ready?"

"Yes. I'm sorry." I give him a sad smile.

I'm sorry for everything.

Get me the fuck out of here.

Sebastian

April and her date walk out of the corridor and to the front desk.

Is he paying the bill? Surely not.

I glance over to their table to see their cocktails are still full, waiting for their return. I watch on as he takes out his wallet and pays the cashier.

She's leaving...*with him.*

I clench my jaw as I feel my temper rise.

"Do you go to the gym?" my date asks.

But I'm too focused on April, whose eyes rise to meet mine before she quickly pulls them away.

She *is* going home with him, so *he* can put out the fire that *I* started.

No.

No fucking way!

I inhale deeply to try and control myself. I can feel my pulse racing as adrenaline surges through me.

Stop her.

I clench my hands into fists on my legs. I get a vision of April and me in the bathroom. Not eight minutes ago...and now she's leaving with him.

"Sebastian?" Marina prompts me.

My eyes flick to her. "I'm sorry." I frown. *Fuck.* "My apologies. I... I didn't hear you."

"I asked if you went to the gym."

"Yes." I sip my drink as my eyes rise to April again. She's waiting for him to pay the bill. He's talking and being friendly to the cashier. "Do you go to the gym?" I ask Marina, focusing back on her.

Who am I kidding? I'm being anything but polite here. This poor woman is the very last thing on my mind.

Why the hell did I agree to this date?

"Yes. I'm a real fitness fanatic." She smiles. "I like to run in marathons too."

My gaze rises to April across the restaurant yet again. Her date puts his arm around her and kisses her temple before they walk out of the restaurant together, arm in arm. My stomach twists as I fight every urge I have to run after her.

Fuck.

I imagine the two of them having sex, and my head feels like it's about to explode.

Go out there and drag her out of his car. Do it now! What the fuck are you waiting for? Don't let her leave with him.

Stop, stop, stop!

Five minutes of insanity tonight will be tomorrow's headlines.

Deputy Prime Minister goes batshit crazy and drags his female lawyer from a car.

I drain my glass, and then I drag my hand down my face. I'm hot and clammy and on the fucking edge of control.

"Are you okay?" Marina asks.

My eyes come back to her. Shit.

I force a smile. "I'm sorry. I just got some news about work, and I'm terribly distracted. Please forgive me."

"Is everything all right?"

I nod, barely able to push the words past my lips. "Just..." I pause as I try to think of a suitable lie. "I have an urgent meeting that has just been scheduled for tomorrow, and I have to prepare. Just running through it in my mind."

"Oh." Her face falls. "What does that mean?"

"Nothing." I smile. "I may have to retire early tonight after we have dinner. Nothing for you to worry about."

"Okay."

That's not a complete lie. I do have something urgent on my agenda for tomorrow.

I need to get April fucking Bennet off my mind.

This has to stop...*now*.

2:00 a.m.

My finger hovers over April's name in my phone.

I'm naked, in bed, with my legs spread.

Alone in the darkness.

I go to dial her number, but then I remind myself that *she's with him*.

I throw my phone to the floor in disgust.

My hand glides through the oil over the end of my hard cock. I've jerked off numerous times tonight, and none of them have tamed the tiger. Nothing on Earth could.

I need her.

I need one thing and one thing only.

April fucking Bennet.

I grip myself with force and begin to stroke hard. My legs part farther. The sound of the slick oil around my fingers echoes throughout the room, and I tip my head back to the ceiling.

I'm wet with perspiration. My grip is painful.

183

If I make it hurt, it will take the need away.

It has to. I can't go on like this.

I turn the incline up on the treadmill and run faster. I've trained hard this morning.

Adrenaline has stolen my sleep, and I'm in a world of regret.

I should have stopped her. I should have dragged her out of his fucking car.

I should have brought her back here and given her what was hers to have.

But I didn't, and it's done now.

And I'm moving the fuck on.

Screw her and her tempting little ass.

I hear my front door open, and moments later, Spencer comes into view. He has two cups of coffee in his hands as well as two papers rolled up under his arm.

"Hey." He looks me up and down as I run. "It's Sunday morning. What the fuck are you doing?"

"Training," I pant.

He screws up his face in disgust and walks back into the kitchen.

I hit pause and walk through the cooldown until I eventually walk out to find him sitting at the table, engrossed in his newspaper.

This Sunday-morning coffee thing we have is a ritual. Charlotte, his wife, goes to church with her father, and Spencer visits with me.

I peel my wet T-shirt off over my head, and I put it in the laundry.

"How was your date?" Spencer asks without looking up.

"Fucked up." I walk to the refrigerator and pour myself a glass of water. "The whole thing is one massive fuckup."

He chuckles as he turns the page. "That good, hey?"

I pick up my phone off the counter and check it. No missed calls. "Un-fucking-believable," I mutter under my breath.

"What is?" Spencer asks, his eyes not leaving his paper.

"I thought she would at least have the audacity to call me." I sip my water. "I mean, she did leave with someone else."

He finally looks up. "Who did? Your date?"

"No, not her. April."

He frowns. "Who?"

"Do you fucking listen to me at all?"

He frowns. "I'm lost."

"The fucking girl. The lawyer from my office. April Bennet."

His eyes widen. "Oh, the Escape Girl."

I sip my coffee and then shake my head.

Spencer puts his hands on his temples. "Hang on, so you went on a date with one woman, but instead you saw April?"

"Yes, and I followed her to the bathroom, and we made out. She was all fucking wet and hot for me, and then she kicked me out and went home with her date."

His eyes hold mine. "You made out in a bathroom *with* your *employee* who was there with another man, all while you were with another woman?"

"Yes! Do you not see my fucking problem?"

"Oh, I see it, you fucking idiot," he tuts. "Are you stupid?"

I take a seat beside him. "And I'm obsessed with this woman. I need to cut this shit out because I have no fucking skin left on my dick. It isn't possible to pull it any more than I already have."

He chuckles and pinches the bridge of his nose. "Christ almighty."

I put my head into my hands in dismay.

"Who is she?"

I look up at him. "You met her already."

"When?"

"At the charity auction, remember? She told you and Masters off."

Spencer's eyes widen. "The insanely hot blonde one."

"That's her, and the worst part about it is that I feel like I already know her."

"What do you mean?"

I shrug. "I can't explain it. There's this familiarity between us. It's so weird because I've never had it with anyone else before. I mean, it's like I know her, but I know I don't." I throw my hands up. "I can't explain it."

"Wait." He frowns. "Did she sleep with Brandon back then?"

"Maybe... No." I shrug. "I'm ninety percent sure she didn't."

"But he liked her?"

"Thought he was in love with her, actually."

Spencer winces. "This shit is too fucking messy, even for me."

I push my fingers into my eyes. "I want this woman, but I can't have her. There's no way I could ever officially ask her out on a date or anything."

"Why not?"

"Come on." I roll my eyes. "Can you imagine the fucking scandal if it were ever found out by the press? She works for me, and she's got a famous boyfriend."

"Jesus." Spencer sighs.

I sip my coffee.

"So she *was* a call girl?" he asks.

"She said I was her first and only client."

"You don't believe her?"

"I have no idea what to believe anymore."

His eyes hold mine. "You really liked her?"

I shrug.

"Well, I'd be finding out what happened with Brandon if I were you," Spence says. "If only for interest's sake."

I exhale heavily. "That changes nothing, though. I'm putting her out of my head once and for all. Nothing good can come of this."

Spence sips his coffee and goes back to his paper. "What are you going to do about your dick?"

"Cut the fucker off."

"Good, do it today." He casually turns the page of his newspaper.

The phone rings, and I wait for Brandon to pick up. Spencer was right. I need to know what went on back then, if only for interest's sake.

"Hey, Dad," he answers eagerly.

"Hello, son." My heart melts at the sound of his voice. I love this kid.

Not such a kid anymore. An adult now. "How are things?"

"Good. Busy. Emma isn't sleeping."

I chuckle. "The joys of a newborn baby."

"God, it's hard."

"How's Mila?" I ask.

"Tired, teary."

I frown. That doesn't sound good. "Is she all right?"

He exhales. "A new baby is just exhausting."

"Yeah. Keep an eye on her, though. You're helping out, right?"

"As much as I can with work."

"Do you need me to come over?"

"Dad," he sighs. "You can't. You're busy enough with your own shit."

"You're more important. Say the word, and I'll be there."

"Thanks." I can tell he's smiling. "How's Bentley?"

I smile at the mention of my beloved dog. "Old and grumpy."

He laughs. "Like you."

"Yeah, yeah." I smile. "Hey, guess who I bumped into?"

"Who?"

I wince as I prepare myself to say it. "Remember April Bennet?"

He falls silent.

I close my eyes.

Fuck.

"She's a lawyer now. She's actually working with one of my lawyers," I say.

"Is she...married?"

"Not sure." I bite my lip. Brandon and I have never discussed April since the day he brought her to my house. He was so angry with me for months afterwards. She was the last thing I wanted to bring up in conversation once things returned to normal.

The way I handled that entire situation is one of my biggest regrets.

"Have you spoken to April since then?" I ask.

"Not once."

"I thought..."

He exhales heavily. "It was one-sided, Dad. I see that now. At the time, I didn't."

I close my eyes as relief fills me. "So you two never...?"

"No. The first time we kissed was at your front door."

I stay silent, unsure what to say next.

"Say hello to her for me," he says.

"I will." I try to change the subject. "Hey, try and talk your mother into coming over, will you?"

"Yes," he laughs. "How long has she got to use her plane ticket?"

"Well, I bought it for her when she got back from when Emma was born. It's valid for twelve months, I think, so another nine months or so."

"Okay, I'll work on her."

I hear the baby crying in the background. "Emma's lungs are working, then?"

"Ha, yes. I'd better go. Thanks for calling. Love you."

"Love you too." I hang up and pour myself a glass of wine.

I sit at the kitchen counter as my mind wanders.

She was telling the truth.

Hmm...*interesting.*

April

I sit in the back of the black Audi with Jeremy. The windows are tinted, as is the case with all the government cars. A security guard is driving.

This is a whole new world to me.

It's Monday morning, and a cavalcade of cars are parked. We are all waiting for Sebastian Garcia to join us. He's in the middle of press conference now, and once he's finished, his entourage is heading to Wales.

There are nine cars in total, including his advisors, his crisis management team—Bart, Jeremy—and his security. This afternoon, he's opening a hospital, has to speak at a luncheon, and then visit a school. Tomorrow, he's going to an opening ceremony at a university, and then he has a string of other engagements over the next few days.

It's been a long weekend after seeing him on Saturday night. He hasn't contacted me since.

Not that I wanted him to, of course. But I do wonder if he ended up sleeping with his date, and that's why he didn't call.

I spoke to Eliza for an hour last night on the phone, and she thinks that I don't have closure between the two of us and that this is the problem, and perhaps she's right. I do seem to have a lot of unsaid words I want to say to him.

Maybe I should just blurt them all out and get it over with.

Bart is in the car in front of ours, so it's just Jeremy and I for the three-hour-long drive. I'm looking forward to getting to know him a little better. He's very guarded with Bart around, but perhaps he's just being professional.

There's a flurry of people on the front steps, and I know Sebastian is close. People seem to run when he's around. His personality dominates those of his coworkers.

It will be very interesting to see him when the Prime Minister returns. At the moment, he seems to be running everything around here.

Sebastian walks out into my view. He's wearing a perfectly fitted charcoal suit with a white shirt and navy tie. His black hair has a little wave to it, and his dark olive skin sets off the whole alluring look.

There's no denying it, Sebastian Garcia is a gorgeous-looking man.

Of Spanish descent, if I remember correctly.

I twist my fingers in my lap as I watch him talk to the woman at his side as they walk down the steps. They're deep in conversation, and he doesn't look up.

The woman is Kellan Chesterfield, his closest advisor. She's well respected and intelligent. She has a master's degree in economics and politics.

She's beautiful with her dark hair and big, pouty lips. Add to that a figure to die for, and I'm not jealous of her at all.

"He isn't into her," Jeremy says casually.

I frown as I turn to look at him. "I beg your pardon?"

"Just in case you wanted to know." Jeremy shrugs.

"Why would I want to know that?" Fuck, am I that obvious?

Jeremy sips his takeaway coffee as we watch Sebastian and Kellan getting into the same car.

She gets to drive with him.

"Well, it's obvious, isn't it?" Jeremy asks.

"What's obvious?"

"I'm just saying that when you're in the room, Sebastian Garcia sees no one else."

"What?"

The car pulls out into the line of black government vehicles. "Oh, come on, April. You must see it."

"See what?" I act innocent because I want Jeremy to elaborate so that I can feed my sick addiction to this man.

"Garcia is into you."

"Why would you say that?"

"The way he looks at you."

"How does he look at me?" I feel excitement stirring deep in the pit of my stomach.

Stop it.

"Like you're the most beautiful woman he's ever seen."

I bite the inside of my cheek. "I don't think so."

"I know so." Jeremy puts his head back against the headrest and looks out of the window.

I twist my fingers on my lap as I carefully plan my next question. Jeremy is the one person who knows a lot about Sebastian.

"I think he has a girlfriend, anyway."

"Nope." He smirks. "Been single for years. Had a wife once, though. Total bitch."

Don't I know that.

"Really?" I act surprised.

"Yeah, and she wants him back."

"Who told you that?"

"It's no secret."

I frown as I try to think on my feet. "I thought I read somewhere that she'd had an affair, though?"

"I think he was away all the time, working. No idea what happened, really." He shrugs. "She'd have to be a fucking idiot to cheat on him. He's totally gorgeous."

I smile, knowing my suspicions were right. Jeremy is gay. "He is," I agree. "Not my type, though."

"Oh, please," he huffs. "Garcia is everybody's type. I bet he'd be all dominant in bed too."

You have no idea.

"Maybe one day you'll find out," I tease.

He chuckles. "I wish." His head goes back to the headrest again. "But I'm taken."

"By Bart? You're not the only one who notices things around here." I smile.

His eyes hold mine.

"Relax." I sigh as I put my head back onto the headrest. "I need a fucking ally around here. Your secrets are safe with me. I've got enough of my own shit going on to worry about you and Bart."

He smiles, as if relieved.

I sigh. "What happens on these trips away, anyway? Tell me everything."

It's 6:00 p.m., and I'm exhausted.

How in the hell is Sebastian doing this? He has constantly been switched on, and when I say on, I mean in the spotlight, being interviewed since 8:00 a.m. He did the press conference this morning, then we drove the three hours down to Wales. He opened the hospital, spoke at a luncheon, did another press conference, and then he visited a school.

He hasn't looked at me once.

Not once.

And I know because I've been watching him all day.

I also know how this is going to go. I'm going to be pining over him now, being all pathetic and remembering how his body felt inside mine. I'm actually glad he's not looking at me. I really am.

But seriously...not even a glance? I mean, fuck me.

Did I completely imagine Saturday night?

We've just arrived at our hotel now. Taylah, Sebastian's PA, is handing out the keys. She came early and organized a group check-in for everyone.

The foyer is grand and large. It's like an old castle that has been done up into a swanky hotel. The bar is off to the left of the foyer and has a large open fire and warm furnishings with a deep red carpet. It's beautiful, like something in a magazine.

One by one, everyone gets their keys and head into the bar. I get to Taylah, and she digs through her bundle of keys and reads from her folder.

"Hello, April." She hands me my key. "Level six, room 212. Your luggage will be taken straight up by concierge."

"Thanks." I take it from her.

"Dinner is down here in the restaurant, pretty much straight away. Let me know if you need anything."

"Okay, great."

I need to go to the bathroom and freshen up. I'm tired as hell. I'm going to sneak up to my room and have a quick shower and a cup of tea first.

Hell, room service sounds good, actually. This political shit is tiring.

I take the lift up to level six and walk down the large corridor. Exotic antique art hangs on the walls, and I smile to myself.

"Wow," I whisper.

I open the door to find an oversized, four-poster bed made from dark wood sitting in the middle of the room. "Beautiful." I walk in, put my handbag down, and look around.

There's a huge bathroom made from cream marble. I pull the drapes back and stare out at the street below. There are little lanterns lighting up the street, and it feels like this is from a fairy-tale book or something.

"Wow. I love this place."

I flick the kettle on and strip off to take a hot shower. I will go back downstairs in a bit, if only to eat.

Once out of the shower, I wrap myself up in the hotel's white robe, and I make myself a cup of tea. Three nights spent in this place is going to be a dream. I turn the television on and am flicking through the channels when I hear a knock coming from somewhere.

I walk over and put my ear to the back of the door.

I hear a knock again, but it's not coming from here. It must be someone knocking on someone else's door down the corridor.

Hmm. I walk back and sit down only to hear the knock again.

Wait, it's coming from the connecting door in my room that I didn't notice before.

I walk over to it, and there's a knock again.

"Hello?" I call through it.

"Hello." I hear a deep voice. "Open the door."

Huh?

I turn the lock and open the door to see Sebastian standing there.

I frown. "What are you doing?"

"Knocking on your door. What does it look like? Yes, I know," he mutters dryly as he walks past me and into my room. "Connecting rooms. What a coincidence."

He's wearing a black dinner suit, ready for his night out. He's freshly showered. God, he smells good.

My eyes widen. "You organized connecting rooms?" I whisper, looking around.

"You don't have to whisper; nobody can hear us. We're the only ones from our party on this floor."

"Oh my God, Sebastian."

"How else am I going to get to talk to you?"

I stare at him, lost for words. "Are you for real?" I whisper again.

"Stop whispering."

I put my hands over my face. "This looks so bad."

"Nobody fucking cares." He sits on my bed. "Sit down." He gestures to my chair.

"What?"

"Sit down. I have to go out, and I want to talk to you for five minutes before I go."

"Sebastian."

"Sit the fuck down and listen to me, April. I'm not leaving until you do."

I glare at him as I drop into the seat.

He sits on the edge of my bed, leans over, and drops his elbows to his knees. "I want to talk to you about the night you came to my house with Brandon."

I clench my jaw as anger fills me. Just the mention of that night drives me mad.

His big brown eyes hold mine, and he exhales. "You have to understand that a parent needs to put their child before themselves. Brandon…" He pauses, and his gaze drops to the carpet. "He'd been talking about this girl he was in love with for weeks. When he turned up, and I saw that it was you…" His eyes rise to meet mine, and he swallows. "It threw me, April. I was so angry at you for betraying him…with *me*. I lashed out."

I open my mouth to say something, but he holds his hand up to stop me. "Let me finish, please."

I stay silent.

"I said horrible things to make you leave. My only intent at the time was to protect him from you. I knew I couldn't deal with you and him, or the possibility that the two of you had been together."

My heart constricts.

"I should never have told him where we met—"

"We didn't meet there," I interrupt.

He rolls his lips. "I wanted him to immediately stop wanting you." His eyes hold mine. "And somewhere in my deranged mind, I knew that if I told him we had slept together, it would kill two birds with one stone. It would make you leave. It would make you not…" His voice trails off.

"Not what?"

He drops his head as if ashamed. "It would end what you had with him."

What?

He raises his chin. "I apologize for that night. I didn't mean to uncover your secrets in the most hurtful way. It was selfish."

I stay silent, unsure of what to say.

"I couldn't stand the thought of you sleeping with him," he whispers as his eyes hold mine.

"I didn't."

"I know that *now*, but back then…" He runs his hand through his hair. "There would be only one thing worse than not having you myself, and that would be watching you with my son."

We stare at each other as a river of regret runs between us.

I drag my eyes away. This is too intense.

"Who is his mother?" I ask.

"My sister."

I frown in confusion.

"Brandon is my nephew. His father left when he was eighteen months old, and I stepped in. He had attachment issues, and I..." He frowns, as if pained. "He's so soft-hearted, I couldn't bear that you hurt him. I thought that you were his first love, and that you were fucking me behind his back."

"So you broke my heart...to save his," I whisper.

"I did my job." His face falls. "I protected my child," he whispers. "And your heart wasn't the only one I broke that day."

He stands and walks to the door.

"B-Brandon never loved me," I stammer. "His heart wasn't broken."

He turns back to me. "I wasn't talking about Brandon." He turns and walks through the connecting door.

It closes with a sharp click

I drop to sit on the bed, shocked to my core. What does that mean?

Fuck.

Bang sounds the door as it closes.

Sebastian is back. I scramble to pick up my phone to see the time.

1:00 a.m.

My mind is a clusterfuck of confusion. I've been overanalysing everything all night.

The way Sebastian spoke earlier sounded like he had feelings for me back then, too.

Maybe I misunderstood.

Maybe he meant to say that Brandon was all that mattered to him.

I guess it doesn't matter now, anyway, but the admission that he had done the wrong thing means a lot to me.

I hear the water turn on next door, and I know he's taking a shower.

Is he going to knock on for me?

I lie in the darkness, on high alert, and I wait.

The thing about thinking that you know what's going to happen is that you don't.

Sebastian didn't knock on my door last night.

He hasn't looked my way once today, either.

In between all his engagements, he's been deep in discussion with Kellan all day through, and I hate to admit it, but it bothers me.

It shouldn't, but it does.

We have had another full day, and now we are back at the hotel. We've had dinner, and we are now in the bar, having a few drinks. Sebastian is sitting with three men and Kellan, while I am at the bar with Jeremy.

It's like Sebastian doesn't know me when we are in public, but then again, I guess he doesn't really. So he's not acting; he's really just telling the truth.

This is all just one big, convoluted mess, and I need to go to bed before I drink too much.

"I'm going to head up to my room," I tell Jeremy.

"Okay." He smiles.

"See you tomorrow."

I walk out of the bar before looking across the room. I don't want him to know I'm leaving. Not that he would notice, anyway.

I take the elevator. I'm having a hot shower, and I'm going straight to sleep.

I'm exhausted.

I wake with a start. The room is semi-dark, but something feels off.

I try to focus my eyes, but I know that Sebastian is in here.

I can feel him...and then I see him.

He's sitting in the corner chair in the dark. He's holding a glass full of an amber fluid, still wearing his navy suit.

"Sebastian," I whisper. "What are you doing?"

Silence.

"Sebastian?" I prompt.

"Breathing you in," his deep voice purrs.

He lifts his glass to his lips and takes a long, slow sip as he watches me.

My heart races in my chest. He's so intense. So serious.

So fucking hot.

"There's nothing more intoxicating than the scent of the woman you want," he whispers darkly.

His tongue darts out and swipes over his bottom lip as his eyes hold mine.

Warning bells go off around me. I know this is all wrong, but hell...

"You want me?" I ask.

"More than anything," he murmurs.

Our eyes are locked, and damn it, why does he have to be such a head fuck?

Why can't he be just a man who I could sleep with without complications?

Why does everything about him scare the hell out of me?

I already know the answer.

I'm too invested.

He puts his drink on the table and walks to me as I lie in bed.

What is he doing?

My breath is shaky when I inhale. *Fuck.*

He sits at my feet and peels the blankets back. His eyes darken when he sees my white cotton nightdress. He slides his hand up my leg, and it comes around to rest at the back of my knee.

He spreads my legs as they bend.

We stare at each other, and I know that I should tell him to stop and go back to his room, but I just can't.

He drops his head and kisses my inner thigh. His dark eyes watch me, as if waiting for approval.

Maybe if I don't watch, I can pretend that I don't know what a mistake this is.

His tongue trails over my skin, up towards my sex.

Fuck.

My breath quivers.

He pulls my panties to the side, and with his dark eyes on mine, his thick, strong tongue swipes through my sex.

Oh God. My back arches from the bed.

He licks me again. "You have two seconds to tell me to stop, Bennet," he murmurs against my sex before he openly kisses me there with purpose.

My back arches off the bed, and I push my hands into his hair, grabbing a handful between my fingers. "Make me come."

15

April

"You want to come?" He flutters his tongue over my clitoris before he peels my panties down.

My back arches off the bed as I try to get a deeper connection.

Sebastian leans up on his elbow next to me, and he slides three fingers deep into my sex. His jaw clenches, and my legs fall open enough for my knees to touch the mattress.

"You want to come, Cartier?" he whispers darkly.

My breath catches at the use of my name from the Escape Club. It's been a long time since I've heard it. I can't believe he remembered.

He massages me deep inside, finding that perfect spot. My body begins to quiver. I'm like a puppet in his G-spot–finding hands, obeying his every command.

He jerks me hard with his palm. "Answer me," he growls.

"Yes," I whimper as the sound of my wet arousal begins to echo around me.

Fuck, he makes me so wet.

He bends and kisses my sex. His teeth graze my clitoris as his fingers work their magic, and I begin to shudder.

He stops, and his eyes hold mine. "Tell me he's gone."

My arousal fades, and I lift my head to look at him. "What?"

He slides his fingers in deep—four this time—and I feel the stretch of his possession.

My head falls back, and my legs rise off the mattress, hanging open in the air.

Ahh, that's so...

"Tell me!" he barks.

"W-who?"

He sits up abruptly and rolls me over onto my stomach. He lies over me, his full weight pinning me down, his mouth to my ear. I can feel his erection digging into my behind through his suit.

"I don't fucking share," he hisses against my ear. Goose bumps scatter over my skin.

And then it all comes back to me.

I remember. I remember everything.

The edge of fear that Sebastian Garcia brings to the bedroom.

You never quite know what's going to happen, whether he's angry or if you'll like it.

Will you make it through to the other side?

The only thing certain is that it's about to blow your fucking head off.

Grabbing my hips, he pulls me up to my knees and comes into place behind me.

He spreads my legs and rubs the backs of his fingers through my sex. I'm swollen and dripping wet. How could I not be? I push my body back to try and get some much-needed friction. He grabs a handful of my hair and drags my head back. Then he slaps me hard on the behind, and I cry out, "Ahh!"

The sound is loud. The sting sharp.

"Don't fucking move," he growls.

I close my eyes, my body throbbing with arousal, adrenaline— a complete out-of-body experience.

I hear the unzipping of his pants. The tearing open of the condom wrapper.

Oh yes.

He puts his hand on the back of my neck and pushes my face into the mattress with force. I smile, and then I feel his tongue over my back entrance. He moans softly into me, as if losing control. He spreads my cheeks and really begins to eat me. I scrunch the sheets up in my fists as I begin to lose control.

Hell yeah. I've missed fucking this man.

He rubs the tip of his cock through the lips of my sex, and then he slaps me hard again. "Answer the fucking question."

I shudder. "I'm going to come," I whisper.

He grabs my hair and jerks my head back, bringing his mouth to my ear. "You come, and see what fucking happens to you."

I turn my head to kiss him, and our eyes lock. Darkness swims between us. An arousal, an emotion, something bigger than what we are.

I've never experienced it with anyone else, but I know for certain that it's something that neither of us can control.

"Kiss me," I whimper. "Please."

He bends and licks my open lips. "Tell me." He twists my nipple hard.

I shudder, and he bites my neck until I cry out. *Oh...*

"He's gone," I breathe. "He's so gone. There's only you."

I feel him smile against my cheek, and then he moves my face towards him and gifts me with a kiss. His tongue dances against mine. His eyes close, and I know that he's right here with me.

Then, as if regaining control, his hand slides between my shoulder blades, and he pushes me back into the mattress with force. With a hand full of my hair in his grip, he slams inside me, hard and deep.

I cry out. He's big. Thick and hard. His possession is unforgiving.

The burn is real.

I'm not an inexperienced woman, but hell, Sebastian Garcia makes me feel like an innocent virgin.

His touch is so different to any others'. His ownership is real.

He grabs my hips in his hands and begins to pump me hard. My entire body is jerking as he hits me.

The bed bangs against the wall, and I glance up and see our reflection in the mirror.

He's still fully dressed in his suit. My innocent white nightgown is twisted up around my breasts. Sebastian tips his head back in ecstasy, and as the dim light reflects off the mirror, I see the shimmer of perspiration across his brow.

"Come inside me," I pant. "I want to feel it. I want to feel it deep. Give me all of it."

He screws his face up, as if losing control.

I want him to come first. I want to blow his fucking brain, like he does with mine. Then I remember how much he likes dirty talk. I push back on his cock and circle my hips in an invitation.

"Fill me up," I whisper.

He grits his teeth and slams in harder. "Come," he commands, knowing he's about to lose it.

"No." I smirk. I like this game. Watching Mr. Garcia coming undone may be my new favourite hobby.

"Fucking come," he grinds out.

I wiggle my behind again. "Make me."

He spits saliva onto my behind, and then he slides his thumb deep into my ass.

I fall still.

Oh, he's a bad man.

I see stars, and the air leaves my lungs.

He pumps me once, twice, three times, and I cry out as I come in a rush.

"*Ah, FUCK!*" His moan is guttural, as if in pain. He holds himself deep inside me, and I feel the telling jerk of his cock. He continues to slam into me as he empties himself completely into me.

I slump onto the mattress, and he falls beside me. We are both gasping for air.

I smile and run my hand through his dark whiskers as we stare at each other. "You got come on your suit," I pant.

He leans in to kiss me. "It was totally worth it."

The door closing stirs my sleep, and I frown into the darkness.

What time is it? Looking around disoriented, I know it must be early.

My arm reaches out to the other side of the bed. It's empty, and I glance over at the crumpled sheets.

I sit up on my elbows and look around my room. The connecting door is shut. I get up and turn the handle, only to find that it's locked from his side.

What?

Is he in there sleeping, or was that him that just left?

I get my phone from the side table and switch it on. It's 6:40 a.m.

My hand drags down my face. He has a breakfast on in twenty minutes, so it was Sebastian who left.

I slump my shoulders in disappointment. I wanted to see him this morning.

He's busy, I guess. He works damn hard. Is every day like this for him?

His schedule is back-to-back, but then I guess that's because Theodore is away, and now Sebastian is doing two jobs instead of one.

I open the curtains to let the light in, and I stare out at the street below. The sun is rising, but it looks cold. I see a man walking his dog, and a woman on a yellow pushbike. She has a breadstick in a basket at the front of her bike.

I squirm, still tender from where Sebastian has been.

A smile crosses my face, remembering last night and how wonderful it was—how wonderful *he* was.

I've never slept with a man like Sebastian Garcia before.

Powerful, dominant, and one hundred percent male perfection.

I remember the way he held my legs back in his take-no-prisoners way, like he owned them. The way he looked at me as he went down on me. The way he whispered in my ear as he gave it to me hard.

I feel myself beginning to throb down below.

Wow.

I stand at the back of the crowd while the formalities take place.

The press is here, and they are all snapping away with their cameras.

After touring three schools this morning, we are now at the university.

Sebastian is opening the new medical wing. The speeches are in full swing, and I puff air into my cheeks as about one hundred people gather around.

Sebastian is standing in line, listening intently. There is a big red ribbon across the entrance doors, waiting to be cut.

Sebastian smiles as he listens to the speaker gushing over the new facility. He's transfixed on what they are saying, and I have to wonder how he holds his concentration for so long.

Who knew that the political campaign trail was so boring? Question after question about policies and budgets, projected incomes and roads, spendings and blah, blah, fucking blah.

Sebastian hasn't glanced my way all day. Although I know, realistically, he can't, I kind of thought he might give me *the look* at least once.

One night, and I'm feeling like this. Ugh, look at me being all needy.

I've been at the back of the crowd, watching all day while he talks in whispers to his advisor, Kellan. She stands beside him, and I don't know what they talk about, but it seems to be a lot.

I'm not an insecure woman. I'm just not. I hold my own and

feel like I could take anyone on. But Kellan is next-level beautiful and captivating. The worst part is that she's intelligent, and even *I* find myself fawning over whatever it is she has to say.

Don't be a pathetic, insecure bitch, I remind myself. *That's not who you are.*

The funny thing is, though, that Mr. Garcia makes me feel more of a female than I've ever been before, and maybe that's not such a good thing when there is another beautiful female thrown into the mix.

My eyes roam over her fitted black dress that shows off her beautiful figure and her high heels and sheer stockings. Her dark hair is pulled back into a ponytail. She's just as interested in the speeches as Sebastian is.

I'm just interested in their friendship, that's all. Nothing unto-ward here. I'm just doing my job. Crisis management.

Hopefully, it won't be my fucking crisis I have to manage, but we'll cross that bridge when we get to it.

Stop thinking ahead. Maybe last night was a one-off thing. Maybe it will never happen again. But deep down, I know that it will. It was too good for it not to. Not that I'm complaining or anything. Earth-shattering sex is totally worth the risk.

I drop my head and smirk. An annoying little voice whispers something deep in my psyche: *It's so much more than sex.*

I stand up and straighten my shoulders. *It* is *just sex, April. Don't even fucking go there.*

Bart digs his phone out of his pocket and then walks away to answer it.

The time comes, and Sebastian steps forward with the cameras snapping away. He cuts the red ribbon, we all clap, and he begins his speech.

"Good afternoon." He smiles gracefully as he looks around at the crowd. "Thank you for the kind invitation. I'm honoured to be here."

My heart swells. He speaks so well in public. He never falters, and he never goes off script. His deep voice captivates everyone in the audience, and I realize it now... I see what they see.

Sebastian Garcia is a born leader. Driven and focused. I've listened to him deliver at least fifteen speeches in the last two days, and every single time, I've been riveted. He's strong and nonapologetic, but his message is good—always good.

I get why they call him the people's politician. He really does put the people and their needs first.

Bart comes back to stand beside me. He leans in and whispers, "We've got a problem."

"What's that?" I keep my eyes on Sebastian.

"Gerhard is at the next venue."

"Meaning what?"

"It's being televised."

I frown, still confused.

"He's only at press releases when he wants to stir up trouble."

"You think he's here about Theodore?"

"Why else would he drive three hours and only attend the televised release? He's going to blow the story out of the water. We're fucked."

I lean in and whisper, "Didn't you say that we have to enter via the back entrance at the next venue to avoid the protestors who are there about the proposed roadworks?"

"Yes."

"Then let the protestors into the press release."

He frowns.

"If they televise the protestors, there won't be airtime left for speculation, will there?"

He raises his eyebrow. "Plant a distraction?"

"Attack *is* the best form of defence, Bart," I whisper as I stare straight ahead. "And the public already know about the roadworks. With the protestors causing havoc, it'll be cut short. No time for questions."

A trace of a smile crosses his face. "I like the way you think, Bennet."

"If Gerhard wants to play games, we'll play them harder."

Bart takes out his phone and walks off to make a phone call in private.

I turn back to Sebastian, and I watch him speak with such conviction and honour. I smile to myself. Maybe I will like this job after all.

Not today, Gerhard.

Not today.

We're sitting at the bar, watching the televised recap of this afternoon's press conference.

The protestors clamber along the side of the streets, yelling abuse while holding placards. We watch on as Sebastian gets whisked out and into a waiting black Audi.

We threw Sebastian to the wolves this afternoon. The press release lasted all of eight minutes, and my plan worked like a charm.

As Sebastian is whisked away, our group smile, chatter, and raise their drinks to the television screen, excited that we held the story. At least for today.

We head back to London tomorrow, back to reality. Who knows what will happen then?

Sebastian is sitting by the fire with three men. He's pensive this afternoon, and I know that the protestors ruffled his feathers. But we did what we had to do. He still hasn't looked at me once, and although I hate to admit it, I'm beginning to feel rejected. "I'm going to head to my room," I say.

"Great work today, April." Bart smiles. "You did good."

"Thanks." I look around at the people I'm sitting with. "Goodnight."

I take the elevator and head back to my room, where I pour myself a glass of wine and run a hot bath.

I hear a knock at the connecting door, and I smile when I open it. Big brown eyes meet mine, and Sebastian steps forward to take me in his arms.

"Finally." He kisses me. It's tender and loving, with just the right amount of suction.

"Hi." I smile.

"Hi," he breathes against my lips. His hand slides beneath my robe, and he cups my behind.

He's different tonight.

Sated.

Last night he was here because he had to be. Tonight, he's here because he wants to be.

"I need a shower," he whispers.

"Okay." I try to step back, but he pulls me closer and kisses me again. "Let me rephrase that. *We* need a shower."

I lie in the darkness and listen to Sebastian's regulated breathing. He's fast asleep, and like the creeper I am, I'm lying on my side, watching him. His dark hair and skin are a contrast to the white bed linen. His big red lips are slightly parted. His thick black lashes fan across his face.

Breathe him in.

He was right: there is nothing more intoxicating than the scent of the person you want.

Just like last night, we fed on each other for hours until our bodies couldn't take or give anymore.

Every time with him just gets better. Every time, I find something new. A deeper connection.

It scares me.

Because, right now, I'm taken back to the twenty-five-year-old who was besotted with the man she's currently staying in a hotel with. The man she hardly knows.

The man she has every reason to despise.

I'm unsure if this is a good thing, but what I do know is that I couldn't stop it even if I tried.

. . .

"I'll have a double latte and a cappuccino, please," I tell the server behind the cash register. "And two turkey, Swiss cheese, and cranberry sauce toasted sandwiches, please."

"Sure thing." She smiles and puts my order into the computer.

It's 3:00 p.m. on Friday. Bart and I haven't had lunch yet. We are across town. He's dealing with a client who is in tears back at her apartment. Her husband, who is currently touring as a drummer in an iconic rock band, has just been arrested in Denmark on pornography charges. Bart is trying to figure out a plan of action and posting bail. How serious the charges are is unclear at this stage.

It's a fucking mess. Who knew celebrities were such nightmares?

This job is exhausting. I've been away all week, and now this. I had to duck out and get us something to eat before we both fainted.

I pay my bill and take a seat as I wait for my order.

I'm not sure what's going on this weekend, or what's going on with Sebastian.

After he kissed me goodbye yesterday morning, I haven't seen or heard from him. And I'm not asking or calling him. The ball is now in his court. If he wants this, he has to pursue it.

I've made it quite clear where I stand. Maybe a little too well.

At the tender age of thirty-one, I'm done with playing games.

Sebastian Garcia lights me up more than any other man ever has—even my ex-husband, and that's saying something because at the time, I thought he was the bee's knees. I've been going over Sebastian's excuse over what happened all those years ago, and looking back at it from his side, I get it.

He had to stand by Brandon. He did the right thing. Even though I got stomped on in the process, what kind of father would he have been if he put a woman before his son? Someone he had known for all of two weeks.

The fact that he put his son—not even his son, but another man's child that he took on—before himself says a lot about his character. There's a lot to like about Sebastian Garcia.

His work ethic, his stance on policies, his intelligence.

His body.

His words come back to me:

There's nothing more intoxicating than the scent of the woman you want.

The woman he wants. Wouldn't that be something? I smile to myself, feeling bashful over how intense our lovemaking was. To say it was incredible would be an understatement.

"Your order is up," the waitress calls to me.

"Thanks." I stand and glance across the restaurant, stopping dead in my tracks.

I sit down immediately so that I'm not seen.

Helena is sitting at a table in the back of the restaurant with Gerhard.

Two of Sebastian's biggest threats...*together.*

Fuck.

What are they doing?

I lift my phone and pretend to take a selfie. Instead, I snap a picture of the two of them together.

I find Sebastian and Bart's names in my phone and send the picture to them, with the caption:

We have a problem.

16

___

April

MY PHONE IMMEDIATELY RINGS, and the name Sebastian lights up the screen.

"Hi," I answer.

"Where are you?"

"In a café in Brixton."

"How do you know who she is?"

"She came into my office once," I stammer.

"Why didn't you tell me?"

"Because of client confidentiality I couldn't, but now that I work for you—"

"What the fuck is she doing with him?"

My eyes roam over to the two of them talking. "That's what I'd like to know."

"Keep an eye on them."

"I can't." I drop my head. "They can't see me."

"Are you in the café now?"

"Yes."

"Go out and watch from across the road or something. See if they leave together."

"Okay."

He hangs up, and I raise my eyebrows. "Goodbye, Sebastian," I mouth to myself.

He's obviously distracted. I guess I would be, too, if I had an evil ex-wife like her.

I collect my order and walk out and cross the street. Damn it, I just want to eat my toasted sandwich while it's hot. I tuck the brown paper bags into my handbag and carry the two coffees by hand. I walk into a dress shop across the street. It has huge windows, so I can watch through them.

Holy crap, have I missed them?

How long can I pretend to look around in these shops for? There are only four opposite the café, and I have been in all of them, all while staring through the windows.

It's been nearly an hour. Did they leave already? I've been watching like a hawk, and I haven't seen anything. What if there was another exit?

Shit.

I can't go back over there in case they are still there and they see me. I also can't leave in case I miss them.

Fuck's sake, what do I do?

I take out my phone and scroll through my numbers. I really don't want to call Sebastian, so I call Bart instead.

"Hey, what's happening?"

"They haven't come out." I look up just in time to see Helena at the register. "Never mind, I see them." I hang up and stand behind the clothes rack.

Helena pays the bill. They walk out onto the street and talk for a moment, and then they shake hands and go their separate ways. I narrow my eyes in contempt. *That bitch.*

It's a business transaction.

. . .

It's Saturday morning. I'm walking out of the gym with a spring in my step. I've just done a boxing class and worked my ass off. Now, I'm about to drop by the grocery shop and pick up some supplies for the upcoming week.

We go away again on Monday, and, quite frankly, I can't wait.

I feel good. I have this buzz of excitement in my stomach, and I know that it has everything to do with a certain man.

I didn't hear from him last night, and that's okay. He would have been stressed out about Helena. Bart called him yesterday with my findings, and we're having a meeting about it next week. With nothing further to go on, we really can't do anything else. But it is interesting to know that Gerhard is sniffing around Sebastian's ex-wife.

Why, we have no idea. But one thing is for certain: we will find out.

I dig my ringing phone out of my handbag and see the name Duke lighting up the screen. My heart drops. He called me last night too.

I can't answer it. I can't be any franker with him than I already have been.

We can't even be friends now because he will always want more, and history tells me that I won't. I just wish he would find someone. I mean, God, he has groupies and beautiful women coming out of his ears. What the hell does he want me for?

I think that's half of his attraction he has for me, the fact that I don't want him.

I've somehow become a challenge, and I don't want to be, because I'm not trying to play hard to get.

I really mean it.

I hit decline and put my phone back into my bag. I've got to be cruel to be kind.

Regret swims in my stomach. Sorry, baby.

. . .

It's 6:00 p.m. on Saturday. I walk through the bar to meet Anna and Penelope. I wave when I see them sitting at a table at the back, and I eventually fall into a seat beside them.

"Hey." I smile.

Anna fills my glass with wine. "Just in time for a toast." She smiles proudly.

I giggle and hold up my glass to theirs.

"To sleazy married-people dating sites," she says.

We all giggle. "Hear! Hear!" I call. "Congratulations."

We're here to celebrate Anna's new job. She just got the position of receptionist at Ashley Madison. Yes, you heard that right. Ashley Madison is a dating site for married people.

"So...tell us everything."

"Well, I start on Monday. I'll be at the head office, on the front desk for a while. If I do well, I can progress to the back of house."

I love seeing her so excited.

"What happens at the back of house, do you reckon?" Penelope asks.

"Orgies," I offer.

"No." Anna widens her eyes. "We are a classy establishment."

"That caters to married people," Penelope teases.

"It's not how it sounds," Anna says. "Once they explained it to me, I kind of got it."

I raise an eyebrow.

"Ashley Madison is for people who are deeply in love with their spouse."

"Oh, please," I scoff.

"It's completely true. They have no desire to leave their marital home, and they are happy in every way with their partner. It's just that their wife or husband doesn't have the same libido levels."

"Ugh." I roll my eyes and take a sip of my wine. "Give me a break."

"You know what?" Penelope says. "I get that. Imagine if you were married to the most amazing man, wonderful dad, and great partner. But then due to bad health or some other issue, he loses his ability to have sex. What would you do?" She looks between us both.

Anna shrugs.

"Would you leave him for a loser that can offer you sex?"

"No," I answer.

"So you would just live the rest of your life without sex?"

I twist my lips. "Hmm."

"This guarantees your partners dignity," Penelope says. "You can have a hookup, discreetly and privately. Nobody is going to find out, and the person you are sleeping with is also happily in love with their partner. You help each other out, purely physically. It's a win-win situation."

"Cheating is cheating," I huff. "I could never condone it. I've been on the other side of it."

"This is different. Your dickhead husband didn't care about you, or he wouldn't have done it with some random chick."

"In my bed." I sneer. "Fucking asshole."

"Cockhead," Anna chimes in.

"Right?"

"All I'm saying is," Penelope continues, "libidos in perfectly happy marriages can be very different too. Sometimes things like these are necessary. If a man is walking around every day and night, horny as hell, and his wife won't put out, what is he supposed to do?"

"Wank," I mutter against my wineglass.

Anna giggles.

"And you can only fuck your vibrator so much." Penelope shrugs. "Nothing beats the touch of a hard man or feeling desired."

"Don't I know it." Anna sighs.

"Anyway." Penelope shrugs. "I get it. I get women who go there. I get men who go there too."

"I'd be happy just to be fucked by someone other than myself," Anna exhales heavily.

God, I want to tell them about the amazing sex I had this week, but I can't, of course. I've decided that I have to keep Sebastian to myself. Nobody can know about us. After this last week away with him, and seeing how good he is at his job, I know I'm not spending time with just anybody.

I'm sleeping with the Deputy Prime Minister of the country, and he deserves my discretion.

There's also the small fact that I will be fired from my job if anyone finds out.

"Oh!" Penelope gasps. "What happened with Garcia?"

"Shh." I look around. "Nothing."

"Nothing?" Anna frowns. "I thought there was all this sexual tension."

"No, he's having a thing with one of his secretaries, I found out," I lie. "They're dating, apparently."

"God." Penelope sits back in disgust. "What a letdown. I was looking forward to that hot gossip, loser."

I giggle against my wineglass.

"Don't worry," Anna says. "He'll probably turn up at Ashley Madison soon."

I raise my glass in the air. "I don't doubt it."

Two hours later, and we're sitting at the bar. We've eaten dinner, had a few drinks, and now two men have come to join us. Penelope and Anna seem to be having the time of their lives, chatting and laughing with them, but I'm just not into it. I'm thinking of back-dooring it soon and going home.

I might call an Uber. I take my phone out of my bag and see a missed call.

April's fool

Excitement fills me, and I hit call, putting my hand over my ear to block out the noise.

"Hi," he answers.

I bite my lip to hide my reaction to the sound of his voice. "Hi."

217

"Where are you? It sounds loud."

"In a bar." Silence. "What are you doing?"

"I was calling to see what you were doing, but never mind. You're out."

"I'm just about to leave, actually." My stomach flutters with excitement, and I get up and walk towards the door of the bar and out onto the pavement. "Why don't you come over?"

He inhales. "I can't... We can't—"

"Be seen together," I cut him off, disappointment filling me.

"Why don't you come here, to my place?" he asks. "I'll have to send my car for you."

"Isn't that risky? If your driver knows..."

"Kevin has been with me for years. You're safe with him. You will have to stay in the car until you are in the garage and the doors are down, though."

"Okay." I smile softly, excited by the prospect.

I get to see him.

"Where are you?" he asks.

"Owen's in Kensington."

"Okay, I'll text you when he's out front."

"Okay."

I run my toe over a join in the concrete as a goofy smile crosses my face.

"See you soon." He hangs up.

I get to see him.

I walk back to the bar and sit back down next to the girls. "Was that Duke?" Anna asks.

"Um..." Shit, although he is the perfect alibi. "Yeah, I might catch up with him."

Anna puts her hand over mine. "Good idea. Screw that asshole Garcia. You're too good for him, anyway."

I fake a smile as I pick up my drink to take a sip. Guilt fills me. Now I'm lying to my friends.

This whole situation is one big fuckup.

. . .

Half an hour later, my phone beeps with a text.

He's out the front. Black Audi.
Your name is Tara.

I have an alias now. How gangster.

"I'm going to head off," I announce to the girls, draining my drink. They and their new friends are deep in conversation.

"See you!" they all call, distracted. They only give me a wave before they go back to talking.

I walk out onto the busy street and see the black Audi parked on the other side of the road. The windows are blacked out. I wait for the traffic to ease before I cross the road, open up the back door, and lean in.

"Hello, Kevin?"

"Tara?"

"Yes."

"Hop in." He nods and faces forward again.

Oh, bit rude. It's like he doesn't want to look at me.

We pull out into the traffic, and my mind begins to wander. How many times does Kevin pick up women for Mr. Garcia? Is this the usual process? Is he told not to look at them?

Stop it.

Twenty minutes later, we pull into Sebastian's fancy street. I remember it well. I walked down it alone and in tears six years ago. My stomach twists at the memory.

For God's sake, just stop being a drama queen, April.

Kevin pushes the button on a remote, and the garage door slowly rises. There's a black sports car parked in one of the spaces.

Kevin drives in and pushes the remote again. The garage door closes behind us.

He gets out and opens my car door, offering me a kind nod.

"Thank you." I smile awkwardly. I can't help but wonder what he's seen in the past.

He walks over and opens the entry door to the house, nodding again.

There's a drill, and he knows it well.

I walk through as my nerves begin to thump. Kevin closes the door behind me.

"Hi, there," I hear his deep voice say.

I turn to see Sebastian walking up the hallway towards me. His hair has more of a curl to it without being styled. He's wearing a black T-shirt and grey track pants. I've never seen him in casual clothes before.

He looks edible, and he smells fucking delicious.

"Hi." I smile.

He kisses me. "Hey." He takes my hand and holds it out to look me up and down.

I'm wearing tight light blue jeans and a fitted navy blazer with a white T-shirt underneath.

"You look gorgeous," he says.

I smile, knowing he's never seen me in casual clothes either. "Thanks."

I hear the garage door begin to open again, and Kevin's car starts to back up. Or is that Sebastian's car? Fuck, I don't even know. It's like I'm in a spy film or something around here."

"Did I interrupt your night?" Sebastian turns me towards him.

I put my arms around his neck. "No. I was waiting for your call."

He drops his hands to my behind. "Oh, you were, were you?"

"Yeah."

Our lips meet again. He takes my hand and leads me down the hall until we get to the living area.

My heart skips a beat.

Fuck, this house. It's full-on luxury.

It's old but perfectly restored. I think back to when it would have been a huge mansion. Who am I kidding? It's a huge mansion today. I don't remember anything about it from the first time I was here, only the street outside, though I only came in the front door and stayed in the foyer.

The ceilings are sky high with beautiful thick curtains draped over the windows. The walls are a warm cream, and the furnishings look like antiques. There is a huge, deep red rug that sits beneath a dark leather sofa.

My eyes roam around the space. I don't think I've ever been in such a beautiful home.

"Sebastian. Your house is…"

He puts his hands into the pockets of his track pants and looks around as if he's trying to see it through my eyes for the first time. "I like it."

I smile and run my finger over the beautiful mahogany cabinet. I really should try to act a little cool here, but I can't even pretend that I'm not in awe.

"Would you like a drink?" he asks.

I nod. "Yes, please."

He turns and walks down a corridor. I tentatively follow, and when we get out into the open, I am floored by what I see.

The back of the house opens up to a huge kitchen and a glass living room. It's modern out here. The walls are white, light, and airy. The furniture is all lighter, too, and the couches are a cream colour. There is a large, open sandstone fireplace with a chimney that goes all the way to the ceiling.

My mouth falls open. "What the hell?" My eyes fly to his.

A trace of a smile crosses his face, and I can tell he's happy with my reaction. "I added this part of the house."

I smile as I point at him. "Because you're an architect."

He chuckles and dips his head. "What do you want to drink?" He walks into the kitchen that's white with marble countertops.

"What are you having?" I ask.

He opens the fridge and peers in with a frown and then closes it again. "I might a have a glass of red."

I glance over to the white couch, knowing that this is a disaster waiting to happen.

I'm a clumsy oaf.

"Okay." I pull out a stool and sit at the counter. We are so sitting over here.

Sebastian turns his back to me to open the bottle over the sink. My eyes drop to his muscular physique. His olive forearms have thick veins coursing up them. I can see the ripples in his shoulders under his T-shirt, and his behind is tight and perky. Christ on a cracker, this man is delicious.

"How old *are* you?" I ask.

He fills my glass. "Too old for you."

"How old is too old?"

"I'm forty-three."

I frown. He's older than I thought. "And you live here alone?"

"Yes." He passes me the glass of wine, and I take a sip. "This is good."

He smirks and clinks his glass with mine. "Life is too short for bad wine."

I bite my bottom lip to stop myself smiling at him like a fan girl. Everything that comes out of his mouth just sounds fucking fantastic. "It is."

He sips his wine. "How old are you?"

"Thirty-one."

He nods. "You never told me you were married."

I get the feeling I'm here for an interview of some sort. "I was before we met the first time."

"And?"

"It was the biggest disappointment of my life."

His eyes hold mine. "Why?"

I shrug. "Walking in on the love of your life having sex with another woman isn't exactly great."

His brow furrows. "What kind of fucking idiot would cheat on you?"

I smile, grateful for his kind words. "The asshole kind, apparently."

He sips his wine and falls into thought.

There's a scratch at the back door, and he gets up to open it. An old brown dog waddles in. He has a curly coat and is a little over-weight. I smile and jump from my stool.

"Who is this?" I drop to my knees and hold my hand out for him to smell.

"Bentley."

The dog comes up to me, and I rub his big old face. He's beau-tiful. "Hello, Bentley." I laugh. "You are a big boy," I say in my baby voice that I save only for dogs. I sit on the floor as I rub behind his ears. "I miss my dog."

"You have a dog?"

"No, my family dog. His name was Digger. He died when he was thirteen. Best dog in the world. Do you have a ball, Bentley?" I baby-talk again.

"Oh God." Sebastian rolls his eyes. "He hates that voice."

"Oh, you love it, don't you, big boy?" I babble on as I rub behind his ears.

"Don't wind him up. He'll be running around the house all night."

"Where's your ball?" I mouth to tease Sebastian.

"Jesus," Sebastian mutters dryly, sipping his drink. I look up to see that he's trying to hide his smile. "He's hungry. I'll feed him." He gets up and walks down the hallway. "Benny, come on."

The old dog waddles up the hall to follow him. I listen on as he feeds him and puts him out.

Sebastian walks back out into the kitchen.

"What did you have for dinner?" I ask him.

He shrugs. "I didn't get around to it yet. I was supposed to be going to my friend's, but—"

"You wanted to see me instead?"

His eyes hold mine. "Something like that. I'll get something later."

"By something, you mean my vagina?" I ask innocently.

He gives me a smile. "Precisely."

I stand and go to the fridge. "I'll make us something."

"That's not necessary."

"I love to cook." I open the fridge and peer in. "It's the one thing I'm good at."

"There's another thing you're very good at."

My eyes flick over to him, and he gives me a sexy wink.

I smile to myself, feeling proud of myself. "What do we have in here?" I see that his fridge is fully stocked. "You cook?"

"I *have* a cook."

"Well." I take out some chicken and put it on the counter. "Now you have two."

His eyes hold mine as the air crackles between us.

I take out some fresh garlic, cream, and bacon. I open the pantry and find some fettuccini. "Do you like carbonara?" I ask.

"Doesn't everybody?"

"Maybe not." I get to washing my hands. "Put some music on, will you?"

"What do you want to listen to?"

I narrow my eyes as I get out a chopping board and knife.

"I'll play your anthem," he says.

"What's that supposed to mean?" I start to chop the onions.

"This was the song that you walked down the catwalk to in the Escape Lounge."

The song "Sexual Healing" by Marvin Gaye sounds through the speaker system.

I stop what I'm doing and glance up. "Was it?"

"Uh-huh."

"How do you remember that?"

"I remember everything about you. You're not easy to forget."

I smile as I go back to chopping. "You do know that I'm going to rob your house while you're unconscious, right?"

He laughs and walks over behind me to refill my glass. Then he pulls my hair to the side and begins to kiss my neck.

I smile as goose bumps scatter up my spine.

"Do that, and I'll tie you up in the basement for a couple of years and use you as my sex slave," he murmurs against my skin.

His teeth graze my neck. "I'm totally down with that." I smile. "Stop distracting me, or you won't be eating."

"Let's skip the main course and start on dessert."

"Sebastian." I turn my head and kiss his big, pouty lips. "You need to build up your energy. I'm hoping that dessert will be a marathon event."

He chuckles, bites me hard, and slaps my behind before he goes back to his stool and sits down.

I turn the hot plates on and begin to fry the onions and garlic. I put the pasta in the boiling water, and we chat and laugh as I cook.

It's not awkward, and it's not sleazy. It feels like I'm meant to be here, doing this with him...whatever this is.

Marvin Gaye's "*Sexual Healing*" plays throughout the house.

If this song is my anthem, I'm making it my bitch.

We've drunk two bottles of wine over dinner.

After washing up, I now have Sebastian sitting in the armchair in his bedroom. The room is lit only by the bedside lamp. His bedroom is big and luxurious, like him.

It wouldn't matter where we were. It's only me and him now, and this desire between us.

Sebastian and I have a lot of things that are good about us, but it's the sexuality, the raw hunger for each other's bodies, that's next-level. He makes me crave a deeper connection, a different kind of dominance. One I've never needed before him. But now that I've had it, I can't get enough.

My eyes hold his as I slowly undress to the beat.

He sits back, legs wide, his hunger real. I slide my jeans down my legs and throw them to the side. I lift my T-shirt over my head and stand before him in a skimpy white bra and G-string. I unhook my bra and throw it to the side, and then I drop to my knees between his legs. He hisses as he sits back, awaiting my mouth.

I spread his legs aggressively and then slide his pants down, followed by his boxers. His hard cock springs free. My stomach flutters at the sight of it, engorged. Its head a deep red, with thick veins coursing up the length of it.

I take him in my hand and kiss the tip. "Hmm." I stroke him, and a rush of cream blesses my body with lubricant.

I want him. *I want every damn drop.*

Getting to let loose on his body is a dream come true. I sit up to remove his T-shirt over his head and throw it to the side. I want full view of this perfection.

He sits back in the chair, his golden skin on show. His broad chest has a scattering of dark over it. His stomach is rippled, and a trail of black hair runs from his navel down to his short, well-kept pubic hair.

His parted quads are big and strong, and I run my hand up his inner thigh, drinking in his beauty.

His eyes hold mine and he cups my face, his thumb slowly sliding over my bottom lip. "Suck me," he mouths.

I smile as I lick up his length. I cup his balls, and holy fucking hell...this is a man that dreams are made of.

I take him deep into my mouth. His eyes darken, and he pushes my hair back from my forehead as he watches me.

I get into a rhythm. My hand follows my mouth. His moans are deep, his quads are flexing, and I can see the muscles in his stomach contracting on the upstroke.

Fuck, yes.

Watching him come undone like this is my new favourite thing.

His breathing becomes laboured, and he begins to shudder as he tips his head back. "Yes," he pants. "Yes. Fucking yes."

He convulses hard, grabs my face, and he begins to fuck my mouth with force.

Damn it, I love this. I smile around him and bare my teeth. He convulses as he comes hard.

Euphoria fills me, and with our eyes locked, I drink him down.

His chest is rising and falling as he gasps for air. I keep on slowly sucking him until he's empty.

"Cartier," he whispers in awe.

"April," I correct him, but he cuts me off with a kiss and moans again when he tastes himself.

He grabs the back of my head and holds me to him as our kiss turns desperate. "Get up here and fuck me."

Sebastian

I sit up on my elbows and look around my bedroom to see it's empty. The sunlight is light as it peeks around the drapes.

"April?"

No reply.

Where is she?

The last thing I remember last night was being wrapped around her like a blanket.

I get up and go to the bathroom. When I go to put on my robe, it's not hanging from the back of my bathroom door. Where did I leave it?

I throw on a pair of boxer shorts and make my way downstairs. I stop midway down the staircase and listen.

I can hear an American voice. I can also smell pancakes.

I frown.

I walk down into the kitchen.

"Ow," April says when she steps over Bentley. "You're in my way, old man."

Wearing my navy robe, she stops what she's doing and holds the saucepan midair as she watches something on the television in the living area. I glance over to see what she's watching. It's CNN, the American news.

I smile and lean against the doorframe. I keep forgetting she's not from England.

She returns the fry pan to the hotplate and continues cooking.

Every now and then, she looks up and stops what she's doing to watch the television.

She goes to the fridge and takes out some fruit before she begins to slice it up. Watching her, a strange feeling comes over me.

This feels normal. Weirdly normal.

I haven't done normal for a very long time.

For ten minutes, I watch her. She talks to the dog and watches the news as she cooks and fusses about. I don't think I've ever seen anything as beautiful and lovely.

She has an air about her. She's confident but innocent, and yet I know she's far from innocent. Quite the opposite, actually.

The woman's a deviant. She fries my fucking brain every time we have sex.

I've never, ever come as hard as I do with her. Every time is better than the last, and I don't know how that's possible, because every time, I swear it's the pinnacle.

She glances up and sees me. "Hey, you." She smiles, walks over, and puts her arms around my neck to kiss me softly.

My heart somersaults at her tender touch. "There's my robe." I smile.

She giggles. "This old thing? I thought it was your grandpa's."

I chuckle as I slide my hands down to her behind, and we stand in each other's arms for a while. Her lips linger over mine before she gifts me with another kiss.

"I made you pancakes."

"Did you?"

"Yeah." She takes my hand and leads me to the stool at the counter. "Sit down and admire my ass while I finish them."

"This, I can do."

"How do you have your coffee?"

"White and one." I watch her make it. "You don't have to cook while you're here, you know."

"I like to cook." Her face falls as she passes me my coffee. "Why, does it bother you?"

228

"No. I mean... I don't want you thinking you have to."

She smiles and serves up the pancakes.

"What?"

"It's so cute that you think I would do something I didn't want to do."

I smirk, knowing that's true.

April arranges the strawberries and bananas on my pancakes.

"Maple syrup?" she asks.

"Please."

She pours it on and passes it over, and then she sits beside me with her plate.

"No maple syrup for you?" I frown.

"No." She bites the food from her fork. "I'm sweet enough."

"Isn't that the truth?"

She puts her hand on my thigh and leans over to kiss me. She's right, though. She is sweet and gentle. Everything I'm not.

My heart constricts as I look at her.

She cups my face. "Last night was wonderful, Seb."

"It was."

We stare at each other for a moment, and an undercurrent of affection passes between us.

Don't fuck this up.

I return to eating. "So, is this where I realize that you've robbed my house?" I bite the food from my fork.

"Aha," she giggles. "I cleaned the joint out last night. Man, you have a lot of shit. My back is sore from carrying it all out to your snooty car."

I smile.

"What are we going to do today?" she asks.

My gaze lifts to hers. *There's a today?*

"Umm." I pause because I don't really know how to answer that. "What do you want to do?"

"Well, seeing as we can't leave the house due to the fact that we're undercover in a secret spy film like *Mission Impossible*..."

I smirk at her analogy. "This is true."

"I thought you could give me a foot massage."

"I think I can manage that."

She leans over and kisses me again. Then she rests her cheek against mine, and it's there again.

This tenderness.

It's so foreign to me, but so comforting and nice.

I pull away from her and return to eating. "What do I get after I massage your feet?"

"You get to cut my toenails."

I burst out laughing at her unexpected answer. "Is this some kind of perverted kink?"

She laughs. "Absolutely, Mr. Garcia. You are in for a treat."

"Can you call the car for me? I need to get home and organize my things for the week," April says.

After watching a movie on the couch together, I dozed off to sleep.

I sit up. "Of course." I walk out and text Kevin, asking him to take 'Tara' home. His response comes back quickly.

With her wanting to leave, I'm reminded what it's like when she's not here. A feeling of loss rolls around in my stomach.

"If I could take you home myself, I would," I say.

She smiles up at me from her place on the couch. "I know, baby." She holds her arms up for me. "Come and cuddle me before I go."

I lie down beside her, and she holds me tightly. I put my head against her shoulder.

I don't want her to go.

She kisses my temple.

"What are you going to have for dinner?" she asks.

"Why don't you stay tonight too?"

She pulls back to look at me. "You can cook your own dinner, Sebastian."

"I didn't mean that. I meant—" I stop myself.

"What?" She brushes my hair back from my forehead.

"We could get takeout, so you didn't have to cook." I swallow the lump in my throat.

Her eyes search mine. "I haven't got my clothes washed for work."

"I'll buy you new ones."

She smiles and kisses me. I know she thinks that I'm joking, but I'm deadly serious.

I wrap my arms around her and hold her tight. So tight, I can feel myself squeezing too hard.

"Stay. I need you to stay, Cartier."

She pulls out of my grip and stands. "Don't call me that. I told you last night. I don't like it."

"It's just a nickname."

"One that brings back terrible memories for me."

I stand, annoyed that she pulled away from me. "How ridiculous. Why would it?"

She watches me. "It doesn't bring back bad memories for you?"

"Nope." I walk out into the kitchen. "I happen to like those memories...a lot better than these ones."

She follows me. "What do you mean by that?"

"Nothing. Drop it."

She puts her hands on her hips. "What the hell? You like those memories better than now? What the fuck does that mean?"

I roll my eyes. "Cut the fucking dramatics. You know what I meant."

"No, I don't. Explain it to me." Her eyes hold mine. "Why do you call me Cartier, Sebastian?"

"You know what? Just fucking go home, April. I'm not in the mood for this bullshit."

She watches me, and I can see her brain working at a million miles per minute. "You liked it when I worked at the Escape Room, didn't you?"

"Shut up. Go home."

"Why would you like me better then..." Her voice trails off, and her face falls. "You're compartmentalizing me?"

"Now you're a fucking shrink? Go the fuck home." I march upstairs.

She storms after me. "You are, aren't you?" She takes the stairs two at a time. "The way you're acting now is telling me that I'm right."

"Just go!" I don't want her here, and I don't want to talk about this.

"Sebastian!" she snaps. "Answer the question."

"What do you fucking know about compartmentalizing?"

"Everything." She throws up her hands. "I wrote the fucking book on it."

"Oh, so now everyone is as fucked up as you, are they?"

"I'm not fucked up." She points to her chest. "And it took me about ten thousand dollars in shrink appointments to be able to admit that."

I walk into my bathroom and slam the door behind me.

She opens it. "Don't slam the fucking door on me."

"Then stop following me!" I yell as I begin to lose my patience.

"Is that what you're doing?"

I stay silent.

"Sebastian?" she asks softly. "You're still thinking of me as your Escape Girl."

I begin to hear my heartbeat pounding in my ears as I stare at her.

She steps back, as if my lack of words physically hurt her.

"So I'm just some girl you pay to have sex with?" Her eyes well with tears.

I clench my jaw. "Don't you dare use tears as a weapon," I sneer. "That's not fucking fair."

Her face falls. "What was last night?"

I stare at her.

She puts her hand over her heart. "While I'm over here falling for you, you think of me as a whore."

I drop my gaze to the floor. I can't look her in the eye.

"Sebastian?"

I keep staring down.

"*Look at me!*" she cries. "Is that fucking true?"

My eyes rise to meet hers. "Just go," I whisper.

Her eyes search mine. "Answer me."

"If you wrote the book on compartmentalizing, you should already know the answer."

Her brow furrows. "I do it to everyone in my life; I hate that I do. I've sought treatment for it for years. And then I met you, the one person I couldn't block out." Her shoulders slump in sadness. "And you go and do it to me."

We stare at each other. "April..."

"What, Sebastian?"

"I'm sorry," I whisper.

Her eyes well with tears again, and she drops her head. "Me too."

She turns and walks out.

I hear her go downstairs, and then I hear the garage door open.

Moments later, I hear the car drive off, and I close my eyes in regret.

Fuck.

April

If there's one thing worse than falling for the wrong man, it's having to work for him once it's fallen apart.

We're in Bristol this week. It's Tuesday night, and Sebastian hasn't said one word to me since I left his house on Sunday.

I'm angry at myself.

How the fuck did I let myself fall for him when I knew it was dangerous?

The worst part is, I know he's not happy either. He's been a cranky bear, and everyone is scared to even talk to him.

We are in connecting rooms, but I'm not sure why. He didn't

knock on my door last night. Perhaps it was too late to change the booking.

I didn't go out to dinner with everyone else. I chose room service alone instead. I'm not much in the mood for socializing. I heard his door open and close about an hour ago, so I know he's in his room alone too.

And it sucks.

I hear a faint knock on the door, and I hold my breath.

Is that him?

The lock is on his side, so I lie still in the dark. I reach up and turn my bedside lamp on, my back to his door when I hear it open slowly.

I close my eyes.

The bed dips as he lies down behind me and pulls me into his arms.

He kisses my temple. "I'm sorry."

I keep lying with my back to him, unsure what to say.

"My demons are dark," he whispers.

I frown and roll to face him. "Then let me chase them away."

"They're too big for us."

I stare at him for a moment. "What are they?"

He swallows the lump in his throat but stays silent.

I cup his cheek in my hand. Whatever he's dealing with is upsetting him. "Baby, talk to me."

His eyes search mine.

"Sebastian."

"I'm fucked up," he whispers.

I lean in and kiss his lips. "Tell me."

His brow furrows. "I can't—" He pauses, and I wait. "I can't perform unless I'm with a prostitute."

I frown, confused.

"Unless I know for certain that there is no future with a woman, I can't even get it up."

I blink, shocked.

Fuck.

17

April

I STARE AT HIM. The way the shadow is throwing off the lamp, I can only partially see his face. I run my fingers through his stubble as I try to think of the right thing to say.

What *do* you even say to that?

"For how long?" I whisper.

"A long time."

"Since you were married?"

"Around then."

I remember Helena that day in my office, and contempt fills my every pore.

What the fuck did she do to him?

His face stays solemn and, not sure what to do, I offer him a crooked smile.

"Have you sought any treatment?" I ask.

"Like a quack?"

"A psychologist."

"They can't help me."

"Who have you talked to about this?"

"Nobody."

"Not even your friends?" I frown.

"No."

A trace of a smile crosses my face.

"Why are you smiling?"

"Because you told me. That must mean something, right?"

His brow furrows, like he's contemplating my question.

I trace a circle with my fingertip on the sheet below me as I think. "So, what you're saying is that not all women you're physically attracted to do it for you?"

"No," he replies without hesitation.

A million things fly through my mind, none of them making sense. "And Cartier does?"

His jaw ticks. "Yes."

I nod.

"But I don't want Cartier."

"Who do you want?"

"You."

I lean in and kiss him softly. This is fucked up, so God knows why I feel relieved.

We stare at each other for a while, and then I ask, "What would happen if I wanted you to make love to me?"

He blinks, and his face twists with a frown.

I give him a moment to reply, and when he doesn't, I answer for him. "Your body wouldn't cooperate?"

"It's not my body that's the problem. The attraction for me is lost."

I nod as I begin to understand.

His face is solemn. He looks so beaten down. I lean in and kiss him. "Thank you for telling me." I hold him close, and I can almost feel his pain through our hug. "This is not so bad. This is okay. We can work with this, Seb," I whisper.

"How?"

"Well." I trace my finger down his nose. "We just take it day by day."

His eyes hold mine.

"And when you need April to be your girlfriend and to kiss and cuddle and hang out with you, she's here."

"And when I need Cartier?"

"She's here too."

His eyes search mine. "Why would you do that?"

I roll over onto my back. "Because I get it. I can't judge. I have my own demons."

He leans up on his elbow. "Like what?"

I stare up at the ceiling. "How long have you got?"

He smiles, encouraging me to go on.

"Well, I can't get close to anyone, for seven years now. I compartmentalize sex. I can't go home to live in America because it reminds me of him and how hard he broke me, even though all of my family and friends are there. I have a wonderful man who I've been sleeping with for four years who loves me and wants marriage and babies, yet I can't think of anything worse. I broke it off with him without one single regret or afterthought. How cold can one person be? And now, to top it all off, I think I've fallen for someone who is in the public eye, and I work for him, so we can never date publicly...and I think he's just as fucked up as I am."

He smiles and pinches the bridge of his nose. Hearing our situation out loud really is comical.

"So, yeah, I can handle your demons." I smile. "I'm not sure if you can handle mine."

"Me neither." He smirks. "You do sound pretty fucked up."

I laugh out loud, and it's cathartic. He laughs too.

After a while, we fall serious.

"Seb."

"Yeah."

"Promise me something."

"What?"

"Can you keep me in the loop?"

He frowns.

"I can deal with anything you throw my way." Maybe this is too heavy to say now, but I need to verbalize it. "But if you want another girl, or if you need another woman, prostitute—whatever you want to call it—it's okay. I'm telling you that it's okay if you need someone else. I completely understand. But you need to tell me beforehand so that I can walk away with my self-respect. If I'm going to do this, I deserve to know where your head is at. And I promise you there will be no judgement or hard feelings. I understand that sometimes—" I pause as I try to articulate what I want to say. "Sometimes the demons are so bad, you need a new weapon."

His face falls, and I know that he understands what I'm saying. I've been there. I've bounced between men, looking for that elusive magic pill that's going to stop the pain.

I lean in and kiss him softly. "That's the only condition I have on our relationship going forward."

"Okay," he whispers, and after a moment he adds, "you have my word."

"Seb." I frown.

"What?"

"How come you told me?"

"What do you mean?"

"Well, you didn't need to tell me this. You could have just played along, and I would have never known."

"I thought I..." His voice trails off.

"Thought what?"

"I thought I owed you the truth, and..." My eyes hold his. "You make me want to be better, April," he whispers. "To get better."

I smile softly as our lips meet, and my entire heart constricts.

This beautiful man.

I push the hair back from his forehead as we stare at each other. "You know, Sebastian, I happen to like you how you are."

He kisses me softly. "That's just because you're fucked up."

I giggle. "Maybe."

He takes me into his arms and holds me tightly. He kisses my forehead before he rolls me away from him and spoons me from behind. For the first time since we met, there's no sexual tension between us. We're just two people lying in bed together, ready to go to sleep.

I can't help but feel that maybe we just entered the friend zone, and there will be no turning back from here. A sadness begins to sink deep into my bones, and I really don't know what will happen between us going forward.

I feel so close to him, yet miles away.

It's like his admission just put him into a precious glass box and I'm unsure of its strength—of what will make it crack. I'm not sure what to say to make it better. I'm not sure if I even want to know what he just told me.

And what does this mean for my heart? Because he's the first man since my husband who I have deep feelings for too. *Oh, the irony.*

Life's a fucking bitch.

We both lie in the silence, lost in our own regretful thoughts.

My mind goes over the hurt that he must have suffered to have been affected so deeply. I think about him going through this all alone for so many years, and my heart constricts.

I fucking hate her.

Like a force from above, I feel my protective instincts infiltrate my body.

Sebastian kisses my temple, and I melt into his arms.

I adore this man.

I've got your back, baby. You can lean on me.

I hear him open the connecting door into his room and pulling it closed behind him.

Waking up like this is lonely.

There's no good-morning kiss. No sweet cuddles.

After the nights are filled with so much emotion, the mornings feel exceptionally cold.

Maybe he thought I was asleep and was trying not to disturb me.

I get up, put on my robe, and go to the bathroom, and once done, I flick the kettle on. After everything that came to light last night, I wonder what happens next.

Do I push him or do I leave him alone?

I stare at the door between our rooms as I try to make my decision.

Fuck's sake, why can't I just like a normal guy for once? A normal, boring guy who is really normal and really boring.

That would be too easy, wouldn't it? It had to be a high-powered politician who has a 747 full of emotional fucking baggage.

Ugh, this is just my luck.

I go over his words from last night. *You make me want to be better. To get better.*

He told me for a reason. He wants me to try.

I drop my shoulders as I steel myself. Okay, let's do this.

I make two cups of coffee before I open the door and walk into his room with them in hand.

He glances up. He's freshly showered, wearing his navy trousers pants and his pale blue shirt, which is still open as he does up the buttons. I can see the ripples in his tanned torso.

My insides clench. He's one hell of a specimen. "Morning." I smile.

"Hi." He glances up briefly as he does up his shirt. His eyes drop back down to his task.

"I made you coffee."

"Thanks. Just put it on the counter." He walks over to his wardrobe, takes out his tie, and begins to tie it.

I drop to sit on his bed, unsure of what to say. "Busy day?" I ask.

"Yes." He throws his tie over his shoulder and walks into the bathroom in a rush.

I twist my fingers in my lap. I can hear him brushing his teeth.

Okay, so this isn't ideal.

I look around his room, wondering what to do.

He walks back out and begins to pack his computer into his laptop bag. He seems annoyed.

"About last night," I say. "Can we talk about it?"

"Nothing to talk about." He collects papers from his desk. "Just forget what I said last night. I'd been drinking."

I frown. No, he hadn't. "What?"

"Just fucking drop it, April."

I stare at him, and I know that he's angry that he told me—that he revealed his weakness.

"You don't have to be a dick," I say.

"And you don't have to be dramatic and whiny at 7:00 a.m. Now, if you don't mind, I'm getting ready for work."

I stand up in a rush. "Don't be an asshole."

"Can I have some fucking peace around here?"

I pick up his cup of coffee. "I'm taking my coffee back. You don't deserve it."

"I didn't ask for it in the first place. I'm well aware that your coffee-making skills are less than mediocre."

I get a vision of myself pouring it over his head.

"Goodbye, Sebastian." I walk back towards my room. "Have a nice day, dear." I smile sweetly.

"Don't give me that condescending fucking tone, April," he growls. "I'm not in the mood for your shit today."

I turn to stare at him in the doorway, trying to understand what's happening right now.

He wants a fight. He's goading me. He wants *me* to push *him* away.

This is him being fucked up.

Hell.

Ignore it, ignore it, ignore it.

Without saying a word, I let the connecting door shut behind me, and I walk into my bathroom to turn the shower on. Moments later, I hear his door slam. He's gone.

I get under the hot water as the adrenaline pumps through my body. Maybe I want to fight too.

Asshole.

"I don't care what it takes. Find a way," Sebastian growls before marching off.

"Jesus. What the fuck is wrong with him today?" Bart sighs.

I widen my eyes as I stare at the computer screen in front of me.

If only you knew.

We've just finished lunch at our hotel, and we are about to hit the road again.

After this morning's hour-long drilling at his press conference, Sebastian wants Gerhard taken off all political reporting. The thing is, we can't control who the media choose for their stories, and neither can he. Sebastian knows that, too, but today he has decided that he can. And who are we mere lawyers to know anything about the law?

Sebastian has been in a mood all day, snapping and snarling at anyone who dares to challenge his opinion, which has been a lot of people. The last press conference tipped him over the edge, and now he's in full rage mode.

"Kellan," we hear him snap as he walks towards the elevator. "I don't have all day."

"I'm coming," she mutters, rushing after him to make it to the elevator.

I bite my lip to hide my smile.

I hate to admit it, but I do love that he's being a prick to her as well.

He steps into the elevator and turns to face the doors. His eyes meet mine, and he remains emotionless as we stare at each other.

The doors close.

"What the hell got under his skin today?" Max says from behind us.

I smirk as I go back to my work.

That would be me.

. . .

It's late—around 10:00 p.m. We didn't get back to the hotel until two hours ago, and then we had dinner in the restaurant. Everyone is now having drinks in the bar and trying to relax before retiring to bed for another full-on day tomorrow.

Sebastian is sitting in the armchair by the fire with a scotch and a cigar. His legs are wide, and his demeanour is all male. From my place at the bar, I watch him lift the cigar to his lips, inhale, and then blow out a thin stream of smoke. He's deep in conversation with four men, and in the ultimate act of fucked-up-ness, I want him.

Him raging around today, snapping and snarling at everything that moved, has awoken my libido, taking it to fever pitch.

I want him to release all that anger on my body.

I want him to punish me for upsetting him.

I take out my phone and text him.

Will you be paying cash or card tonight, sir?

I see him dig his phone out of his pocket and read the text. His eyebrow rises, and he slowly sips his scotch.

Cash

I reply.

Your date will be waiting in the suite for you in thirty minutes.

His tongue darts out, and in slow motion it sweeps over his bottom lip. His eyes rise to meet mine, and he gives me the best 'come fuck me' look I've ever seen.

It's dark, dangerous, and hot as fucking hell.

I'm going to get it.

Nerves dance in my stomach. Another text from Sebastian comes through.

I'll have a full service. And make that ten minutes.

I drain my glass, and without looking up, I stand and leave. I need a two-minute shower, six minutes to prepare myself, and then another two minutes spare to freak out. I really should be more clued up on hooker talk before I make a booking.

Full service. What the hell does that mean?

I'm sitting on the end of the bed, freshly showered, wearing the hotel's oversized white bath robe.

I drag my hand down my face, wondering what the hell I'm doing.

Every fibre inside of me is screaming that this is wrong, and yet, like a sacrificial lamb, I sit here waiting for him to come and pay me for sex.

Sebastian Garcia is all kinds of fucked up. He doesn't want sex unless it's with a prostitute.

And what does it say about me that I'll take his money?

I'd take his last damn cent if it means I get to hold him for the night.

I've never been so disgusted with myself in my life. Why does it have to be him?

Why can't I feel this way about Duke?

I drop my head into my hands, preempting the regret.

I already know how this story ends, and it isn't good. This isn't going to be one of those happy love stories where everything gets tied up in a little red bow at the end.

I imagine myself crying on the floor, broken.

Again.

My mind takes me back to the last time we were together and how hard and fast I fell. How badly it ended.

I should know better. I *do* know better.

I hear the door in Sebastian's room shut, and I close my eyes.

He's here.

My heart begins to beat faster. Just knowing he's near sends my adrenaline into overdrive.

This is messed up.

I'm as bad as he is.

Maybe worse.

I stand and put my ear to the adjoining door. I can hear the shower turn on in his bathroom. He's showering.

For me.

I push my fingers into my eye sockets as I try to calm myself down.

Shit.

I rush and take out the bottle of champagne from the fridge and pour myself a glass. I down it in one go. I pour another glass so fast that it sloshes over the sides, and I lift it to my mouth with a shaky hand.

Calm down.

What is it about Sebastian Garcia that affects me so much?

I tip my head back and drain the glass again.

Fuck.

I refill my glass and sit down on the bed. *Act cool.*

There's a knock on the door, and I close my eyes. Here we go.

"Come in," I call.

The adjoining room door opens, and there he stands. Dark hair, olive skin, big red lips, and in the same hotel robe that I'm wearing.

His eyes find mine. "Hello." His voice is cool, detached.

Nerves flutter in my stomach. "Hi."

He lifts his chin in approval. I know he can tell that I'm nervous, and he likes it.

"Can I come in?"

I gesture to the room with my hand. "Please."

He walks in and closes the door behind him. He stands at the end of the bed. His hands are in the pockets of his robe. "What are we drinking?"

I frown because suddenly there are no words in my brain. "Champagne."

His dark eyes hold mine, waiting.

"Would you like some?"

"Yes." He stays still on the spot.

I pour him a glass and pass it to him.

"Thank you." He takes it from me, and with his dark eyes holding mine, he lifts it to his lips and slowly sips. Then he licks his lips.

"So, *Cartier*..." *Fuck.* "What do you have in store for me tonight?"

I frown, confused.

Huh?

"I want to know what I'm getting for my money." His voice his deep and husky. I glance down to see his large erection tenting his gown.

Dirty bastard.

"This is my first job, sir," I whisper, playing along. "You are my first client."

Arousal dances like fire in his eyes, and he dusts my bottom lip with his thumb.

"Take it off."

I frown.

"I said, take it off," he demands.

I slowly untie my robe and open it. His eyes drop down my body.

"Drop it."

I pull it back over my shoulders and let it fall. It pools around my feet.

His eyes drop to drink me in, and he gives a slow, satisfied smile. "Better."

He reaches out and cups my breast. His thumb dusts back and forth over my erect nipple, and his eyes meet mine.

"Are you nervous?" he asks.

I nod.

"Don't be." He cups my face in his hand and leans in to slowly kiss me. His tongue sweeps through my parted lips as my feet float from the floor. "I'll look after you," he whispers.

Will you?

He kisses me again, this time deeper, and my eyes close in reverence.

My body is covered in goose bumps. If this is our last night together, I'm going to make it count.

"How can I please you?" I whisper up at him.

"By breathing."

My eyes search his.

Why say romantic things if you don't mean them?

It's easier when he's hard and fast. At least then it's only about sex and orgasms—an equal exchange of power. That, I can handle.

This, I'm not so sure about.

He grips my hair with both hands as he kisses me harder this time, and my face screws up against his.

The emotion between us is a tangible force.

I don't even need sex. Him standing here and kissing me like this is enough.

His lips drop to my bare shoulder, and he walks around behind me.

He lifts one of my legs to rest on the ottoman at the end of the bed. With his lips on my neck and his teeth in my skin, his hand dusts between my legs. He parts me with his fingers.

Goose bumps scatter all over again.

He bites my neck hard as he slides his fingers through my wet flesh. Our arousal is pumping hard between us, bouncing off each other like a rubber ball.

I can feel how much he wants me. He's aching for it.

So am I.

He kisses me over my shoulder as he slides in two fingers, his other hand cupping my breast.

He works me, and then slides another finger in. Damn...the burn of three thick, strong fingers fucking me is hot and addictive. The sound of my wet arousal hangs in the air.

Instincts take over, and I lift my leg higher. I want more.

Deeper, thicker, longer.

He gets rougher, both with his teeth on my neck and his fingers. I know we are both close to coming, and he isn't even inside me yet.

"Sebastian," I whimper.

His lips take mine as I slide my hand under his robe and stroke his thick cock. It's dripping with pre-ejaculate.

Fuck.

My eyes roll back. He feels so good.

I grip him hard, and he hisses. Our kiss becomes frantic, and I jerk him almost violently.

He shudders.

I smile against him as he loses control. In one swift movement, he bends me over the bed and onto my knees before he slams in hard.

I moan deep.

He repositions my hips and pushes my back down towards the mattress. "Drop your shoulders."

I do as I'm told, opening myself completely to him. He spreads my lips with his fingers.

Then he's riding me, hard and unapologetically. The sound of our skin slapping together echoes around the room, and I glance up into the mirror in front of us. He's naked now. When did he take his robe off?

His olive skin glistens with a glow of perspiration, but it's the look of sheer ecstasy on his face that makes me lose my head.

"Give it to me," I moan.

He slaps me hard, and I cry out as my body contracts around him, the orgasm so strong, it steals my breath.

"Fuck," he growls. "*Fuck, fuck, fuck.*" He holds himself deep, and I feel the telling jerk of his cock deep inside of me.

I shudder as the aftermath takes over me, and he falls down on top of me as we both gasp for air.

Then there's silence.

Say something.

I close my eyes against the sheet beneath me, overwhelmed with emotion.

Please say something. Anything.

Sebastian

The soft moan from beside me wakens me. April is in my arms.

I stiffen and ease back, and April instinctively rolls towards me to snuggle in tight. She's warm, soft, and vulnerable.

She's everything that I'm not.

My polar opposite, and yet she's the same.

I listen to her regulated breathing as I lie and stare up at the ceiling. With every inhale of her breath, my chest tightens a little more.

The attachment I feel to her isn't healthy for either one of us.

But it's so nice lying here with her. Five more minutes won't hurt.

I close my eyes to try and force myself to relax.

In, out...in, out...in, out.

I repeat the breathing mantra in my head to try and calm myself, but it's hopeless.

My heart begins to hammer as an uncontrollable panic takes over. It starts at my toes, and like a tidal wave, I feel it rise up and over me.

I close my eyes to chase the demons away.

Stop it.

The sound of my pulse beats loudly in my ears.

The tightening of my chest.

The lack of air in my lungs.

I can't stand it any longer.

Waking up with April Bennet starts my day with a panic attack. The kind that's unforgiving and makes me feel like shit.

I hate that I can't wake up with her.

I hate that I'm so fucked up.

I slide out of bed and gather my clothes together before I carefully open the adjoining door to my room. I take out my wallet and hold it in my hand. I need to pay her. I stare down at the cash in my hand.

What am I doing?

Uncontrollable panic sets in.

I carefully open the adjoining door to my room. I'm as quiet as I can be, because there's only one thing worse than sneaking out of April's room in the morning to do the walk of shame, and that's her waking up and me having to explain myself.

Because I can't.

What could I possibly say that makes this okay?

I take one last look at the beautiful woman sleeping without me, with her creamy skin and blonde hair splayed across her pillow.

So alluring, so perfect.

Toxic.

I need to get as far away from her as possible.

Now.

I rush from the room and close the door behind me as quietly as I can. I lean up against the back of it in the darkness of my room, my chest heaving as I try to catch my breath in the silence.

What's happening?

What the fuck is wrong with me?

I want her. I crave her. The nights in her arms are incredible. But every morning, I wake up completely freaked out.

She's the mindfuck of all mindfucks.

April Bennet isn't good for my mental health, and I know in my heart of hearts that I'm not good for hers.

This has to stop.

18

April

I WOKE up when Sebastian jerked away from me.

I pretended to be asleep so that I didn't have to hear the lies.

I feel sad for him.

I know that he wants me. Our chemistry together is undeniable, and I know that, on some level, he cares.

He just can't do this, even though he's trying.

I can feel him fighting with himself. The decent thing for me to do would be to take a step back and give him some space.

But knowing all too well how the fucked-up mind works means that he will probably go back to his gentlemen's club to try and fuck me out of his system. I also know that if he crosses that line, that's it for us. We will both be the person we regret letting go. The ones that got away.

I exhale, knowing this is a no-win situation.

Stay and fight, I push him away.

Give him the space that he needs, I lose him anyway.

Maybe this is too hard, and we were never meant to be. That's the logical answer.

I go to the door and put my ear against it to listen. I can hear the shower running.

Should I go in there and try and talk to him now?

But what would I say?

Hey, can we try and work this out? Because you're the first person that has made me feel not dead inside.

I drop my head. It's not all about me. It has to be about him too. I can't force this. I can't fix him. He has to do this by himself.

My forehead rests on the back of the door as I think. I should just leave it.

If I don't know what to say, I probably shouldn't say anything at all.

I need to think on this further. I push myself off the door and get into the shower. Let's see what the day brings.

Three school visits and two hospital openings are a long time to watch someone to see if they look your way. I can confirm that Sebastian has not. Not even a glance.

And that's fine. It's totally fucking fine. I don't need him to look my way.

He did, however, make riveting conversation and laugh with every other female in the room.

Screw him.

Sneaking out every morning like he's embarrassed that we slept together.

What the hell is wrong with me?

Actually, I don't even need to ask myself that. I've worked it out.

I'm the queen of self-sabotage.

Nice men who love me, I care for but don't want. Assholes who want to pay me for sex and have me at their beck and call, I crave.

No more.

I'm done with men. Fuck them all, I say.

Not literally. There will be no fucking.

No fucking whatsoever.

I'm becoming a nun. I am way too old for this shit.

The car pulls to a halt outside our hotel, and I climb out with Bart. It must be the day for it, because he and Jeremy had a fight at lunch too.

I wasn't supposed to hear it, but I couldn't help it, seeing as I was sitting with them, although I was pretending to be on the phone. Jeremy is pissed because Bart told him he's going away for the weekend with his wife. Jeremy completely lost his shit and threw his bread roll into his soup. It even splashed on my shirt.

He got up and stormed off, and we haven't seen him since.

Where the hell he went, I don't know.

We waited for a long time in the carpark while Bart tried to call him. He didn't answer. Now, Bart is furious, and I'm scared to speak in fear of saying the wrong thing.

But I am confused. Surely, the fact that Bart even *has* a wife should be reason enough to be pissed. Why would a weekend away trigger him when he goes home to her every night?

Who knows? Maybe Jeremy has a wife at home too. Nothing surprises me anymore.

I can't talk or place judgement. I win the prize for messed-up love.

I don't love Sebastian.

Fuck's sake.

The whole world has gone to hell on a broomstick.

I take the elevator up to my floor and walk down the large corridor to my room.

We've come back to get ready for a function tonight, and it's the very last thing I feel like doing. I have no idea where Sebastian is, nor do I care.

I open the door to my room and instantly see that the adjoining door between our rooms is open.

Oh, it suits him now.

I narrow my eyes. *Don't even.*

Calm, calm. Keep fucking calm.

I'm angry, more than I should be, but I don't like being treated like crap, and I'm not playing this game of his.

He comes around the doorframe, a glass of scotch in hand, dressed in his black dinner suit. "Hello."

I roll my lips to hold my snarky tongue. "Hi."

"Why are you so late getting back?"

I widen my eyes. *Why are you such a prick?* "We had to wait for someone."

He gives me a slow, sexy smile. "Well, I'm glad you're back."

Ha. Horny, are you, fucker?

"I'm tired. I'm going to have a nap." I gesture to the door. "Do you mind?"

A smirk crosses his face. "Do I mind?"

"Closing the door."

"This one?" He taps the door with his palm.

Yes, that one, you dumb fuck. What other doors are there? "Please."

He walks into my room and closes the door behind him. I stare at him flatly.

He sips his scotch and raises his eyebrow.

I cross my arms over my chest. Seriously, just go away.

"Is there a problem?" he asks calmly.

"You tell me."

He holds his hands up and shrugs sarcastically.

I smile sweetly, the psycho part of my brain now activated. "I'm tired. Please leave."

"How could you possibly be tired? You slept like a log all night."

I glare at him.

You'll be sleeping like a dead person soon. "Sebastian," I sigh. "I am not in the mood for you today. If you don't want to argue, I suggest you leave me alone."

"What's turned you so pissy?"

"Oh my fuck!" I snap in exasperation.

Before I explode, I turn my back to him, go to the fridge, and fill a glass full of wine. This damn man is turning me into an alcoholic. I usually never drink on a school night.

"You're angry with me?"

I take a sip, still standing with my back to him.

"Is this about last night?"

I spin towards him, all systems firing. "What could I possibly be pissed about, Sebastian?"

"I don't know. You're the one who offered—" He cuts himself off.

"Offered my services?" I ask. "Is that what you were going to say?"

"No," he says too quickly.

"I'm not pissed about last night." I open the sliding door and walk out to sit on the balcony. He follows me out and sits on the chair beside me.

I stare out over the city as I try to work out what I want to say. I don't even know.

I'm trying so hard not to be a drama queen, but damn it, I hate feeling like this.

"Why do you do that?" I ask.

"Do what?"

"Sneak out."

"I don't want to wake you."

I raise an eyebrow. "Really?"

He exhales. "I don't need—"

"I know," I cut him off. "You don't need drama, and you don't need me, but you like using my body for sex. I get it, Sebastian. You've made it more than clear on many occasions."

"I don't like your tone."

"And I don't like feeling like fucking shit."

"So don't." He shrugs.

I stare at him. "What does that mean?"

"If I make you feel like shit, don't see me anymore." He sips his scotch, as if he doesn't have a care in the world. "Go back to your boyfriend...the football guy."

My nostrils flare as I struggle with my overactive emotions. *He really doesn't care.*

"You know what?" I practically spit, losing the last of my patience. "I wish that I stared at *him* all day, waiting for him to look my way. I wish that I picked up *his* shirt from the floor and inhaled it just so I could smell him. I wish that I stayed awake all night watching *him* sleep because I thought he was the most beautiful human I've ever seen. And most of all, I wish to God that I felt for him what I do for you, Sebastian, because *he* deserves me." I angrily wipe the tears from my eyes, embarrassed that I care for him as much as I do.

His eyes hold mine.

"And I hate that you make me needy and whiny, because this isn't who I am. The shoe is always on the other foot, and I hate that the person I care for doesn't give a fuck about me."

His brow creases. "Why would you say that?"

"Because it's true."

"What do you want me to do, April?" He stands, outraged. "Whisk you away for a month in Italy? Follow you around like a puppy? Get on bended knee and propose? I don't know what preconceived ideas you have on how relationships should be, but I can assure you, I am not about that. And if you're not happy, then don't put me through your bullshit drama. I won't fucking put up with it."

Wow.

I shake my head with a roll of my eyes.

Typical asshole.

He throws his hands up in the air. "What's it going to be? You want me as I am or not at all? Because that's all I've got to offer."

I glare at him.

"Fine." He slams his drink down on the table so hard that it sloshes all over the sides. "Go back to your boyfriend, because unlike me"—he holds his fingers up to air quote me— "*he* deserves you."

He storms out and slams the door behind.

The room falls silent, and I close my eyes in disgust.

Fuck.

The ballroom, now loud and filled with jovial chatter, is host to a charity function for a local hospital.

I'm sitting with Jeremy, and boy, are we fun to be around, each of us now silent and sulky. Bart's loud laughter can be heard all the way from over at the bar. I look over and see he's talking to Sebastian, as well as a few other men. Each of them is laughing and having fun without a care in the world.

Fuckers.

I look back at Jeremy, who is forlorn and miserable.

"I have to ask... What do you see in Bart?"

He shrugs. "I wish I knew."

I glance back to the bar to see Bart is telling an animated story. The men around him are hanging off his every word. Whatever he's saying is apparently very funny.

"I overheard your fight with him today at lunch."

Jeremy rolls his eyes and sips his wine. "Sorry."

"Don't apologize, although you'll have to explain it to me, because I'm confused as hell."

He drops his forehead into his palm, his elbow resting on the table. "That makes two of us," he mutters dryly. "I met Bart at a conference in Atlanta about seven years ago. I was a PA to another lawyer at the time. We were out with a large group and, one by one, they dwindled off and went home. It ended up being just the two of us left in the bar. We drank and laughed, and somehow the conversation turned to our sexualities. I told him that I was gay and that I'd never been with a woman. He told me that he was straight and that his only regret in life was that he hadn't experimented in college like everyone else. He'd always wondered what it would be like to be with a man, but now that he was older, it was never going to happen. The more we drank, the more we clicked. The chemistry was like nothing I'd ever felt before."

I imagine the scenario as he explains it. I can almost see the two of them alone in a bar.

"He told me he and his wife had fallen out of love, and that they had decided to separate. It was completely amicable, and they were only friends now. He said he loved her like a sister and that it was sad for both of them because they had four young children together. Having a separated family wasn't anything either of them ever imagined."

His eyes rise to mine, and I offer him a soft, reassuring smile as I put my hand over his.

"When we were walking back to our hotel, he kissed me." Jeremy drops his head, as if ashamed.

I squeeze his hand. "And?"

"And it got heated outside my hotel room. I told him that he was married and that he should go home. I didn't see him again for the rest of the conference. I heard that he'd left at some point because he fell ill. But I knew the real reason was that he was disgusted with himself for making out with a guy."

Bart's loud laugh drifts over from the bar again, and my eyes rise to him. I exhale heavily. Sebastian is now smoking a cigar. I watch him lift it to his lips and inhale as he listens to Bart.

Fuckers.

"Six weeks later, Bart turned up at my office. He told me that I was all he could think about, that he was going insane over me, and that he had left his wife because of it."

Jeremy exhales, clearly frustrated. "We went out for dinner then back to his new apartment. Everything was still in boxes. We ended up having sex."

I watch him struggle, knowing he's ashamed.

"It was the best fucking sex I've ever had. I'd like to tell you that it was nothing special, but we fell madly in love. From the moment he first touched me, I was done for. We were inseparable, and I moved in eight weeks later." He stares off into the distance.

"So you live together now?"

He raises his eyebrow and sips his wine. "Not long after I moved in, he started having trouble with his eldest daughter."

"Didn't she like you?"

He scoffs. "Bart would never admit to being with a man. To everyone else, I was his roommate. Nothing more. When his kids would come over, he would treat me like he didn't even know me. I understand why, but that didn't make it hurt any less.

Anyway, his kids were desperate for Bart to get back together with their mother. His eldest daughter, Heidi, became depressed. It was a terrible time. Bart was worried sick, and I was worried too. I'd gotten to know his children, and I cared for them as well. They are great kids."

He drains his drink in one gulp. There's a lot of pain in this story. I can feel it oozing out of him.

"When Heidi was twelve, she tried to commit suicide."

My face falls.

"It was...horrendous. Poor Robyn and Bart."

"Robyn?"

"Bart's wife."

"You know her?"

He nods. "Not something I'm proud of."

Hell, this story is a doozy.

"Heidi nearly died. It was touch and go. She spent two weeks in intensive care. Thankfully, she survived, but when she got out of hospital, all she wanted was for Bart to move home to be with her."

My heart drops.

"And he did what any father would do: he moved home to be with his daughter."

"God, Jeremy." I sigh.

"Bart told me it wouldn't be for long—that he wanted me to go and work for him so that he could spend his days with me because we couldn't be apart."

"Where do you live now?"

"I'm still in our apartment with all our things. He comes over most nights for an hour or so, when he's at the"—he holds up his fingers to air quote— "gym."

"Fuck."

"He kept telling me that he's still there because of Heidi, and I believed him. I mean, I spend more time with him than anyone. All day, every day; every night, we make love; and on the weekends, we often go away. But a few weeks ago, I went to a function with a friend and Bart didn't know I was there. He was there with Robyn." He pauses. "I was watching them from the shadows."

"And?"

"The way she was looking at him. Their body language."

"What?"

"They're sleeping together again. I know it."

"Hell." I drag my hand down my face.

Jeremy smiles flatly and holds his champagne glass up. "So there you have it. My fucked-up love life. I'm in love with a married man who I sleep with most days and who swears his undying love for me. One who is going away to New York with his wife next week for his anniversary without his kids. You can figure out why I'm upset."

"How do you know he's going away with her? Maybe it's a mix-up."

"Robyn called me to see if I had any ideas on what she could buy them for their anniversary. Told me all about the romantic weekend away that Bart had organized for her."

"Fucking hell," I whisper, wide-eyed. "This is a nightmare."

"Right?"

"What are you going to do?" I ask softly.

"What I always do." He sighs. "Give him an ultimatum. Tell him that's it. He will leave, and I will miss him so much that I will nearly die from a broken heart. In a few weeks, he will tell me how he can't live without me and beg me to come back. I will believe him, even though I know nothing's changed." Jeremy twists the stem of his wineglass and stares at it.

"You deserve better than this," I tell him.

"I know." His eyes meet mine. "But have you ever loved someone so much that you would literally die to be with them?"

My eyes rise to Sebastian. He lifts the cigar to his lips and smiles sexily at the woman he's talking to. "Maybe," I admit quietly.

Jeremy's eyes follow my line of sight. "What's going on with you and Garcia?"

"Nothing."

Hearing Jeremy and Bart's miserable story has given me a reminder of what my life will be like in six years if I stay.

"Sebastian has issues, and I can't save him, as much as I wish I could."

Bart and Sebastian laugh out loud, and Jeremy and I look over to their group.

"Do you want to get out of here?" I ask.

Jeremy pushes his chair out. "Where do you want to go?"

"Anywhere but here."

My phone rings, waking me. I'm disoriented. It's dark. I sit up in a rush and glance at my clock. It's 5:35 a.m.

"Hello," I answer.

"April, I need you in the function room immediately," Bart says firmly.

I wince because I'm still half asleep. "What's wrong?"

"Theodore has escaped from rehab."

"W-what?" I snap. Is this a bad dream?

"Just get down here. We've got a fucking disaster of epic proportions going on."

I push the blankets back in a rush. "Okay, on my way."

I hang up and walk to the adjoining door. Sebastian didn't knock last night. In fact, I didn't even hear him come back. I put my ear to the door.

Silence.

He's probably already downstairs with Bart.

I quickly shower and make my way down to the function room we are currently using as an office. Already there are Bart, Jeremy, a few security guards, three police officers, and Kellan Chesterfield.

"Hi." I throw my laptop bag on the desk and look around. "Where's Sebastian?" I ask.

"A car is just picking him up now," Bart says, pulling out a map. "So, Theodore was last seen here." He points to the map. Everyone leans in to take a look.

I frown. "What do you mean, a car is picking Sebastian up?"

"He didn't stay here last night. I've spoken to him; he's on his way," Bart replies, distracted.

Jeremy's eyes meet mine.

Where the fuck did he stay?

"April, get on the phone to the CEO of the facility. I want the security footage."

"Yes, sir." I begin to Google the number of the facility.

The doors bust open, and Sebastian marches in flanked by security guards. He's still wearing his dinner suit from last night. His black bow tie is undone and hanging around his neck. He's dishevelled, and it's obvious he's been asleep.

His eyes find mine across the room. He glares at me. I glare right back.

You. Fucking. Asshole.

19

April

I DROP MY HEAD. My furious heartbeat hammers in my ears.

I have no words for this man.

How could he?

What the hell is going on? I know he has feelings for me. *I fucking know it.*

Coward.

My cheeks heat with anger, and I try to focus on what I'm supposed to be doing. Sebastian tears off his bow tie and throws it on the desk as he sits down. I pretend not to look at him as he dials a number on his phone. He holds it to his ear and waits.

"Pick up." He hangs up and then dials another number.

I stare at my phone, pretending to Google whatever crap it is that I'm supposed to be searching for, but there is no searching going on. There's only dread and red rage fury.

He slept with someone else last night. It's obvious.

I know we aren't Romeo and Juliet or anything, but fuck, I thought we were more than that.

"April, how are we going with the surveillance?" Bart calls, making me jump.

"Coming." I fumble with my phone. I'm completely flustered and on the edge of control.

Fuck...*focus.*

With shaky hands, I type into Google

Number for Aletta Rehab.

"You all right?" someone whispers. I turn to see Jeremy.

"Yep," I snap, outraged that I'm even being asked this question.

"Can someone please explain to me how a person escapes from a maximum-security rehabilitation facility?" Sebastian growls. "What the fuck kind of establishment is this place?"

Jeremy glares at Sebastian. "He's fucked," he whispers.

I bite my bottom lip so hard that I nearly draw blood. "I don't care," I lie.

"Yeah, sure, I believe you."

Not helping.

"Will you stop? I don't have time for this crap, and I don't care what he fucking does. He's an asshole."

Jeremy rubs my shoulder sympathetically and walks back over to his desk.

"Has anyone spoken to Leona?" Sebastian calls.

"No," Bart replies.

"Wouldn't calling his wife be the obvious fucking thing to do?"

"We've been trying. She isn't answering."

"Is she in the country? April, get her on the phone."

"I'm doing something else," I reply.

His eyes rise to meet mine. "Well, stop what you're doing and get Leona on the phone."

I glare at him, and he glares right back.

I keep doing what I was doing.

Don't push me, asshole. I am *not* in the fucking mood for you today.

"Did you get her?" I hear him ask.

I keep Googling.

"April!" he shouts. "Did you get her?"

"No, I did not," I growl. "I am doing something else, and I don't appreciate your tone, Mr. Garcia. Do not raise your voice at me again."

The room falls silent, and he narrows his eyes. "I asked you to do a task."

"And I am already doing something else. Perhaps you could ask one of the twenty other people in the room to do it. I am not your secretary, Mr. Garcia. I am a lawyer. Stop insulting my intelligence." I turn my back on him and march from the room.

My heart is hammering.

How dare he?

He makes me fall for him, fucks with my head, and then when I ask him about it, he ends it. Then he goes and sleeps with someone else to get over me.

That's it. We are finished.

Done.

"Good evening, Aletta Private Facility," the receptionist answers.

"Hello, this is April Bennet. I'm a lawyer who represents Theodore Holsworthy. I need to speak to the head of security, please."

"Yes, of course. One moment, please."

I hear Sebastian's voice bellowing from the conference room behind me as he directs his anger at someone else. I roll my eyes.

Fucking hell. I need a new job.

Stat.

Sebastian

I walk into the café at 7:00 a.m.

Masters and Spence are already in our regular seat at the back. "Hi."

"Hey," they both reply.

I take off my jacket and fall into my seat.

Julian is reading the morning paper and, as usual, Spence is smiling up at me.

I exhale heavily. Has there ever been a more faithful friend?

Spencer Jones, my biggest cheerleader, and the sweetest man on Earth.

Masters flicks his paper in the air before turning the page. "This time next week, we'll be on a plane."

"Fuck, yeah. Five days in paradise." Spencer smiles as he raises his coffee cup in the air. "Good thinking getting married in the Maldives, Ricco. Just what I fucking need."

I roll my eyes. "I doubt I'll even be able to go."

"Can I get your usual?" the waitress interrupts me.

"Yes, please."

"What do you mean, you won't be able to go?" Spencer asks. "We have had this weekend planned for twelve months."

"Yeah, don't fucking start," Julian agrees. "You're coming."

"Yeah, well... I'm having the week from hell."

Julian rolls his eyes. "So dramatic."

"Right?" Spencer chimes in.

"Listen, fuckers." I lower my voice to a whisper and lean towards them. "Between you and me, the fucking Prime Minister has done a runner from rehab."

"What?" they both gasp.

"Where is he?" Julian frowns.

"If I knew that, I would go there and give him a swift uppercut to the throat. I don't have time for this shit."

Spencer screws up his face. "You really don't know where he is?"

"No idea. We have security and police searching for him everywhere. If the press get a hold of this, he's completely screwed."

"I don't understand. I mean, he's always been a bit of a loose cannon, but..." Julian's eyes hold mine. "What's happened to tip him over the edge?"

"His wife left him."

"Of course she did." Spencer throws his hands up in the air in disgust. "There's always a fucking woman involved."

"Will you keep your voice down?" I hush them.

"Sorry."

They both look around guiltily.

"What happened?" asks Julian.

"Gardener?" Spencer blows into his coffee. "Was it the fucking gardener? I'm telling you one thing, there is a very good reason my gardener is eighty." He taps his temple. "It's called forward thinking, boys. Take notes."

"Or just plain slave labour." I roll my eyes.

"Your fucking gardener is eighty. Christ almighty, you're an asshole." Julian winces. "Poor bastard is going to have a heart attack."

"Anyway," I cut them off. "Theodore is missing, and I'm having to hold the fort. I don't know how long I can cover for him. Unless he turns up very soon, I seriously doubt I can come away next week."

"Fuck's sake." Spencer sighs. "I only called Ricco yesterday and told him you were bringing a plus-one."

My face falls. "What? Why the fuck did you do that?"

"Now you can bring your new girl." He smiles sweetly.

"You are such a fuckwit," I whisper angrily. "I am not bringing her. Besides, she's now my old girl. It's well and truly over."

Masters rolls his eyes as he sips his coffee. "Another one bites the dust."

"What the fuck did you do, you idiot?" Spencer fumes. "You like her. You really like her."

I glance over to Julian, who smiles and winks. He loves watching Spencer lecture me over women. It's his favourite pastime. Not too long ago, it was him on the receiving end.

"I didn't do anything. She just isn't the girl for me."

"Oh, fucking bollocks," he says. "Fine." He rearranges the napkin on his lap with renewed purpose. "I'll invite a date for you. I have a million women lined up waiting."

"I don't want a fucking date, Spence. Stay out of my business." I sip my coffee. "Stick to your pregnancy sex."

Julian rests his face on his hand and smiles dreamily. "Is there anything better than pregnant sex, though?"

I wince as I get an image of a heavily pregnant woman having sex. The thought is disturbing. "I can think of a million things, you fucking pervert."

"So, what happened with June?"

"April, you idiot," I correct him.

"I knew it was a month." Spencer shrugs. "April. What happened with April?"

"Nothing. I fucked it. I'm moving on. End of discussion."

Spencer's eyes hold mine. "What did you do?"

"Will you get off his fucking case?" Julian snaps. "Leave the poor bastard alone."

"Thank you," I sigh.

"Well?" Spencer asks again.

"It was too hard."

"Nothing worth it is easy," Julian says.

"You're supposed to be on my side, fucker."

Julian holds his hands up in surrender. "I'm just saying."

"Don't."

"Here you are." The waitress smiles as she puts our breakfast on the table in front of us. "Three omelettes."

We thank her, and the boys forget all about me as they begin to eat and chat. I eat my breakfast in silence, my mind miles away.

It's with April. It's always with April.

I feel like shit.

April

I watch the dial in the elevator as it goes up the numbers, my mind filled with poison.

Did he think of me while he was inside of her?

Was I anywhere in his thought process? Or am I imagining something that isn't there?

The worst thing is, deep down, I know he cares. I know we have something, and we shouldn't, because we hardly know each other.

Every time I'm in the room with him, my heart is on standby, waiting for him to look my way, waiting to smell his cologne. To feel the power emanating from his body. To feel my own physical reaction to him. The goose bumps, the butterflies, the flush of my cheeks when he makes eye contact. Every little thing means so much.

And it sucks. I fucking hate this.

I've waited seven years to feel something for someone. Anything.

It's ironic that I've fallen for someone who has as much baggage as I do.

Maybe even more.

Poor Duke, is this how I made him feel?

It makes me sick to my stomach. I inhale deeply to try and fight off the nausea.

The unwelcome vision of a woman on her knees in front of him plays like a horror movie in my psyche.

Was it dark and moody, or were the lights on?

How many times did he come?

Oh.

I remember the way he puts his hand around my throat when he fucks me. The darkness in his eyes. His primal urge to dominate.

The fire and fear he lights up in me.

It's wrong. I know it is.

So why does it feel so right?

I close my eyes, knowing there are no winners here. This will never work. Sebastian Garcia is an entity all of his own.

And I am an island.

The elevator doors open, and I drag myself up the corridor. I close my eyes as I brace myself to knock on the door. *Come on, you can do this.*

I knock twice.

"Come in," Sebastian's strong voice calls.

I open the door and walk in as I act unaffected. "You wanted to see me?"

"Yes." He points to the chair with his pen. "Please, take a seat."

I stare at him, wondering if I can lie across his desk in protest until he wipes the last week away from my memory. I sit down. "What is it?"

His dark eyes hold mine, and for an extended time we stare at each other.

"You wanted to see me?" I prompt.

"Yes." He regains his composure and holds his pen in his hands. "How are we going with the security footage?"

"I've done the report, but it appears that he stole a security card from a cleaner's trolley and simply walked out in the middle of the night."

"And none of his credit cards have been used since?" He frowns.

"No."

He rubs his pointer finger over his lips as he thinks. "I'm beginning to get worried."

"Me too."

He leans back on his chair, deep in thought. "Let's hope they find him today, hey?"

"Yes." I nod.

There's no denying that this situation is dire. Not because he's the head of the country, but because he is a human being with depressive addiction problems who is missing.

Sebastian and I remain silent, unsure what to say next.

"Is that all?" I ask.

"You know..." His eyes hold mine. "You *are* better off without me."

I stare at him.

"I can't be what you need, April."

But you are.

Emotion rushes through me like a freight train, and I turn my head to evade his gaze. Damn it, why does he make me so weak?

"If I could fix this, I would. I can't," he continues.

Liar.

"Okay." I square my shoulders. I don't want to be here, listening to his lame excuses for one minute longer. I stand. "Is that it?"

A frown creases his brow.

"I won't bother you again, Sebastian," I say.

He looks disappointed, but what does he want me to do? Beg to be his prostitute so that I can clear his conscience? As easy as it would be to carry on having no-strings sex with him, I can't do it.

I care too much.

I'm already hurt. I can't imagine the state of my heart if I let this continue. Maybe this is God punishing me for treating Duke the way I did for all those years.

This is how he felt about me. The roles were reversed but the scenario was the same.

One person was in love. One person wasn't.

"Is that it?" Sebastian asks. "Is that all you've got to say?"

I stare at him, my heart aching. He wants me to take him back on his terms...and I want to.

He slept with someone else.

"Goodbye, Seb." I force a smile. "I hope you find what you're looking for."

His face falls, and I turn and walk from his office.

That's it. It's over.

My phone vibrates on my kitchen counter. I pick it up and smile. It's Jeremy.

I know this is last minute and you probably already have plans, but do you want to grab a drink tonight?

I don't feel like going out, but maybe I could do with it. Sitting around here all alone and being depressed isn't helping.

I text back.

How about dinner and a few cocktails? I don't want a late one.
I have a million things on tomorrow.

I don't, but I can't stand the thought of being locked into a big night.

Sounds great. I'll book somewhere.
How's 7:00 p.m.? Do you like Italian?

I smile and reply.

Yum. See you then.

"Hi, honey." My mom's happy voice smiles down the phone.

"Hi, Mom." I get a lump in my throat. What is it about mothers? I can be as fierce and cold as they come, but the moment I hear my mom's voice, I revert back to the scared child I am.

I just want her to hug me and tell me it's going to be all right.

"How are you, sweetie?"

"Good," I lie. I feel emotional and sad, and I don't want to talk about it. I know I need to get off the phone. I don't want her to worry about me. "Mom, I'm just with friends, can I call you back?" I lie to her again.

"Okay, darling. Are you going out tonight?"

"Yes, just for dinner. Italian."

"Sounds delicious. Have fun, I'll call you tomorrow."

I close my eyes because damn it, times like this I just want to be at home with my family. Lying on my parents' couch and eating all the chocolate.

But reality's a bitch. I'm here in London, all alone.

"Bye, Mom, love you."

The phone clicks as she hangs up, and I go to the fridge. I guess I'll just have to eat chocolate on my couch instead.

"What's in these cocktails?" I smile as I eye my glass.

"I don't know. Good shit." Jeremy shrugs.

We are at Belsito, an Italian restaurant in Kensington. It's a trendy little place, not far from my house. Dinner was beautiful, dessert was divine, and don't even get me started on how good these cocktails are.

It turns out that Jeremy and I have a lot in common. We've laughed and chatted, and we have not spoken one word about two certain people that we know. I know he's not bringing up Bart on purpose, and I'm doing the same. I don't want Sebastian's and my sordid details out there. I've only said we had something for a little while and it fizzled out. But I know he knows there was more. It's awkward for both of us. I work with both men, and so does he, so it really is a case of 'the less you know, the better'.

Although I must admit I'm kind of hating on Bart for the way he's treated Jeremy. He deserves so much better.

"What have you got on tomorrow?" Jeremy asks.

I let out an overexaggerated sigh. "Boring crap. Housework. Washing and grocery shopping."

"Yeah, same." He sips his drink. "Have you heard from Garcia?"

"Nope, and I don't expect to."

A set of car keys come flying onto the table with force, causing Jeremy and I to jump.

"What the hell are these?" a voice growls.

We both look up to see Bart, his face red and furious.

Jeremy squares his shoulders, clearly preparing for battle. "What are you doing here?"

"Mind telling me why your Porsche turned up at my house on the back of a truck today?" Bart fumes.

"I returned it."

"Why?"

"I don't want it anymore."

"It was a gift!" Bart snaps.

"Then give it to your *wife*."

Ouch.

Bart's eyes bulge and then fall to me. Oh crap, he's wondering what I know about the two of them.

"Umm. I'm going to get going." I stand.

"Good idea," Bart says, his eyes firmly locked on Jeremy.

"Sit back down." Jeremy grabs my hand.

"No, I really need to go." I bend and kiss Jeremy's cheek. "See you on Monday."

I take out my purse. Bart holds his hand up. "I've got it." He slinks into my seat, not wasting a single second.

"Are you sure?" I frown.

"Completely." He just wants me out of here.

"Okay, thanks." I give Jeremy a wave, and he narrows his eyes at me.

Sorry.

I head outside to the taxi rank. The line is long, and thunder rumbles in the air. Fuck it, I'm not in the mood for this shit. I take out my phone and order an Uber. I cross the street away to wait for its arrival.

I can smell the rain as it comes, sprinkles and then heavier and heavier.

Damn it.

I wrap my cardigan around myself and peer up the street, letting out a defeated sigh. At least Bart is pursuing Jeremy and trying to make amends.

Polar opposite of my situation.

Sebastian doesn't give a literal fuck about me.

He's a douche.

But deep down I know he's not. Only to me, which is worse, I guess.

I shake my head. I hate that I keep thinking about him. I'm

going over and over the last week, wondering if I overreacted, trying to analyse his behaviour and what it all means.

Fucker.

The car pulls up beside me, and the window rolls down. "April?" the driver asks.

"That's me." I smile and get into the backseat just as the rain comes down.

I stare out the window as we pull into the traffic, glancing back at the restaurant to see if I can see Jeremy and Bart. I wonder if they'll get through this.

I face forward again.

Oh well. What doesn't kill you makes you stronger, right?

With my track record, I should be Godzilla by now. Strong enough to take down the world.

The car pulls into my street. "Just up on the left," I tell the driver. I catch sight of someone sitting in a parked car when we drive past. I turn my head.

Wait, was that...?

The car draws to a stop, and I climb out. "Thank you." I close the door and squint my eyes to focus on the car.

What?

Before I can stop myself, I march across the road in the rain and knock on the window. Sebastian looks at me and winds it down.

"What are you doing here?" I snap.

"Stalking you. What does it fucking look like?"

20

April

MORE ATTITUDE.

I give up. I throw my hands up in the air in disgust. "Go home, Sebastian." I turn and storm towards my building.

Wait a minute.

I stop and look around the street before I march back to his car. "Where is your security?"

"Don't fucking start."

My eyes widen. "Are you stupid? You snuck away from your security guards?"

"I had to see you."

"And now you have." I hold my arms out wide in exasperation. "Go home, you idiot!"

Furious, I turn and march towards my building. This man is the living end. What's next?

I'm so glad taxpayers' money is funding his security team.

What an asshole.

I hear his car door slam and the alarm beep, telling me he's locked it.

I walk faster, but he runs to keep up with me. "Will you wait?"

"No." I march up the front steps and swipe my key. The doors open, and Sebastian is hot on my heels.

I walk into the elevator and turn towards the front. "If you don't have anything worthwhile to say, Sebastian, don't bother." I'm wet and angry. This man is beyond infuriating.

With his cold eyes locked on mine, he gets into the elevator and turns to face the front too. We ride to my floor in silence with adrenaline screaming through my veins.

Is my apartment a mess? I don't even remember how I left it, and he hasn't been here before.

Great.

I open the door with him standing behind me. I walk in and look around, relieved that it's not as messy as I imagined it would be.

He remains silent.

If he's here and wanting to talk, he'd better make it worthwhile.

"Do you have something to say?" I ask.

He stares at me for a moment. "Where were you tonight?"

"I went out for dinner."

"With who?"

"A friend. Don't go there, Sebastian. Not after what you've done this week. Don't you dare."

"What's that supposed to mean?" He gasps.

"You deny it?"

"Deny what?"

"Seriously?" I drop my head into my hands. Honestly, this is pointless. "Just go home."

When I look up, his eyes search mine. He seems unsure what to say. So lost and sad.

"Seb," I sigh.

His lips twist, like he's holding something in.

Empathy fills me. I don't know what's going on with him, but he's struggling with whatever it is.

"Are you going to say something?" I ask softly.

He looks around the room, unable to make eye contact.

"Sebastian," I urge. "Look at me."

His hands are clenched into fists by his sides, and he drags his eyes to meet mine. "Don't give up on me," he whispers.

I get a lump in my throat. "*You* gave up on *me*."

We stare at each other.

"I just—"

"Did it work...sleeping with her? Are you over me now?"

"It's not what it looks like."

I roll my eyes. "Please," I mutter under my breath.

"I stayed at another hotel so that I wouldn't get on my knees and beg you."

"Beg me for what?"

"For you to feel the same as I do!" he cries, as if outraged.

"And how is that?" I scoff. "I'm not a mind reader, Sebastian. Stop talking in riddles."

"You think I like this?" He throws his arms in the air "I hate being like this, and I hate that I fucking care about you."

I frown, surprised. Okay...not what I was expecting him to say. "When you didn't come back..."

He screws up his face in disgust. "How the hell could I sleep with someone else, April, when you're all I can fucking think about? I let you assume that because I knew it would make you walk away."

"Why is this so hard?" I whisper. "It shouldn't be this hard."

"I don't know."

I step towards him, and he takes a step back as if I'm some wild animal. I know for certain that if I want this to work, I have to step up and help him. He can't do this alone. He's broken. Maybe more than I am, and that's a lot.

I hate his ex-wife for what she's done to him.

"Seb," I say softly. "You're looking into this too much. You need to stop thinking about the past...or the future. There is no pressure or expectation between us."

He cups my cheek, and his scared eyes hold mine.

"Just think about now, because that's all we have," I tell him.

His chest rises and falls.

"If you want us to have a chance, you need to talk to me," I whisper.

"You don't want to know the fucked-up shit that's in my head."

Emotion overwhelms me, and suddenly, I do. I want to know everything about this beautiful man. The good, the bad, and the ugly.

There's a feeling between us. A closeness. An understanding.

Fear.

I sit down on the couch, not sure what to say, and he sits opposite me. He places his elbows on his knees and drops his head as he wrings his hands together. He's clearly stressed out.

"Would you like a drink?" I ask.

He nods.

I get up and look in the fridge. "I only have wine."

"That'll do."

I pour two glasses and pass him one. I drop back into my seat, and we both take a sip in silence.

"Where do you want this to go?" I ask. "In a perfect world, what happens in this story, Sebastian?"

"We work it out."

"That's what you want? To work it out?" I repeat to make sure I heard him right.

He nods as he swallows.

Progress.

"That's what I want, too, Seb."

A frown creases his brow, as if he's surprised by my answer.

I think back over my history and all the therapists I've seen over the years. None of their advice ever seemed to help me. One particular therapist comes to mind. He always wanted me to abstain from having sex because he thought it was counterproductive to me building any form of intimacy.

"You know what's wrong with us?" I ask.

He raises an eyebrow. "Enlighten me," he mutters dryly.

"We skipped a step. We went from cute flirting in a coffee shop one day, to you choking me and fucking my brains out in a brothel the next."

A trace of a smile crosses his face. He likes that memory.

"We missed the dating stage, Seb. We never built that friendship, or the trust that goes with it."

He frowns, processing my words.

Yes, this is it.

"Think about it," I say with renewed purpose. "We are so good together physically, but emotionally, we're useless. We're either fucking hard or fighting harder. There's nothing in between. No light and shade. No relationship can endure that, no matter how much we want this to work out."

"We can't change the past, April. I wish that I could."

I smile softly, hopeful for the first time all week. "But we can."

He frowns.

"What if we went back?"

"You've lost me."

"Your hang-up is based around sex, am I right? You only respond to one-night stands and paid sex, and then in the morning, you freak out because you think you owe me more."

He exhales heavily as if disgusted, and I know that I'm right.

"So let's take it off the table completely."

"What?" He screws up his face.

"Let's be together and not have sex."

"An attraction like ours can't be tamed, April. It's not that simple."

"We could try."

"Why would you want to do that? Sex is the only fucking thing that does work between us."

I stand and walk over to sit on his lap. I brush the dark hair back from his forehead and kiss him softly. "Because I know we are better than this."

I look up into his big, beautiful brown eyes, so tortured and flawed, and I kiss him again, our lips lingering over each other's.

"I can't be with you and not..." His voice trails off. "I wouldn't be able to—"

"Baby, listen to me." I take his face in my hands. "We have something, and it's far from perfect, but it's worth trying for. From the moment we met, I knew it was special, and sure, we've both made monumental mistakes, and you've been a real fucking asshole at times."

He twists his lips to stop a smile.

"But in the end, it's how we navigate things from here that matters, isn't it?"

He runs his hand tenderly down my back as he listens.

"And besides, Rome wasn't built in a day," I say hopefully.

"I'm sorry you have to deal with my bullshit," he murmurs.

My heart constricts, and I push his hair back from his face. "This isn't your fault. Never, ever apologize to me for being honest. I know better than anyone that the mind can be a dark place and that we have no control over the things that shape us. To be honest, Sebastian, I don't even know how I'm being so normal right now. It's usually me who's the fucked-up one."

He smiles as his tongue slowly slides through my parted lips. I open my eyes to see that his are firmly shut.

The tenderness dancing between us like a song.

Maybe we do have a chance.

We kiss again and again, and arousal rolls in as we hold each other.

No sex!

Short-term pain for long-term gain. Ah, what am I doing? I pull back from him.

"No sex, remember?"

He raises an eyebrow. "Come on, you have to be joking. There is no way we won't have sex. The attraction between us is way too strong."

"I want to try. If not for you, for me."

He frowns.

"You're not the only damaged one here, Seb, and I know this is it for me. I need to sort my shit out now or give up on relationships altogether. I'm thirty-one."

He gives me his first genuine smile of the day, and my heart melts. "You have plenty of time."

"Ha, you just say that because you're old."

He chuckles. "Perhaps."

I know if I keep sitting on his lap and kissing like this, I'll be bent over the couch in two minutes flat. I stand, and he swiftly pulls me back down onto his lap.

"Not yet," he says. "I haven't held you for four days, April. I need more time." He holds me tightly with his head to my chest, and I smile as hope blooms.

Sweet Mr. Garcia is in a league of his own.

I don't get him often. It makes me cherish it more when I do.

His lips drop to my nipple, and he gently tugs it with his teeth.

"Hey." I pull back from him. "Remember: no sex."

"It was a nibble. My cock was nowhere near the Motherload."

I giggle. "The Motherload. Is that what we're calling it now?"

"Maybe." He smiles. "It has a ring to it." He bites my nipple again.

"Stop." I laugh.

I refill our glasses and pass him his. He holds it up in the air, and I clink mine to his.

"What are we toasting?" I ask.

"To the most ridiculous social experiment of all time," he mutters dryly. "Motherload abstinence."

I burst out laughing, and he laughs too. We fall silent as we stare at each other, the air circling with something new.

Hope.

He looks around my apartment. "So, what do we do now?"

I haven't hung out with anyone on a platonic level for a really long time. It's always been sex driven. "I have no idea." I shrug. "Watch porn?"

"Works for me."

I giggle. "You're a sex maniac, Mr. Garcia."

"And you're excellent in bed. We're perfectly suited."

"No, you're next level."

"You can talk. I've never met a woman like you. You're more sexually charged than I am."

My mouth falls open as I fake horror. "I am not."

He raises an eyebrow.

I pinch my fingers together. "Little bit."

"I'll last longer than you will." He smirks.

I smile goofily over at him. I like this game. And of course he'll last longer than me. He doesn't have to look at his beautiful body like I do.

"Let's place a bet on it."

"What's the prize?"

"Hmm." I think for a moment. What's something that he would never want me to do? Okay. "If you cave before me, you have to let me fuck you with a strap-on dildo."

He snorts wine up his nose. "What the fuck?" he splutters as he launches into a full-blown coughing fit. He slaps his chest, mortified. "That's not fucking happening."

"Well, then, keep your cock away from the Motherload."

He throws his head back and laughs, and I do too. It feels so good to laugh together.

He falls serious. "What do I get if I win? Which I will, by the way."

"What do you want?"

"Hmm, the possibilities are endless." He narrows his eyes. "Let me get back to you on that."

"Or not. We both know I'm going to win, anyway."

His eyes darken, and the energy is there again between us.

It's atomic.

I need to change the subject. "We have to go back to your house," I say.

His face falls. "Why?"

"Because, as your legal representative, we both know you being here isn't a wise move. Especially with Theodore missing. If something were to go wrong and it came out that you'd snuck away..."

He rolls his eyes.

"I'll pack a bag and come to your house."

He opens his mouth to say something and then swiftly shuts it again.

"What?"

"Nothing."

"Say it."

"I'm playing in a golf tournament tomorrow."

"And?"

"I have to leave ridiculously early."

"Sebastian, I'm more than capable of amusing myself for a few hours."

His dark eyes drop down my body as if imagining something. "Doing what?"

"Not that." I widen my eyes. "Get your mind out of the gutter."

"Apparently, my body isn't allowed in it, so..." He shrugs. "Come on, let's go."

I walk into my bedroom and take out my overnight bag from the closet. Sebastian walks into my room and looks around. He walks to my shelves and carefully studies my photo frames. "Who's this?"

"That's my sister Eliza, and that's Nathan."

He picks it up. "She looks like you."

I smile. "She does."

"And the guy?"

"That's her partner. He's a surgeon."

He nods and places the frame back on the shelf. "Who's this?"

"My parents."

He places it back on the shelf, and then he picks up a rock. "What's this?"

"My lucky rock."

He smirks. "You have a lucky rock?"

I smile, feeling bashful. "Uh-huh."

He turns it over and looks at the bottom. "What luck has it brought?"

"I found you."

His eyes rise to meet mine, and he smiles softly. "You did." He places it back on the shelf. "But I found you the first time."

I think back to him coming to the coffee house for my bad coffee, day after day. "You know, there's been a lot of weird coincidences between the two of us," I say.

"Such as?"

I bite my lip to hide my smile. "You said that exact line the day we met."

"I did?" he asks, surprised.

I nod.

"What were the coincidences?"

"I saw you in the street the morning we met. You gave money to a homeless man on the street. After that, you came into my café."

He smiles softly, as if remembering. "Then I met this gorgeous blonde with a hot, tight ass."

"Who made great coffee—"

"Horrible coffee," he cuts me off.

"You kept coming back because it was so good."

"I was trying to warn people away. Duty of care to humanity."

I giggle. "And at the same time, I was broke and looking for another job."

He doesn't like this part of the story. "Don't remind me."

I hesitate, unsure if I should go on, but I want to go over this with him. We haven't discussed it all. "And you came to the club."

He pulls my hips towards his. "And I choked you out."

"You did more than that. You blew my mind."

The air between us crackles with electricity.

"And we spent a wonderful two weeks together, until..."

He tucks a piece of hair behind my ear. "Enough of the train wreck. I don't want to talk about it," he murmurs against my lips as he kisses me softly.

"I fell for you then, and you threw me to the side."

He stiffens and pulls back from me. "Why are we going over this shit?"

"Don't you ever think about these things?"

"Not if I can help it."

"Why not?"

"Because all I see is a whole lot of reasons why we don't work."

I hold my hands out wide. "And yet, here we are."

Our eyes are locked.

I take my overnight bag down and begin to throw my clothes into it. I pack my toiletry bag, a few clothes for tomorrow, and even some work clothes for Monday. I don't know why I feel the urge to lay it all out on the table for him, but I do.

"This is our last chance, Seb. If we don't get it right this time, I'm going home to America, and I'll never see you again."

"Is that a warning?"

"No."

"Then why bring it up?"

"I want you to know why this is important to me. I'm not being overdramatic, but I need to strip us back and try again for real this time."

He exhales heavily. "Why would you even think of this crap? It won't work. Sex has nothing to do with our problems."

Maybe he's right and this is totally ridiculous. "My therapist told me to do this for years, and I never wanted to. But tonight, I've been thinking maybe it was just the person I was with at the time."

"Oh." He fakes a smile. "That makes me feel so much better. You couldn't stop having sex with him, but you're more than happy to stop it with me." He walks towards my bedroom door. "I don't want to hear your fucking bullshit, April. Are you coming to my house or not?"

"Having a conversation is not bullshit, Sebastian," I call after him.

"Listen." He puts his head back around the doorframe. "I like having sex. If I wanted a platonic therapy session, I would go to an exuberantly expensive therapist for useless advice."

I roll my eyes.

"And don't roll your eyes at me," he snaps.

Seriously, this man is an idiot. Can't he at least understand where I'm coming from?

"Well, I'm doing this for me," I huff.

"That's great. You do your little thing for you, and I'll be jerking off beside you for me."

I roll my eyes again.

"And don't be surprised if some of my semen finds its way into your virginal mouth."

I smirk.

"I'm just saying." He holds his hands up. "The term 'choked out' may have just found a new meaning."

"Why are you such a sex maniac? All you think about is coming."

"Because you're insanely hot. Now, hurry the fuck up or I'm leaving without you." He walks out of the bedroom, and I hear him grab his keys and head for the door.

I smile after him. My deep and meaningful Mr. Garcia wasn't exactly sweet and understanding, but it's a start.

And that's all I'm asking for.

"April!" he groans.

I pick up my bag and head for the door. "Coming, dear."

I hear the shower turn off as I lie in bed, and my stomach flutters. Sebastian and I made out in the garage before we even got inside, in the kitchen, made out in the hallway, halfway up the stairs, and it is crystal clear that I didn't think this plan through at all.

We are hot together, and maybe he's right.

I just want to fuck him already.

No.

He walks out of the en suite bathroom with a white towel around his waist. My eyes drop down his thick, rippled torso, and my breath catches.

Sebastian Garcia is one hell of a beautiful man.

His eyes find mine, and he unwraps his towel and lets it fall to the floor.

Fucking hell...perfection.

He's tall, dark, rippled with muscles, and has the biggest brown eyes I've ever seen. This man is the epitome of sexuality.

His thick, hard cock hangs heavily between his legs, and he climbs into bed beside me. He lies on his back and puts his hands behind his head.

Arousal begins to flood through my body.

"Anything you want to do?" he asks casually.

I swallow the lump in my throat as my eyes linger over his engorged cock. Thick veins are coursing up the length of it. "Nope."

"Okay." He sits up and takes a bottle of lube from his bedside. He clicks it open and holds it up. "Last chance."

I begin to throb.

"Knock yourself out," I whisper as I turn on my side towards him. I rest my hand on my elbow to get in position to watch the show.

He lies back against his headboard and spreads his legs wide. I watch on as he squirts lube on his hard cock and gives himself a long, strong stroke.

Fuck.

He runs his hand up over his end and then back hard to the base. His hooded eyes find mine. "You going to kiss me while I do this, baby?" he whispers.

I shake my head. I know if I touch him anywhere, it's all over.

The sound of his voice all husky and hushed...it's the sound of the devil.

His strokes get harder, and the muscles in his arm and chest flex as he works himself.

Oh hell...this is the dumbest plan in all of history.

What was I thinking?

He widens his legs as his breathing picks up. I sit up, unable to act uninterested.

Fuck me.

He tips his head back and moans, and I swear, I feel it between my legs. I've never met a man so sexual. Harder and harder, the bed begins to move beneath me to the sound of his moans. I sit still, transfixed to the best porn I've ever watched.

The lube is loud, slurping and cracking.

Driving me wild.

"April, fuck, baby, get on me," he whispers.

Oh God, *I want to.*

"Keep going," I pant.

With his eyes locked on mine, he clenches his teeth and really lets himself have it. I can tell by his breathing that he's close.

I hold my breath, and he moans, deep and guttural, as hot white semen spurts across his stomach.

I stare at him in awe, and then without thinking, I drop my head and drag my tongue through his arousal.

Our eyes are locked.

I lick again and again, until his hand goes to the back of my head as he watches on.

I want him so bad.

His grip on my hair tightens, and he clenches his fist, dragging my face to his. "Kiss me." His lips take mine, and he moans when he tastes himself.

We kiss as if we have all the time in the world.

Oh, I'm lost.

This beautiful man does things to me.

"You taste good," I murmur against his lips. He pulls me over to lie on top of him, his arousal wet beneath me. I'm throbbing with want, wet and swollen.

Our heartbeats soar together as one.

"I need to sort you out," he breathes as he holds me close.

"No, baby." I kiss him again. "I'm waiting."

"For what?"

"For more."

His eyes search mine. An undercurrent of emotion runs between us.

I don't know how I made it through that without touching him.

I know what I want.

I'll try anything to get it.

"April." I feel a soft kiss on my lips. "I'm going, sweetheart. I'll be home in a few hours."

My eyes flutter open. "Okay." I wrap my arms around his neck. Sebastian is freshly showered and decked out in golf clothes. He smells delicious.

"What time is it?" I frown.

"Early. Go back to sleep."

"Okay." I smile, and with another soft kiss, he leaves me.

I hear the garage opening and closing before he drives away.

I'm not sure how long I doze for after he leaves, but I don't fall back into a deep sleep. Once awake, I pick up my phone and scroll through aimlessly. I hear a click in the distance.

Bentley sits up as if hearing something too. He walks to the door, his ears pricked.

I hear something downstairs.

Is somebody in the house?

I'm heading towards the door when I hear another sound. Fuck...what is that?

I see a small security screen iPad attached to the wall near the door of Sebastian's bedroom. I've never noticed it before. There are little pictures of each room in the house, and right on the bottom-left screen, I see movement.

What?

I lean in to get a better look. I watch the figure—they're dressed in full black with a balaclava on—walking down the hall before they go into the office.

I hold my breath as the person pulls off the balaclava, and my eyes widen in horror.

Helena, Sebastian's ex-wife, is in the house.

My heart races as I watch the screen. What the hell is she doing here?

She opens the top drawer of his desk and rattles around it, obviously looking for something.

Fuck.

I grab my phone and dial Sebastian's number, but it just rings and rings.

"Pick up," I whisper.

The call ends, and I dial the number again. It rings out again.

I watch on as Helena begins to go through the drawers.

I can't even go down there because I don't want her to see me.

I imagine her face when she finds me here, and the assumptions she'd make.

Oh shit.

"What the hell is she looking for?" I grip my head in a panic.

She moves to the filing cabinet and pulls on the drawers. They're all locked.

She searches through the desk drawers, eventually pulling out a small set of keys.

Oh, no, you don't. I don't know what you're looking for, but you're not fucking getting it. Especially not on my watch.

That's it!

After I tiptoe over to the double doors and sneak out onto the balcony, I dial 999.

"Hello, what service do you require? Fire, ambulance, or police."

"Hi," I whisper. "Police."

"Putting you through."

The phone rings, and someone picks up. "Hello, Police."

"Hi, there is an intruder in my house," I whisper.

"Where are you?" the man asks calmly.

"I'm outside on the upstairs balcony, and the intruder is downstairs. I'm watching them on the security cameras."

"Do they know you're there?"

"No, I don't think so. Please send someone quickly. I have no idea what they are doing."

"What's your address?"

I quickly tell him the address.

"A car will be there shortly. Stay where you are. Is anyone else in the house?"

"No." My heart is hammering in my chest. "The house belongs to Sebastian Garcia, but he isn't home."

"The politician?"

"Yes, that's him."

A thought comes to me. What if Sebastian comes home and he finds her in his office, looking through his things? He'll go mental, and who knows what she is capable of.

"Oh my God, please hurry," I whisper.

"Stay on the line."

"No, I've got to watch her on the security cameras inside. Hurry!" I hang up and turn my phone on silent. I quietly open the doors and sneak back inside, just in time to see her wrestle with the keys. She turns back to the desk, and Bentley walks in. She kicks her foot out to get rid of him, and I see red.

Don't mess with the dog, bitch.

He approaches her again and she kicks him. Something snaps inside me.

Fury is running through my veins, and before I know it, I'm standing at the office door.

"What are you doing?" I snap.

She's now going through the filing cabinet. She looks up and falters.

"Who are you?" she asks,

I'm your worst fucking nightmare.

"Wait." She frowns, trying to work out where she knows me from.

"I'm the cleaner. Get out."

She narrows her eyes, not believing me for a moment.

Shit, I don't actually want her to get out. I need to keep her here until the police turn up.

"I asked you what you were doing," I growl.

"Who are you?" She sneers.

I cross my arms over my chest. "It doesn't matter who I am. What the fuck are you doing here?"

"I came to visit my dog." She pushes something behind her back.

"Liar."

Uneasiness falls over me. What does she have in her hand? Is it a letter opener?

She wouldn't...

Is she dangerous?

Shit.

"What's behind your back?" I demand to know.

"Nothing."

The sound of sirens roaring up the street takes over, and as I look towards the window to see the police, she makes a run for it. I chase her at full speed, out of the office and up the hall. As we run into the kitchen, my toe catches on the rug and I fly headfirst into the granite countertop.

Searing pain tears through my skull. My vision blurs, and I fall to the floor. I hear the front door bust open in the distance.

Muffled voices.

Panic.

Pain.

Darkness.

21

Sebastian

THE ECHO of the club connecting with the ball can be heard as it echoes around us.

Julian raises his eyebrow, smirking, happy with his shot.

"Fuck you," I mutter in disgust.

I go through the clubs in my golf bag, sizing up the distance I have to hit the ball to. Hmm, which one?

I decide on the nine iron. I take it out and clean the head.

Spencer pulls his towel out to do the same, and he winces. He holds the hand towel to his nose and pulls it away in disgust. "Fuck, this stinks like shit."

I take a ball out and walk to the tee off.

Spencer smells his hand towel again. "Oh, fuck me. It smells like a sweaty whore bag."

I position myself to hit the ball.

Behind me, I hear Spencer inhale it once more. "No, sweaty ball sack. Smell this, Masters." He holds his towel out towards Julian. "Does this smell like sweaty ball sack or sweaty whore bag?"

"How would I fucking know?" Julian asks dryly. "I've never smelt either of those things."

Spencer chuckles, clearly amused.

"Shut up," I mutter as I line my club up. I pull it back over my shoulder, and just as I'm about to take a swing…

"It stinks really bad," Spencer says, interrupting my concentration.

I hit the ball, and it goes careering off to the side.

"Fucking hell, Spencer!" I snap. "Shut the fuck up. I'm taking off my shot because of interference."

He holds his hand towel towards me. "If you would just smell this thing, you would know what I'm saying."

I snatch it off him and stuff it in the garbage bin as I walk past it.

"Good riddance," Spencer huffs to the bin behind me.

We walk off towards my ball. "So, April has decided that we aren't having sex anymore," I say.

The two boys screw up their faces. "Why?"

I shrug. "I don't fucking know. Something about intimacy or some bullshit."

"What has no sex got to do with intimacy?" Masters asks.

"You tell me. Apparently, her therapist has been telling her to do this for years, but she hasn't wanted to do this with anyone else before me."

The boys' eyes meet mine.

"Yeah, that's what I thought too. Basically, I'm the only one she can stop having sex with. The old boyfriends still got it." I exhale heavily. "And get this…she even made a bet on it. If I give in and have sex with her, she wants to fuck my ass with a strap-on dildo."

Julian's face falls in horror while Spencer throws his head back and laughs hard. "Fuck me, Seb. For someone with such an innocent name, she sure is a fucking deviant."

I roll my eyes. "Well, rest assured it isn't happening."

"What isn't?"

"None of the above. No fucking of her or any fucking of me."

We get to my ball, and I drag it out from the tree. We hear a phone ringing somewhere.

"Whose phone is that?" Masters asks.

"Not mine," I reply. "I accidently left mine in the car."

A ding sounds. Someone has a text message.

Spencer digs his out of his golf bag and reads the text. "Oh, get fucked." He drags his hand down his face. "Not that. Anything but fucking that."

"What?"

"Charlotte wants to go to Edward's for dinner."

Masters and I chuckle. Spencer's brother-in-law is the bane of his existence.

"Happy wife, happy life," Masters replies casually. "It could be worse. She could want to fuck you with a dildo."

They both burst out laughing, and I roll my eyes...again.

Fuckers.

"You ride that thick fake cock, big boy." Spencer winks at me.

Masters gyrates his hips and pretends to slap something.

I exhale heavily as I take my next shot. "I don't know why I tell you losers anything."

"Because you need us to take you to the hospital when she breaks you in."

They laugh again.

I slam my club back into my golf bag and storm off in the direction of my ball. "I need new friends."

Four hours later, I get into my car to find my phone where I left it, on charge.

I pick it up.

7 Missed Calls - April

That's weird. She never calls me. I dial her number.

"You've reached April Bennet. I'm sorry I can't get to the phone

296

right now. Please leave a message, and I'll call you back as soon as I can. Have a nice day."

"Hi, babe. I'm on my way home now," I leave on her voicemail.

An hour later, I pull into my street to see two police cars parked in my driveway. The front door of the house is open, and I can see people moving around inside. "What in the world...?"

April.

I pull up and rush inside. "What's going on?"

The policeman turns to me. "Mr. Garcia?"

"Yes."

"It appears you had a home invasion."

"W-where's April?" I stammer.

"She's been transferred to Memorial Hospital by ambulance."

"She's hurt?" I gasp.

"She called emergency services because someone was in the house. When the patrol car got here, they found her unconscious."

My eyes widen. "What the fuck?"

"We're dusting the house for fingerprints, but unfortunately, the security cameras weren't recording. Do you have any idea why they were off?"

"That's impossible. They're always recording."

"Yes, but—"

She's hurt.

"Not now!" I yell as panic sets in. I turn and run to my car. I take off at speed.

Has she been shot?

I grip the steering wheel with force, and I drive like a maniac.

This isn't happening.

The traffic is backed up, and I run my hands through my hair in frustration. "Come on!" I yell.

My phone rings through my car speakers. It's Spencer.

I click accept. "Oh my fucking God!" I yell. "There's been a break-in at my house. April is hurt. She's gone to the hospital in an ambulance."

"What the fuck? Is she okay?"

"I don't know, I'm in traffic, and..." I peer up the road to see that the traffic is static for miles. "Fuck it!" I punch the steering wheel.

"Which hospital?" he asks.

"Memorial."

"I'll meet you there."

I hit the end button and do a U-turn in the middle of the road. Cars honk their horns. I drive up and over the curb and cut the corner to take a shortcut. Twenty minutes later, I screech to a halt outside the front of Memorial Hospital. I get out of my car and run to the reception area.

"Hello. A-April Bennet has been brought in by ambulance..."

The lady fakes a smile, as if annoyed by my rudeness. "Hello."

"Yes, hi." I widen my eyes. I don't have time for you, bitch. "Where is she?"

The woman slowly types the details into her computer, and then she waits.

"Well—"

"I'm looking, sir," she cuts me off. "What was the surname?"

"Bennet."

She looks again.

"Oh my God...will you hurry up?" I snap. "I don't have time for this."

The woman's eyes rise to meet mine and then slowly go back to her computer.

For fuck's sake.

"Here she is," she replies, monotone. "She's still in Accident and Emergency."

"Where's that?"

"Go back out through the front doors and turn right. It's about fifty meters. You will see a large Accident and Emergency sign."

"Thank you." I run out the doors, down to A&E, and over to reception. "Hello, my girlfriend April Bennet has been brought in by ambulance," I pant.

The nurse looks up and does a double take. "Mr. Garcia?"

Oh no, she recognizes me. "Yes. Where is April, please?"

She types into her computer.

For fuck's sake, doesn't anyone know what is going on around here?

"Take a seat, sir. I'll have a nurse come out and get you."

"I need to go in now!" I snap. "It's an emergency." My eyes hold hers. "Please."

She exhales, stands, and opens the security door. "This way, please."

I follow her down the corridor and into what looks like a triage room. There are numerous beds in one huge room. Each bed is surrounded with a curtain.

"This way." We go to a cubicle, and she peers in. "Hello." She smiles. "I have April's partner here."

"Yes, come in," a male voice replies.

The woman pulls back the curtain, and my face falls. April is lying in bed with a deep-purple and black eye. She offers me a sleepy smile. A doctor is with her.

"Oh my God." I rush to her side, bend, and kiss her temple. "Are you all right?" I whisper as I brush the hair back from her forehead.

She nods with a soft smile. "I'm fine, Seb."

"You are not fine. You've suffered a serious concussion," the doctor interrupts.

"What happened?" I ask.

"Someone broke into the house."

"They hit you?"

"No," she huffs. "I chased them and tripped on the rug. I fell into the marble kitchen counter."

My eyes widen. "You chased them?"

"Excuse me," the doctor says. "I'll be back in a moment." He walks out of the room, and I bend and kiss April's forehead. "I'm so sorry. I left my phone in the car, and—"

"Sebastian, it was Helena."

I pull back to look at her. "What?"

"It was Helena in the house. I was watching her from upstairs through the surveillance cameras. She was looking for something in your office, then she kicked Bentley. I snapped and marched down there."

I frown, imagining the scenario.

"Sebastian, she had something hidden behind her back. She took something from your filing cabinet. I was chasing her to get it back."

My blood runs cold, and my heartbeat pounds in my ears. "What was it?"

"I couldn't see, but she got it out of the filing cabinet."

"Have you told anyone else this?" I whisper.

She shakes her head. "No, I wanted to talk to you first. She didn't recognize me."

Adrenaline surges through my veins. "Don't tell anyone. Say you saw nothing."

"It will be on the cameras."

"They weren't recording."

"Why not?" April's eyes widen. "What are you going to do?"

What needs to be done.

The curtain flicks open. "Time for your CT scan." The nurse smiles.

"Don't you worry." I bend and kiss April on the temple, faking a smile. "Rest, my love." I push her hair back from her forehead. "I'll wait here for you, okay?"

She gives me a weak smile before she's wheeled away.

I put my hands on my hips and turn to face the wall. My heart is pumping hard, and fury fills my every cell.

This time, Helena has gone too far.

22

Sebastian

"I swear to God, we need to get this bitch snuffed out," Spencer whispers as he blows into his coffee cup.

I roll my eyes. "Who says 'snuffed out'?"

"I do."

"Right, because you're so gangster," I huff. "Spencer Jones, Mafioso."

"Yeah, well, this fucking bitch has got it coming. I could be gangster if I wanted to be. I could totally get her snuffed out. Surely Masters knows some hit men who owe him a favour?"

I look around guiltily. "Keep your voice down," I whisper.

"What did she take? That's what I want to know," he asks. "What the fuck was she doing in your house, and how did she get in if the locks weren't touched?"

"That's what I want to know too."

We both fall silent as we think.

"Helena doesn't do anything without an agenda," I say.

"I know, but what is it?" Spencer asks.

"Money. It's always about money with her."

"What about how she chased her?"

I get a vision of April chasing Helena out of the house, and I smile, impressed. "She's a ballsy bitch, I'll give her that."

"Mr. Garcia?" A doctor walks around the corner.

"Yes?" I stand.

"April's tests are all back. She has a heavy concussion but is clear to be released into care. Are you okay to stay with her, or should I call family?"

"I'll look after her. Is everything okay?"

"Thankfully, she'll make a full recovery. I've written up a prescription for pain meds. She'll have a headache for a few days. She's very lucky."

"Thank you." I shake his hand. "I really appreciate it."

The doctor leaves us alone, and I turn to Spencer. "Do you want to come in and say hi?"

He thinks for a second. "No, it's okay. I'll meet her properly some other time. She wouldn't be in the mood for me. Send her my best wishes, though." He shakes my hand. "Keep me posted." He heads for the door.

"Spence?" I call, and he turns back. "Thanks."

He flashes me a smile, and with a curt nod, he turns and leaves.

If ever there was a faithful friend, it's Spencer Jones.

The late-afternoon sunlight shines through the window. April is fast asleep on my bed, and I'm sitting on a chair in the corner of the room.

No locks were broken, which can only mean one thing. Helena had a key.

How?

The locksmiths should be here soon. I've had my security company working on the alarm systems all afternoon. Apparently, the recording function was turned off from inside the house about three weeks ago, which means this isn't the first time Helena has been here.

What the fuck does she want?

I haven't been able to ask April any more questions—she's still sleepy—but I have this lead ball in the pit of my stomach.

If April had hit her head any harder, she may have...

I close my eyes.

I'm sickened that things have gone the way that they did.

"Seb?" April whispers.

I get up and move to sit on the side of the bed. "I'm here, baby." I take her hand in mine, bend, and softly kiss her cheek. "I'm not leaving. Go back to sleep."

She smiles sleepily and closes her heavy eyelids once more.

I hold her hand as I stare at her beautiful face. She has the bluest black eye I've ever seen.

So many thoughts are running through my mind. So much hate and resentment. Feelings that I never thought I'd have for someone I once loved.

What was Helena looking for?

Tomorrow, we have to talk to the police, and a decision needs to be made as to what I want to do with this. I know what I want to do.

I picture my hand around Helena's throat. Nothing would give me more pleasure than strangling that bitch.

If only...

April

The delicious aroma of bacon and eggs wakes me from my slumber.

I stretch and look around Sebastian's bedroom. Jeez, what day is it?

I feel like I've been zonked out for a week.

I get up and go to the bathroom. As I'm washing my hands, I look in the mirror and cringe. My eye is closed, and it's so bruised, it's a deep blue. I gently pat the swollen, sore tissue around my eyebrow and wince in pain.

Hell, I did a good job of it, that's for sure.

Damn it, I wish I had caught that bitch and punched her square in the face.

How dare she come here?

I wash my face and try to open my eye, but it throbs. Bloody hell, how do boxers do this all the time? Black eyes are surprisingly painful. Even my eyeball is sore.

I tie my hair back, pull on Sebastian's robe, and make my way downstairs towards the kitchen.

I'm starving.

I find Sebastian in the kitchen. He's stirring something in a frying pan, wearing navy pajama pants and a white T-shirt.

He looks up and gives me a breathtaking smile. "Here she is, Rocky Balboa."

I smile as I make my way over to him. He takes me into his arms. "Clumsy Balboa, more like it." I peer into the frying pan to see an omelette. "That smells delicious."

He kisses my forehead. "How are you feeling?"

"Good." I shrug. "A little embarrassed, if I'm honest."

"Why?"

"Because at the most crucial moment of all time, I fall over and clock my head. I should have caught her."

"Are you sure you fell over?"

"Yes."

His eyes hold mine, as if not believing me for a second. Wait, he doesn't think...

"She wouldn't beat me in a fight, you know," I say as I put my hands on my hips.

He bites his bottom lip to hide his smile.

"I'm pretty tough, Sebastian."

"I have no doubt." He kisses me softly. "Never pictured you for a brawler, though."

"Yeah, well, some people trigger me."

He chuckles. "Hungry?"

"Starving." I look at the clock on the wall and step out of his arms. "Shit, we're late for work."

"Not so fast." He pulls out the stool at the kitchen counter and sits me down. "I've cancelled the trip away this week, and we're both working from home for a few days." He puts two cups of coffee on the counter.

He never has a day off. "Why?"

"Because you look like the evil dead, and I'm playing nurse." He passes me a fork.

I smile goofily as I take it from him. "Oh." I take a bite of my omelette. "This is good. Thank you."

He flicks the tea towel over his shoulder and watches me eat.

"Are you eating?" I ask.

"I ate two hours ago."

"Oh." I shovel another mouthful in. "So, what was she looking for?" I ask.

He twists his lips. "I have no idea."

"She took something; I know she did."

He pulls out the stool beside me and sits down. "Tell me exactly what happened, from the beginning."

"I was upstairs, and I was drifting in and out of sleep. I rolled over to get my phone, and Bentley was on the floor beside me. He sat up with his ears pricked up, as though he heard something. Then I heard something. I thought you must have come home." I shrug. "I walked out into the hallway, and I saw the security screens. Someone was walking up the hallway, dressed in black with a balaclava on."

"A balaclava?" he gasps.

"Yes, like full robber's kit. I was freaking out. I called you, and you didn't answer. I kept watching the screen, and the person walked into your office."

He listens intently.

"Has she been here before?" I ask.

"Never."

"Well, she knew where she was going. It wasn't like it was her first time in the house."

"Hmm."

"Anyway, she got into the office and took off her balaclava. At that point, I was relieved."

"Why?"

"Because it wasn't a serial killer."

"Trust me, a serial killer is the lesser evil." He widens his eyes.

"She started going through your desk drawers, and I was freaking out. I didn't want her to see me, and I couldn't get you, so I went out onto the balcony and called the police. Why weren't you answering your phone?"

"I left it in the damn car."

I roll my eyes. "Then she was trying to get into your filing cabinet. She got the keys, and then she tripped over Bentley, so she kicked him."

"She *what?*"

"She kicked him."

"How hard?"

"Not really hard, but enough for me to march down there. When I got there, she was rummaging through the top drawer. She put something behind her back."

"What did it look like?"

"A piece of paper, I think. I don't know for sure, but it was from the back of the drawer. I'll show you."

"Eat your breakfast first."

"No." I march down to his office and pull out the drawer. The dividers are spaced apart at the back. "Here. Whatever she took, it's from around here."

The divider heading reads:

Bank Statements

"Why would she want a bank statement?" I ask.

"To see how much money I have." He frowns, deep in thought.

"Why would she want to know that?"

"I don't know." He takes my hand. "Your omelette is going cold."

"I'm sorry I let her get away." I sigh as I follow him up the hall.

"Don't you worry about Helena. She's not your problem." He sits me back down at the kitchen counter.

I pick up my fork. "Yeah, well, she's messing with the wrong woman."

He smirks.

"If she wants to get to you, she has to get through me." I thumb my chest.

He breaks into a breathtaking broad smile and reaches up to touch my eye socket. I wince.

"It's such a relief to have a brave, burly bodyguard," he says.

I smile, embarrassed. "Don't let this black eye fool you, Seb. I am one tough motherfucker."

"I know."

"And if I wanted to take her down, I totally could."

"Of course you could, sweetheart." He tucks a piece of my hair behind my ear as he smiles lovingly at me.

"Don't look at me like that. I'm hideous."

"I happen to think you look lovely."

"Are you making fun of me?"

"One hundred percent. You're hideous."

I giggle, and he leans over to kiss me. "Eat your omelette before I make you eat dick."

It's midafternoon and, like teenagers playing hooky, we are back in bed. It's warm and dark, and we're nestled up together underneath the blankets. Sebastian is leaning on his elbow, lying on his side, facing me. I'm wearing panties and a T-shirt, and his hand is roaming over my body as his eyes hold mine.

It's the weirdest thing. We haven't had sex for a long time—maybe a week—and yet I've never felt closer to him. There's an unspoken tenderness passing between us. The same one that used to turn up when we'd lie in each other's arms after we'd made love. Only now it's there all the time.

Maybe the therapist did know what she was talking about?

"Maybe I should take your temperature," he whispers as his lips softly take mine. He slides my panties down my legs to take them off.

I smile against his lips. "You really should."

If I were stronger, I would tell him to stop, but I don't want him to.

I need him.

This.

He spreads my legs, and his fingertips slowly trail up my inner thigh. Our eyes are locked, and the air between us is electric. He dusts the back of his fingers over the lips of my sex, and a trace of a smile crosses his face. "Just as I suspected, thirty-seven point two," he whispers.

I giggle. Best thermometer ever.

Unable to control it, my legs spread wider, and I put my top leg over his body to completely open myself up to him.

In.

I want you in.

His fingers start to circle my lips, and I hold my breath.

Deeper and deeper.

Oh...

He slowly slides a thick finger in, and we both inhale sharply as his lips take mine.

He adds another finger, and my eyes flutter closed. He takes both fingers out and explores again. He circles them over my back entrance, and I hold my breath again. "Why don't we have sex here?" he asks. His voice is soft and husky. Aroused.

"That's not my thing. We will never have sex there."

"Have you done it before?"

I give a subtle shake of my head. "No."

His eyes blaze with desire, and I can almost hear his psyche screaming with excitement. "Why not?"

"It's too much."

"Too much what?" he whispers as he bends and bites my

nipple through my shirt. He slides his thumb deep into my sex, his fingers still exploring that forbidden zone.

The double pleasure sensation makes my mouth fall open as we stare at each other.

"I'm saving that for my forever man."

He smiles as he kisses me, his pinkie inching in a little. The feeling of his thumb pumping deep inside of me and his pinkie finger hovering there does things to me, and I moan with a shudder.

The need for a deeper connection steals my breath.

Fuck, yes.

He bites my bottom lip. "Don't tell me you don't want this. I can feel the need in your body." His tongue delves deep into my mouth as he kisses me passionately, and I can't deny it. When he touches me there, it feels too good. Who am I kidding? Every touch from Sebastian Garcia is out of this world.

He rolls over me and spreads my legs just as the doorbell rings from downstairs. He frowns and keeps kissing me, but it rings again. His phone begins to buzz on the side table.

"Fuck off!" he snaps, annoyed at the interruption.

The doorbell rings once more, and another text comes in.

"Check who it is?" I whisper.

He sits up and reads his phone. It's a message from Bart.

I'm at your front door.

He rolls his eyes and sits up. "Bart's here."

"Oh God." My body is screaming out for more. "It's okay, you go."

He exhales heavily and stands. He leans down, and with his hands on the mattress above my head, he kisses me. "Don't move a muscle."

"You think I'm just going to lie here with my legs spread, waiting for your return?"

"You'd better." He stands and rearranges his dick in his track pants. He pulls an oversized sweater on and checks himself in the mirror. "Don't want to be scaring Bart with my hungry dick," he mutters.

I lie still, all hot and flustered. "I'm pretty sure Bart's seen hungry dicks before."

"True."

Ahh, so he knows Bart is gay. Another piece of the puzzle I didn't know. I wonder if he knows about Jeremy.

He disappears downstairs, and I lie in bed. I hear him open the door, followed by Bart's distinctive voice.

I sit up so I can listen. Their voices are muffled. I quickly get dressed and head to the door and out into the hallway.

"Well, what was she doing here?" I hear Bart ask.

"Looking for something," Sebastian replies.

"Like what? Where was she?"

"My office. I'll show you the drawer she was in." I hear them walk down the hallway and into Sebastian's office.

I wonder how long Bart has been dealing with Helena's bullshit. He's been with Sebastian for a while, but I don't think she's done anything like this for years, although I could be wrong. I slink down to sit on the top step as I wait for them to finish.

What *was* that bitch doing here?

I get a memory of her hiding something behind her back. Damn it, why didn't I grab it from her? What was it?

Their voices become loud again as they walk towards the front door.

"You tell me now," Bart says. "If there are any skeletons you are hiding, anything that you could think of that she could dig up, I need to know."

"No. Nothing new," Sebastian replies.

"It's okay if there is, but I need to know now so that I can act before the story hits."

Shit.

I can't sit here and pretend like there's not something he

should know. It's only a matter of time before Helena works out who I am. Bart is my boss. He deserves the truth.

I stand and walk down the stairs. Sebastian glances up and sees me, and his face falls.

Bart looks up, startled, and frowns. "April?" I give him an awkward smile, and his eyes flicker to Sebastian in question. His eyes come back to me. "What happened to you?"

"I had an altercation with a kitchen countertop," I say. "There is something you should know, Bart."

Bart raises his eyebrow, already knowing what it is and seemingly unimpressed. "Go on..."

"I was here when Helena broke in. She didn't know who I was, and I pretended to be the cleaner."

He exhales heavily.

"I chased her, tripped, and hit the kitchen counter. I ended up in the hospital. The police are coming over this afternoon for questioning."

He puts his hands in his suit pockets, and his eyes drift to Sebastian for clarification.

I glance over to see Sebastian is glaring at me with a thermonuclear anger.

Huh?

"Do you have something to tell me?" Bart asks, looking between us.

Sebastian twists his lips, and his unimpressed eyes hold mine.

"Yes," I reply. "I've been seeing Sebastian on a personal level for a while. We met years ago and have recently reconnected." I shrug nervously. "We are...together."

"You didn't think to tell me this before you started?" he snaps.

"With due respect, I didn't realize we would be working with Sebastian." My eyes flicker between the two of them. "I'm resigning from your team, effective immediately. I'm going back to my normal duties."

Sebastian's jaw clenches as he glares at me. "You don't need to resign."

"Yes, she does," Bart interrupts. "You think I need this publicity nightmare? The Deputy Prime Minister is sleeping with his legal counsel. For fuck's sake, what are you two thinking?" He sighs. "I should have been told."

"I'm telling you now," I hit back. "And for the record, we *are* dating, so you need to get over it and handle Helena."

"I'm really disappointed, April. I didn't think you were the type to sleep with a client. This will not look good on your résumé."

"Watch your fucking mouth," Sebastian barks. "She isn't sleeping with a client. You heard her. We're together. And she's right! You just fucking worry about Helena."

I bite my lip to hide my smile. Hope runs through me.

"What am I supposed to say when the story breaks about you two?" he retorts.

"There is no story," I reply sharply. "I don't work for him now. I'm just a regular lawyer that he's dating. There is no headline story here anymore, Bart. What you need to work out is what the hell Helena took from this house."

"Are you really going to give up the opportunity of a lifetime?" Bart asks me.

"I would give up any job on Earth to be with him." My eyes find Sebastian's, and his brow furrows.

It's true, I would.

I have.

"Fine." Bart rolls his eyes and makes for the door. "I'll be in touch." The door slams on his way out.

"Are you serious?" Sebastian growls.

Huh? He's angry?

My face falls.

"How dare you?" He turns and marches into the kitchen. I run after him like a puppy.

"W-what do you mean?" I stammer.

"You didn't think to discuss this with me before you blurt it out to the fucking world?"

I open my mouth to say something, but no words come out.

"Is this your master plan?" he yells. "Railroad me into a relationship?"

"*What?*"

"We have never discussed coming out about us. And you
resigned from your fucking job. What the hell was that?" he cries.
"Are you deaf, dumb, or just plain stupid?"

My eyes bulge as I put my hands on my hips. "Listen here, you
asshole," I growl. "I don't know who the fuck you think you are,
but I will tell my boss the truth. And for the record, we are in a
fucking relationship, so you'd better grow the fuck up and appreciate it."

"Or what?"

"Or you'll see what fucking happens, that's what!"

"Do not threaten me, April."

"I'm sick of your childish bullshit, Sebastian." I turn and march
towards the stairs, and he follows me like a bull.

"What does that mean?"

I turn on him like the devil. "It means that you had better man
up. Grow some balls and let yourself love me or step the fuck back
so that someone else can."

He narrows his eyes. "Another threat?"

"That one's a promise, asshole."

"Stop calling me asshole."

"Then stop acting like one!" I yell back. I take the stairs two at a
time.

"You may as well go home!" he cries after me. "I will not be rail-
roaded into anything, April. What next? You demand I marry
you?"

My anger explodes.

I get to the top of the stairs and see his runners sitting in the
hall. I pick one up and hurl it down at him. He ducks out of the
way, deflecting it to the side. It hits the wall with a thud. "I'll go
home when I'm good and ready and not a minute before!" I shout.
Nobody makes me angrier than this fucking stupid man.

Ouch, yelling hurts. I put my hand over my eye.

"What?" he yells.

"You're hurting my eye!" I cry.

"Well, you're hurting my fucking brain!"

"Impossible, you don't have one." I march up the hall and into his bedroom, and I slam the door hard.

I flop onto the bed in disgust. Adrenaline is pumping through my body.

Fuck you, *asshole*.

I snuggle into my pillow. It's dark, and I glance over to see the clock. 8:00 p.m.

Shit, I've been asleep for hours.

I lay here and listened to Sebastian slamming things around downstairs for a while, and then I must have drifted off. The house is silent now, and I wonder if he is over his tantrum yet.

I get up and go to the bathroom. I wash my hands and go back to bed.

I pick up my phone and text my mom and my sister. I scroll through Instagram for a while before the bedroom door opens, and Sebastian comes into view.

His eyes find mine, and without saying anything, he walks into his wardrobe.

I roll my eyes. Great, now he's sulking and getting dressed to go out.

I lie still, waiting for his next tantrum. He is the last-word freak. He won't let this go.

I know he won't.

He's right, though. I should have discussed this with him first, but in my defence, I was just being honest.

Sebastian walks out of the wardrobe completely naked and leans against the doorframe. My eyes drop down to see that he's rock-hard.

Huh?

We stare at each other for a moment.

"You have no idea what you're asking."

Uneasiness falls over me. "What do you mean?"

He pushes off the wall to come and stand in front of me. His hard cock is only inches from my face.

"Sebastian..."

He pulls my T-shirt over my head and throws it to the side. He grabs my foot and drags me to the side of the bed as his dark eyes hold mine.

I swallow the lump in my throat. I know this look. It's the one he used to give me at the Escape Club. The one where he fucks me like he hates me. Truth be told, he probably does.

He reaches down and puts his hand around my throat, gripping it hard as we stare at each other.

Electricity crackles between us.

"I have needs," he whispers.

Excitement tears through me. This is wrong, but holy fuck, it's hot.

"So do I."

I spread my legs. His grip around my throat tightens as my heart hammers in my chest.

"Having a boyfriend like me..."

I know.

I give him a nervous nod. Somehow, I don't think my no-sex rule is going to apply here tonight.

He's angry, and I know that we need this.

This is next level.

He bends and spits on my sex, creating a lubricant. Then he bends and licks me there. I nearly convulse on the spot. What the hell?

How is he so hot?

He rises and slides his tip through my wanting lips, then slams into me. The burn of his possession stings, and I whimper.

Our eyes are locked as he holds his weight off me with one hand, the other still tightly around my throat.

"Seb," I whimper, and he squeezes harder.

"Don't."

I'm silenced, the darkness taking over.

Oh God... This is what I crave, the darkness within him.

Sating the darkness within me.

His thick cock begins to pump me hard, the sound of his moans echoing around the room. All I can do is clench around his beautiful body.

He won't kiss me, instead licking my parted lips. The pleasure building between us is like a fire.

His raw dominance, his thick cock...*my heart free-falling from my chest.*

He flips us so that he is sitting, and I am over him. We come face-to-face as we stare at each other.

"I love you," he whispers, as if pained.

My eyes well with tears because, hell, if this isn't the best 'I love you' I've ever had.

"I know."

His face falls.

"I love you too," I whisper.

23

Sebastian

THE DRONE BUZZING in the background wakes me from my slumber. I wince, roll over, and turn off my alarm.

I lie for a moment to get my bearings, and I look around. I'm alone in bed. Where is she?

Thoughts of last night run through my mind. I close my eyes in disgust.

Fuck.

A moment of weakness has ruined everything. I get up and walk to the bedroom door and listen. I can hear CNN in the distance, and April talking to Bentley.

She's downstairs. Relief fills me, and I frown as the realization hits me.

Stop it.

I shower, get dressed for work, and make my way downstairs. I find April in the kitchen, drinking coffee as she cuts up fruit.

She looks up and smiles. "Hey, you."

"Hello." I stand on the spot.

She raises an eyebrow, and I raise one back.

"Are you going to kiss me good morning?" she asks.

And so it begins.

I exhale and walk over to her. She takes me in her arms, rises on her toes, and kisses me softly. I feel it in the pit of my stomach, and I pull out of the kiss. "I have to go. I'm running late."

"It's only 6:45 a.m."

"Early meeting."

She smiles up at me.

"What?"

"Are you in the middle of a freak-out right now?"

I swallow the lump in my throat. It's a strong possibility. "No."

"Are you regretting anything?"

I hesitate for a moment, and she raises an eyebrow.

"Nope."

She smiles up at me as she runs her hand over my suit-covered cock. "Do you still love me?" she asks.

"Oh, for fuck's sake, April. Enough of the lovey-dovey crap. You caught me in a moment of weakness. We don't have to go on and on about it."

She giggles and rearranges the lapels of my suit jacket. "Okay."

"What are you doing today?"

"Well, I can't go into the office with this black eye. I'll go home and work from there."

My eyes hold hers. "Stay here."

"Why?"

"I've arranged security for you."

She frowns. "Why?"

"Have you looked in the mirror lately?"

"Sebastian, it's okay. I'm safe."

"That's debatable."

"Do you think she's going to try and hurt me?"

I rearrange the cuff links on my sleeves, trying to act uninterested. "I don't know what that woman is capable of, but I'm not taking any risks."

She smiles proudly, as if knowing something I don't.

I turn towards my coffee machine and flick it on. "So, you will stay here?"

"Yes, dear."

"And you won't leave without security?"

"No, dear."

"Stop patronizing me, April. I don't like it." I fill my cup, and her arms come around me from behind. She kisses my back.

"Do you want to go out to dinner tonight?" she asks.

"No."

She lets out a deep sigh and steps back from me.

Fuck, *I'm being a prick.*

It's not her fault that I'm fucked up. I turn and take her into my arms. "I can bring home dinner, if you like."

She acts uninterested when I kiss her cheek.

"Anything you want. Text me when you know what you feel like." I kiss her to try and sweeten the deal.

"What we had last night was pretty good," she says casually.

"All right." I take a sip of my coffee. "Choked-out chicken it is."

She laughs out loud, and it brings with it a warm, fuzzy feeling. She has the most beautiful laugh I've ever heard.

She kisses me and pushes the hair back from my forehead. "I'm feeling like the luckiest girl alive today, Seb."

My heart swells before I quickly recover. "Yeah, well, you do have a brain injury." I hug her. "I have to go."

"Okay."

I grab my keys and briefcase, and I take one last look at the woman wearing my dressing gown in my kitchen, with her messed-up hair and black eye. I've never seen anything so beautiful.

It's me who's feeling lucky.

"Next question," I snap, and point to another reporter. Fuck, I hate this part of the job.

"Can you release any further details on Theodore's condition?"

"Not at this stage," I reply. "Next question."

"Is he having a mental breakdown?" someone yells.

No, but I might if they keep this up.

"Theodore is suffering from exhaustion. There is no need for concern, he just needs to rest," I lie. "He will be back at work before you know it."

Fuck it, this can't go on. We need to fess up that he's a loose cannon with a drug problem and admit that he's missing. Where the hell could he be? We have so many people out searching, and with every day that passes, my fear for his welfare escalates.

At first, I thought he'd just gone on a bender with a wild woman. Now, I'm not so sure. His phone has been switched off for weeks. He hasn't touched his credit cards, although I know that he does have others in different names so that he can escape the press when he wants to disappear. I guess his plan has worked a little too well this time.

I wish I paid more attention to those fake names when I saw them way back then. Never in a million years did I think this would ever eventuate.

"Are you going to supersede the Prime Minister?" someone calls.

"No." I look around. "Next question."

April

The warm afternoon sun is beaming down on me in Sebastian's backyard, and I smile up at the sky. The rare London sunshine is a delight.

Bentley is stretched out beside me. I think I've found my own little piece of paradise.

I love this house.

I can see why Seb is so attached to it. My mind goes back to Helena and the fact that she's been in here. We are still trying to work out how she got a key. Apparently, a few weeks ago, she turned up at Sebastian's sister's house to 'see' Bentley when she had him. Putting the pieces together now, Seb and his sister think that she was there to steal the key to Seb's house, because she turned up again a few hours later, saying that she left her scarf there. That's when he thinks she went and got a key cut and was sneaking it back in.

Bitch.

I wonder what she was looking for.

I walk back into the house and wash my coffee cup with my mind ticking. What does he have that she wants so badly? I walk down to Sebastian's office and pull out the filing cabinet drawer that she had opened. She was searching somewhere at the back. I go to the area I think she was looking, and I read the dividers.

Bank Statements

I take them out and lay them across the desk to look through all the dates. There's nothing missing. All the statements are here. I go to the next divider and go through them. Nothing missing.

Hmm.

I look again and again, and I get to a drawer right at the back. I lay them all out and frown. The statement goes from March, April, May, and then it jumps to July.

There's a statement missing here.

I turn it over and read the back, and then I read the front.

It's a credit card statement from six, nearly seven years ago. I slip into the seat and roll my fingers on the desk as I think. What would she want his credit card number for?

What does she want?

I text Sebastian.

Cancel your credit card ending in 507.
Helena has the number.

A reply instantly comes back.

Already done

x

Good.

I narrow my eyes as contempt fills my every cell. If you want to hurt him, bitch, you'll have to get through me.

It's just gone 7:00 p.m. when the garage door goes up.

I called Seb earlier. I wanted to cook dinner for the two of us. Takeaway choked-out chicken didn't sound appealing. I have a baked dinner in the oven, and I've had a productive day. I vacuumed the house, did some washing, took a nap, and I made a little surprise for Sebastian, which could go either way, but it had to be done. I guess I'll soon find out by his reaction. I hope I haven't overstepped the mark.

I know I have, but I needed to do this for me.

I stir the gravy and take the large baking dish out of the oven. The heavenly aroma of roast meat and vegetables fills the house. I'm wearing my new favourite outfit: Sebastian's dressing gown. My blonde hair is in a messy bun, and I have no fucks to give about my appearance. This man makes me feel comfortable in my own skin. He likes me best like this.

I like me best like this.

He appears and leans against the doorframe, watching me. His big brown eyes find mine across the room, and he gives me the best 'come fuck me' look I've ever seen. Wearing a navy suit and a crisp white shirt, he is the epitome of dreamy. My heart skips a beat.

"Hi," he purrs.

"Hello, Mr. Garcia." I smirk.

He pushes off the wall, and in one swift movement, he has me in his arms.

He gently pats my blue eye socket. "Does it still hurt?"

"No. It's getting better."

"How was my girl's day?" He kisses me with suction and dominance.

Just delicious.

"Better now."

He unfastens the tie of my dressing gown to reveal my naked body. His eyes drop to my toes, and he licks his lips.

"Mine too."

He stands back and cups my breast, his thumb dusting back and forth over my erect nipple. His hands slide down around to my behind, and he kisses me as he pulls my body against his hard cock.

Oh, *this man.*

"Dinner." I smile against his lips.

"Is right here." His lips drop to my neck, and his teeth graze my skin. Goose bumps scatter up my spine.

I tip my head back to allow him greater access. No matter how hard I try, I can't resist him. "Seb." I smile goofily up at the ceiling. "I've made you dinner. In fact, I've made you a lot of things today."

He pulls back to look at me. "Such as?"

"A surprise. Now sit down while I serve."

Sebastian rolls his eyes and takes a seat at the bench. I pour us both a glass of wine and pass his to him. He takes a sip, his eyes lingering on my face.

"What?" I smirk.

"I like coming home to this."

"To what?"

"You, half naked in my kitchen."

I giggle and point to him with the tongs in my hand. "That's because you're a sex maniac."

He taps his lap. "Come."

I go to him and put my arms around his neck. He slides his hands in under my robe and holds me tightly. We stay here for a while, and it's nice. There's a closeness between us, and it's not hurried or passionate. It's comfortable.

Homely.

Something I've been searching for, for a very long time.

"What's this surprise you made me?" he asks.

Oh crap.

"Umm... Well..." I really don't know how this is going to go down. Knowing Sebastian, it could very well be the drop of an atomic bomb. "I was thinking about everything today, and how..."

He listens.

"I know that it's not... I mean, I don't want you to ever go through that again." I stumble over my words, trying to make this come out in the right context.

"April," he says in his deep, commanding voice.

"I made you something. Of course, you will need to get Bart or someone you trust to check it," I babble on.

Nerves dance in my stomach.

"April..." he warns impatiently.

I push off his lap. "I'll just go get it." I walk up the hall and into his office to retrieve the ten-page document in his printer. I walk back out and hand it over.

He frowns as he looks down at it in his hands.

"It's a prenup agreement," I announce.

His eyes rise to mine, and he raises a pissed-off eyebrow.

Oh crap, he thinks it's about me. "I mean, it's not for me or anything. It's for you to have for the future. Like, if you ever meet the right person. I don't want you to get ripped off ever again, Seb."

Unimpressed, he throws it on the table and stands. He goes to the cupboard, takes out a glass, and fills it with scotch. He takes a sip as his angry eyes hold mine.

"Are you angry?" I ask.

"Yes, I'm fucking angry," he growls. "If you want to leave, just do it." He drains his glass.

I open my mouth to say something, but no words come out.

"I cannot believe you would have the fucking audacity to draft a premarital agreement for my future wife to sign," he says.

"Sebastian..."

"Don't." He fills his glass again.

"This is for your own protection. I won't let another woman rip you off."

"I don't want another fucking woman!" he yells.

Oh crap, he thinks I'm leaving.

"Then I'll sign it," I stammer. I grab the pen from the shopping list on the fridge. "Here, I'll sign it right now."

Fuck, this is going bad.

Real bad.

I flick through the pages to the back and quickly sign my name on the dotted line. I'm half expecting him to throw me out into the street. "There, see?" I smile. "It's done."

He glares at me.

"Sebastian, I don't want your money, not one penny. But if I'm going to stay here in your house and be with you, I need to have this for my own sanity. I want us to go into this relationship unencumbered."

He storms past me, heading towards the stairs.

"Where are you going?" I call after him.

"To take a shower. Do you want to do up a premature legal agreement for that?" he yells.

I roll my eyes. Smart-ass.

He marches up the stairs, and I slump onto my stool. I thought I was doing a good deed—that he would be happy.

Premature legal agreement.

I exhale heavily. I guess not.

I peer into the oven and glance at the clock. Sebastian has been upstairs for half an hour. Is he even coming back down?

Too soon.

It was too soon, you idiot.

What the fuck was I thinking?

I honestly thought he would be happy that I took it upon myself to do that.

I hear the stairs creak, and I stir the gravy to act busy. He walks in and takes a seat back at the kitchen counter.

"Are you ready for dinner now?" I ask with my back to him.

"Yes, please," he replies curtly.

Big baby.

I dish out our food and place it in front of him.

"Thank you."

"You're welcome." I smile through gritted teeth.

I sit down, and we eat in silence while I repeat the mantra, *hold your tongue, hold your tongue.*

Eventually, he breaks the silence. "I'll have my own lawyer draft an agreement."

"That's fine," I say, trying to keep a straight face.

We eat in silence again.

"And I don't like being pushed into anything," he states.

"Okay."

"You will not be moving in here until we discuss it."

I roll my eyes. He's pissing *me* off now. "That's fine, Sebastian. I don't want to move in here, anyway."

His eyes rise to meet mine.

"What?" I scoff. "It's okay for you to say it, but if I agree, I'm in the shit."

He raises an eyebrow and goes back to his dinner.

"I was only trying to protect you," I say.

"I don't need your protection," he snaps.

"Really?" I scoff. "From where I'm standing, you kind of do. You're a very wealthy man, Sebastian. Don't be a fool."

He gives a subtle shake of his head. "You're fucking infuriating, April."

"And you're a big baby." I stand and pick up my plate.

"Where are you going?"

"To eat my dinner in front of the television." I walk out into the living room and sit down on the couch. I begin to eat my dinner on my lap. "And I might write up a contract for this too!" I call out.

If he wants to be a dick, I can be a bigger one.

"Write up a contract that you have to suck my cock every day!" he calls from the kitchen.

"If you check the fine print of the already-written contract, you will see that it is me who gets head on the daily," I call back. "I'm not stupid, you know."

"Could have fooled me," I hear him mutter.

I smile to myself, and I know that he will be smiling too.

"And you're washing the dishes," I call.

"I can't hear you."

I smile, knowing our fight is over.

I think that maybe I won.

I lie back in the deep, hot water as the steam rises. I think this is the deepest, most luxurious bathtub I've ever seen. Sebastian has been fussing around downstairs. He washed up and fed Bentley. God knows what he's doing now.

It's the strangest thing. We have these disagreements, but never once do I consider going home, which is weird. Usually, that's my first response.

He walks into the bathroom and takes off his sweater.

"What are you doing?"

"Getting in. What does it look like?"

I smile and scooch over. He slides his track pants down his legs, and I'm gifted with a full frontal from my Adonis.

His skin has a beautiful honey hue. His chest is broad with a scattering of dark hair. His stomach is ripped with muscles. My eyes drop lower to the well-kept, black pubic hair and his large family jewels. No matter how many times I see him naked, I'm always taken aback by his beauty.

He climbs in the opposite end and rearranges us so that I am lying between his legs. He takes the soap and begins to wash my legs. I stay silent as I wait for him to say something. Eventually, he does.

"I have a wedding in the Maldives this weekend."

Oh no. A weekend without him. "Okay."

"I leave on Thursday and get back next Tuesday."

I nod. Damn it. He's going away for work tomorrow for two nights, so that means I won't see him for a week.

"I'd like you to come and meet my friends."

"To the wedding?"

"Yes."

I smile goofily.

He remains straight-faced as he soaps up my feet. "I'm going away for work tomorrow, remember? I won't see you for an entire week otherwise."

"Oh, I had forgotten about that," I lie as I act casual. "I'll have to see if I can get off work."

Bang work. If they don't give me time off, I'll leave. Not really, but still.

"I have a lot of time in lieu owed to me, so it shouldn't be a problem."

He nods as his eyes search mine, and I know that he has a million things that he wants to say that will never leave his lips.

"I'm sorry about the contract, but you need to know that I'll protect you, even if you don't want me to." I slide up over his body so that I am lying on top of him.

"I hate that you think this is about money. I don't care about the money."

I melt and kiss his big, beautiful lips, running my hand through his thick dark hair. "This is about freedom, Seb," I say softly.

He frowns, not understanding.

"I need to know that we are on the same page. You need to remember that I lost everything to an ex-husband too. That contract protects both of us."

He blinks. "You think I would take your money?"

"No. Not that I have a lot, anyway." I pause as I try to get the wording right in my head. "But if there ever came a day when we decided to go further..."

"Define further."

"Elope or something crazy. This way, the legalities are already taken care of."

"Elope?" He frowns.

"Well, I'm never having a white wedding again. What a crock of shit that was."

He smiles softly.

"My next wedding will be just me and my husband. It will be for us and us alone. No witnesses, no bullshit, no lies, and no fear of losing everything again."

He kisses me as his arms slide up over my back, and I know that he likes that answer.

"I just need you to know that I'm not here for what you have, Seb. I'm here for what you are."

He pushes the hair back from my face as we stare at each other. "I love you, April Bennet," he whispers.

I smile. "I know."

His lips take mine, and I'm lost.

Sebastian Garcia is special, and he's all mine.

Sebastian

I'm sitting at the table with two of my colleagues. It's been a full-on day with press conference after press conference.

We are at a dinner function filled with five hundred people, but all I want to do is go back to my room to call April. I'm over this political shit for the day. I hate staying away from home. I've had enough.

Bart appears through the crowd and pulls out a seat at our table. "Seb."

"Hello."

"I had a look over that contract you gave me this morning."

"And?"

"It's watertight. She did a good job. I say sign away."

I knew she would have done it right. "Thank you."

A waiter arrives at the table with a tray of drinks. He places them down one by one. "Here you are."

"Thanks." I drain my glass and pick up my new one as I glance at my watch. Another hour and I'm out of here.

Pound, pound, pound, goes my head.

Searing pain ricochets through my skull.

Fuck.

I drag my eyes open to see the room spinning, and I quickly clench them shut again.

Oh...

My stomach rolls, and I sit up in a rush. Perspiration wets my skin.

What the hell, I feel sick. I stumble to the bathroom and throw up violently. My body is shaking, as though dealing with some kind of fever.

Fuck.

I get into the shower and under the hot water. I lean up against the tiles. I have zero energy. Why am I so hungover?

What did I drink last night? I frown, trying to remember.

Huh?

My mind is blank. The last thing I remember was sitting at the table in the bar.

But...

I frown as I try to clear my brain fog. How did I get back to the hotel?

I get out of the shower and dry myself. I wrap my towel around my waist and walk back into the room to look around for my things.

My phone vibrates on my side table.

I pick it up. "Hi."

"How's my man this morning?"

"Good morning, Miss Bennet. Where are you?" I ask.

"In bed."

I smile as I walk into the wardrobe to retrieve my suit. "I wish I were there. My bed was lonely without you."

"Mine too," she purrs sexily. "What happened to you last night? I thought you were calling me when you got back to the hotel."

Huh?

"Wait..." I frown. "Did I speak to you last night?"

"What do you mean?"

"It's the weirdest thing, I can't recall anything." I take the coat hanger with my suit on it and lay it out on the bed.

"You called me three times. How much did you drink?" she asks.

Three times! What?

I search my mind for some kind of memory. "I don't remember speaking to you at all."

"What?" she asks.

"Did I sound drunk?"

"No, but you were very lovey-dovey."

"Define lovey-dovey."

"Telling me how much you missed me and stuff. You were as cute as. It made me miss you more."

I screw up my face. Cute as is not my style.

I stay silent for a moment as I try to reconcile last night. No, nothing. I change the subject. "What are you doing today?"

"I have to go into the office to pick up some files. I'm going to work from home for the rest of the week. This eye of mine looks horrendous."

"That's a good idea."

Where's my wallet? It must be in my suit trousers from last night. I look around the room and see my suit crumpled on the chair. Fuck, I must have been drunk. I always hang my suit up when I take it off.

"What's on today for you?" she asks.

"Not much. Same shit, different day." I walk around the room with my phone to my ear. "We have to find Theodore as a matter of urgency. Apparently, there's been a possible sighting in some country town. Who knows if it's a genuine lead." I pick up my pants from the floor and feel around the pockets for my wallet. It's not there.

"I can't wait for the weekend. What do you think the dress code will be for the wedding?" she asks.

Where's my fucking wallet?

"I don't know. It'll be hot, so something cool, I imagine." I continue to look around. "Your birthday suit works for me."

She chuckles, and I smile. I pick up my suit coat and feel around. I locate my wallet in the inside coat pocket. I pick up my white shirt from the floor, and my stomach drops as I stare at it.

Red lipstick is smeared across the collar.

What the fuck is that?

April chats away as the room begins to spin. I look around in a panic.

What happened here last night?

My eyes go to the coffee table, and I see a silver wine chiller with an empty bottle of champagne sitting in it. There are two glasses beside it—one still half-filled with champagne. Two glasses...

My stomach drops.

"Seb?" April asks, and by the tone of her voice, I can tell she's asked me a question.

"Sorry, what did you say? I couldn't hear you."

I drag my hand through my hair as I walk over to the bed in a panic. With my phone to my ear, I angrily toss back the blankets to inspect the sheets.

"I just said that I can't wait to see you," April whispers huskily.

I close my eyes. "Me too. Listen, babe, I have to go. I'm running late."

"Okay, have a nice day."

My heart beats hard and fast. This can't be happening.

"Love you."

I screw up my face. *Don't.*

"You too."

I hang up in a rush and pick up the pillow to smell it. The strong scent of perfume cements the evidence, and I throw the pillow against the wall in disgust.

What the fuck did I do?

24

Sebastian

THE ROOM CONTINUES TO SPIN. I walk into the bathroom and lean on the sink. I stare at my reflection in the mirror. My face has a sheen of perspiration, my hair is tousled, but it's the disgust in myself that makes my stomach roll.

No.

I may be a lot of things, but a lying cheater *I am not.*

Fuck, this is a nightmare.

What the hell went on last night? I search my brain for a recollection of anything.

Let me think, I was sitting at the table.

Bart came over and sat down.

He told me that April's contract was good to go and that I should sign it.

Then...

I screw up my face to concentrate really hard.

Nothing.

I need to see Bart. I know for sure that he was there. I march back out into my room and retrieve my phone. I dial his number, but it rings out. I glance at my watch. It's still early. Maybe he's in the shower.

I call Melody, the tour manager.

"Hello."

"Hello, this is Sebastian. Can you tell me what room Bart is in, please?"

"Hi, Sebastian. Let me check."

"Okay."

I wait on the line until she comes back. "He's on level 6, room 624."

"Thank you." I hang up, throw on my suit, and five minutes later, I'm walking up the corridor towards room 624. Jeremy is approaching from the other direction.

"Morning." I nod.

"Good morning," he replies, and we both stop once we get to room 624. "Are you here to see Bart?" he asks.

"Yes."

He looks at me deadpan, and I can feel an undertone of anger. "Me too."

I fake a smile. Great. Don't tell me that I'm arriving in the middle of a domestic. I'm not in the mood for their fighting shit this morning. I turn towards the door and knock.

Jeremy stands behind me, waiting for the door to open.

I knock again.

"Looks like he's not here," I say, half relieved.

"Stand aside. Melody just gave me a key." He holds the card up to the scanner.

"That's not necessary." I get the feeling that something is going down between them. "I'll come back later."

The lock releases, and Jeremy pushes the door open. Bart is fast asleep in bed with a naked woman on either side of him.

"What the hell are you doing?" Jeremy cries from behind me.

My eyes widen.

Fuck.

Jeremy marches in, picks up a jug of water, and pours it over Bart's head. "How could you?" he cries.

Bart wakes with a jump. He looks around, confused and shocked. "What's going on?" He jumps back when he sees the woman. "Who are you?" he cries.

The woman smiles and stretches. "Hi, baby," she purrs.

"How could I be so stupid?" Jeremy cries before he marches from the room.

"Jeremy!" Bart yells. "I don't know..." He scurries out of bed and falls onto the floor, disoriented. "What the fuck is going on here?" He's naked with scratch marks all over his back and a large love bite on his neck. Red lipstick is smeared all over his face.

Hell, this is bad.

"I swear to you..." Bart cries. "I don't know." He looks around the room, completely shocked by what's going on. He wraps a towel around his waist and chases Jeremy out into the corridor. I hear Jeremy going ballistic, with Bart hot on his heels.

Hang on. The same thing that happened to me has happened to him.

I think we were drugged.

I walk over to the bed. "Who are you?" I yell at the women.

"What?" They wince as they screw up their faces.

"What did you put in our drinks?" I demand.

"What are you talking about?" The blonde one scowls as she climbs out of bed. She's naked and has a killer body.

I grab her by the arm. "I'm calling security. Right now."

She rips her arm out of my grip. "What are you talking about, you idiot? I'm a call girl. Bart ordered us and paid for the entire night. Check his credit card if you don't believe me."

What?

Oh hell.

Bart comes marching back into the room. "Get the fuck out of here!" he cries to the two women. He storms into the bathroom and slams the door.

They both look to me for direction.

"You heard the man!" I snap. "Leave. Now."

They collect their things, and I walk to the window to stare down at the street so I don't have to look at them while they dress. Disgust fills my every pore. I've never had anything against working girls. They've always excited me.

Today, it feels wrong. *I feel dirty.*

I turn back to them. "Were either of you in my room?"

"No."

"Tell me the truth," I growl.

"Your security guard came and dragged you away before the fun even started."

I close my eyes in relief.

Thank God.

The girls dress, and they leave in silence.

I knock on the bathroom door. "Bart?"

He stays silent.

"They're gone."

He opens the door. Devastation is written all over his face.

"I think we were drugged."

His eyes widen. "You too?"

"I woke up and remembered nothing. I know for certain that I hadn't had that much to drink."

"What the fuck?" He begins to pace. "Who would do this?"

I shake my head, totally confused. "I don't know. Who would gain anything by setting you up with two prostitutes?"

Bart stares at the wall for a moment and narrows his eyes as they fill with contempt. "I know."

"Who?"

"My *fucking* wife."

"Surely not." I stare at him. "You really think she'd stoop this low?"

"She'd do anything to make Jeremy leave me." He drops his head. "And I think he just did."

April

I glance up at the mirror behind the cash register. Oh man, I look like a freak.

Who wears their sunglasses inside shops? Women with black eyes, that's who.

I'm supposed to be working from home today. I worked all morning, but this afternoon I've snuck out in search for a dress for the wedding this weekend.

I have to look perfect. I am meeting Sebastian's lifelong friends, after all. I hope this bloody black eye fades before then.

I think I found the perfect dress. First store, first dress I tried on. When is shopping ever this easy?

"Next," the cash register girl calls. I step forward, and my phone vibrates. I look down to see the name.

Jeremy

"How are you today?" The cashier smiles as she takes my dress and rings it up.

"Good, thanks. How are you?" I stuff my phone back in my bag. I'll call him back later.

It's just gone 9:00 p.m. when I climb into bed. I turn the television on in my bedroom and lie back. Time for some trash TV. My phone rings, and the name *April's Fool* lights up the screen. I was wondering when he was calling me.

"Hi there," I answer with a smile. "I thought you'd forgotten me."

"I'm downstairs. Buzz me in."

I sit up in a rush. "What? Really?"

"Uh-huh."

I run to the security camera and see him standing there with his overnight bag. Excitement fills me, and I push the buzzer as fast as lightning. I glance around at my apartment. Shit, it's pretty messy. Oh well, it is what it is.

I do a little jig on the spot and open my front door as I wait for him. *He's here.*

Gah, I'm seriously pathetic over this man.

Oh crap, my dress I bought for the wedding is laid out on the chair. I quickly roll it up in a ball and throw it in the linen cupboard. I don't want to seem too eager.

The elevator dings, and he comes into view wearing his custom grey suit, carrying his black leather overnight bag. He looks every bit like the walking orgasm that he is.

His eyes find mine, and he gives me a slow, sexy smile. "Miss Bennet."

"Here I am." I do a little wiggle on the spot. "Looking hot in my flannelette pajamas."

He chuckles and takes me into his arms to kiss me. "Flannelette works for me."

"What are you doing here? I thought you weren't back until tomorrow."

"You wouldn't believe the day we had." He takes my hand, and we walk into my apartment. "I need a shower."

"Okay, have you eaten?"

"Yeah, we had something on the way home."

We walk into the bathroom, and he strips off his clothes and gets under the shower. I sit on the toilet to talk to him.

"So, what was so bad about your day?" I ask.

"Get this." He soaps himself up. "Remember how I said I didn't remember speaking to you last night?"

"Yeah."

"I think I was drugged."

"What?" My eyes widen. "By whom?"

"Bart's wife."

My mouth falls open.

"You can't tell anyone this."

"I won't. What happened?"

"I woke up and couldn't remember anything. I started freaking out, so I went to see Bart. I got to his hotel room at the same time as Jeremy, and when we opened the door, Bart was asleep with two naked girls beside him. He was covered in lipstick."

My eyes widen in horror. "Oh no."

"But he doesn't remember anything either."

I frown. "What?"

"His wife had him drugged and ordered hookers. Then she called Jeremy this morning saying that she couldn't get in touch with him and asking if he could check on him for her."

"Hang on, why weren't they together in the room, anyway?" I ask.

His eyes hold mine.

"Yes, I know about Jeremy and Bart." I scoff in a rush. "Everybody knows. It's not half obvious."

He shrugs, relieved that he didn't reveal that secret. "How would I know? It's a fucking weird setup if you ask me. Married to a woman with a boyfriend on the side."

I roll my eyes. "Sleazebag." My mind goes to Jeremy. "Oh no, poor Jeremy. Shit. He called me today, and I didn't pick up."

He keeps soaping himself up. "So, yeah, Jeremy and Bart had a huge fight, and Bart was freaking out and screaming at his wife on the phone, who swears it wasn't her."

"Wait a minute. Why were *you* drugged?" I frown.

"I was unlucky enough to be sitting next to him when the drinks arrived, I guess."

The hairs on the back of my neck stand to attention. "What did you do last night?"

"Nothing, thank fuck. I was freaking out for a while there, but I spoke to the security guard. He found me drunk in the bathroom, and he walked me back to my room early."

I stare at him. Something is off with this story. "So you weren't with the women?"

"No."

"Why did you think you were at first?"

340

"There was lipstick on my collar." He keeps washing himself.

Alarm bells start to ring. "Where did the lipstick come from?" I ask.

"The girls in the bar. Apparently, they came over and were trying to talk to me, getting all flirty. Thankfully, I got the hell out of there. Poor Bart didn't have the same fate."

I stare at him as I imagine the scenario he is setting. Hmm. Interesting.

"Fucking nightmare." He exhales heavily. "I'm glad to be home, put it that way."

"How do you know the security guard walked you home?" I ask.

"I saw him, and he told me that he walked me to my room and that I got into bed while he was still there. I checked all the details, don't worry."

"And nobody else was in your room?"

"No. I told you that."

I don't like this.

"Bart needs to go to the hospital and get drug tested. This is a criminal offence," I tell him.

"He is going. That's why we came home early."

"Well, you should go too."

"I'm fine. Nothing happened to me."

"How do you know? What if something did? What if you had sex with one of those hookers? What if they took photographs? What if this is some elaborate blackmailing scheme? You're the Deputy Prime Minister, Sebastian. If anyone is a target to be blackmailed, it would be you, and not that stupid sleazebag Bart."

"I would know if I had sex with someone, April."

"How? We have so much sex that you wouldn't be able to feel a change in your body."

He rolls his eyes and continues to shower.

I stare at him. "I want you to go and get tested."

"I'm not. Drop it." He puts his head under the water and begins washing his hair. "All I'll be doing is wasting six hours at the hospital for no reason."

Ugh, infuriating, *stupid twat.*

I walk out into the kitchen as my mind goes into overdrive.

Something is off.

Darkness looms around the corners of my bedroom, just like the shadows in my mind.

Sebastian is fast asleep, lying on his side, facing me. I watch as his chest rises and falls, the flutter of his lashes, and his lips that slightly part when he breathes in.

I've never been so besotted with someone before. Sure, I've been in love and been in lust, but with Sebastian, it's different. Everything is magnified. The speeches he gives, the way he looks at me, the way he wears his suits...even the way he smells.

I have this overwhelming feeling that something isn't right. Something is going on in the background, and I need to work it out before it blows up in my face.

Protecting him is all that matters.

I've been in the pits of hell, and I am weathered for any storm, but I can't let it go.

I can't drop this feeling, no matter how hard I try.

I will not allow that witch Helena to hurt him ever again.

I get a vision of her in his office last week. The entitled way in which she hid whatever it was behind her back, as if she was owed something. How dare she come here with an agenda?

I hate her.

Maybe more than I hate my ex, and that's saying something. At least he accepted the divorce and, sure, he wouldn't move out of our house, but he was never vindictive.

Sebastian stirs, and his eyes flutter open. He reaches for me and pulls me closer. "Why are you awake?" he whispers in his husky voice. He holds me cheek to cheek.

"Bad dream."

He kisses my temple. "Go back to sleep, baby. I'll protect you."
He rolls me over and nestles in behind me. I hear him slip back
into regulated breathing as he dozes back off.

But who'll protect you, my love?

I stare at the wall, adrenaline coursing through my veins. I'm
filled with conviction. I know what I must do.

And I will.

I rearrange the lapels on Sebastian's suit jacket. "I'll walk you
down. I want to grab a coffee."

"Okay." He tugs at my hips, bringing my body against his
crotch. Can we ever just hug without it being sexual?

Obviously not.

"You do make it very hard to leave, Miss Bennet." Our lips meet
in a tender kiss. I smile up at my handsome man and run my
fingers through his thick black hair.

"I'm looking forward to our weekend away." I smile.

"Me too."

He takes my hand and leads me out of the door. We take the
elevator and walk out onto the street, where we see the black car
waiting for him. We head towards it.

"April!" a voice calls. We turn to see Duke.

My heart drops as I come to a stop. "Duke."

Oh, crap.

Sebastian tries to drop my hand, and I grip it harder, keeping
him close.

"Duke, this is Sebastian."

Duke nods, and Sebastian forces a smile. "Hello."

He tries to release my hand again, and I hold it with white-
knuckle force.

"Are you two...?" Duke frowns as he looks between us.

"We are," I reply.

Sebastian rolls his lips, uncomfortable with this conversation.

"Can I speak to you?" Duke's eyes flick to Sebastian. "Alone?"

Sebastian tries to escape my viselike grip, and I squeeze it in a silent warning. "No, Duke, I'm sorry. There is nothing further to say. We've been over it a hundred times."

"I... I can't move on," Duke splutters.

Sebastian drops his head. "I'll leave you two alone."

My heart breaks, but I keep a hold of Sebastian. He needs to be here for this conversation. I don't want him to feel insecure all over again.

"I'm in a relationship with Sebastian, Duke. I'm sorry that we didn't work out, but you need to accept my decision."

Duke's nostrils flare, and his angry eyes find Sebastian. "She'll never marry you. She doesn't want children. She'll spit you out like she did me."

Sebastian stares at him, remaining silent.

"Duke," I sigh.

"Tell him," Duke spits. "Tell him you never want to live with someone. Tell him you never want to get married."

Sebastian tries to pull his hand free. "Stay here, Sebastian!" I snap, losing the last of my patience.

"No." He pulls away and walks towards the car.

My eyes find Duke. "You and I weren't right for each other," I say softly. "And I know that for certain now that I've met Sebastian. You will understand, too, when you meet the right person. I promise you."

"She will never marry you. She's broken!" Duke calls to Sebastian, losing the last of his control.

Sebastian stops and turns back towards us.

Oh God, could this conversation get any worse?

"We'll see," Sebastian replies sharply. "You will respect her decision and stay away from her."

My eyes flick to Sebastian.

"Goodbye, Duke," he snaps. "My condolences, but we won't have this conversation again. This is your first and last warning: stay away from her. April, let's go."

He takes me by my hand and ushers me into the back of the

waiting car. The door shuts behind us, and I stare at Duke on the pavement as we pull out into the traffic.

Sebastian sits beside me, his steel gaze looking out the window as we drive.

"Did you write up that prenup for my protection or to prove to yourself that you're serious about this?" he snarls.

I swallow the lump in my throat, remaining silent.

A bit of both.

He glares at me, as if reading my mind, and I wither a little. "April is going to my house," he announces to the driver.

I frown. "But—"

"You will be spending the day at my house. You can work from there. Like it or not."

Jeez.

"And if he dares come near you again—"

"Okay, okay, Sebastian," I whisper. "Calm down."

His cold gaze returns to the streets flying by, and I feel my heart rate slowly return to normal. I watch him and try hard to hold in my smile.

Caveman Garcia is hot.

"Flight 121, boarding," the attendant announces throughout the airport.

It's Friday morning, and we were supposed to leave for the Maldives for the wedding yesterday, but Sebastian had to work late last night.

It's okay as long as we get there at some point. I don't care when.

I'm wearing a fitted black dress with a denim jacket and white slip-on shoes, trying to be casual and dressy at the same time. I have my bag packed, my body primped to perfection, and my nerves firmly intact.

I'm meeting Sebastian's friends this weekend, and I know how important they are to him. First impressions are everything, and I really want to make a good one.

I have this thing that when I'm nervous, I go quiet, and I know it makes me appear rude.

Remember to talk, remember to talk.

"Let's go." Sebastian takes my hand, and we walk out through the gates. It's a smaller plane than what I've ever been on before. That would be just my luck, finally meeting the man of my dreams only to die in a fucking plane crash.

He glances over at me and frowns. "You all right?"

"Yep."

"You're quiet."

I shrug. "Perhaps a little nervous."

"Nervous?"

"What if your friends don't like me?"

He gives me a breathtaking smile and pulls me to him. "How could they not?"

He kisses my temple as we walk. "I like you, and that's all that matters."

It's just after 2:00 p.m. when the plane comes to a stop on the runway.

"We're here." I bounce around in my seat.

Sebastian smirks, picks up my hand, and kisses my fingertips.

"What's the first thing you're going to do when you get there?" I ask.

"April Bennet."

I giggle. "No, I mean, like do, do. Like a doing thing."

He raises an eyebrow, amused by my childlike excitement. "April Bennet."

I smile as I pull his face to mine and kiss his big, pouty lips. "Thanks for bringing me."

The seatbelt sign goes off. "Let's go have some fun."

"Okay." I stand so quickly that I hit my head on the overhead. "Ouch."

"Careful," he warns.

We walk up the aisle, and as we get to the doors, we are hit with a wall of heat. It's like a blazing-hot oven.

I gasp as the air leaves my lungs.

"What in the sauna do you call this?" Sebastian mutters under his breath.

"Right." I get the giggles as we walk down the plane's stairs. "Please tell me we have aircon in our room."

"I fucking hope so. My balls are hard-boiled in these jeans."

I burst out laughing, and he laughs too. Oh, it's so nice to be somewhere different together. So much of our time together has been spent in the shadows.

I feel like we are finally a real couple, doing grown-up couple things.

Hand in hand, we walk over the tarmac and into the airport. Once through security, we see a man standing with a sign that reads:

Garcia

I hunch my shoulders together in excitement.

"Hello, Mr. and Mrs. Garcia?" the driver asks.

Mrs. Garcia.

"Yes," Sebastian replies.

"This way, please."

"Thank you." We follow him out to a black Audi, and we climb into the backseat.

Woohoo, we're on our way.

An hour later, we turn off the main road. The landscape is tropical and well-kept. It's super beautiful. We come to a large circular driveway, and the driver pulls over.

"Here we are." He gets out and retrieves our bags from the trunk, leaving us to walk to reception.

It's all open air, and I can see through to the huge, exotic resort pool that's surrounded by deck chairs and waiters delivering cocktails to people. Behind all that is the most beautiful, crystal-blue water I have ever seen. The sand is white.

Wow, this is Heaven.

"What ocean is that?" I ask Sebastian.

He looks out and rolls his lips. "Indian Ocean."

"Really?" I frown. I take out my phone and Google it.

What ocean surrounds the Maldives?

"Indian," he repeats.

"Just checking."

"Do you have to check everything I say?"

"Uh-huh."

Indian Ocean

"Oh." I sigh, slightly dejected. I was sure it was something more exotic. It sure does look like it. I've never seen water so blue.

Sebastian gives me a sexy wink in an 'I told you so' statement.

I smirk.

"Can I help you?" the receptionist asks.

"Yes, checking in, please."

"Of course." She smiles, her eyes lingering on Sebastian. "What was the name?"

"Sebastian Garcia."

Her eyes widen. "Oh, yes, of course, sir. You're from the United Kingdom. We've been awaiting your arrival. The extra security is in place. Please let us know if anything isn't up to your standards."

Sebastian fakes a smile, unimpressed. "Thank you." He hates a fuss, and I know that his security team back home would have organized this without his consent.

"Did you have a good flight?" she asks, her eyes lingering a little too long on my handsome man.

He did, bitch. *Back off.*

I fake a smile too. And hurry up about it.

"Paulie will show you to your room." She hands over the key. "You are in the North Wing Penthouse." She gestures to the left. "If you go around past the pool and restaurants, your penthouse is on the oceanfront."

"Thank you."

Paulie steps forward and nods. "This way, please." We follow him out through the gardens, and we cut through a pool area.

"Seb!" someone calls.

We turn to see a blond guy waving. He starts to jog over to us. Seb smiles and waves back.

Scratch that. A blond *god* is jogging over to us. Square jaw, blond hair, and ripped abs.

Jeez, *who is this?*

"Hey, you made it," he laughs and shakes Seb's hand.

"This is April," Sebastian introduces me. "This is my rent-a-friend, Spencer Jones."

I chuckle as I shake his hand.

"Hey." He smiles. "Nice to finally meet you."

"You too." I smile and hunch my shoulders. *Awkward.*

"Come see the others," Spencer says, gesturing to the pool.

"We're on our way to our room," Seb replies.

"It will only take a minute." Spencer grabs my hand and begins to drag me towards the pool. "Look who I found!" he announces to the others.

A man looks up from his deck chair, and his big brown eyes meet mine. Okay, fuck. Who the hell is that gorgeous specimen with his dark hair, square jaw, and...eish, power for days? "Julian Masters, this is April."

I smile as I nervously shake his hand. Jeez, strong hands too.

"This is his wife, Brielle." She's pretty and natural-looking—younger than me, by the looks of it.

349

"Hello." I smile.

"And this hot-as-hell woman is my wife, Charlotte." Charlotte is heavily pregnant and wearing a bikini. Her stomach is huge.

"Hi." I smile.

Oh, great. They're all lying around together in their swimsuits. This is my worst fucking nightmare.

The two women jump from their deck chairs and kiss me.

"It's so great to finally meet you, April," says Brielle.

They both kiss Sebastian on the cheek, and he affectionately rubs Charlotte's stomach. I can tell that they're close.

"Okay, we have to go to our room. This poor guy is waiting for us," Sebastian says.

We look over to see Paulie waiting patiently under the palm trees.

"See you later," Sebastian calls.

I give them a wave, and we both turn and follow Paulie.

We make it to our apartment, and my mouth falls open.

Wow.

It's directly on the sand, overlooking the beach, with huge, open bifold doors running along a gigantic deck. It's made of timber with a thatched roof, and it looks like it's come straight out of an island-holiday brochure.

It's possibly the most beautiful place I've ever been.

"This is the bedroom." Paulie shows us through. The four-poster bed is strategically placed in the middle of the room, with a large green marble bathroom just off it, with an oversized sunken bathtub.

But it's the glass wall view I can't get over. There's aqua-blue sea as far as I can see.

"You have twenty-four-hour room service for anything that you need. Just dial 9."

"Thank you."

"Is there anything else I can do for you?"

"No, thank you," Sebastian says as he tips him.

Paulie leaves us alone, and Sebastian's eyes find mine.

"Seb." I smile. "This is incredible."

His eyes glow with tenderness. "It is, isn't it?"

I know he isn't talking about the place. He's talking about me.

He takes me into his arms and kisses me, slow and tender, leading me down the path that we travel, where nothing else matters but each other.

I know I've been in love before, and I know I must have felt like this, but I don't remember this closeness. The attachment between us is so deep.

"Let's go swimming in that Indian Ocean," he murmurs against my lips.

"But...your friends?"

"...Are a little too much sometimes, even for me." He kisses me deeper, his tongue curling around mine. My feet lift off the floor. "I want you to myself today."

My heart flutters. It's as if he can sense that, after the chaotic and busy week we've had, I need time with him alone. Just the two of us.

"We'll go out with them tonight." He walks me back to the bed. "But today, you're all mine."

If Heaven were a day, this would be it.

We swam, we lay in the sun, we made love, and we took a late-afternoon nap to the gentle sound of the waves lapping against the shore.

Sebastian is the most relaxed I've ever seen him. There's not a mobile phone in sight. In fact, I think he even switched it off. That's unheard of.

But now we have dinner with his friends.

I hold my arms out. "Do I look okay?"

I'm wearing a fitted, strapless grey dress and sandal heels. My blonde hair is down in beach waves, and my makeup is minimal.

I'm relieved that I gave myself a little bit of a spray tan. I would have looked like an anaemic snowman if I hadn't.

Sebastian smirks at me. "You look beautiful."

I inhale deeply.

"Stop it." He takes my hand and lifts it to his lips to kiss my fingertips. "It's just another dinner. This is not like you. I've never known you to be nervous before."

"Well, this is important."

"Why?"

"Because..." I shrug. "They're your friends, and I know that first impressions count."

He pours me another glass of champagne. "I have a plan." He passes the glass to me, and we toast.

"Such as?"

"You drink copious amounts of cocktails to eradicate your nerves."

I smile against my glass.

"And I'll take advantage of you when we get home."

I giggle. "I think you've taken advantage of me a few times today already."

"You took advantage of me." He slides his hand down my body and up under my dress. He cups my behind, and I smile as I sip my champagne.

The man is a bona fide sex maniac.

He puts his mouth to my ear. "How does that sound?" he whispers.

Goose bumps scatter up my spine. His fingers slip under the side of my panties, and he glides his fingertips through my sex.

"Hmm." My eyes flutter closed as I take another sip of my champagne. "Keep talking."

He bites my neck with force at exactly the same time as he impales me with two thick fingers.

Oh...

My knees nearly buckle out from under me.

His dark eyes hold mine as he works me, his thick fingers touching my most secret place. "Oh, my girl loves to fuck my hand."

My eyes close.

He jerks his hand hard. "Doesn't she?"

"Yes," I whimper.

He lifts my leg to rest on the chair, and he starts to really work me. Two fingers... then three, his teeth grazing my neck, biting my ear, and his quivering breath skimming my skin.

Four fingers...

Ouch.

I clench around him, and he smiles against my neck.

"You have no fucking idea how hot you feel stretched out like this."

My body shudders, and I bear down on him.

He puts his mouth to my ear. "You're going to come on my tongue tonight." He growls. "Hard."

Oh yes I am.

I shudder, and he takes his hands out of my pants and stands up straight. With his dark eyes fixed on mine, he sucks his fingers dry.

I pant as I melt into a puddle.

"I want to come now," I whisper.

"No." He straightens my dress and pulls it down. He neatens up my hair.

I pant as I watch him, my sex still buzzing from the beating he's just given it.

Wet, swollen, and utterly stretched.

Needy.

"Later."

25

***

April

HAND IN HAND, we walk into the outside garden restaurant. I feel like I'm going to vomit...or come. Damn Sebastian for making me horny. As if I weren't wound up enough already.

"Garcia!" voices call as we walk through the restaurant.

Sebastian smiles and waves, and we head towards the table.

"You didn't tell me that you knew everyone in the Maldives," I whisper.

He smiles at everyone sitting as we arrive at our table. "You do know that this is the pre-wedding dinner, right?"

"Oh." I fake a smile as I glance around at all the eyes fixed firmly on me. "I do now."

This is hell on a stick. Everyone he fucking knows is here.

Great.

He pulls out my chair and I sit down. He slides in beside me. We're sitting at a small table for six. His four friends are already here.

"You remember Julian and Spencer, Brielle and Lottie."

"Yes." I smile. "Hello."

"Hi." They all smile and stare at me like I'm a freak in the circus.

"What were you two doing all day?" Spencer asks. "We were waiting at the pool for you. How rude. I would have thought you would make more of an effort, April."

"They were getting busy," Julian mutters.

My face falls, and the girls burst out laughing. "Spencer, stop it," Lottie says.

I put my hand on my chest in relief. "Oh my God, don't tease me. I'm nervous enough," I admit.

Sebastian rolls his eyes. "Don't be nervous about these fucking idiots. Nobody to impress here."

"Hey!" Brielle chimes in.

"Watch your mouth." Lottie laughs.

"Two jugs of sangria," the waiter says as he puts two huge jugs of some exotic-looking red drink on the table.

"Yes, thank you." Brielle smiles. "Keep them coming."

Charlotte rolls her eyes. "Oh, this is just great."

"Just keep making babies for me, babe." Spencer gives her a sexy wink as he rubs her pregnant stomach.

She fakes a smile at him and fans herself with a paper fan. "When I have this baby, Spencer, I'm going on a bender for a week, and you're babysitting the entire time. Breastfeeding and all."

Spencer raises his glass to her. "Yes, dear."

I can't help but smile as I watch them. He adores her, it's obvious. He has a likeable, naughty-boy charm about him.

"How long have you got to go?" I ask.

"Ten weeks." She smiles.

"First baby?"

"No, fourth."

My eyes widen. "Wow."

She seems nice and has a real toffy English accent. I wonder where she's from.

I turn my attention to Brielle. "Do you have any children?"

"Yes, five."

"Five?" My eyes widen, unable to hide my shock. God, these women are full-on breeders.

"Three are ours, and two are my stepkids."

I think I pick up an accent.

My eyes drift to Julian. He must have had kids with someone else before.

"Although they like Brielle more than me," Julian mutters dryly.

"We all do," Spencer replies casually against his glass of sangria.

"Am I picking up an Australian accent?" I ask.

"Yes. I'm an Aussie. Tell me about you."

Julian smiles as he watches her. It's obvious he's smitten too.

"I'm American." I smile. "Lawyer."

They all hang off my every word. I shrug bashfully.

"How did you two meet?" Charlotte looks between us.

"Ah." My eyes find Sebastian. He's sitting back, enjoying the show, not a word to be heard. *Cut in any time, fucker.* "We met in a café about six years ago. We dated briefly then, but it didn't work out."

Sebastian's, Julian's, and Spencer's eyes meet, and I know his friends know the real way we met.

Screw it. He wants to be honest with his friends, so do I.

"Actually, that's not all of it. After we met in the café, I worked in a strip club, and Sebastian came in."

A broad smile crosses Julian's face, and he glances over to Spencer, who is also wearing a goofy grin.

"Steady on," Sebastian chokes.

The girls' eyes widen.

"I'm telling you two the truth because I can't lie, and I know that Sebastian has already told the boys. I want to be honest with you both right off the bat."

Charlotte slaps Spencer's arm. "Why didn't you tell me?"

Brielle's mouth falls open when she turns to Julian. "You knew this?"

Sebastian holds his hands up in surrender. "It was the one time I went to a strip club, and she was working behind the bar to put herself through law school," he stammers.

I look over to see Julian is smirking into his drink, his eyes holding mine.

He's impressed that I told them the truth.

So am I.

"Oh, I like you." Charlotte gasps. "Somebody pour her another drink. I want to hear all the strip club stories."

Spencer playfully puts his hand over my glass. "Let's not."

We all laugh. Maybe this night won't be so bad after all.

They actually seem nice.

Sebastian

I watch as April chatters and laughs with the girls at the other end of the table. This is so weird.

The girls never like anyone I date. Not that I ever bring them to anything like this, I guess. I've taken dates to black tie balls before, but Brielle and Charlotte have always been guarded and not overly friendly.

They're different tonight. Or maybe it's just that it's April.

Unassuming and pretty, she oozes warmth and kindness. But most of all, she's intelligent.

"So, what's the plan if you go into early labor while we're here?" April asks.

"I don't know." Charlotte looks over to her husband. "What's the plan, Spence?"

He shrugs. "Freak the fuck out." He puts his hand over his mouth so the girls can't hear. "And then getting rolling fucking drunk," he mutters under his breath.

Julian and I laugh. Spencer is hardly drinking due to Charlotte's condition, in case he needs to drive somewhere in an emergency. He wants the baby to come more than anyone.

"You can call me and Sebastian," April slurs in her 'I've had way too many sangrias' voice. "I'm good in emergency situations, and Seb always knows what to do."

I smile against my wineglass. When do I always know what to do?

Never.

"And besides, my cat had kittens," she continues.

"Trust me, this pussy is a lot bigger than yours. We need back-up," Spencer mutters dryly.

We all burst out laughing.

Charlotte slaps him on the arm. "Spencer."

Brielle goes to stand and stumbles back on her chair, crashing spectacularly backwards into the garden bed.

"Fucking hell," Julian mutters, jumping up.

April bursts out laughing, and she scrambles to pick Brielle up. She grabs her hands and begins to pull her out of the hedge. They're laughing loudly as they fumble around, and everyone is looking our way.

"No more for you. We're going home," Julian says as he pulls Brielle to her feet. "You could have broken your neck." He smooths down her dress and straightens her up.

"But we're going dancing," Brielle slurs. Her hair is wild, and she has the devil in her eyes. Jeez, I think she's even drunker than April.

Drunker. Is that a word?

"Yes. Dancing!" April gasps. "Let's go." She grabs Charlotte's hands and pretends to slow waltz with her. "Bubba loves to dance." She bends down to Charlotte's stomach. "Don't you, cutie pie?" she says in a baby voice.

"Oh God." I roll my eyes. "That's it. We're out, too, April."

Brielle sidesteps and stumbles again on her heels. Just as she's about to fall back in the garden, Julian catches her. "Home," he demands, putting his arm around her.

"Yes, good idea." She looks up at him lovingly. "What have you got for me, big boy?"

Julian winces, and Spence and I burst out laughing.

I take April's hand. "Come."

"*Noo.*" She laughs. "Don't be a party pooper, Seb. Me and the girls are out on the town. Aren't we, girls?"

"There is no town," Julian replies.

"Yes!" Brielle calls from under Julian's arm. "I'm going out, Jules." She goes to pull away, and he takes her arm in a viselike grip. "Home time, Bree." He pulls her along. "You've had enough."

Brielle puts her hand to her mouth, whispering while she's being pulled along like a child. "He's being boring."

"What's new?" Spencer mutters.

We walk through the gardens back to our apartments. The girls are on each arm of Charlotte, chatting and giggling, tottering along like drunken sailors.

The boys and I are walking behind them, rolling our eyes at their antics, and a strange thought crosses my mind.

This is the first time that this has ever happened.

The three of our partners, getting along and having fun. Actually, having more fun than us.

Weird.

Julian slaps me on the back when we get to their hut. "Good luck with that one tonight."

"Oh." Brielle frowns. "I don't feel so good." She holds her stomach. "Jules, I feel sick."

"Christ almighty." He winces.

I chuckle. "I think you're going to need some luck yourself... and a bucket."

He helps her up the stairs, and Spence and Charlotte say their goodbyes. I take April's hand, and we continue to walk to our room.

She hiccups in an exaggerated way as she looks up at me, and I smile down at her. Even blind drunk, she's adorable.

"I like your friends." She beams.

"They like you."

"Really?" She seems surprised. "Because I like them."

"Yes, you just told me."

"Did I?" She frowns.

I lead her up the stairs, and she sways as I unlock the door.

"Are you all right?" I ask.

She nods. "Yep." She hiccups again.

"Why did you drink so much?"

"It was Charlotte," she slurs.

I frown. "Charlotte?"

"Yes. I had to drink for her too."

I chuckle. "That makes sense." I lead her into our room. "Bed."

"No, I need a shower." She rises on her toes to kiss me. "Can you run us a shower, babe?"

I smile against her lips.

"You owe me an orgasm." She smiles sexily and cups my cock in my pants.

Blood starts to swirl around my body. Now, *that* I can do. Even drunk, this woman is hot for it. "All right."

I walk into the bathroom and turn the shower on. I retrieve the towels, undress, and get under the water to wash myself. I give myself a few sneaky strokes.

Hmm, yes, I feel like this. I imagine how good she's going to feel around me.

"April." I smile. "Come and get it."

Silence.

"April?" I frown. What's she doing out there?

Silence.

I walk out of the bathroom and around the corner to see her curled up on the end of the bed, still in her dress, fast asleep.

I exhale heavily. This is not what I had planned.

I pick her up and put her to bed, taking her shoes off. I pull the sheet up over her and kiss her forehead as I brush the hair back from her face.

I frown as I stare down at her. I didn't realize how much I've been missing by being alone. This weekend has opened my eyes, and I feel like this is a turning point in our relationship.

I bend and kiss her again. I kiss her shoulder, her cheek, her arm, and I just can't get close enough.

I lie down beside her and hold her in my arms. She's dead to the world, fast asleep, but it makes me feel better by holding her close.

The longer I hold her, the stronger my need becomes. I get up and return to the shower. I see the lube and squirt some into my hand.

No use wasting this boner. I may as well help myself.

April

I sit in the sun, my sunglasses on. I'm somewhere between Heaven and hell.

Being hungover is bad.

Feeling near death from alcohol poisoning while sitting in the sun at a wedding is the fucking worst.

We are on the beach, sitting on the chairs that are lined up in pretty rows as we wait for the bride to arrive.

I am in a world of pain with absolutely no sympathy from Sebastian.

Bree is worse, and Charlotte thinks this is the funniest thing that has ever happened.

Brielle has been throwing up nonstop all morning.

"Oh." Brielle sighs and holds her head. "I swear to God, I'm literally dying here. If I even see a bottle of sangria again, I'll throw up. That shit is the Devil."

"It doesn't come in a bottle," Julian says, staring straight ahead. "It's a cocktail."

She rolls her eyes, annoyed by his response. "How come you're not sick, April? Do you have an iron stomach or something?"

"Trust me, I am," I whisper.

Not a lie. I really am feeling as sick as a dog.

"Some people can handle their liquor," Julian replies.

"Did you bring me any water?" she asks him.

"Do I look like I have water?" He holds his hands out.

"Seriously, Jules, if you love me, you will go find me some water. I'm so dehydrated, I'm turning into a sultana."

Julian rolls his eyes.

Sebastian smirks, and I can tell that Julian and Brielle's conversations often keep everyone entertained.

"And if you love me, you wouldn't expect me to fly all the way to the Maldives to be your hydration slave. Your condition is self-inflicted. Suck it up, princess," Julian replies flatly.

Spencer drops his head and chuckles.

Sebastian glances over at me and gives me a soft smile. I reach over to take his hand and pull it into my lap.

This all feels so natural and not at all what I expected. I really like his friends. They're my kind of people. The girls are around my age, and we have a natural rapport. Spencer and Julian are dry and witty.

Spencer is soft and swoony, and Julian is a hard-ass, although I kind of get the feeling he's a big softy underneath too.

And then there's my man, Sebastian Garcia.

Tall, dark, handsome, guarded, and damaged.

Perhaps the most beautiful man I've ever been with. In terms of looks, definitely, but it's his heart that has me convinced. He's like an onion. With every layer that I slowly peel back, I get a little more from our relationship.

He's deep and caring, bossy and dominant, with a huge heart.

I know he said that he loves me, and in his own way I know that he does, but his walls haven't come completely down yet. I guess it's just going to take time to build that trust between us. For me too.

But I have faith it will come. What's between us is too good for it not to. By admitting what we're both feeling, it's a big step in the right direction.

And now with his friends...

He lifts my hand and kisses my fingertips. I smile over at him.

The way he looks at me is just *everything*.

"Get a room, you two," Spencer whispers. "I'm about to vomit in my own mouth here."

"That makes two of us," Bree moans as she holds her temples.

"Don't even think about it," Julian warns her.

"Oh, please do," Charlotte whispers. "That will be the highlight of my life if you vomit here at the wedding."

"Do it on the groom," Spencer whispers. "Let me film it."

I drop my head and giggle. Brielle's hangover is hilarious.

"Hurry the fuck up." Sebastian looks around. "It's two thousand degrees. What are we waiting for?"

"The bride." Charlotte widens her eyes to accentuate her point.

He exhales heavily, unimpressed. "Ah. Her."

The music starts, and we all stand and turn to see a beautiful bride walking down the beach, wearing a classic white dress and a veil. With long dark hair, she looks every bit of the wedding fantasy.

"Oh no." Brielle drops her head and fans her face. "I think I'm going to throw up."

"How lovely," Julian murmurs, faking a smile at the oncoming bride.

I bite my bottom lip to stop myself from bursting out laughing. Even sick as a dog in ten-thousand-degree heat, I'm having so much fun.

We walk along the beach on our way home from the wedding. It's nearly 1:00 a.m. We've had the most amazing afternoon and night at the romantic beachside wedding.

There's been laughter and dancing. Sebastian has been utterly gorgeous, and I've been swooning at his every word.

The moonlight is dancing over the water now, and the breeze is blowing through my hair. We stop walking and look out to sea.

Sebastian takes me in his arms, and I stare up at him. Our lips slowly meet, and, unable to help it, my eyes close. I'm giddy over this man.

Like a wave in the ocean, attachment is beginning to flood through us. It's exhilarating and terrifying.

Real.

Sebastian stares down at me, and it's as if he can read my mind. A frown creases his brow. "What?" he asks.

I swallow the lump in my throat. I don't want to admit that I'm petrified of loving him—that this is all going to go south, and that the next time my heart breaks, it might be beyond repair.

When I'm alone, I'm safe. Nobody can hurt me.

But...

"I don't want to be that person anymore," I whisper.

Our eyes are locked. "Me neither," he says softly.

He kisses me, and I know that he feels the same. Unbridled fear is running between us like wildfire.

"Sebastian," I whisper. "Promise me that we won't fuck this up."

"You know that I can't."

My eyes search his. He reaches up and tucks a piece of hair behind my ear.

"I *can* promise you two things," he says.

The wind whips through my hair. "Such as?"

"That you have me." He takes my hand and places it over his heart. I feel the warmth of his chest. "And that I'm trying my hardest." He leans down and kisses me softly. "You make me want to be a better version of myself. The old version... Before—" He cuts himself off.

"What's that old saying?" I stare up at him. "Love like you've never been hurt."

"I wish I could." His eyes search mine. "How do you do that?"

I shrug as emotion overwhelms me. For some reason, I tear up because, fuck,

I wish I knew.

He sits down on the sand, and I sit down beside him. We both stare out at the sea in silence.

I feel like I'm on the precipice of heartache.

Relationships are hard when both people are whole. Relationships are barely doable when one person is broken. But both parties... How could that possibly work?

"Why did you stop seeing Duke?" he asks.

I frown, surprised by his question. "Because I didn't love him."

"How did you know that you didn't love him?"

"Because it didn't bother me if he slept with anyone else, which he did. We had an open relationship. Not that I ever slept with anyone else. I would never put a title on our relationship. I hated the thought of being tied down and trapped."

"How does that differ to how you feel about me?"

"Because—" I pause. "From the first moment I saw you in the street with that homeless man, I could see you."

"For what?"

"For who you really are."

He stares at me.

"I'd been dating all these supposedly great guys who said they loved me. Then there was you, telling me you didn't want me, acting like you hated me, treating me terribly, wanting me to be your whore...but deep down, I always knew."

He drops his head as if overwhelmed with emotion. "Knew what?"

"That you and I would end up together on a beach on the Maldives one day."

He breaks into a slow, sexy smile. "Hungover?"

"Only one of us is hungover."

His eyes twinkle with a certain something. "The other one is smitten."

I smile at the beautiful man in front of me. His eyes oozing with honesty. His hair windswept and wild. "I do love you, Seb. So much."

"Show me." He rolls us over so that I'm on top of him.

I sit up, my legs on either side of him, our most sensitive parts touching. I stare down at the beautiful man shining in the moonlight. "You'd better undo that fly on your pants, Mr. Sandman."

He chuckles, and I go up on my knees to give him room to move. He struggles and unzips his suit pants. "Now what?" He smiles up at me.

I pull my panties to the side. "We do this." I slide down onto him.

He looks up at me in awe. "I like that we're doing this."

I smile, the double meaning not lost. "Me too."

Buzz, buzz, buzz, buzz.

Hmm, what's that?

"Hello," Sebastian answers in a husky voice. He stands and walks over to the window and peers out onto the street below as he listens to whoever is on the phone. "Is he all right?"

He falls silent.

I rub my eyes as I watch him. Who's he talking to?

"I'll be on the first plane home." He nods and turns. His eyes find mine. "See you soon." He hangs up.

"What's going on?" I ask.

"They found Theodore."

I smile. "Great."

"He's dead."

26

April

I BLINK IN SURPRISE. "WHAT?"

"He committed suicide. They found his body in a rental car in a forest in the north."

My heart constricts. "Oh no. When?"

"It looks like a while ago. Probably as soon as he went missing."

"God," I sigh sadly.

"I have to go home." He walks into the walk-in wardrobe and retrieves his suitcase.

"Of course."

"You're having a good time. Stay with the others. Fly home with them, and I'll meet you back in London." He puts his suitcase up on the desk and begins to throw his things into it.

"No, I'm coming with you." I stand and retrieve my suitcase.

"It's not necessary," he mutters, completely distracted with his packing." I can feel his stress levels skyrocketing by the second.

"Seb." I hug him from behind. "I'm leaving with you."

He turns and takes me into his arms. We stay silent for a while, just holding each other.

Suicide. Is there a worse death? So much sadness. So much pain.

"I'll pack our things. You organize the flight," I say with renewed purpose.

"Okay." He kisses me. "I'm sorry."

"Don't be." I smile up at him. "Promise me that we can come back here."

"I promise." He pulls out of our hug and gets on his phone. "Hello, I need two seats on the first plane to London." His eyes flick over to me. "Yes, chartered, if possible."

He listens. "Three hours?"

I nod.

"Yes, okay, thank you."

The plane lands on the runway. We've arrived in London.

I look over to Sebastian, who has said two words the entire flight home. He's staring straight ahead, leaning back against the headrest, lost in his own thoughts. There's a deep sadness within him. It's circling around the both of us, taunting me with the happy weekend we've lost.

I wish I could say something worthy, something to make this all better, but there is nothing, so I stay silent.

Apparently, there are already whispers in the media. Bart has also called ahead to tell us the press is at the airport, waiting for an update from their beloved Garcia. I guess they realize that if he's coming home early, something big is going down.

Poor Theodore.

How the hell does Sebastian announce to the world that Theodore is now dead when he's been assuring them that he was fine?

I drag my hand down my face. God, this is a fucking nightmare.

I feel guilty for leaving Bart alone in this when he needs me most. Maybe I'll work behind the scenes for him this week.

The plane comes to a stop, and Sebastian stands and fusses

368

around in the overhead. He retrieves his suit bag and goes to the bathroom to freshen up. When he returns, his thick black hair is neat, his suit is crisp, and his beautiful face is grim.

He's ready for business.

There are two versions of Mr. Garcia: The one the world knows, the hard-ass workaholic who has a secret penchant for high-class hookers. Then there's my Seb, the loving man who makes me feel like the most beautiful woman on Earth.

I hate that the world doesn't get to see the real him, but I know that this is how he is.

Guarded.

I smile softly, hoping that he can feel my affection for him. He has the worst week coming up, and nobody can help him through it. He and he alone will face the press. It is his voice that everyone will turn to for guidance in such uncertain times.

The doors are opened, and the cabin crew and pilot shake Sebastian's hand as they stand by the door.

"Thank you." He nods.

I smile and follow him down the stairs, hanging back a little, unsure where I am supposed to be. Sebastian stops and turns back. He holds his hand out to me.

I frown at him. He wants to be seen together? He's usually so private.

"Are you coming?" he asks, hand outstretched.

"Are you sure?"

"Yes."

I take his hand, and my heart begins to hammer. This is it. The announcement of our relationship.

The doorman opens the door, and we walk into the airport.

Cameras flash. People run.

"Mr. Garcia, is it true that the Prime Minister is dead?" someone calls.

Sebastian exhales and pulls me along quickly.

"Is this your new wife, Mr. Garcia? Have you been on a honeymoon?"

Sebastian rolls his lips, unimpressed as we march along.

"What is your name, miss?" someone yells. "What does your ex-wife think of your new girlfriend?"

What?

Sebastian stops and turns back to the man who called it out. He glares at him. The man takes a step back, unsure of the consequences. Sebastian's chest rises and falls, and I know it's taking all his strength not to smack the man in the mouth. I give Sebastian's hand a subtle tug, and he turns back to me. We start walking towards the exit to where our car is waiting.

"When are you having a press conference?" someone calls.

We walk out through the front doors, cameras still flashing. We arrive at the waiting black car.

God, this really is horrendous.

I drag my hand through my hair. What must I look like?

Sebastian opens the back door of the SUV, and I slide in. He closes the door behind me.

What?

I peer out of the tinted windows to see what he is doing, speaking with the photographers. His face is angry, and whatever he is saying, they are all taking notes.

He turns and gets into the car beside me. He slams the door.

"Drive!" he orders.

"Yes, sir."

The car pulls out into the street.

I turn and look out the rear window to see the camera flashes disappearing into the distance.

I turn back to face forward, my heart still hammering in my chest.

I glance over to see Sebastian's elbow resting on the car door, his hand on his temple. He's staring out at the passing traffic, miles away.

Poor Theodore.

Good morning, babe.

Wishing you luck for today xoxo

A text bounces back from him.

Missed you this morning. I didn't want to wake you.
Call you later. Love you

xo

I smile. *Love you.* Two little words that mean so much. I get up and shower, make my way downstairs, and turn on the television.

I make myself some coffee and toast, and then I hear the headline on the news.

"A press conference has been called by Sebastian Garcia and is scheduled for today at 11:00 a.m. Mr. Garcia, who flew in from the Maldives last night with his partner April Bennet, is in damage control amidst allegations that the Prime Minister has passed away."

I stare at the television. There's footage of us walking hand in hand out of the airport last night, and people firing questions at Sebastian.

I drop to the couch. *Shit.*

My phone beeps with a text. It's Jeremy.

Oh my God, we need to have lunch today.
I have so much to tell you.

My God, we do. I have so much to tell him. I spoke to him only briefly last week. He was still waiting for the blood tests to see if Bart had been drugged or not. I wonder what the hell is going on with those two. I reply:

Sounds great.

I smile and wave when I arrive at the restaurant.

Jeremy is sitting at the back with two cups of coffee already on the table.

"Hello, gorgeous." He smiles broadly.

I kiss his cheek. "Hello. It's so good to see you." I sit down. "Is this my coffee?"

"Yes." He winks. "Just as you like it, although I would have preferred wine. I took the liberty of ordering us lunch. I knew you would have to get back."

I reach over and take his hand in mine. "Oh my God, what's happening? Every time I call you, Bart is there, and you can't speak."

Jeremy rolls his eyes in an overexaggerated way. "That fucking bitch drugged him and set him up with those hookers."

"Who?" I screw up my face.

"His wife."

"Why, though?"

"To break us up. She's had her suspicions about us for a while now. He hasn't been sleeping with her, so she's assuming that he's sleeping with me."

I sit back, not buying it for a second. "But she's still married to him. Wouldn't that mean that he cheated on her as well?"

"Look." He sips his coffee. "I know how this must look from the outside, but his drug tests came back, and he definitely had Rohypnol in his system."

"The test was positive?" I frown, surprised.

"Yes."

I stare at him. "That means Sebastian was drugged too."

"Well, thankfully, the security guard got him home safe."

"Hmm." My mind goes into overdrive. "Why do you think it was Bart's wife?"

"Only she would organize female hookers. Anyone else who was trying to hurt him would have known his taste was towards men."

"True."

"And she called me in the morning, saying that she hadn't been able to contact him, asking me if I could go to his room to check if he was okay."

I narrow my eyes. "What a bitch."

"Anyway, I don't care." He smiles sarcastically. "She put her own nail in the coffin. He's left her for good now."

I blow into my coffee. "So he's moved in with you?"

"No." He shrugs. "Thinks we should live apart for a while. Date and get back to trusting each other."

I frown. "That's weird."

"I know." He looks around. "I keep feeling like there is another part to this story."

"What do you mean?"

"There is something else going on with him, but I just can't for the life of me..." His face falls as he stares at something across the restaurant.

I look over to where he is looking. "What is it?"

"Look who's in town," he whispers, anger oozing out of his every pore.

I frown as I look back over to where he is staring. "Who?"

"Nicolas Anastas."

"Who's that?"

"See the two men sitting near the bar?"

I look over to see two men. One, a gorgeous European man, and the other with curly brown hair. "Which one?"

"The Greek god."

"Oh." I smile as I stare over at him. "Perfect analogy. He is, isn't he? Who's he?"

"He's a psychologist and an acclaimed author. He's also loaded and quite famous. He lives in America. Lived in London for a couple of years a while back, and he and Bart became good friends. Bart's his solicitor."

I raise my eyebrows. "Hmm."

"It was he who first made Bart question his sexuality."

"What?"

"He told me that whenever he was with Nicolas, he found himself aroused and dreaming of them having sex together. He thought about him all the time."

My eyes widen in horror. "Bart told you that?"

"This was long before we got together, but..."

"You think Bart and Nicolas have reconnected?"

"Well, if he's back in town, I know they definitely will have seen each other. He only comes to London to see Bart."

Oh hell.

I puff air into my cheeks. "With all due respect, Jeremy, Bart seems like a pretty fucked-up guy. You can do a lot better than him."

"I know." He sighs sadly. A waitress walks by. "Excuse me," Jeremy says. "I've changed my mind. Can I see the drinks menu, please?"

"Of course." She smiles.

I watch Jeremy for a moment. "Why are you still working for him? Why are you still with him? How many chances are you going to give the man?"

"I love him."

"Sometimes, love isn't worth the payoff." I sigh. "Look at you. You're gorgeous and in the prime of your life. But you're in love with a married man who has now finally left his wife, yet he still isn't willingly returning to your bed."

"He loves me, April. I know he loves me."

"I don't doubt it, but it seems that he needs time to get his shit together. Perhaps he needs to sow his gay wild oats or something before you and he can plan a future."

He exhales heavily. "Maybe."

Jeremy's eyes drift back to the other side of the restaurant. I look over to see the Greek god standing to pay the bill. He's tall and powerful, dominant.

"He's gorgeous." Jeremy sighs.

He really is.

I reach over and take Jeremy's hand in mine. "So are you, and you're so young. Too young to be putting up with this fucking bull-shit. You have your whole life ahead of you."

Jeremy exhales heavily as his eyes find mine. "Enough of my disastrous love life. How's Garcia treating you?"

I smile, grateful for the change of subject. "Surprisingly well."

The week has been strained. I've hardly seen Sebastian. His stress levels are at an all-time high. He leaves before I wake in the morning, and he gets home late at night.

Meeting after meeting, press conference after press conference. I've been working and coming straight back here.

He insists on me sleeping at his house, even though he's hardly here. He says he's not sleeping without me and that it is nonnegotiable. I can't say that I'm upset about it. I don't want to sleep without him either. We turned a corner in the Maldives. I'm not sure where that corner leads to, but I'm down for the ride.

Parliament is going to vote on Friday, and word has it that Sebastian is going to be elected as the next Prime Minister of the United Kingdom.

Tonight, we are meeting the gang at a restaurant for dinner. I'm ready, dressed, and waiting to go.

Where is he?

My phone beeps with a text from Sebastian.

Sorry babe, running late.
Kevin will pick you up in five minutes.
I'll meet you there.

I reply.

Okay

The headlights swing into the driveway, and I grab my coat. Well, this is new, meeting his friends without him beside me. He'd better not be too late. I make my way out and smile at Kevin before I get into the backseat.

"Hello."

"Hello, April. Lovely night, isn't it?"

"It is."

He reverses the car out, and we pull into the street. I watch the traffic zoom by, and I think back to all those years ago when I was hiding around the side of Sebastian's house while he went inside with Brandon.

Brandon. Now, there's a blast from the past. Sebastian hasn't mentioned him to me at all. Hmm, I'll have to remember to ask about him later.

Twenty minutes later, we pull up at the curb. Kevin parks and gets out of the car. He then opens the door for me.

"Have a lovely night," he says with a warm smile.

"You too. Thank you." I make my way inside and look around. The restaurant is bustling. Chatter and laughter fill the space. There's a big bar in the centre of the room with chunky metal stools around it. Huge brass lights hang down low, creating a trendy vibe. I catch sight of Spencer at the back of the restaurant. On closer inspection, I see the others are sitting with him. I make my way over.

"Hello."

"Hi." They all smile.

Spencer pulls out the chair beside him and taps it.

"Thanks." I slide into my seat. "How are you feeling?" I ask Bree.

"Oh God." She winces. "I'm still not right, and I am never drinking again."

"Big week, huh?" Julian says.

Spencer fills my glass with wine and passes it to me.

"I'll say," I agree.

"How's he going?" asks Spencer.

"He's okay." I shrug. "Very busy and stressed, but that's to be expected."

"I still can't believe that Theodore has died. Do they know any of the details? Was he murdered?" Charlotte asks.

"Good grief." Spencer huffs. "Murdered? This isn't an action movie, Lottie, calm down. Why do you think everyone is fucking murdered? If I go missing, you'll all know who did it."

Everyone laughs.

"I'm not sure about any of the details," I lie. I don't know what Sebastian has told them, but I'm not oversharing.

Julian's eyes hold mine and, once again, I'm reminded that if Sebastian knows something, Julian and Spencer do too. He tells them everything.

The group continue to talk conspiracy theories. I look around the restaurant; it has a really cool vibe. My eyes roam over the crowd and then stop when I get to the bar. I see a familiar person sitting with another woman.

My blood runs cold.

Helena.

What is she doing here?

Sebastian walks through the front door, towering over everyone around him, and flanked by security. Wearing a dark suit and a pale blue shirt with tie, he looks as handsome as ever.

Sebastian Garcia cannot hide in a crowd, and it has nothing to do with being the Prime Minister.

My eyes immediately drift back to Helena to see if she notices him. Right on cue, she glances up and sees him. Her face lights up, and she smiles softly.

Huh?

That doesn't look like the face of the woman who hates him.

My skin begins to crawl.

I watch on as she stands and walks towards him. He glances up and his step falters when he sees her. She approaches him. Her face is hopeful, and then she smiles and says something. His security guards step forward and Sebastian holds his hand up to them as a warning to stay back.

Helena rises on her toes to kiss his cheek, but he turns his head away from her.

Cold and hard, in front of everyone who is watching.

My stomach twists. I know how much his dismissal hurts.

Helena drops her head.

God...

And for the first time ever, I feel sorry for her.

It's one thing to have a marriage break down, but to fuck it up so badly with a man like Sebastian Garcia must take you to a new level of regret.

How would you ever forgive yourself for losing him?

I watch her watching him.

"Shouldn't it, April?" Brielle asks, snapping me out of my thoughts.

"Oh, sorry." I return my attention to her. "I beg your pardon. I didn't hear you."

"I said that sangria should be used as a weapon in war."

I giggle and raise my glass to her. "Agreed."

Sebastian appears at our table. "Hello." He smiles and loosens his tie.

"About time, fucker." Spencer smiles.

Sebastian sits down beside me and leans over to kiss my cheek. "Hello, sweetheart," he whispers, his finger running up the back of my neck. "Sorry I'm late."

"Hi." I smile bashfully. God, he's a beautiful man. I glance up to see the rest of the table—and the restaurant, for that matter—are watching our interaction. I blush, embarrassed. Sebastian reaches over and, in one sharp movement, pulls my chair towards him. He takes my hand and places it over his thick quad.

He picks up a menu. "Just so you all know, I'm eating everything in the house tonight. This is my breakfast, lunch, *and* dinner."

"You haven't eaten at all today?" Charlotte gasps. "Sebastian, that's so bad for you."

"Don't worry, I'm sure he had a liquid lunch," Spencer mutters dryly, raising a brow.

They continue talking, and my eyes fall back to Helena. She's sitting back at the bar now, watching our interaction.

Have his friends seen her? Do they shun her too?

Once upon a time, this would have been her sitting at this table in my place.

I wonder what it feels like to watch us from the outside.

I can't imagine.

And for the first time, I get it. I get why she won't walk away and leave him alone.

I understand why she's hanging around and trying to cause trouble to gain his attention.

Because any attention from Sebastian Garcia would be worth it.

She's still in love with him.

It's late, and we are lying in bed. Sebastian is watching the news, and I'm pretending to read. The reporters on the television are speculating about Theodore's death, going on and on and on about the possibilities and who will be voted in as the next Prime Minister.

But my mind is firmly on Helena.

I'm not sure if I should bring this up, but the poison is burning a hole inside of me. I have to say it out loud.

"Why didn't you tell me that Helena is still in love with you?" I ask quietly.

He pauses before answering, his gaze firmly on the television. "Because it doesn't matter."

"To whom?"

"To everyone. Least of all her." He continues watching television.

I think for a moment as I watch him. What does that even mean?

"Has she ever asked you to take her back?"

"Every time I speak to her."

Ouch.

"Is that why she does all these things? Is it some sort of revenge to try and hurt you?"

He shrugs, clearly uninterested.

"Sebastian, I don't understand. Explain this to me. I thought you hated each other."

"I don't want to talk about this tonight. Seriously? You think I don't have enough on my plate at the moment, April? Now I have to deal with your insecurities."

"Just forget it." I exhale heavily and put my book down on the nightstand. I roll over and turn my back to him. Another thought enters my mind. Why haven't I asked this before? "What did the police say?"

He stays silent.

I roll over to face him. "When she broke into this house, did they charge her for breaking and entering?"

His jaw clenches, and his tongue glides over his bottom lip. He's annoyed.

Uneasiness fills me.

"We had no evidence. The cameras weren't working."

I frown as I stare at him. "She wasn't charged?"

"No."

"But you could have had a restraining order put on her. You did that, though, right?"

He reaches over and puts his hand on my thigh. "I've done everything right by you, April," he says. "You have no reason to doubt me."

"Answer my question, Sebastian."

He hesitates, but eventually answers, "No."

I stare at him for a moment. I open my mouth to say something.

"Don't," he warns. "This conversation is over."

I blink, surprised.

Wow.

I roll over and turn my back to him. I can't believe him.

I inhale deeply and close my eyes as I try to chase the demons away, because those bitches are scared and reading more into this than they should.

How could they not?

He's still protecting her.

He switches the television off and snuggles in behind me. His body is close to mine. He kisses my shoulder, and I stare into the darkness.

There are secrets between us. I can feel them lurking.

What isn't he telling me?

We lie in silence for a while, and eventually he says, "Good night, sweetheart. I love you."

Do you?

"Good night," I whisper.

But it's not a good night. It's a terrible night.

Sebastian's ex-wife still loves him...and maybe, just maybe, he still loves her.

The alarm goes off.

Sebastian bounces out of bed and walks into the bathroom, leaving me in the darkness, my mind a clusterfuck of confusion. I hear the shower running, and I go over what we talked about last night, though it's not what we spoke about that has me concerned. It's what he wouldn't discuss that's triggered me.

I get up and walk into the bathroom. His eyes meet mine for a brief moment before he turns away and continues to wash himself.

I sit up on the bathroom vanity. Eventually, he turns off the shower and gets out. He begins to dry himself with a black towel.

"Can we talk about last night?" I ask.

"April." He dries himself aggressively. "I don't have the mental energy to fight with you this week."

"Why are you protecting her?"

"For fuck's sake!" he cries. "Are you listening to me at all? Press conferences, police questioning, federal taxation issues, organizing a funeral service and dealing with the entire fucking country's questions." He throws up his hands in disgust. "I'm so stressed out that my head is about to explode, and you're carrying on about a woman I divorced seven fucking years ago. The Cabinet is voting for a new Prime Minister today, and I'm the front-runner." He wraps his towel around his waist. "Do you have any fucking idea the amount of pressure I'm under?" He marches out into the bedroom and into his walk-in wardrobe.

My shoulders slump. God, he's right.

This week is not the week to talk about anything of importance. I scrunch up my face in regret.

You idiot.

He dresses in his suit, acting angry, while I sit on the bed and watch on in silence. He stands in front of the mirror and does up his tie. My stomach somersaults. How can an angry man putting a tie on be so sexy?

I get up and go to him to take over his tie tying. "I'm sorry."

His eyes meet mine. "I just—"

"I know, babe." I rise up on my toes and kiss his big lips. "I'm just being an insecure cow."

"You have me, April. You know that you have me."

"I know." I smile up at him. He's right, I do know that I have him. There's no question about that. "No stress tonight, I promise."

His hand slides around to my behind, and he pulls my hips towards his waiting dick. "What I really need is a good stress reliever." He gives me a pump with his hips.

"You're a sex maniac, Mr. Garcia."

He gives me a slow, sexy smile. "And you are excellent in bed." He pumps me with his hips again. "Which is why we're perfect together."

"Well..." I rearrange his collar. "I will be at my most excellent best tonight, sir."

His dark eyes hold mine. "I'll look forward to it."

. . .

8:00 p.m. and I look at myself in the full-length mirror. Holy hell on a cracker, who am I?

Determined to give Sebastian a stress-relieving night, I went to the adult shop today and bought myself a sexy little hooker outfit.

Little being the operative word.

I'm wearing black suede thigh-high boots, black leather crotchless panties, and a black leather bra with the boob parts cut out. I have on a full face of glamourous makeup complete with fake lashes, red lipstick, and I'm wearing a long, dark wig, with a red satin ribbon tied strategically in a bow around my neck.

I'm unrecognizable, even to me.

I'm nervous seeing him like this. What will he think?

Who am I kidding? I know he'll love it.

The man's a fucking deviant.

I walk downstairs and pour myself a shot of tequila. I want it to be a complete fantasy for him, sensually as well as visually. I remember back in the day when I saw him at the Escape Club. He would always be smoking a cigar and drinking strong liquor. I go to his bar and take out one of his cigars and light it. I inhale and the smoke fills my lungs.

Hmm, it's been a long time since I enjoyed one of these babies.

I won't even smell like me. The tequila, the smoke, the look of me...they all bring back memories of when we first met. When he was a bad man, and I was pretending to be a bad girl, though I didn't have to pretend too hard. I loved every second of our time in the club. It was the ultimate fantasy...for both of us.

I place a chair in front of the door, and sit down, spread my legs, and wait.

I see the headlights come into the driveway, and I smile darkly as I inhale the cigar.

Mr. Garcia, come to Mummy.

Game on.

. . .

The door opens and Sebastian closes it behind him. He walks in casually. He frowns when he smells the cigar smoke, and he glances up, stopping in his tracks. He inhales sharply, and I know that he likes what he sees. I take a long, slow drag of the cigar and blow a stream of smoke.

"Cash or credit?" I whisper.

He drops his briefcase on the floor. "Cash." He takes his jacket off and throws it to the side with urgency.

I hold my smile. Oh, he likes it all right.

He jerks his tie loose and puts his hand on my chin to lift my face to his.

Electricity crackles as we stare at each other.

I inhale the cigar slowly, and he drops his lips to mine. He inhales the smoke I breathe out.

Fuck.

He licks my open lips and then slowly unbuttons his shirt, his eyes never leaving mine.

His thick, broad chest comes into view, as well as his muscular stomach and the trail of black hair that disappears down into his pants.

He takes the cigar from me and pours himself a glass of tequila. "Get on your knees."

I drop to the floor on my knees, and he unzips his pants and steps out of them. He falls into my place on the chair. He spreads his legs and leans back, inhaling the cigar, drink in hand as he watches me.

His cock is thick and heavy between his legs, engorged with the large risen vein through the centre.

He inhales his cigar again. "Suck. My. Cock," he mouths. The smoke drifts out of his mouth and dances in the air.

Fuck, he's a dirty bastard.

I spread his legs and kiss his inner thigh. He grabs my face aggressively. "I'm not paying to be fucking kissed," he growls.

Jeez.

My arousal begins to hammer, and I lick up the length of his cock. Dark eyes watch me.

"All of it," he mouths.

I take him into my mouth. The taste of pre-ejaculate hits my tongue, and my eyes flutter closed.

He hisses sharply. I flick my tongue over the end of him, teasing as I go, and he grabs the back of my head and pushes me down, forcing me to take all of him.

I gag.

"There's nothing hotter than the sound of a woman choking on my cock," he whispers.

Bastard.

I bet he's heard that sound a million times before.

With both hands on his thick quads, I deep-throat him. He sits back, legs wide, cigar in hand, watching me.

Emotionless and cold.

Detached.

I can feel the arousal building between us. He's rock-hard, and with every stroke of my tongue, my body gets wetter.

He tips his head back and drains his glass of tequila before he pushes me back. "Come." He holds out his hand.

I stand, and he leads me up the stairs. I smile, knowing just how hard his cock is and how good I'm going to get it.

We get to the top of the stairs, but instead of turning right to his room, he leads me to the left.

Huh?

We walk into the last guest bedroom down the hall, and I frown. I came into this room once when we first met. It has a king-size bed and its own bathroom, and the floor is hardwood instead of carpet. I thought it was odd that it was so different to the rest of the house.

He closes the door behind us and turns towards me.

His eyes are ablaze with desire. There's something different about him tonight; I just can't put my finger on it.

He pulls the blankets back, revealing leather sheets.

Huh? What is this?

"Get on the bed."

I hesitate.

"Now," he orders.

I lie down on the bed. He grabs my hands and brings them up over my head. He pulls the curtains behind the bed to reveal four sets of handcuffs attached to the iron bedframe.

What the hell?

He handcuffs me to the bed with a cold detachment.

My heart begins to hammer with confusion.

What's going on?

He goes to the door and locks it with a key, and then with the same key unlocks a wall-length cabinet.

The air leaves my lungs as the colour drains from my face.

Every sex toy known to man is in here, as well as bottles of lube. Huge dildoes, a sex doll, whips, and bondage gear.

Panic runs through me.

What the fuck is this room?

He takes out a bottle of oil and pours it all over me. It splashes all over the leather sheets.

Dark eyes hold mine.

"Don't tempt the Devil, Cartier. You may not like him."

27

April

Uneasiness fills me.

I'm all for role-play, but...

I swallow a nervous lump in my throat.

He straddles my body and, starting at my toes, he slides up over me. My body begins to relax as his hard dick makes its presence known. His intention unwavering, he does it again, this time stopping at my chest to straddle my body. I'm trapped beneath his strong thighs.

Who's he kidding? I fucking love the Devil.

Bring it.

He begins to rub his hardened cock through the oil between my breasts. His ripped abdomen glistens in the light. My hands are tied above my head, and I stare up at him in awe.

No matter how fucked-up Sebastian Garcia is, his touch silences me every single time.

He grabs my face and brings my ear to his mouth. "So, you want to be my whore?"

I pant, my eyes closing.

His hand tightens on my face as he jerks me hard. "Answer me," he growls.

"Yes," I whimper.

"You want to use your beautiful, creamy cunt to make me happy?"

Fuck. How is he so filthy?

If dirty talk were an Olympic sport, Sebastian Garcia would be the king of the world.

I nod. "Yes."

He licks the side of my face. "Here's how this is going to go," he whispers as his tongue dances near my ear. Goose bumps scatter up my spine. "You're going to clench yourself around my cock so hard that you nearly snap it in two."

I swallow the lump in my throat, on the edge of fear.

"Do you understand me?"

I pant.

"Last warning."

"Y-yes," I stammer. "I am. I mean, I will."

He kneels over my face and rubs the tip of his hard cock over my lips. Pre-ejaculate and oil smear across my face.

His chest is rising and falling as he looks down at me, his dark hair hanging over his face and his muscles glistening with oil. But it's his eyes that are turning me inside out.

He's running on instinct; the need to fuck in him is so hard now that nothing else matters.

His filter is gone, along with his restraint.

I don't know if I've ever seen something so *arousing*.

He leans on his elbow beside me, and he kisses me hard as he pushes my top leg up so that it rests by my shoulder. Then his hand glides down my body, through the oil and over my breasts. Lower...lower.

His thick fingers find that sweet spot between my legs, and he opens my lips as far as they'll go. I inhale sharply. His eyes hold mine as he stretches me open.

Every time we have sex, he surprises me.

Nothing is ever the same with this man. As soon as I even think about getting comfortable, he ups the ante, taking it to a higher level.

He gives me more.

His tongue dances seductively against mine. I'm writhing beneath him. My eyes can't stay open, and my arms are beginning to hurt from being tied above my head.

I moan into his mouth, and then his teeth begin to roam along my jaw. He bites my neck.

Fuck.

He takes my nipple in his mouth and bites it hard. I cry out, and his eyes flicker closed.

He's getting off on my pain.

Huh?

Uneasiness begins to flow through me. This is new territory. It's a Sebastian Garcia I haven't met before.

He sucks his way down my body, moving lower and lower until he reaches his goal. He stops and spreads me wide, and he stares at me.

I hold my breath as I look up at the ceiling. What is he doing?

I lift my head to watch him. His body is down on the bed now, parallel to my sex. He slowly drags his fingers through my flesh as he lies on his side, completely preoccupied with his task.

"Seb," I whisper.

"Don't come."

Huh?

His mouth comes over me, and he sucks hard. So hard that it smarts, and I curl my legs around his head to try and escape him.

"Open," he growls as he slams my legs down on the mattress.

Oh...

His thick tongue glides up and over my sex, and then he lifts my hips and licks my behind, his hungry eyes holding mine.

He wants me there. Jeez.

He swirls his tongue again, and I shudder. Fuck, I swear I'm going to come so hard that I'll pass out. This is too much.

Then he's all in as he holds my hips up, deep tongue and whiskers on me. I'm all over his face.

He's in places that he shouldn't be, and, oh, it's too good. I shudder again.

"I said don't fucking come." He bites my clitoris, and I jump.

"*Ouch*."

"I'll give you fucking *ouch* in a minute." He flips me over so that I am on my knees. My wrists sting from the pull of the handcuffs. He shuffles me around and lifts me onto my knees, and then he spreads them apart.

He gets up, and I hear the cupboard door open. *Oh no.* What is he getting?

My heart begins to hammer. The bed dips again when he kneels behind me.

I drop my head to the mattress and hold my breath, unsure, aroused, and about to have a heart attack.

His tongue flutters over my back entrance, and I close my eyes as heat begins to pump through me. Hmm.

God, this should not feel as good as it does. He really begins to eat me, and I clench, needing a deeper connection. He must be able to sense it, and he slides three of his thick fingers into my sex.

I moan as my body begins to ripple around him. My hips have their own agenda, and I push back onto his face.

This is wrong but *so* fucking hot.

He slides a finger into my ass, and I moan.

No.

He adds another finger, and my eyes roll back in my head.

"Don't come," he growls.

What?

I moan again.

Crack.

He slaps me hard, and my eyes shoot open.

"Don't you dare fucking come."

I can't stop it. I convulse and scream into the mattress.

"You're going to pay for that," he threatens.

He puts the tip of his cock at my back entrance and begins to push forward.

"No. Sebastian!" I yell.

He stops, and silence falls between us

I can hear him panting and gasping for air. He's struggling as he tries to control his urge to fuck my ass.

Prolonged silence.

What is he doing?

He grips my hip bones, and I know he's on the edge of control. I wiggle my hips a little to bring him back to the moment. It works. He slaps me hard, and then he bends to lick me again. He moans into me, and hell, has there ever been a hotter sound?

I smile against the mattress. I thought I'd lost him there for a moment.

He gets up, and I frown. What's he doing now? I hear something tear, and I glance over my shoulder to see him rolling a condom on.

What the hell? He's really into his role-play.

Horror dawns.

Maybe a little too much.

Is this how he fucks his whores? Is this what he does to them?

He slaps me hard again, and I wince in pain. *What's with the slapping?*

I'm not sure I like this.

The bed dips, and he kneels behind me. He glides his tip over my back entrance and through the lips of my sex.

"Do you know how hot you look from this angle?" He rubs his fingers over my behind. He's still desperate to have me there.

With one knee on the mattress and one foot on the floor, he slowly pushes himself into me and lets out a deep, guttural moan.

My heart constricts.

He isn't having sex with me now. In his mind, he's fucking a stranger.

He's with a prostitute.

I scrunch my eyes shut. *Be careful what you wish for, April.*

"Good girl," he whispers, and kisses my back. "Just like that." He leans over and begins to ride me, his hips working in short, thick pumps. "You love my cock, don't you, my dirty little girl?"

I close my eyes. Hell, sometimes I wish I didn't.

He moans.

"Your cunt feels so hot and creamy," he whispers darkly. "Clench for me, baby. Break it."

My body releases a deep shudder. I'm going to come again to the sound of his dirty talking.

I'm as fucked up as he is. I'm loving this shit.

He grabs a handful of my hair and pulls my head back as he slams into me.

I cry out, the air knocked from my lungs.

Then he's riding me hard.

The bed is hitting the wall, and the sound of our skin slapping together is echoing around the room.

Ouch. I close my eyes to try and deal with him.

My body begins to burn. His moans are loud, and, God, this is full on.

I've never been fucked like this before.

Rough...*so rough.*

He's a lot of man to take.

I whimper, and he grabs the back of my head and pushes my face into the mattress. With both hands, he manoeuvres my spine so that my shoulders are down on the bed, leaving me handcuffed and completely at his mercy.

He brings his feet to either side of my body and squats over me. His cock is so deep inside, and his hands are pushing my back down with his deep, fast, punishing pumps. My eyes roll back in my head.

Thump, thump, thump goes the bed on the wall.

Oh no, I'm going to come.

He begins to moan, deep and guttural, and I smile into the mattress.

Here he goes. I can feel it building.

He hisses loud and holds himself deep, and then he cries out as he jerks hard.

In the final showdown, he pumps me so hard that I might just break.

I cry out as the last of my resilience is stolen from me.

I slump onto the bed, my eyes filled with tears.

He drops his head to my back, as if collecting himself, and then he reaches up and releases the handcuffs.

Without a word, he gets up and walks into the bathroom.

I pant to myself.

I sit up and put my head into my hands.

What was that?

I get up and walk into the bathroom to see him with both hands leaning on the bathroom vanity. He's staring at his reflection in the mirror, his chest rising and falling as he tries to catch his breath.

He's wet with perspiration, his hair and eyes wild.

He looks up, and his cold eyes meet mine. He tears off the condom and throws it in the waste bin, as if disgusted.

What?

I don't know what's going on here, but this is fucked up.

I turn to walk out of the bedroom and down the hall. I hear him marching out after me.

"Don't you leave me!" he cries.

I turn to face him.

He's panting with crazy fear in his eyes.

"I'm working on it." He shakes his head. "I'm... I'm working on it," he stammers. "Don't leave me. Please," he begs. "I swear I'll change."

My face falls.

And I thought my demons were bad.

I go to take him in my arms. "It's okay, baby," I whisper. He drops his head to my shoulder, and I hold him.

He's distraught. Close to tears.

"It's okay, I'm not going anywhere," I tell him.

He holds me so tightly, and he seems distraught over it.

"It's okay," I whisper against his hair. "It's okay."

We stand like this in the hallway for a long time—his head on my neck, and my arms protectively around his shoulders—until we have to move. "Come on, let's have a shower and wash this oil off," I whisper up at him.

His haunted eyes hold mine. I lean up and kiss him softly. He screws up his face against mine.

Whatever has him scared must be bad. He's petrified that I'm leaving.

"Come on." I lead him down to the bathroom, and we get into the shower. He takes the soap into his hands and begins to wash the oil off my body in silence, leaving me to stare up at him.

I don't know what the hell just happened, but I'm not pushing him.

Whatever it is, he'll tell me when he's ready.

He washes my sex, and I wince. His face falls. "Did I hurt you?" he asks quietly.

"No."

He clenches his jaw as if stopping himself from saying something.

I kiss his big, beautiful lips. "It's okay, baby."

"Nothing about this is okay."

I hold his face in my hands. He looks so sad and lost as the water beads on his face in the steamy room. We wash each other in silence, and we eventually get out. He dries me off first and then himself, and we get into bed.

I hold him in my arms. Tonight, it's different. His head is on my chest.

We lie in silence as I run my fingers through his hair. Every now and then, I kiss his forehead in reassurance.

"It wasn't her fault," he whispers into the darkness. I frown. "I was too much for her."

I don't want to throw him off before he tells me what he's talking about, so I choose to stay silent.

"In the months leading up to the divorce, I couldn't..."

Helena. He's talking about Helena.

I kiss his forehead again, trying to encourage him to open up.

"She was small. I was big. I liked it rough, she—"

"Didn't?" I murmur.

"She kept pulling me up during sex. In the end, I—" He pauses, and I know that the memory is still painful. "I was so scared that I was going to push her too far that I couldn't turn my mind off." He kisses my breast, and I hold him tightly.

"She wanted vanilla. I needed chocolate."

I exhale as the jigsaw puzzle finally falls into place.

"You stopped having sex with her," I whisper.

"I was just trying to get my head around it. Every time we would have sex, I couldn't come. I was too controlled—too in my head. In the end, I didn't even want to go there. It was too stressful for me. I'd have anxiety for the next two days, worrying that I'd been too rough with her."

I hold him tightly. "Baby," I whisper.

He blames himself.

"She started to think I didn't find her attractive anymore."

"Did you?"

"Of course I did. I loved her."

My heart constricts. *Ouch.*

"We fought."

I kiss his temple as I brush the hair back from his forehead.

"I started going away for work. I thought the distance would make us better."

"Did it?"

"She thought I wanted to get away from her—that I didn't want sex because I was seeing someone else."

My heart drops. I already know how this story ends.

He stays silent for a long time, lost in his own thoughts. "In the end, it turned out our gardener had the vanilla she needed."

That bitch.

"This is why you protect her, because you feel responsible?"

"She was hurt."

"She went to another man, Sebastian."

"Because I couldn't—"

"Because *she* couldn't," I cut him off.

He exhales heavily.

"Is that why you like call girls? Because you know they can take it rough? Because you know that there is no chance you can hurt them?"

He stays silent, and I know that it is.

I think for a moment, and then I smile. "Maybe this was God's way of saving you for me."

I feel him smile against my chest. "My sweet coffee girl who fucks like the sexiest whore I ever met."

I giggle. "You know, I can't regret how we met, not even for a moment, because I don't believe we would have worked out if we had stayed together back then."

He leans up on his elbow. "What about now?"

"I've been looking for a man to deliver me straight-up chocolate fudge all my life."

He chuckles and then falls serious. "I'm not too much for you?"

"You're perfect for me," I whisper as I kiss him. "I always knew something was missing, Seb, and it wasn't until I slept with you that I found out what it was. I need you like this; I need this darker form of lovemaking...more than anything."

He screws up his face against my lips. "I love you. Promise me you'll never leave."

"I promise." My heart somersaults. His words are so heartfelt. He really does love me. I can feel it pouring out of him.

This poor, beautiful man has been to hell and back, all because he was too sexual for his prim and proper adulterous wife.

"I do have one bone to pick with you, though," I say.

"What's that?"

"That sex doll has got to go."

His mouth falls open in fake horror. "Belinda? Spence bought me her. She's a Vero 5000."

I smirk at her name.

"Her pussy has twenty-four settings." He raises his brows to accentuate his point.

I laugh out loud, and he does too. "I'm not sharing you with a twenty-four-setting pussy."

He kisses me softly.

"But the big blue dildo...he can stay." I smile against his lips.

"Yeah, no. That fucker's gone."

Sebastian

"I've got to go, babe." I take April in my arms and hold her tightly. God, I love this woman. I hug her harder.

"Good luck today."

I exhale heavily. Nerves are coursing through my veins. "Thanks. It's being announced at 9:00 a.m."

"You're going to win the vote." She smiles as she rearranges my collar. "I can feel it in my waters."

"If I don't, it's a good excuse to quit politics."

"Then you can be my full-time sex slave." She smiles up at me.

"I'm already your full-time sex slave." I pump her with my hips.

"We'll go out and celebrate when you get home, regardless of the outcome." She smiles.

"Okay."

I kiss her and make my way out to my car. It feels so weird. Tonight, I'll return to the house either as the Prime Minister of the United Kingdom or completely retired from politics. I've already made the call. If I'm not voted in, then I'm walking away.

We sit in the boardroom as the votes are read out. My mind is heavily on Theodore today.

Where is he now? Did he find the peace he was looking for?

When did I last speak to him? I discreetly take my phone out of my pocket and put it under the table on my lap. I go through my call register and scroll back as I search for his name. I'm scrolling and scrolling when something rolls past. I frown, stop, and scroll back up.

Huh.

Outgoing call - Helena - April 4th - 8 minutes

When did I call Helena?

What?

I look at the date and frown. When was that? Did I butt-dial her by accident or something?

I think back to the date. Why does that sound familiar?

I do the math.

My heart drops.

That's the night I was drugged.

My heart begins to hammer in my chest, and the room spins. I don't remember anything about this.

Why the hell did I call Helena? And what the fuck did we talk about for eight minutes?

"The next Prime Minister of the United Kingdom is Sebastian Garcia," the speaker announces.

I glance up to the sound of applause, completely rattled. The room is in a standing ovation. I stand and fake a smile. "Thank you."

What did I talk to Helena about?

Fuck.

28

April

I SIP my coffee as I watch the television on my work computer. The office is abuzz with excitement as everyone waits for the final vote. They're all doing the same as me, watching the coverage live from their desks.

The footage shows the candidates all sitting in the House of Lords in what looks like a courtroom. The commentators are rattling on about who they think is going to win, and how Garcia is the front runner.

Garcia.

I smile proudly. It seems so surreal that this is my life—that I am dating *the* Sebastian Garcia.

To me, he's just a guy who gave a beggar in the street money, and then he bought a bad cup of coffee. It seems like forever ago that we met, and we've been through so much bullshit, but somehow, he made me fall madly in love with him.

And, oh, do I love him.

The footage hones in on Sebastian.

This is it.

"*The next Prime Minister of the United Kingdom is Sebastian Garcia,*" the speaker announces.

"Yes." I clap my hands in excitement. The rest of our office breaks out into cheers and loud yelling.

I watch on as Sebastian glances up to the sound of applause. He looks completely rattled, and I laugh at his shocked face.

The room performs a standing ovation, and Sebastian rises to nervously dip his head and smile. "Thank you."

I well up with tears as I watch him take the podium. He's so humble.

With his dark hair and olive skin, and his big, beautiful heart on display for the rest of the country, I could just die with pride.

"He did it." Jeremy laughs as he comes around the corner. He hugs me and nearly knocks me from my feet. "He did it!" he cries.

"I know." I put my hands over my mouth, hardly able to believe it. "He did. I can't wait to speak with him," I gush.

Jeremy lies back on the chair in my room, wearing a goofy grin. "Look at you, all in love with the Prime Minister and shit."

I giggle as I turn the television coverage off. "Who even am I?"

"The envy of every woman."

I pick up my pen, and an idea springs to mind. "Don't plan anything for lunch break today."

"Why, what are we doing?"

"Buying a congratulatory present."

"Like what?"

"I don't know. Something special that Sebastian can keep forever. A keepsake."

"Hmm." He narrows his eyes. "I'll brainstorm. We need to blow his fucking mind with this gift." He walks towards the door and turns back. "Lunch at one?"

I smile. "Sounds good."

My phone rings and the name Eliza lights up the screen. I smile and pick up.

"He did it," she cries.

I laugh out loud. "I know."

"And can you engrave those?" Jeremy asks.

I smile to myself. We've just bought Sebastian the most beautiful set of cuff links from Tiffany's. They are simple, gold, and complete with diamonds in the classic pattern on each one. I know he will love them.

"Yes," the jeweller replies.

"How long will that take?" I ask.

"Around twenty minutes."

I cringe. "I have to be back at the office. I have a client coming in."

"I'll wait for them for you," Jeremy offers.

"Really?" I smile. "You're the best." I kiss his cheek because he really is. I swear he spent all morning googling these damn cuff links and where we could buy them from.

He nailed the brief. These are perfect.

It just completely filled my credit card, but who cares. It's for Sebastian.

My phone rings.

April's Fool

I quickly kiss Jeremy, and with a quick wave, I walk out of the store.

"Congratulations, Mr. Prime Minister." I smile.

"Can you believe it?"

"I can. I'm so proud of you Sebastian."

"Thank you, it means a lot."

"I guess you're busy?"

"Swamped. Listen, I know we said that we were going to celebrate tonight, but—"

"It's okay if you have something on," I cut him off, and my

heart drops. I can't help but feel a little disappointed. I wanted to give him my present.

"Well—" He pauses. "My parents have organized a little get-together for my close family and friends."

I frown. His parents?

They live here? Why hasn't he mentioned them before?

"Oh."

"So I'll pick you up on my way home."

"You want me to come?" I squeak.

"Of course."

I open my mouth to say something, but words fail me. I mean, it's one thing to meet the parents and family, but to do it in front of everyone on the night he has been elected Prime Minister of the entire fucking country is my worst nightmare.

"I'll be there about seven."

"Okay, sounds great," I lie.

"See you then." He hangs up.

I begin to power walk back to the office in complete panic.

Shit.

Fuck me fucking swinging, what the hell do I wear to this?

A family party at his house...*argh!*

I text Jeremy.

Sos. Help!

Sebastian is having a family celebratory party tonight.
What the hell should I wear?

My phone instantly rings. It's Jeremy.

"H-hello," I stammer.

"He just threw this on you?"

"Yes, and I'm meeting his parents. What will I wear?" I shriek in a panic.

"I don't know. I'll have a look for something. Leave it with me."

"I'm going to get you fired."

"Oh, like I care. My boss is an asshole."

I widen my eyes. "One you happen to be dating."

"Yeah, that's right, so he can suck my dick. I'm taking an extra hour for lunch. What's he going to do, fire me? He's probably staring into Nicolas Anastas' big brown eyes as we speak."

"You know, one day you'll be my assistant and not his." I smile gratefully.

"Hurry up about it, will you? I'm sick of his bullshit."

"Ha-ha, okay, I'm working on it. Thank you."

I hang up and rush into my building. Who knew that Jeremy would become such a lovely friend?

I take the elevator and watch the dial going up. If Bart *is* sleeping with Nicolas behind Jeremy's back, I'm going to go postal.

That guy's a fucking asshole.

7:00 p.m.

I read the text from Sebastian.

Pulling into your street now.

I reply.

Okay, I'll come down.

I run into my bedroom and take one last look at myself. I'm wearing a fitted chocolate-coloured dress that Jeremy bought me from some fancy designer store, as well as black heels. Gah, my bank balance got fucked up the ass today, but who cares?

I'm meeting the parents.

My blonde, shoulder-length hair is down in loose curls, and I'm wearing natural makeup.

I grab my purse and my coat and make my way downstairs.

The black Mercedes wagon is parked at the curb, and Sebastian is standing next to the back door. He sees me, and his face breaks into a breathtaking smile. I practically run and jump into his arms. He laughs as he holds me tightly, and I can tell how excited he is too.

This is a special day.

He opens the back door, and I slide into the seat. He gets in beside me and closes the door. His lips find mine and he kisses me softly as the car pulls out into the traffic. "Hello, Miss Bennet. You look lovely."

"Hi." I dig his present out of my bag. It's wrapped in black parchment paper with a gold ribbon bow. "I got you something."

He holds it in his hand. "Why?"

"Because I'm so proud of you, Seb." I well up. "This is huge." I roll my eyes. "Oh my God, I'm so emotional over you today." I smile, embarrassed. "I keep tearing up every time I think of what you've achieved."

His face softens, and he takes my cheeks in his hands and kisses me tenderly. "Thank you. I love it."

"You haven't even opened it yet."

"I already know I love it." I watch on as he unties the bow and unwraps it. He frowns when he sees the Tiffany's box. He opens it, and his eyebrows shoot up. He pulls the cuff links out and stares at them in the palm of his hand.

"They're engraved." I smile.

He turns them over and reads the inscription.

4.5.21

I love you

April

His mouth falls open as he stares at them. "I love them, and I love you." He quickly begins to take out his current cuff links and change them over. I smile proudly. I think he likes them.

Ten minutes later, we arrive at his house. The lights are all on, and nerves simmer in my stomach. Kevin steps out of the driver's seat and opens the back door.

"Thank you," Sebastian says.

"Thanks." I smile.

"Have a good night, and congratulations, sir," Kevin replies.

"Thank you." Sebastian smiles as he takes my hand. He leads me up the front path to the house and opens the door.

"Surprise!" everyone yells.

The house is full of balloons, and streamers are hanging from the ceiling. Sebastian laughs as we walk in. There are about thirty people here, and everyone is hugging him and laughing. Oh, it's a happy time.

"This is April," he announces to everyone.

I fake a smile as all eyes fall on me. I just want the earth to swallow me up.

"Hello, April!" everyone calls, and they all break out into excited chatter.

I glance over and see Brielle and Charlotte. I make a beeline for them.

"Hello." I smile and kiss them on the cheek. "Thank God you're here," I whisper.

Brielle takes my hand in hers. "Wouldn't miss it for the world."

We stand back and watch on as, one by one, everyone hugs and kisses Sebastian. Everyone is so excited for him.

Eventually, his eyes find mine, and he smiles tenderly across the room.

I just melt.

"God, the way he looks at you," Charlotte whispers.

"Right?" Bree sighs. "I miss that new 'in love' look. Now, I just get the 'I'm going to nail you to the bed' look."

Charlotte and I laugh.

Sebastian comes over and takes my hand to kiss my fingertips. "Come." He leads me to the other living room, where he presents me to others.

"Mom, Dad, Violet...this is April. April, these are my parents and my sister."

"Ah." His mother smiles. She's beautiful with dark hair. She also looks kind. "Hello, my darling." She's softly spoken and has a Spanish accent. She kisses my cheek. "Finally, we get to meet you."

"Hello." I smile, feeling a little better.

His father steps forward, and my heart somersaults in my chest. He's Sebastian's double: tall, olive-skinned, and decidedly Spanish-looking, only he's older with grey hair. He's a very good-looking man.

"Hello, April. It's lovely to meet you." He shakes my hand.

"And this is my sister, Violet." Sebastian smiles.

"Hello." I smile.

She fakes a smile. "Hi."

My heart drops. Not exactly a warm greeting.

Sebastian's phone rings, and a name lights up the screen.

Jameson Miles

Huh? What the hell?

He knows Jameson Miles? Surely that's not the same media tycoon from New York that I've heard of.

"Answer it," his father says.

"Say hi to Jay from us." His mother smiles.

Sebastian answers the phone. "What do you want?" He smirks, as if something is funny. He listens and then bursts out laughing. "You could be onto something there." He holds his hand over the phone. "Miles says the UK is now in serious trouble." He laughs as he listens again. "Thanks."

I smile as I watch him.

"They went to boarding school together in Italy," his sister tells me.

"Oh."

Someone calls his parents away, and I am left alone with Violet.

I sip my wine nervously as I wait for her to say something.

"So, you're Brandon's friend?"

Ah, shit. This is Brandon's mother. She knows about me, the sex club, and all the other sordid details. That explains a lot.

"I am. I mean, I was." I shrug. "Unfortunately, we've lost touch."

She nods and bites her lip, as if holding her tongue.

I stare at her, and I can feel her animosity for me.

I have to say this. I know that I have to lay it out on the table right now.

"Look, Violet. I know that Sebastian and I didn't meet under normal circumstances."

"No, you didn't."

"I just want you to know that Sebastian was the only man I ever saw at that club, and I was never romantically involved with Brandon. It was all a big misunderstanding. Brandon is a wonderful person, but he misread the situation. I know that it probably doesn't matter to you anyway, because if I were you, I would have already made up my mind of what I thought of me too."

She glares at me.

"But I love Sebastian. I would do anything to make him happy."

Her eyes hold mine.

"I know you're still friends with Helena, and I understand your animosity towards me."

"I'm not friends with Helena. I tolerate her." She huffs. "Barely."

Shit, she wants to fight. This is going bad.

Bad, bad, bad.

I nod, unsure what to say next.

"I just want someone to love Sebastian like he deserves to be loved," she says.

I nod again. "I want that too."

"If you hurt him..."

"I won't."

We stare at each other.

"I'd like it if we could be friends." I shrug.

She looks out over the other people here.

"I only want what's best for him," I say.

"And you think that's you?"

"Yes," I reply without hesitation. "Nobody could love him more than I do. If we've gotten over all the obstacles we've had thrown at us and still feel like this about each other, I know it's special."

She exhales heavily, conceding defeat. "Don't make me regret giving you a chance, April."

"I won't."

"You need to talk to Brandon."

"I know." And I really do know. It's been on my mind lately. "I was going to call him, but I don't know what to say."

"You start with hello."

"Good advice."

She gives me her first genuine smile. "It is nice to finally meet you. You're not what I expected."

Relief fills me. I think it's going to be okay. "Thank you. You too."

The night has been fun, and people are just starting to leave. Brielle and I are tidying up the kitchen, and Charlotte is sitting at the kitchen counter.

Sebastian walks into the kitchen, talking on the phone.

"Thanks for calling, Son. I love you." He smiles as he listens. "Yes, I'll put her on." He holds out the phone to me. "It's Brandon. He wants to speak to you."

My eyes hold his, and he raises a brow. I know this is it. If I want a real future with Sebastian, which I do, I need to fix things with his son. I can't hold a grudge for the pain he caused me. I have to let it go.

No ifs or buts about it.

I take the phone from him. "Hello, Brandon," I say, hopeful.

"Hi, April."

I close my eyes at the sound of his familiar voice. I hold my finger up to the girls and walk out into the backyard for some privacy.

"How are you?"

"I'm good," he replies. "Long time, no speak."

I close my eyes and smile as hope runs through me. It feels like things are finally falling into place.

It's just gone midnight when we finally get up to the bedroom. The night has been filled with cheers and happiness. Sebastian must have received at least thirty phone calls from people congratulating him.

Seb puts his phone on to charge on the bedside, and his eyes find mine across the room.

"You look tired." I smile.

"Delirious," he sighs, taking his jacket off. "Shower and bed."

He walks into the bathroom and turns the shower on.

"Come on, babe," he calls.

I smile as I undress. What is it with us two? We never shower alone anymore.

Always together.

I walk in and get under the hot water. Sebastian takes me into his arms. I close my eyes against his warm shoulder, his big arms wrapped around me.

"I could go to sleep right here." I smile sleepily.

"Same." We both lean on each other, warm, safe, and relaxed. Alone for the first time today.

"I like your family." I smile up at him.

He soaps up his hands and begins to rub them over my body. "They like you."

"It was a good day, huh?"

He kisses my lips. "The best."

. . .

The phone lights up the darkened room from the bedside. It vibrates on silent with an incoming call.

The sound of April and Sebastian chatting in the shower echoes throughout the room.

The phone rings and then stops.

It begins to vibrate again, the name lighting up the screen:

Helena

29

April

Three Months Later.

MATHEW, my bodyguard, holds the back door of the black Mercedes wagon open for me, and he gives me a kind smile as I walk out of my building.

"Hello, Mathew." I smile.

"Good evening, Miss Bennet." He closes the door behind me after I slide into the backseat.

He gets into the driver's seat, wearing his customary black suit and earpiece. He looks every bit of the handsome bodyguard.

We pull out into the traffic, and I glance behind me to see the second security car following us.

My life has changed dramatically.

I'm dating the Prime Minister of the United Kingdom.

My beloved Sebastian Garcia.

Security guards are ever present, his work schedule is ridiculous, and we live between two houses. Staying at my place is completely out of the question now. Security risks are things I can no longer ignore. Not that I can actually call it my place anymore.

It's more like an empty apartment with furniture in it. I haven't slept there in three months. Depending on our schedule, sometimes I go weeks without even calling in. My potted plants live at Sebastian's place, along with all of my clothes and personal belongings. He keeps asking me to end my lease and fully move in with him, but I just want to wait a little bit.

We've only been together for a few months, and even though I know that this is forever for us, I want to try and at least act a little cool.

Not that I can.

I'm completely and irrevocably in love.

The traffic whizzes by as I stare out the window, and I smile to myself. If only I knew back then what I know now.

My marriage breakdown...

The darkest and most horrible days of my life, when I thought that dying would be easier to get through than to live another day in pain...

They were all just stepping stones *to him*.

He was always my grand plan—the man I was supposed to find.

I've never known a love like this. So pure in all its essence.

This man owns my body and soul. He's my best friend, my confidant, my protector.

The love of my life.

And we're not perfect. Far from it.

To the outside world, I'm sure we appear to be.

The Prime Minister who dates the lawyer...both madly in love.

On paper, the perfect duo.

But we have deep psychological flaws, both damaged in our own way. He's insanely jealous of any man who looks my way, and he's so innately sexual with me that it borders on being a sex addiction.

And I... Well, I have nightmares where he goes back to his ex-wife.

Horrible dreams where I wake up drenched with perspiration and gasping for air.

Because, damn, if that ever happened, I wouldn't survive it. I've been through a lot of things in my life, but *that* I couldn't cope with.

Some nights, my insecurities get so bad that I dread going to sleep. I can't handle the thought of seeing them making love in our bed.

It feels *so* real.

I think that's a huge part of my problem: that they make love, not fuck.

I hate that he loved her first.

It kills me.

But I'll never tell him. I would never admit any of it because I know this isn't about her or anything he's done. I have no reason to be insecure.

It's about me and the damage my ex-husband caused when I found him in my bed with another woman.

The way he looked up at me while he was still inside of her.

My heart constricts.

I close my eyes to try and block out the memory, but the pain still lingers.

The cut is so deep, I don't know if it will ever heal. My breath quivers on the inhale as I stare out into the night. I hate that it still affects me after all this time.

Every text Sebastian receives, I wonder if it's from her.

Every time he's late home, I wonder if he's been with her.

And it's just ridiculous because I know Sebastian would never do that to me, and I know that she hasn't contacted him at all, but my gut won't lose this feeling that the other shoe is about to drop.

I don't trust Helena, and to know that she wants him back just adds salt to my wound.

I'm not an insecure person—I never have been—but I think I just love Sebastian so much that my vision is clouded. My sister

Eliza says this is totally normal after coming out of a divorce and that, in time, I will get over it.

I will not let my fears poison our love. So, for now, I'll hold it all in and keep it to myself.

I'll act brave.

Because Sebastian Garcia's love is worth being brave for.

The car pulls up to our destination at 10 Downing Street. The Prime Minister's official residence. We don't live here full-time, only choosing to stay here when a function is on. That usually turns out to be around four nights a week, and Bentley stays here with us. The security team ferry him from place to place.

I smile to myself. Bentley is the most spoilt dog in all of parliament history.

The car door opens, and I step out. "Thank you," I say to the driver.

I walk up to the front door, and it is opened immediately.

"Good evening, Miss Bennet." A guard nods.

"Good evening." I walk through the grand, circular foyer to another two guards that are standing to attention by the door.

They, too, nod in greeting. "Good evening, Miss Bennet."

"Hello. Where is he?" I ask with a smile.

"In the gymnasium."

"Thank you." I take the steps upstairs and walk into our apartment and kick off my heels. I put my handbag down on the side table and see Bentley fast asleep on his bed in front of the fire. I pat his sleepy head.

"Oh, you are so lazy, aren't you?" I smile. "Are you a lazy boy?" I ask in my best baby voice that I save especially for him.

I glance at my watch. The function doesn't start for another two hours. I have plenty of time to get ready. I'll go and see Sebastian.

I walk down the stairs, past the two guards and along a huge corridor. I turn the corner and see another two guards sitting outside the double doors. They startle when they see me and immediately stand.

"Don't stand on my account." I smile.

They both dip their heads. "Good evening, Miss Bennet."

"Hi." I can hear loud music echoing from inside the gym. "Is he alone?"

"Yes."

I open the double doors and hear the deep beat of the music playing. I raise my eyebrow.

One of the security guards drops his head to hide his smile. I glance in to see that the light in the room is diluted; only the exit signs over the door provide light. I see Sebastian on the other side of the room, totally engrossed in his chin-ups.

I close the door behind me and walk in unnoticed.

The song "Goosebumps (Remix)" by Travis Scott is playing, and I smile. Sebastian loves this song. He says it reminds him of me when we first used to meet back in the club.

I lean up against the back wall as I watch him, the beat to the music deep and sexy.

Sebastian's legs are bent at the knee, and he pulls himself up on the bar. His T-shirt is wet.

Up, down, up, down, up, down.

His ass is tight and taut. Mighty fine.

How much strength does it take to do this many chin-ups?

He drops to the floor and bends over with his hands resting on his knees. He pants as he rests, and I smile as I watch him.

Hmm...

He motions to reach up again, but his shirt must be constricting him. He takes it off and throws it on the floor.

He pulls himself up, and I see every muscle in his back contract. The sheen of perspiration catches the light. *Oh.*

I feel myself flutter.

I turn and hit repeat on the sound system's iPad on the wall.

I watch him go up and down, his muscles contracting, with my heart in my throat.

Unable to help it, I step forward. Our eyes lock in the mirror but he keeps going with his chin-ups.

The sexy song plays on in the background as I walk over and stand in front of him.

He pulls himself up as I slide my hands up his perspiration-clad body. He eases himself down, and I do the same. His biceps and shoulders are pumping.

Just like my blood.

Our eyes are locked. It's just him and me.

Hell, he makes me forget how to breathe.

He rises up and down, his dark eyes locked on mine, and I cup his groin. I kiss his stomach, and run my hands up over his rock-hard abs and then lower.

He's hardened.

I inhale sharply, and he lets go of the bar and jumps down.

In one sharp movement, he has me pinned to the wall, his hand wrapped tightly around my throat.

His mouth moves to my ear. "Did you come in here to feed my cock?" he whispers darkly.

I stare at him. His knee parts my legs, and he pushes his hard erection into me as he bites my ear. "Answer the fucking question," he growls.

Goose bumps scatter up my arms, and I smile. So appropriate with the song that's playing. "Yes."

He slides his hand up my thigh and slips my panties to the side. He inhales sharply when he feels how wet I am. And then, without warning, he impales me with three thick fingers. I whimper into the darkness and glance at the door.

The guards are just outside.

He works me hard as he stares at me. He has the strongest fingers ever...

Fuck.

I grip his damp shoulders and, *oh...*

In one strong movement, he lifts my legs, spreads them wide with his strong hands, and pins me to the wall, his cock sliding deep inside my body.

My eyes flutter closed when he bites my neck.

Goose bumps...every time.

He puts his filthy mouth to my ear. "Feed me."

I text Sebastian.

Where are you? We have to leave

He replies:

I'm coming. What's the rush?

I roll my eyes. I told him this ten times already.

*Hazel is only awake for another hour.
We are on a hard time limit.*

He replies.

FFS, I'm coming around the corner

I flit around in excitement. We're going to see Charlotte and Spencer's new baby girl.

Hazel Grace is four weeks old, and to be completely honest, I'm obsessed with her.

She's my favourite hobby.

She's sweet, chubby, and she smells like Heaven, all while wrapped in a pretty pink blanket.

Sebastian's car pulls up out the front. I grab my coat, run out, and jump in.

"Hi." I kiss him quickly. "Took your frigging time."

"Calm down, woman," he says as we pull out into the street.

"I told you to be quick," I gasp. "I can't hold her if she's asleep, Sebastian. It's rude to get someone's sleeping baby out of bed on a visit."

He rolls his eyes. "Your obsession with this child is creepy."

I smirk. "Maybe." I bounce in my seat. "Drive faster."

He exhales in exasperation as he glances into the rearview mirror at the security car trailing us.

"If I've missed her, I'm blaming you," I scoff.

"Babies sleep, April. If you missed her, you'll just have to wait until the next visit."

"Less talking, more driving."

Twenty minutes later, we pull up at Spencer and Charlotte's, and I practically run inside.

"Is she asleep?" I ask as soon as the door opens.

"I kept her up for you." Charlotte laughs and passes the perfectly pink little bundle to me.

"Oh." I stare down at her.

Sebastian walks in and puts his arm over my shoulder, staring down at her with me. "Isn't she perfect?" I whisper.

He smiles. "She is."

"Well, she is my child. What else would you expect?" Spencer says when he walks into the room and kisses my cheek. "Hey, baby."

I drop to sit on the couch and smile down at the beautiful baby in my arms.

She's the epitome of wonderful.

Everyone chats and talks while Spencer makes us tea, but I just stare down at Hazel. I glance up to see Sebastian sitting opposite me, watching. "You're creepy," he mouths.

"I don't care," I mouth back.

I wipe off the last of my face cleaner and throw the cotton ball in the waste bin before I stare in the mirror. I look at the small wrinkles around my eyes. Hmm, I need some new turbocharged eye cream or something.

I turn the shower on and undress.

"Seb?" I call.

He stays silent, so I poke my head around the bedroom door to see he's engrossed in the news on the television.

"Are you getting in with me, babe?"

"No." His arm is above his head, and his eyes stay fixed on the screen.

"Okay." I shrug and get in under the hot water. He must be tired. He's been really quiet all afternoon. I wet my hair, pour shampoo into my hand, and begin to lather it up. Is there anything better than hot-water therapy? I really don't think so.

"Do you want a baby?"

My eyes spring open. "What?"

"I said"—Sebastian is standing in the steam-filled room—"do *you* want a baby?"

My mouth falls open in surprise. "Um." I hesitate. Oh, jeez. "Well..."

Sebastian raises an eyebrow and waits for my answer. "It's a yes-no question, April."

"Well, mine's not really a yes or no answer."

"Meaning what?"

"It's a complex question."

He puts his hands on his hips. "How?"

"I don't want *a* baby." I pause before feeling brave enough to say the rest. "I want *your* baby."

His eyes search mine.

I exhale. "I mean, I know—"

He cuts me off by stepping forward into the water, still fully clothed, and he takes me into his arms.

"What are you doing?" I frown.

"Marry me."

30

April

I STARE UP AT HIM. *What?*

"Why not?" he asks. "We both know that this is it for us. You love me, and I love you."

My mouth falls open. "You're serious?"

"Deadly." He smiles down at me before leaning in and kissing my lips.

"Seb."

"Say yes, April." His tongue sweeps through my parted lips.

I smile against him. "This is—"

"Say yes."

"Yes."

He pulls back to look at me. "Friday."

I frown. "Friday, what?"

"We marry on Friday."

"Friday?" I gasp.

"You said we could elope."

"When did I say that?"

"When we started dating."

"That was a flippant comment." I shake my head in disbelief. Is this conversation really happening? "I'm working on Friday, anyway."

"All right, next Friday."

I blink in surprise as shampoo begins to run down my face. "Next week?" I tip my head back to wash this stupid shampoo out of my hair before I'm blinded.

"No point dragging it out." He takes his wet T-shirt over his shoulders and throws it on the floor. He drags his pants down and kicks them to the side. "Kiss me."

"Sebastian, let me wash this damn shampoo out."

He brings his hands up to do it for me. I open my eyes to see him smiling down at me.

I smirk.

"Friday," he mouths.

"*Next* Friday," I remind him.

"In secret, in Spain."

"Spain?" I squeak.

Hell on a cracker, this man is full of surprises tonight.

He takes me into his arms. "I want to marry the woman I love in the country I come from. The land where my ancestors roamed."

Oh, my heart.

I don't know if I can even take time off from work, but seriously, who fucking cares? "Okay." I smile. "Next Friday, in Spain, just you and me."

He smiles as his lips meet mine. "Mrs. Garcia."

My stomach somersaults. Did that really just happen?

I can't even...

"Sebastian, are you high?"

"Next Friday." His hands slide down to my behind. "I will be."

Cloud nine is a great place to be.

I sit in my office and stare into space, wearing the goofiest of all goofy grins. I keep envisioning Seb in the shower last night, under the water in his clothes, asking me to marry him. The way he was so hopeful and gorgeous.

It was unexpected, and yet it was perfect at the same time. It wasn't just romantic but madly romantic. There was no ring, but I don't even think I want an engagement ring.

A simple gold band would be perfect.

He is perfect.

He's right; we know this is it. We are meant to be. There is no point in waiting.

The last few months have been a dream come true. We argue and squabble. We laugh and love and take care of each other.

This really is it.

I know that we're being selfish by eloping.

We've both been there and done the white-wedding thing before, and in the long run, it meant nothing. Both marriages failed.

I wonder where the ceremony will be. I text him.

Dear Mr. Garcia,
What will I wear to our wedding?
Will it be at a registry office or somewhere more weddingy?

A reply bounces straight back, and I smile. He usually never gets my texts for hours.

Dear Soon-To-Be Mrs. Garcia
Whatever you wear will be perfect.
P.S. 'Weddingy' isn't a word.
Xo

I smirk and reply.

Perhaps if you are going to correct my English, sir, we could play
teacher and naughty student tonight?
What are you wearing?

He replies.

You're on detention, young lady.
Punishment will be handed out for your misdemeanors.
I will be wearing my new wife.

xo

I spin on my chair with glee. Oh, I'm so excited.

Knock, knock.

I glance up to see Jeremy sauntering in. I quickly close my phone down. Sebastian has sworn me to secrecy.

"Hey." I smile.

Jeremy exhales heavily. "I hate men."

"Men as in Bart, or plural as in all?"

He slumps into the chair at my desk. "He didn't come home last night."

My eyes widen. "What do you mean, he didn't come home? How do you know?"

"Well, I don't know for certain, but he always calls me when he gets home, no matter what the time."

"Right?"

"And he told me he was meeting Nicolas for dinner, but then... no call."

"Well, he told you about Nicolas." I frown. "Surely if he had something to hide, he would have kept that a secret."

"Unless he's acting transparent."

I roll my eyes. "Seriously, Jeremy, what are you doing with this guy? Nobody is supposed to feel like this when they're in a loving relationship."

"I know," he sighs.

"Do you want to have lunch today?" I smile.

"Where at?"

"Your pick."

He exhales heavily. "Can we have all the carbs?"

"Uh-huh." I frown. On second thought, what the hell am I wearing to this wedding? Oh, who cares? Sebastian likes me how I am, anyway. "Yep, all the carbs, and maybe even a cocktail."

"I do love you." He stands and gives me a wink before walking out.

"Jeremy!" I hear Bart call. "Can I see you in my office for a moment, please?"

"Sure," Jeremy replies.

I see them walking down the corridor, and Bart's office door shuts behind them.

I wonder what lies Bart's going to tell him now, the selfish prick. Jeremy has got to get out of that relationship. It's toxic.

Another night, another gala.

My life with Sebastian is glamourous and always busy. He has so many engagements, and, of course, I always attend. He won't go anywhere without me.

"You ready, sweetheart?"

"Just a minute," I call as I slip my stilettos on.

I take one last look at myself in the mirror. I'm wearing a fitted black strapless dress. It's simple but lovely. My hair is up, and for once, I'm wearing red lipstick as well as dangly diamante earrings.

I actually look pretty good.

I walk out to see Sebastian standing near the door. He's wearing a black dinner suit and bow tie, and his hands are in his pants pockets. His eyes drop to my toes, and he gives me a slow, sexy smile. "Well, hello there."

I put my hands on my hips and do a little twirl. "You like?"

He steps forward, taking me into his arms. He bends and kisses my breast through my dress. "I do." He begins to nibble his way up to my neck.

I giggle. "Behave, we have to go. We're late already."

He takes my hand, and we walk down the stairs and into the large foyer. One of the security guards looks up at me and smiles, completely forgetting where he is.

I feel Sebastian stiffen on my arm.

We get to the bottom of the stairs and Sebastian stops still in front of the guard.

He raises an eyebrow. "And?"

The security guard grimaces, knowing he's been caught perving. "Yes, sir."

"First and last warning," Sebastian says as we walk past.

Oh, jeez.

We walk out the front doors. The black Mercedes wagon is waiting, and the driver is holding the door open. "Good evening."

"Hello." We both smile and get into the back of the car.

Sebastian takes my hand in his lap as we are whisked into the night.

I stare over at my beautiful man. Protective and jealous.

Just how I love him.

Half an hour later, we are at the Governor's Charity Ball.

It's an exciting night for all of us. This is Charlotte's first night out after having their baby. She and Spence aren't staying for long, but it's great that they're here all the same.

We've been hanging out a lot with the four of them. The girls are hilarious, and the boys are inseparable. We have a lot of fun together with them and their kids, especially now that I'm obsessed with baby Hazel.

I had dinner with Penelope and Anna this week, too, and it's been so hard not to blurt out to everyone all the exciting news about next week, but we really want to do this alone.

As Sebastian said, we can celebrate with everyone when we get back, and there's no chance of anything being leaked to the press. That's the very last thing we want to deal with.

"Oh, hell," Spencer whispers, dipping his head. He holds his forehead to hide from someone. "Seven o'clock."

We all look up to see a woman smiling. She waves and begins to walk over. Sebastian's face falls, and Julian drops his head. "Here we fucking go," Julian mutters.

Brielle's eyes widen, and Charlotte bites her lip. Whoever this woman is, she's obviously the topic of conversation.

"There you are," the woman gushes to Sebastian. "Where have you been hiding?"

He fakes a smile, stands, and kisses her on the cheek. "Hello, Angela, nice to see you."

She's attractive with dark hair, a lovely figure, and she's way overfriendly. Sebastian turns straight to me. "Angela, please meet April, my girlfriend."

Her face instantly drops. "Hello." She looks me up and down.

Oh, *she's rude.*

"Hello." I smile. My surprised eyes flick up to Bree and Lottie to see that they're both smirking, clearly amused. Have I missed part of the conversation?

"Hmm." Angela's eyes stay glued to me. "Sebastian, you haven't been around in a long time. The children would love to see you."

"Ah, yes." Sebastian widens his eyes. "I'm very busy." He gestures to me. "With April."

"Doing boyfriend stuff," Spencer interrupts.

Julian drops his head to hide his smile.

Angela's eyes hold mine. "Where do you live, April?"

"With me," Sebastian fires back.

Spencer smirks as he looks up at her.

Okay, who is this woman, and why does everyone think everything she says is amusing?

She turns back to Sebastian. "So, are you going to come over to see us?"

"Umm." Sebastian's eyes flick to me. "I can't. April doesn't like me going out."

"Taskmaster," Julian mutters.

"She locks him up," Spencer adds.

My eyes widen, and I laugh. What the hell? "Not at all, Sebastian. You can go and visit whenever you want to, sweetheart."

"Okay then," he dismisses her. "Thanks for that."

She rises up on her toes, clearly excited, and smiles between us. "I'll see you soon, Seb."

She walks off, and everyone snickers.

Sebastian pinches the bridge of his nose, disgusted. "Don't even."

"Who was that?" I ask, holding up my hands. "Actually, let me guess."

"Oh, please do." Spencer laughs.

"I'm guessing you've"—I screw up my face as I try to think of a nice way to say this—"been with her?"

Sebastian closes his eyes, and I know I've hit the nail on the head. The others chuckle.

"And who *is* she?" Spencer asks.

Sebastian stands. "I can't talk right now; I'm dancing with April. Do not disturb us

anymore with your boring topics of conversation."

They laugh.

I stay seated and smile as I look between the others. "Why, who *is* she?"

Sebastian widens his eyes at them in warning.

"Tell me," I demand.

"Let's just say...he kept it in the family."

Sebastian pulls me to my feet. "Dancing, my love." He drags me away. "Ignore these fuckers."

"Do the words' ex-sister-in-law' ring any bells, Garcia?" Spencer calls after us.

My eyes widen as he pulls me along. "Sister-in-law? Ex... You slept with Helena's sister?" I gasp as we get to the dance floor.

He takes me into his arms and then winces. "Shh, dancing."

"Sebastian!"

He screws his face up. "Maybe a little bit."

427

My mouth is open as I stare up at him. This is so unexpected.

What the hell? This is a nightmare. This is horrendous, and the confirmation I've been searching for.

He doesn't love her anymore.

He couldn't.

Like a tangible force, I feel the fear leave my body.

Oh, thank God.

He acts serious, holding back a smirk. "What?" He spins me, bends, and kisses me softly. "What do you want to say? You're disgusted, appalled..."

Impressed.

"All those things." I try to control my smile.

He shakes his head. "Not one of my proudest moments. There were copious amounts of alcohol involved, and I was clearly still in my angry stage."

"Does Helena know this?"

"Who knows, and who cares?" He spins me around, and I laugh out loud.

This is the best news I have ever heard.

"I thought you felt sorry for her." I frown. We haven't discussed Helena since that night when he had the meltdown. I haven't wanted to bring her up, though I've thought about it way too often.

"I did in the beginning, but then she got nasty and slept with everyone. She took me for everything I owned, and"—he shrugs casually—"it was quite cathartic, actually. Unlike her sister, Angela is a good person. We were friends for a long time, and it symbolized the beginning of my new single life."

I smile up at him like a groupie. This is groundbreaking information for me. I was scared that he still loved her a little, but this proves that he doesn't. There is no way he would have ever done that if they weren't over for good. He has super high morals.

He slept with her sister.

I bite my bottom lip to hide my goofy smile. Best news ever.

. . .

I'm lying on my side, staring at Sebastian in the dark. It's late. We went to the ball and then came home and made love.

He rolls on his side to face me. "What are you thinking about?"

"I can't believe you slept with Helena's sister."

He closes his eyes. "Please don't remind me."

"I thought you felt sorry for her?"

"I did in the beginning." He pauses, thinking for a moment. "You know, it was weird."

"What was?"

"The way my marriage ended."

"Why?"

"Well, she had this hang-up that I didn't find her attractive anymore, so she started acting differently."

"What do you mean?"

"I don't know. She became flirty around my friends. Wore different clothes. It was like she was crying out for attention. And I could see it happening before my eyes, and I knew why she was doing it. But—" He cuts himself off.

"You didn't try to stop it."

He rolls his lips. "After, I blamed myself. I was devastated. But the day I asked her to stop using my surname, she got nasty."

"How?"

"She started sleeping with people I knew. She took me for everything financially, and she even tried to get Bentley. She was hell-bent on hurting me in any way she could."

"Did she?"

"Yes." He exhales heavily. "Each little thing she did cemented what I had feared all along."

"What was that?"

"That I never really knew her."

I frown, surprised by that statement.

"It's one thing to love someone, but to realize that you loved someone who never existed is the worst betrayal of all."

"I don't understand. How didn't you realize you weren't compatible before you got married?"

429

"She was very inexperienced, and I thought..." He exhales heavily. "I only saw what I wanted to see. They say love is blind."

"What did you think?"

He shrugs. "I don't know what I was thinking, really."

"Do you think you will ever be rid of her?" I ask softly.

He shrugs. "Surely her drama will end soon. I'm assuming when she meets someone, it will have to."

"I have a confession," I whisper.

"What's that?"

"I'm relieved that you slept with her sister."

"Because you're a sicko." He smirks.

"Obviously." I giggle. "I thought you still loved her."

He screws up his face. "Why would you think that?"

"Well, you told me this sad story about how she was the victim, and how you regretted it, and it was all your fault."

"I only told you why we ended so that I didn't do it again with us." He leans in and kisses me softly. "Helena is not a nice person, April. The things she has done to me since our divorce are evil through and through, and I don't have feelings for her at all. But what kind of person would I be if I didn't recognize my own mistakes in the breakdown of that relationship? It takes two people to ruin a marriage, and I was far from perfect. If I told you that I was, it would have been a lie."

I smile softly, relief flooding through me.

"The night I told you about Helena and me was the night I was particularly hard on you in the bedroom. I thought I'd done it again, and that you were going to leave me too."

"I like hard in the bedroom."

"Like I said, sicko."

"Takes one to marry one." I smile.

He rolls me onto my back and holds my hands above my head as he kisses me.

"This time next week, you'll be mine."

"I already am."

. . .

Fairy tales do come true; I know that for sure now.

When I was a little girl, I dreamed of feeling like a princess, being swept away by my prince.

And I have been.

When Sebastian Garcia tells you that he's taken care of it, he really has.

It's late on Friday night, and we are in Toledo, Spain—the place where Sebastian's ancestors walked.

The golden walls of the iconic Cathedral of Toledo are lit with hundreds of candles, while I stand in the waiting room wearing my fitted floor-length cream evening dress.

The church is huge. The priest, Sebastian, and I are the only three here.

There are, of course, ten security guards outside, but I'm trying my hardest to forget about them.

The wedding waltz begins, and I close my eyes. *This is it.*

With a deep, shaky breath, I push open the heavy door and walk out into the church.

Sebastian is standing at the altar. He turns and gives me a breathtaking smile. He's wearing my favourite black dinner suit with the silk lapels and bow tie.

I slowly walk towards him in time to the music.

Seeing him there, waiting for me with that look in his eyes...

I just want to run.

My heart explodes with love for this man, and my eyes well with tears. We fought hard to win this battle. To overcome our fears.

I make it to the end of the aisle and Sebastian takes my hand. He bends and kisses my cheek. "Hello, my love."

"Hi." I smile bashfully. The way he looks at me is so intense; there's no mistaking his love for me. My eyes flick to the priest, and he smiles at the two us. "Estamos reunidos para celebrar la unión de dos almas," the priest says.

"We are gathered here to celebrate the union of two souls," Sebastian says as his eyes hold mine.

Oh dear God...we're getting married in Spanish. Sebastian is translating.

Emotional overload.

My eyes fill with tears, and I blink so that I can see him.

"El amor es precioso, el amor es bondadoso," the priest says.

"Love is precious, love is kind." Seb smiles softly.

"El amor es un lenguaje que no se puede aprender. Es intrínseco, vive dentro de nuestro ser."

"Love is a language that cannot be learned. It is intrinsic, it lives inside of us."

I smile softly over at my beautiful man.

"¿Qué es lo que buscas, hijo mío?" the priest asks.

"What is it you're seeking, my child?" Sebastian's eyes hold mine. "Amor eterno. Eternal love."

Gah...

This is too much. I wipe a tear as it rolls down my cheek.

"¿Sebastián García, quieres a April Bennet para tener y sostener a partir de este día?"

"Do you, Sebastian Garcia, take April Bennet, to have and to hold from this day forward?"

"Sí, quiero. I do."

"¿Y tú, April Bennet, quieres a Sebastián García para tener y sostener a partir de este día?"

"And do you, April Bennet, take Sebastian Garcia to have and to hold from this day forward?"

"I do."

Sebastian smiles and rocks up onto his toes, as if proud.

"Que el Señor los una por la eternidad," the priest says.

"Let the Lord join you for eternity."

"Repite después de mí, con este anillo me caso contigo. En la enfermedad y en la salud, en la riqueza y en la pobreza, por el resto de nuestra vidas."

"Repeat after me, with this ring, I thee wed. In sickness and in health, for richer, for poorer, for as long as we both shall live."

The priest passes us the two gold rings, and Sebastian slides the thick gold band onto my finger. "Te amaré hasta el final. Esta es mi promesa," he whispers in his husky voice. "I will love you until the day I die, April. This is my promise to you."

Oh...

I take the ring and slide it onto Sebastian's finger.

"Ahora los declaro marido y mujer, puedes besar a tu novia."

"I now pronounce you husband and wife, you may kiss your bride," Sebastian repeats.

We smile softly at each other. He takes my face in his two hands and we kiss through overwhelming emotions.

We've come so far. It feels like a lifetime ago that we met in that club.

So much to get to where we stand tonight.

I love him so much.

We made it...

Mr. and Mrs. Garcia.

We walk up the boardwalk and my eyes widen. "*This* is where we are staying?" I gasp.

Sebastian lifts my hand to his lips. "Well, not right here, but this *is* how we get there, yes."

My mouth falls open. A small landing leads to the largest yacht I've ever seen.

Four men stand in line as they wait to greet us. The one in a white suit and fancy-looking hat dips his head. He looks important; he must be the captain of the ship...yacht, whatever the hell this thing is. "Good evening, Mr. and Mrs. Garcia."

Mrs. Garcia... What the hell? I let out an unexpected giggle. "You're the first person to ever call me that."

Sebastian smiles warmly and winks at the captain before shaking his hand. "Thank you."

He takes my hand and leads me across the boardwalk and onto the yacht. A man holds out a silver tray with two glasses of champagne, and we each take one. The glasses are crystal and heavy. "Thank you."

The waiter gives me a kind smile. "Canapés and cocktails are to be served in fifteen minutes on the deck, Mrs. Garcia."

Excitement shoots through me. *Mrs. Garcia.* I'll never tire of hearing that.

"Okay, thanks." I don't know where to look first; this is over-the-top opulence. My eyes meet his. "Sebastian," I whisper. "Are you kidding me?"

He smiles proudly as he looks around. "Only the best for my girl." He leans in and kisses me tenderly, and I melt against him. How did I get so lucky?

I pull out of his arms to look around the ground floor. There's a huge, luxurious living area with dark timber floors and exotic-looking custom rugs, a dark twenty-seater wood dining table, and a black mini grand piano in the corner.

Piano...on a boat. What the hell?

The furnishings are the very best money can buy, all in different shades of cream with scatterings of emerald green and navy blue.

Where do you even buy furniture like this?

Crystal lampshades are strategically placed, and chandeliers hang from the ceilings.

Frigging hell, this is next level.

I glance out onto the deck and see huge outdoor couches, deck chairs, and an oversized hot tub. And we're having cocktails there in fifteen minutes.

Ahhhh...kill me now. I'm dead.

Sebastian leads me up the stairs, and my mouth drops open once more. This is the most beautiful bedroom I have ever seen. His eyes meet mine, and I smile softly. "I suppose I can spend a week in this dump."

He takes my champagne off me and walks me backwards towards the bed. "I'm sure we'll find something to do."

I giggle against his lips. "We have canapés being served on the

434

deck in ten."

"Do I look like I care?" he murmurs against my lips. His teeth drop to my neck.

"Can we at least pretend to be normal?" I laugh as I look at the ceiling.

"We are on our honeymoon. For once, we are supposed to fuck all day. It's the official festival of come."

I burst out laughing. "The festival of come? Good Lord, you are a born romantic, Mr. Garcia."

"I know, it's a gift." He laughs, too, and I take his two hands in mine and step back from him. "Thank you." I look around. "This is...perfect."

"Like you."

I kiss him softly. "Like us." We hold each other, and there's this beautiful intimacy in the room. "Let's just take our time and enjoy our night. We'll never get this back. I'm not rushing a thing."

His eyes twinkle with a certain something, and I know that he agrees. He picks my hand up and kisses it. "I love you."

My eyes fill with tears. "I love you."

"Why do you get so teary when you say that?"

I shrug, embarrassed. "Because—" I cut myself off.

"What?" He takes my face in his hands. "Tell me."

"I didn't know I could love someone as much as I love you."

His eyes search mine.

"I thought I was in love before...but I hadn't even scratched the surface."

He smiles softly. "Thank you."

"For what?"

"Waiting."

I frown.

"For me to get my shit together. I haven't been the easiest man to...love."

My heart bursts. "Sebastian, you are the easiest man in the world to love."

He kisses me softly and takes my hand in his.

435

"Cocktails on the deck are waiting." I smile.

"Cock in bed is a much better option, in my opinion," he mutters dryly. "But whatever."

We make our way downstairs and out onto the deck. The yacht has now left the dock, and we are slowly heading out towards the sea. The sun is just setting, and the sky is a beautiful hue of pinks and reds. Oh... This is magical.

The waiter appears with a silver tray. "Here you are, Mr. Garcia. Top-shelf margaritas, Gran Patron Tequila as requested."

"My wife's favourite." Sebastian smirks.

He remembered.

I giggle as I take my margarita from the tray and sip it. Oh wow...that's the stuff.

Heaven in a cup.

The waiter leaves us alone, and Sebastian holds his margarita to mine in a toast. "To many happy years, my love."

The yacht, the sunset...the dreamy husband.

This is utter perfection.

I smile and hold my drink in the air. "With many more of these."

It's late, the crew have retired, and the captain is belowdecks. A second security yacht is a few hundred meters behind us.

We are in the hot tub, surrounded by darkness, the gentle lapping of the ocean sounds in the distance. The cool wind is dusting our skin.

Sebastian has me straddled over his body as we kiss, his hands on my hips, dragging me over his thick hard cock. With his eyes locked on mine, he undoes the ties of my bikini bottoms and takes them off. His fingers drop to my sex, and he slowly begins to work me. Our kiss turns desperate.

I've wanted him all day.

The feelings between us are too intense.

With two fingers deep in my sex, he slides his other hand

around. His fingers begin to explore the part of me that he doesn't know.

My behind.

We stare at each other as he rubs me there, the forbidden zone, where he hasn't been allowed to go.

He slowly slides the tip of a finger in, and I shudder as we stare at each other.

Arousal is pumping heavily between us.

"It's our wedding night," he whispers as he kisses me in a silent plea.

"You want that as your wedding present?" I ask.

His eyes are dark, unwavering. "Yes."

He keeps working me, back and front...and God, I can hardly keep my eyes open from the feelings of pleasure.

"You're so...big, Seb," I whisper against his lips, unable to hide my fear.

"I won't hurt you. I promise." His fingers keep going, keep pushing my limits, amping up my arousal, and hell...this feels so fucking good.

He lifts his hand out of the water and holds it out to me. "See this gold band?" he whispers.

I look down at his wedding ring.

"This means I will always protect you," he murmurs. "You have all of me, April. And now, I need all of you."

I stare at him, and I know this is it.

The moment in time where I hand myself completely over to someone.

But he's not just someone. He's my husband, Sebastian, the love of my life.

I know that this means a lot to him. It's more than the sexual act, it's symbolic.

"Okay..."

He frowns. "Okay?"

I smile. "Don't give me time to second-guess this."

"Okay." He sits up with renewed purpose and grabs my bikini bottoms and puts them back on me.

"What are you doing?" I ask as he ties them up at the side.

"Taking you to bed."

I swallow the lump in my throat. Oh hell, here we go.

There isn't a chance that this isn't going to hurt. He's big...huge. And... Well, ...fuck.

I didn't think this through.

With my bikini back in place, Sebastian steps out of the hot tub and holds a towel up for me. He wraps me in it and then leads me upstairs by the hand. We walk into the bedroom, and he flicks the lock, his eyes meeting mine.

I stand before him, my heart hammering in my chest.

The sound of the engine is a drone in the background. His eyes are blazing with desire.

Sebastian Garcia always brings it to the bedroom, no matter what the circumstances.

No matter where we are.

This is who he is. I know what I'm in for unbridled pleasure, guaranteed.

Regardless of that, this time, I can't help but feel a little nervous.

He takes my bikini off, and with the towel dries me carefully and then lays me on the bed. He spreads my legs and leans down and kisses me there. As if completely focused on his task, he gets up immediately and goes to his suitcase and takes out his toiletry bag. He removes a bottle of lube and puts it on the bedside table. My eyes widen when I see it. "You packed lube?" I frown.

"Boy Scout." He smirks.

"Always prepared?"

"Optimistically so."

I giggle and a little of my nerves dissipate.

This is something he's thought about. He really wants this.

He slides his shorts down, and his large, thick cock springs free, engorged and rock-hard. It hangs heavily between his legs,

438

and he gives it a few slow strokes as he kicks his shorts to the side. He lies down beside me and leans up on his elbow, his lips take mine, and he kisses me. His eyes close, and he's wearing a soft smile. He has this aura of happiness around him. "This is going to perhaps...sting," he murmurs against my lips as his fingers find that spot between my legs.

"Is this my pep talk?" I whisper.

"Yes." He smiles and then falls serious. "We can't stop once we start."

My eyes search his.

"It will be quick, and once I'm in..."

My heart begins to pump hard, and I know I have to stop overthinking this. "Sebastian, just do it."

He gives me a dark smile and disappears down my body, his teeth grazing my skin all the way. He spreads me apart with his fingers and licks me deep with his thick tongue, and I close my eyes to deal with him.

I don't know how the hell he's got such a strong tongue, and fingers for that matter.

So strong.

Is there a hot-fuck training camp that all men should know about? If not, there should be.

He licks me deep, and I hold my hands on the back of his head as I writhe beneath him. He can make me come like this in sixty seconds. Sebastian Garcia is the king of oral.

And not just because he does it so well—it's because he loves it.

He does it for him.

His eyes close in pleasure as he takes everything from me, and all I can do is watch on, helpless to the pleasure. He rolls me over, gets behind me, and pulls me up onto my knees by my hips.

He spreads me and begins to lick me there, a flutter, a lick, a slow kiss.

My eyes close, and my mouth hangs open as I give him full access to me. This is as intimate as it gets. He slides his fingers into my sex as he continues to lick me there, and pleasure begins to build, my body taking on its own agenda and pushing back onto him.

He kisses my cheek, and then I hear the click of the lube bottle as it opens.

Fuck, *here we go.*

He spreads the lube over my behind and rubs it in, through the lips of my swollen sex too, smearing it all over.

Up and down, up and down. I feel like a well-oiled machine. Wet and waiting.

He nudges his cock at my opening and sits it at the entrance, then his fingers get to working in my sex as he begins to pump me there.

"Push back on me," he whispers, his voice hoarse, and I know it's taking all his control to take this slow.

With his hand on my hip bone, he pulls me back onto him as he shows me how he wants me to move, his dick just parting my entrance.

The smart of his ownership runs through me.

Oh... Ouch... I drop my head to the mattress.

His fingers that are now pumping me deep in my sex begin to take over, and I want more. I push back a little further and feel the sting as his tip goes right the way in.

He moans, deep and guttural, and it spurs me on.

I want this to be good for him.

I lift myself back up onto my hands and push back a little further.

He inhales sharply. "That's it, baby," he moans, his voice unrecognizable. "That's it."

I push back a little further, and it hurts. "Oh..." I whimper.

"It's okay." He leans down and kisses my shoulder. "Take your time, sweetheart." His fingertips begin to circle over my clitoris, and I shudder. This...this is too much.

To feel his oiled-up fingertips, the ache of my needy sex, his body just inside mine.

So there...but not nearly enough.

His fingers circle and swirl through the oil, and I begin to build.

I'm going to come.

Hard.

I grit my teeth and push back. Sebastian moans as his hands grip my hip bones; he's grappling for control. "That's it." He pushes out as if in pain.

Hearing his guttural voice does something to me, and suddenly, I need this. I need to be taken here. "Fuck me," I whisper over my shoulder at him.

His eyes darken.

"Sebastian, I said fuck me," I demand.

He grips my hip bones in his hands and pushes forward hard. His body slides deep inside mine, and searing pain shoots through me as I am speared into the mattress.

Oh...fucking hell.

He stays still to let me acclimatise, then leans over and kisses my shoulder. "Kiss me." I turn my head, and his lips take mine. His fingertips continue to circle over my clitoris, and I feel the pleasure build. "More," I moan into his mouth, "I need more."

He slowly pulls out and slides back in. I smile, grateful that it didn't hurt as much this time.

"You all right?"

"Yes."

I push my hips back in a silent invitation, and he hisses as he begins to slowly ride me with short, shallow pumps, and I stare into space as I learn to deal with the new sensation. The lube slaps between us.

"Fuck yeah," he whispers darkly. "Oh," he moans. "So fucking good."

I smile, knowing that dark part of his brain has been activated where there's no turning back.

His pumps get deeper, thicker and...oh.

My toes curl.

This is good...*so good.*

What have I been missing?

We get rougher, deeper, and I begin to moan, unable to hold it in. The intensity of this is overwhelming, and I'm almost scared to come. "Sebastian," I cry out.

He gives it to me, hard and fast, and I lose my head as I claw at the sheets. I scream as the most intense orgasm I've ever had tears through me.

"Fuck," he cries as he holds himself deep. I feel the telling jerk of his cock as he comes hard inside of me.

We pant as we fall to the mattress, the waves of pleasure so strong that I shudder uncontrollably. I'm shell-shocked, and he's kissing me all over as if overwhelmed with love and emotion.

So much devotion.

I open my eyes to find his big brown eyes watching me.

I smile softly.

He bends and nips my shoulder with his teeth. "Fucking hot." He kisses me. "Can we do that again?"

I giggle as he pulls out of my body. Oh... It feels foreign with him gone. I liked him in there. "Not today, naughty husband." I smile as I hold him. "Not today."

The scent of the ocean, the heat of the sun, the sheer fantasy of my honeymoon is a dream come true

We lie sunbaking on the deck of the yacht on our second to last day in Spain. We've had the best week, swimming, shopping, and sightseeing all day. Dancing and dining at the most beautiful restaurants and making love all night.

Sebastian speaking Spanish to everyone we meet has literally fried my brain.

I am officially married to the hottest man on Earth.

Pure fucking Heaven.

We're lying on towels on the deck, and I glance over at Sebastian. He's holding his hand up and looking at his thick, gold wedding ring. He's been doing it all week.

I roll over onto my stomach and face him. "What do you think about when you look at your ring?"

He shrugs.

I lean on my elbow. "What?"

"I swore to myself that I would never get married again."

"And yet, here we are." I watch him continue to stare at his ring. "Why did we get married, if you were so against it?"

"Because it was you."

My heart swells.

"And because—" He frowns before cutting himself off.

"What?"

"I want a baby too."

I smile over at him in surprise. We both knew that I wanted a child, but I didn't know he did too.

He rolls over towards me, runs his hand up over my arm. "I don't want you taking the pill anymore. I want to try and start our family straight away." He leans in and kisses me, his lips brushing tenderly against mine. "What do you think?"

I smile and run my fingers through his thick black stubble. "I think we should get to baby-making activities, right now."

He chuckles and rolls me onto my back, then spreads my legs with his knee. "Already on it."

We walk down the stairs of the plane and onto the tarmac. The honeymoon is over.

Sebastian takes my hand in his, and we walk through the airport. Photographers are here, waiting. Bart released a photo of the two of us yesterday to the press, announcing our marriage, and Sebastian wanted to get this over with.

This is their photo op. The quicker they get the first photo of us as husband and wife, the quicker they leave us alone.

Cameras flash, people cry out our names, and Sebastian whisks me through the airport and into the back of the waiting car. It's a flurry of activity, and the door shuts behind us, and he turns to me.

"Are you ready to start our new life together, Mrs. Garcia?" he asks.

I smile over at my handsome man. "Am I ever."

Sebastian

Knock, knock.

"Come in!" I call. It's my first day back at work, and everybody wants something from me.

My head of security walks in. "Sorry to interrupt, Mr. Garcia."

"That's fine. How can I help you?"

He pauses, choosing his words carefully. "We have a situation downstairs."

I raise an eyebrow. "Such as?"

"Your...ex-wife is here, demanding to see you."

I wince. "What?"

"She's crying. Screaming the place down, actually."

For fuck's sake, I know how dramatic she can be. I've seen it many times. "Does she know that I'm here?"

"Unfortunately, yes."

I exhale heavily. I may as well get this over with. I can't say I'm surprised. "Bring her in."

"Very well, sir." He leaves, and I let out a deep exhale. I'm not in the mood for this today.

Five minutes later, the door opens, and Helena walks in.

She's been crying, and my stomach twists. If we were on better terms, I would have called her so that she heard the news from me first.

But we aren't, so I didn't.

She sits down at my desk. Her eyes hold mine.

I hold a pen in my hands. Guilt fills me. No matter how much animosity there is between us, regret still lingers when she's hurt.

444

"Hello, Helena."

"You married her?"

"Yes."

Her eyes well with tears. "How could you?"

I bite my bottom lip to stop myself saying something hurtful. "Helena, I will not have this conversation with you. Our marriage ended seven years ago."

"She's no angel," she whispers angrily.

The hackles on my back rise. How dare she? "What do you mean by that?"

"Don't act stupid. I know who she is."

"And who is she?"

"She's a lying whore."

"She is nothing of the sort, and watch your fucking mouth. *She is my wife*."

"Go to hell."

A sarcastic smile crosses my face. "Any chance of that ended with our divorce."

"Are you happy with what you've done to me?"

"And what, pray tell, have I done to you?" I fume.

"Taken my name, my money...the life I was supposed to have."

I smirk at the audacity of this woman. "You're mistaken. It was you who took my money. I'm now happily married to the love of my life, and you *will* accept it." I lose the last of my patience with this woman. "Move the fuck on, Helena, and leave us alone."

Her cold eyes hold mine. "Last chance, Sebastian."

"For what?" I smirk. "To understand how pathetic you really are? Too late."

She takes an envelope out of her bag and passes it over to me.

"What's this?"

A trace of a smile crosses her face. "Open it and see."

I open the envelope and pull out an A4 photograph. It's of April and me in the Escape Club all those years ago. April isn't looking at the camera, but I can see clearly that it's her.

My eyes rise to meet Helena's.

She pauses for effect. "You know, the security system was surprisingly easy to hack." She smiles sarcastically. "The beloved Prime Minister and his pure wife. The first lady, Mrs. Garcia, the lawyer," she says quietly. "The dirty whore you paid for sex."

My stomach drops.

No.

"You have forty-eight hours to hand over ten million pounds, or you and your whore will be exposed to the press."

Sebastian

I FROWN IN DISGUST. "WHAT?"

"You heard me. Ten million, and I'll disappear so you can carry on with your pathetic life."

"Even if I had access to that kind of money, which I don't, I'm not paying you one fucking penny," I growl.

"Okay." She stands. "Then prepare for the press release on Wednesday." She turns towards the door.

"Helena!" Panic sets in. "Wait."

She turns towards me.

"Why would you do this?"

"You know why."

"I don't give a fuck about me, but what reason could you possibly have to destroy April? She's a good person who has worked fucking hard for her law degree. You can't do this to her. Hurt me all you want, but leave April the fuck out of it."

She tilts her chin upward. "Do you really expect me to feel sorry for her? She catches your eye in a brothel, makes you fall in love with her, all the while sleeping with your son?"

I stare at her, shocked. How does she know all of this?

"You've got it wrong. She isn't like that. She was never even working in that club."

"Proof is in the footage, Sebastian, and I *am* going to go public with it. Unless you part with some of your precious money. Because, let's face it, it's only a matter of months before she takes it all in your impending divorce, anyway." Her calculating eyes hold mine. "She doesn't love you. She never did. Wake up, Sebastian, you fool."

I clench my hands at my sides, my anger hitting a crescendo. I've never had so much contempt for anyone in my life. "Get out." I sneer.

"Forty-eight hours."

I step towards her, unable to help it.

She smiles sarcastically. "Hit me. I dare you."

I turn my back to her because if I don't, that's exactly what I will do. "Get out."

She stays still.

"Get the fuck out!" I yell.

The door clicks when she leaves, and I inhale with a shaky breath.

"Fuck, fuck...*fuck!*"

I pick up my phone and call Bart.

"Hi," he answers.

"Get over here now. We are officially in a crisis."

"Hello, Porscha?" Bart says. He's on speakerphone with the manager of the sex club. "It's Bart McIntyre calling. I'm a lawyer acting on behalf of a very high-profile client."

"Yes, hello, Bart," Porsha replies.

Bart glares at me. He's furious, and *so am I.*

This is my worst fucking nightmare. I sit back in my chair, pinching the bridge of my nose.

Please, let me wake up.

"My client has just been delivered photographs of himself in your club with an Escape Girl."

"What?"

"You heard me. There's video evidence."

She gasps. "Oh no..."

"He's being blackmailed for ten million pounds. Do you mind explaining to me how the hell someone got this footage?"

"Um—" She pauses. "I'm so sorry. Our system was hacked three or four months ago and then again this week. We assumed they were after credit card details, but thankfully none of those were compromised."

"I'll tell you what was fucking compromised. My client's identity!" he snaps. "If this goes live, I will be pressing charges against you to the full extent of the law. You can kiss your fucking club goodbye."

"Oh my God!"

"How does this happen? What the hell do your clients get for their exuberant fees if not their privacy?"

"Ah..." She's rendered speechless. "My sincerest apologies. I just don't know what to say. We were assured by our IT team that nothing was taken."

"They lied. I'll be in touch." He hangs up on her.

Speechless, I put my head into my hands.

"You know..." Bart begins to pace. He's furious. "When I asked you if you had any skeletons in your closet, the fact that you met April in a brothel may have been one of them, Garcia!" he yells. "How did I not know about this?"

"Watch your fucking mouth," I growl. "You are speaking about my *wife*. She is not a prostitute. She worked there one time, and it was the fucking time I met her."

"Do you have any idea what this is going to do to the political party?"

"I don't give a fuck about the political party," I cry. "I'm not worried about myself. I couldn't care less about my stupid fucking job. I'm worried about April! If this gets out..." I shake my head, the fear in me so present that I can barely push the words past my lips. "She will always be the prostitute who slept with the Prime Minister. She will never shake this. It will be the end of her career."

He stares at me.

"Do you know how fucking hard she worked to fight her way back?" My voice cracks, betraying my hurt. "This can't get out, Bart. It can't. I won't let it. I will not let her be portrayed in this manner. Not now, not ever."

"Then you have to talk to April." He sighs sadly.

"If I tell her, she won't let me pay it. I know her. Her morals are too high, especially when it comes to my ex-wife. She would rather die than give that woman one penny."

Bart closes his eyes. "Fuck's sake."

We both sit in silence as we think.

"What do I do?" I eventually ask.

"There's no proof that, even if you do give Helena the money, she won't go to press, anyway."

"I know, but at least it might buy me some time."

"For what?"

"In case you missed it, I got married last fucking week, Bart!" I stand in a rush. "Do you really think this is how my new wife wants to spend her first week of marriage?"

"Stop putting everyone else's needs before yourself. This is ten million pounds, Garcia."

"I don't care about the money." I throw my hands in the air.

He holds his hand out in defeat. "Then, there's your answer."

I stare at him.

"You're going to pay her the money, regardless of how stupid you know it is."

"What do you want me to do? Throw my wife to the slaughter?" I lose my temper. "Get out!" I bark. "If you have nothing more to say, get the fuck out."

Bart exhales heavily. "This is a bad idea."

"Tell me the alternative. Give me a better fucking plan, Bart. Because as of this moment, you've got nothing."

He stares at me, thinking. "What if I barter her down?"

"How?"

"I'll email her. Tell her you can't get that amount of money. Ask if we could negotiate a deal of sorts."

I scratch the back of my neck in frustration. I don't want to give this bitch a single penny.

"At this point, she's clutching at straws. She would have no idea that you're willing to pay. I'll tell her we have someone who can prove the photos have been manipulated and are fake—that she isn't going to get any traction with this story. I'll try and get her to agree to a few million and sign some kind of assurance that she won't go public. Ten is ludicrous. It's out of the question."

"I can't believe this is happening."

"Leave it with me." He walks towards the door.

"Bart!" I call, and he turns back. "Thank you."

He nods, still unimpressed. "I'll be in touch."

I climb out of the car just as April bounces out the front door. I look up, and my breath catches at the sight of her beautiful smile.

"Hello, Mr. Garcia." She smiles as she kisses me.

"Mrs. Garcia." I smirk.

I hold the car door open, and she gets in.

We are on our way to dinner with our friends to celebrate our marriage.

What a fucking joke.

What I should be doing is packing April up and moving her to the moon.

I have this sick lead ball in my gut telling me that shit's about to get bad, and there's no way to stop it. My world is spinning out of control on its axis.

If I tell April, her name is dragged through the mud and her career is over.

If I don't tell April, she is protected.

But I lie to her.

Damned if I do, damned if I don't. Fucked up, either way.

We sit in the back of the car as the driver whizzes through the traffic.

April's chatting and laughing, being her gorgeous self, while I sit emotionless, watching her. Her hand is resting on my thigh, and I look down at the gold band on her finger. The one that matches mine.

I close my eyes in sadness. All my life, I waited for a love like this.

"What's wrong, babe?" She lifts my hand to her mouth and kisses my fingertips.

"Just tired, darling," I lie.

"We won't stay late."

"No, it's okay. I'm fine. We can stay as long as you want."

She bounces around in her seat. "I'm so excited to see everyone."

I fake a smile. "Me too."

The procession of security cars pulls up outside the front of the restaurant, where a photographer is waiting. The driver gets out and opens the back door. I climb out to the flashes of the camera, and I help April out by taking her hand.

"Mrs. Garcia!" the photographer calls. "How is married life?"

"Wonderful." She smiles.

My heart drops, and we walk inside to see our friends sitting at the back. They all stand. April holds her hand up and wiggles her fingers to show them her ring, and the girls dance with excitement as we approach the table.

"Congratulations." The girls laugh as they kiss us.

The boys shake my hand and slap me on the back.

"You old dog," Spencer jokes. "Why weren't we invited?"

We sit down. April is laughing and chatting. She's so happy, and I just want to die a slow, painful death.

Because I should. My terrible taste in ex-wives should be a death sentence.

Spencer watches me and gives me a subtle frown. Masters, too.

They know me too well for me to hide anything from them.

"You guys want to get cocktails at the bar with me?" I ask.

"Yep." Their chairs are both out before· I've finished my sentence. We take the girls' orders and walk over to the bar. We stand in the corner at a small round table as we wait for them to be made.

"What is it?" Spencer whispers.

"You can't tell anyone," I whisper back. "Swear on your life."

"What?"

"Helena has video footage of me in the Escape Room with April."

Their eyes widen.

"She wants ten million or she's going to the press."

"What?" Spencer shrieks.

"Keep your voice down." I look around.

"What the fuck?" Masters whispers. "How did she get it?"

"Their systems got hacked. Can you imagine the fucking head-line? 'The Prime Minister and the prostitute who is now his wife'."

Julian's and Spencer's eyes widen in horror. If my files have been hacked, hell, we're all fucked.

"Christ almighty, what are you going to do?" Julian asks.

"I say we kill this bitch." Spencer punches his fist. "For real this time."

"Will you be fucking serious for one minute?" I hiss.

"Who says I'm not?" he huffs.

"I think I'm going to pay the money."

"What?"

"Have you got a better idea?" I whisper. "I won't have April dragged through the mud."

"Fucking hell," Julian mutters.

"How does she sleep at night?" Spencer whispers. "God damn

it, she's a real fucking mole. I mean, I always knew it, but this is some next-level crazy shit."

"Drinks are up," the waiter calls.

"Not a word to the girls," I whisper.

"Yep," they both reply, and we walk back to the table.

I sit down and place April's drink in front of her.

She looks over at me lovingly. "Thank you."

I smile and take her hand in mine. I kiss her fingertips and glance over at the boys. Their traumatized faces say so much.

I'm fucked.

I watch her chest rise and fall as she sleeps like the angel she is.

April's blonde hair is splayed across her pillow. Her big, pouty lips are slightly parted.

There's a peace that she brings.

I've never loved anyone as much as I do her. I didn't even know that it was possible.

I keep going over and over the ramifications of not paying this money.

I imagine the media circus that will surround us, the judgement on my beautiful wife, watching her deal with the criticism, and her heartache.

The end of her career. The end of mine.

Our families and future children knowing how we met... That's if we even make it through this to have children.

She will blame me, and how could she not? I blame me for having an ex like Helena.

I can't do it.

I won't risk April at any cost. I would give my soul to the Devil if it meant that she remains untainted.

I know this is wrong, but I don't care. I'm giving Helena the money.

I'll deal with her later. She *will* pay for this.

But right now, I need time.

454

April

I wake when I hear the shower turn on. It's early morning, and I smile as I stretch.

Life is good.

Sebastian's phone beeps with a text on the side table. I reach over and pick it up.

Your withdrawal is ready, Mr. Garcia
We look forward to welcoming you at 1:00 p.m.
Bank of Britain

I frown. Huh?

What does that mean?

I hear a fuss out in the hallway, and a vase smashes. I get up in a rush. Bentley has brought his lead up to try and make us go for a walk. It got caught on the side table and has knocked the vase over.

"Hey, what are you doing?" I ask.

He looks up at me innocently, and I smile. I can't be angry with such a cute face. "Come on. Let's get the dustpan." I make my way downstairs and grab the dustpan.

This is the last thing I feel like doing. Good morning to me.

11:50 a.m.

Jeremy walks into my office and closes the door behind him.

I glance up. "Hey."

He looks like he's just swallowed a fly. "If I knew something... something bad...would you want to know?"

I frown. "Like what?"

"Okay." He winces. "So, does that mean yes?"

"Yes."

"You know how I think Bart is seeing someone else?"

"Yes."

"Well, don't judge me, but I didn't see him again last night, and

455

I was going crazy all night. This morning, I illegally logged in to his email for evidence."

"Jeremy," I whisper. "You can't do that."

"Sebastian is being blackmailed by his ex-wife," he blurts out in a rush. "Bart's been negotiating a deal with her."

My eyes widen. "*What?*"

"She has footage of you two in a strip club. Sebastian has to pay her ten million pounds today at 1:30 p.m. in a hotel room or she is going to the press."

"What?" I explode.

"Shh." He looks around guiltily. "I'll lose my job if Bart finds out that I told you."

I think for a moment. That text this morning from the bank...

I forgot all about it.

What the hell?

"That stupid fuck," I whisper.

"Who, his wife?"

"Sebastian." I get out of my seat. "Sit down," I demand.

"What?"

"You log in to that email right now. I want to see exactly what the fuck is going on."

1:40 p.m., and I'm standing in the shadows of the broom closet on Level 3 in the London Hilton. I had to book a damn room on this floor to get up here, but I don't care.

Drop-off of the ransom money is apparently anytime now, and I'm waiting for Sebastian to arrive. I don't think I've ever been so fucking furious in my entire life.

Why didn't he tell me?

The elevator dings, and I lean back against the wall. Sebastian walks out with a duffle bag, and my eyes glow red.

You are so dead.

He walks to the door and knocks. I begin to creep up behind him. The door opens, and Helena stands before him.

"Have you got the money?" she asks.

"Oh, he's got the fucking money, all right," I snap.

They both turn towards me, shocked.

I push past them both into the room. Helena tilts her chin, but Sebastian looks like he's seen a ghost.

"Give me the money and get out," Helena says.

"He's not giving you a single fucking penny!" I snap. I glare at Sebastian, and he rolls his lips.

"She's got footage," Sebastian replies.

"Ha." I huff. "She hasn't got shit."

"Yes, I do. I'm going to the press. Now get out." She tries to snatch the bag from him.

"Do not give her that fucking bag!" I yell. "She's lying."

"How do you know?"

"Because I have the footage," I snap. "I'm the one who hacked the system. I wiped all the footage of the two of us months ago, so you can go to hell, you scheming fucking bitch."

Sebastian's and Helena's eyes widen.

"You hacked the system?" Sebastian whispers, shocked.

"Of course I did. I wiped everything with you on it," I snap. Adrenaline is coursing through my body. "There was one image that was encrypted that I couldn't get, but it had nothing about the club on it. That's the only picture she's got."

Sebastian gasps. "It was you?"

"Call the police," I demand.

Helena's face falls.

Sebastian's eyes are wide as he looks between the two of us.

"Call the fucking police!" I scream at him.

He takes out his phone.

"Did you tell her?" Helena asks him in an eerily calm voice.

He frowns.

"Did you tell her about our night together, Sebastian?" She turns to me. "Do you know?"

Uneasiness falls over me. "What are you talking about?"

"Sebastian called me from Bath a few months ago. Said that he was moving forward with you, and he wanted to say goodbye to me properly. Begged me to come see him. He wanted to make love to me one last time...the way I needed it. We never got that last goodbye, and it was something he always regretted."

"I did not," he scoffs.

"What story did you go with, Seb?" she asks softly. "Did you tell her you were drugged? Or did you go with the 'fell asleep' excuse? We couldn't decide on that night."

We never got that last goodbye, and it was something he always regretted.

What...

My heart begins to hammer in my ears.

"You stupid girl," she sneers. "You think you have this all sewn up, don't you? You think you have everything sorted."

I stare at her, contempt dripping from my every pore.

"Well, guess what, April?" She smiles sweetly. "I have the one thing that you don't."

I glare at her.

"I have his baby." She turns to Sebastian. "I'm fourteen weeks pregnant with your child."

32

April

SEBASTIAN'S FACE FALLS, and he steps back as though hit with a physical blow.

"Oh, please," I scoff. "Is that the best you've got?" I roll my eyes, disgusted. "You're a fucking insult to my intelligence."

She smiles. "Am I? Or is it you who's the stupid one?"

"Do you really think that we're that gullible to believe anything that comes out of your lying mouth?"

I glance over at Sebastian. He's staring at her, rendered speechless.

"Give me the money and I'll disappear. You have my promise," Helena replies.

The hide of this woman.

I step towards her, fury raging through my blood like never before. "And I have a promise for you, Helena," I whisper. "Actually, I have two. One, you will never get another single cent from my husband. And two, you picked the wrong damn woman to mess with. I will not stand for one more single minute of your fucking shit, so get out my face before I put you behind bars." I lose the last of my patience. "Do you understand me?"

Sebastian's chest is rising and falling, his fists clenched at his sides.

I turn towards the door. Sebastian is still frozen on the spot.

What the hell is he doing?

"Sebastian!" I bark. His eyes come to me as if snapped out of a trance.

"Yes?" he says.

"Sebastian, don't be a fool," Helena replies. "You know what's going to happen if you don't leave that bag here."

Sebastian's eyes hold mine, and I raise my eyebrow.

Don't even think about it, fucker.

He storms towards the door, bag in hand, and marches out into the hall.

We walk down and get into the elevator in silence. The doors close behind us, and I take out my phone to call Bart. He answers on the first ring.

"April."

"*This* is your crisis management, Bart?" I huff.

"How—"

"Yes, I stopped it," I snap. "Bring a plainclothes police officer to Sebastian's. We're pressing charges. We need to release a public statement this evening. You need to prepare for it."

"April."

"Nonnegotiable, Bart. Attack is the best form of defence. This has gone too far. It's only a matter of time before the story breaks, and you know it. Our statement needs to hit first."

Sebastian drags his hand through his hair. He looks like he's about to pass out.

I hang up the phone, and he looks over at me, his eyes searching mine. "April..."

"Don't," I whisper angrily. My blood is literally boiling. "How could you be so fucking stupid?"

He opens his mouth to say something, but the elevator door opens. The security guards are standing around, waiting for their precious Prime Minister.

We both fake a smile as we walk out and get into the back of the waiting car.

Sebastian

"To my place."

"Yes, sir." The car pulls out of the hotel, and I reach over to take April's hand, but she flicks me away. My heart drops.

She's furious.

Who could blame her?

The phone call.

Oh no. My stomach rolls.

I feel sick.

The car weaves through the heavy London traffic. My mind goes back to that morning in the hotel when I woke with no memory.

I see the silver wine chiller and the two crystal glasses.

I remember the scent of perfume on my sheets. At the time, I was terrified, but then, as soon as the security guard said he walked me back to my room, I dismissed my fears. I put it down to two glasses being delivered as standard practice, and the scent on the sheets as a strong washing powder, but now...

Why didn't I get drug tested?

I thought there was no use wasting time at the hospital when no harm had been done. I thought it was about Bart and his wife —that I had accidently had a drink meant for him.

What if...?

Fuck.

I close my eyes as a dark sense of dread fills me.

This can't be happening.

April

We walk in the front door to find Bart standing in the foyer. Sebastian brushes past him and walks straight into the kitchen,

"Are you serious?" I ask Bart. "Where are the police?"

"They'll be here in half an hour, and don't give me your crap, April. We were only trying to protect *you*."

"By giving her six million pounds?"

"It *was* ten," he splutters. "If this story broke about the two of you, the ramifications would be horrendous."

"Oh my God. How could you even contemplate caving in to her demands?"

"She has footage, April."

"No, she doesn't," I snap. "She was lying."

"How do you know?"

"Because I had the club's system hacked months ago, and I wiped all traces of Sebastian from the security footage."

Sebastian walks back into the foyer with a glass of scotch.

"Why would you do that without clearance?" Bart asks.

"To protect him." I throw my hands up in disgust. "Like you should have done. What the hell has he been paying you for, Bart? I would have assumed that you would have already wiped his sordid-history slate clean."

Sebastian tips his head back and drains his glass.

"As soon as she broke into this house, I knew she was up to something, and I couldn't go on about it because it would be assumed that I was being the jealous new girlfriend. Why the hell wasn't she charged back then for breaking and entering? I always assumed that she was." I throw my hands up again. "I cannot believe the advice he has been given in regard to her."

"Ex-wives are an entity of their own."

"And you would know." I huff as I begin to pace. "You lead by such great example, Bart. Did you know that Helena is now threatening that she's pregnant with Sebastian's child from the night that you and he were drugged?"

His eyes widen. "Is she?"

"No!" I bark. "Another lie."

"Fucking hell." He drags his hand down his face. "Why didn't you tell us you hacked the system? How do you even know how to do that?"

"Because it's illegal, Bart, and I didn't do it by myself. Penelope, my friend, did it. She's a computer scientist. I didn't tell you because I assumed that I would have been told if there was a privacy breach. Never in a million years did I imagine that this stupidity would occur."

"Calm down," Sebastian says.

"Calm down?" I growl. "Calm down? How can I fucking calm down?"

Sebastian and Bart exchange looks.

"This is what's going to happen," I reply as I look between the two of them. "When the police get here, you're going to tell them that Helena has tried to blackmail you with falsified images of you in a strip club. You have all of the emails as proof. You are going to show them the cash you withdrew to give to her."

Sebastian rubs his forehead.

"She has images," Bart replies. "We've seen them with our own eyes."

"She has *one* image. I couldn't delete that one image because it was on the very edge of the tape, and we couldn't work out how to do it. But I know for certain it wasn't incriminating, or that it even showed it was in a strip club. It could have been from anywhere, and my face wasn't visible. We did a trace and deleted footage of every night Sebastian was ever there for his entire membership." My eyes flick to Sebastian. "That conversation is coming later."

Sebastian winces.

I know how often you went there, fucker.

"You're also going to tell them about the night in Bath when you were drugged and the pregnancy threat," I continue. "I want them to investigate where her mobile phone was on that date. We need to prove she's lying."

"April," Sebastian whispers.

"Sebastian!" I snap as he hits the last of my patience. "Do. Not. Even," I warn him. "We press charges, and then we issue a state-

463

ment saying that you have been through a blackmail ordeal using falsified images," I say in a rush.

"Issuing a statement isn't needed," Bart replies.

"You know that if we don't, she will. We need to cut her off at the chase," I reply. "We won't say that the blackmail was from her, but at least if the statement is out, our story stands."

Sebastian drops into his chair, unable to stand.

Knock, knock.

I look between them. "I have to go upstairs. I can't be here without butting in and telling them what you two should be saying. I'll ruin the whole thing."

"Yes, go," Bart says. "We've got it."

Sebastian's eyes search mine, and I force a smile. "See you soon." I take the stairs two at a time, and I wait at the top, just out of sight,

I hear Sebastian open the front door. "Hello, please come in."

The police were here for hours, going through everything. The questioning was in depth, and I imagine it was very stressful for Sebastian.

Then the public relations team arrived, and the house was full of people as they organized the statement that was to be released to the press. It was a whirl of activity down there, and I should have perhaps been involved. After all, I used to be part of that crisis-management team.

But I couldn't. I stayed upstairs and cried like a baby to my sister on the phone. She wants to come over to be with me, but she's heavily pregnant and can't fly.

I feel so alone and compelled to stay out of sight tonight. I didn't want to see anyone.

And perhaps, if I'm being completely honest, I'm embarrassed that my husband is being accused of fathering a child while he was with me.

I feel sick to my stomach.

What if it's true?

It isn't.

He wouldn't do that to me—I know he wouldn't—and besides, I'm sure men can't ejaculate while unconscious.

Everyone left about an hour ago, but Sebastian hasn't come upstairs yet.

I don't know what he's doing down there. If I were a better person, I would go and comfort him; he's had a really stressful day.

But I can't help but feel resentment towards him.

By protecting her, he gave her a gun to shoot me.

He knew what she was capable of and yet he never pressed criminal charges.

I don't understand why. I never will.

I keep seeing Helena's face when she asked me if he'd told me about the night that they spent together, and that he had decided that he was moving on with me and so he wanted to say goodbye to her properly. He wanted to make love to her one last time.

It makes sense.

We had just told each other that we loved each other. Things had just turned serious between us. If ever there was a turning point in time when he had decided that we were going to be more, that was it.

I know that it's stupid, and I know she's making it all up, and it never happened, but my insecurities are at an all-time high.

I've been that wife before who never thought that her husband was capable of such things. The one who would have defended his honour with her life.

Unfortunately, I no longer hold the ability to go gung-ho into publicly defending any cheating-husband allegations. No matter what the story is, no matter how much I want to, I will remain silent.

I did all I could to protect him, and he hasn't protected me.

I hear the top step creak, and I close my eyes, pretending to be asleep. I don't know what to say to him, so this is the easy option.

The bed dips, and I feel him push my hair back from my forehead. He bends and kisses my temple.

"Do you know how much I love you?" he whispers.

I get a lump in my throat because, damn it, *I love you too.*

So much.

I open my eyes, and we stare at each other in the darkness.

"Are you okay?" I eventually whisper.

He nods, but I know that he's not.

"Have a shower and get into bed, babe." I sigh. "It's over now. You need to sleep."

His eyes hold mine, and I get the feeling he wants to say something.

Gone is my powerful Mr. Prime Minister. This man is scared.

I hold my arms out, and he lies down to hug me. He holds me tightly, and I can feel his anxiety oozing out of him.

"It's okay," I whisper against his hair.

"Nothing about this is okay," he murmurs.

I hold him close. "I know, but tomorrow we will have more perspective. We're both tired and emotional right now. We need to stop thinking about it."

"You're right." He drags himself up, showers, and then climbs in behind me and pulls me close.

After a while, I hear his breathing regulate as he drifts off into an exhausted sleep. His big arms around me are comforting. I don't know what tomorrow will bring. Hopefully, a sense of calm.

For the first time today, I feel myself relax.

I wake before the sun and quietly slide out of bed. I put on my robe and sneak downstairs. I make a cup of tea and turn on the television to watch the news.

I already know the headline. Let me rephrase that: I'm dreading the headline.

In breaking news, Prime Minister Garcia has been involved in an extortion attempt.

Sebastian Garcia has been threatened with falsified images of himself soliciting prostitution in a high-end brothel if he didn't pay ten million pounds.

A warrant is out for an arrest, but as of yet, the perpetrator remains on the run.

A defamation case is being lodged as this goes to air.

Fuck.

Panic runs through me.

There are a lot of people who know that Sebastian went to strip clubs years ago.

He was on a lot of women's radars because of his skills in the bedroom. They all knew his name back then, and he isn't easily forgotten.

What if someone else comes forward?

There's no footage; I know that for certain.

"It's okay," I whisper to myself. "This statement had to be made."

If he is to survive this scandal, we had to come out swinging.

The news keeps going on and on about it, and I hear the shower turn on upstairs.

He's awake.

I keep watching the news, and I make him a coffee.

"Hello," he says from the doorway. I glance up and immediately hold up the remote to turn the television off.

Wearing his perfectly fitting charcoal suit and a crisp white shirt, he looks the epitome of Mr. Smooth.

"Good morning." I smile.

He walks over and takes me into his arms. He kisses me softly, his lips lingering over mine.

He doesn't say anything, but what is there to say?

Both of us are unsure what's going to happen with Helena, the loose cannon still on the run. We are both on tenterhooks.

I want to fight and yell and carry on like a child at him for getting us into this position with her, but then I remember that he was only trying to protect me, and my past is just as sordid as his.

He went to that club... but I worked there.

And nobody else besides the two of us would ever believe that he was my first client. *My only client.*

He has the weight of the world on his shoulders, and I'm not adding to his stress levels, no matter how selfish I want to be and put the blame on him.

I know I can't.

"I made you a coffee," I say.

"Thanks." He rolls his lips and picks up the mug. "Are you all right?" he asks.

I force a smile and nod. "Yep," I lie. "Are you?"

"Uh-huh."

We stand with our coffees in our hands, staring at each other in some kind of fucked-up, silent standoff. Both of us knowing that the other isn't okay. Both of us unwilling to bring up Helena's pregnancy revelation.

My anger and his stress aren't a good combination, so I'll play nicely until I can act like an adult.

"I have to go," he says.

"Yes. Go." I smile, grateful that I won't have to try and bite my tongue for much longer. I really need to get a hold of myself.

Why didn't you just get drug tested?

How could you be so selfish? How could you put me through this?

"See you tonight." He kisses my cheek. "I love you."

I fake a smile, battling anger, disappointment, and blind-rage fury. "You too."

He turns and walks out the door. It closes quietly, and my eyes well with tears.

Disappointment runs through me.

Say something, you asshole. Reassure me.

For fuck's sake, reassure me.

Sebastian

I walk into the restaurant to see Spence and Julian in our normal seats at the back. I make my way over to them and fall into my usual spot.

"Fucking hell, Garcia," Spencer whispers. "You've aged me by fifty years."

"Right?" Julian mutters into his coffee.

"Did you find out anything more?" I ask them.

I called them both last night when everyone had left. We spent an hour on Google together, trying to find out if it's even possible to have an erection while unconscious.

"Nope." Spencer sighs. "Just that it is possible and probable, if stimulated, to get an erection and blow while unconscious."

I drag my hand down my face. "I have this really bad feeling." I pick up my coffee with a shaky hand.

"It will be fine."

"She'll leave me."

"April won't leave you." Spencer sighs. "She loves you."

"I should have told her when it happened."

"You didn't know what it meant," Julian huffs. "None of us would've ever imagined this could happen. Helena is lying; I'm sure of it. Stop worrying about it. You've got bigger fucking issues. Have you seen the news today?"

"There is no bigger issue than having a baby with my ex-wife," I whisper angrily. "I couldn't give a flying fuck about my job. Imagine that...newly married while my ex-wife is carrying my baby. Do you really think that's going to fly with April?"

Spencer glares between the two of us. "Helena's a bona fide fucking cunt."

I put my head into my hands.

"How *is* April?" Julian asks.

"She's acting fine. She's strong. But I know as soon as this blows over, I'm getting it with both barrels. That's if there is no baby. Can you fucking imagine if there is?"

"Well, if there is, you need to have her charged with rape," Spencer whispers.

"Ha." I scoff. "And everyone would believe it, wouldn't they? It's my ex-wife. Her word against mine, and we all know how this fucking looks."

"Christ almighty," Julian whispers. "This is a disaster."

I walk through reception.

"Good morning, Mr. Garcia."

"Morning."

I walk into my office and lock the door. I put the code into the safe, and I go to my briefcase to take out the passport. I flick through it, seeing the name and photo of my beloved.

April Bennet

Without hesitation, I put the passport into the safe, slam it shut, and relock it.

I need an insurance policy.

She can't leave me. I won't let her.

April

The car pulls into the garage around 7:00 p.m.

Sebastian hasn't called me once today. That's a first. I know he's probably busy being pulled from pillar to post, but with everything that's going on, I would have thought...

I've made dinner and had a glass of wine.

I feel unusually nervous to see him. My heart hammers in my chest when he comes into view.

"Hello." I smile.

"Hi, babe." He bends and kisses me, and then pulls immediately out of my arms.

Oh.

He sits on the chair and rests his elbows on his thighs. His head is hanging low, and he looks at the floor.

The hairs on the back of my neck stand up as I watch him. Something's up.

"I called her," he says quietly.

I frown. "Who?"

"On the night I was drugged, my call register shows that I made an eight-minute call to Helena's number," he says softly.

Emotion rushes through me.

His eyes rise to meet mine. "And there were other things."

My heartbeat pumps loudly in my ears. "Like what?"

"There was a..."

"A what, Sebastian?" I snap.

"A bottle of champagne with two glasses beside it." He shakes his head. "But that's standard practice, isn't it?"

"And what about the bedsheets?" I whisper.

His eyes search mine as his nostrils flare.

My vision blurs, and I drop my head as pain sears through me.

"I-I didn't think it meant anything," he stammers in a panic. "It wasn't even on my radar. I don't—"

I step back from him as if hit by a physical blow.

"I swear to you, April"—he shakes his head—"I don't remember anything. I promise you."

I get a lump in my throat as I stare at him; it's big and painful and hurts all the way down.

I thought he was the love of my life, but he's just like the rest of them.

A liar.

I need to get away. I can't be here. I turn, and he jumps from the chair and wraps me in his arms from behind.

"Don't. Don't!" he begs. "April, please listen."

We struggle as he tries to hold me against my will. I turn, and with all my strength, I push him off me. He goes flying back.

"Stop it!" I cry.

"Please," he begs. "I don't remember."

"You remembered to lie to me, though, didn't you? That was the one detail you did get right."

"Because I love you. I thought it meant nothing."

We stare at each other, me with contempt, him with fear.

"Well," I whisper. "It looks like you might have your baby after all. It just won't be with me."

His eyes well with tears. "What does that mean?"

My anger peaks. "It means stay the fuck away from me!"

33

April

I MARCH to the bedroom to get dressed. I don't know where the hell I'll go, but I need to get away from him.

"Where are you going?" he calls.

"Out."

"There are cameras out there."

I tear through my overnight bag, looking for a shirt. Damn, this living between two houses pisses me off. "Do I look like I care?"

"April..."

"So help me God, Sebastian, stay away from me. I'm so furious with you, I can't even stand it."

"I didn't lie to you. Ever," he argues. "I saw the call on my register in the seconds before I was elected. The cameras were on me, and then with everything going on, I completely forgot about it. And I thought the other things were standard practice."

"So when *were* you going to tell me this?"

"I'm telling you now."

Gah.

This man is fucking infuriating. I yank my pants on.

"Where are you going?"

"I told you. Out."

"I don't want you leaving the house."

"And I don't want to be here with you, so tough fucking shit."

I grab my handbag and open the front door in a rush. I glance down and see four security guards standing around on duty. They have no idea of the Armageddon going on up here.

Damn it, if I leave, they're going to have to come with me.

They have to. It's policy.

Why the hell is Sebastian the Prime Minister? It's annoying and damn inconvenient.

Fuck it, what do I do now?

I'm so angry that I can't see straight. The very last thing I want to deal with is being followed as I drive around the streets, trying to calm myself down.

I close the door and turn to see satisfaction flash across Sebastian's face.

My God, I'm about to go postal.

I inhale deeply.

Calm, calm. Keep fucking calm.

I storm back to the kitchen. I dish my dinner onto a plate, grab a knife and fork, and pick up the bottle of wine. I don't need a glass. I'll drink it straight from the damn bottle. I march back up the hall.

"Are you not eating with me?" he calls.

I slam the bedroom door shut.

No, I'm not, *fucker.*

I turn the lock.

And you're officially in the doghouse.

I wake alone.

The bed was lonely last night, and I feel sad today.

I've been married for a few weeks, and look at the fucking mess my marriage is in.

Who knew that my capability of marrying asshole men would be so high?

I roll over and stare at the wall as I try to brace myself for the upcoming day. I have to go to work and deal with a million questions from everyone about the scandal that's all over the news.

That's the last of my worries.

A baby. *His baby.*

My chest constricts. I couldn't stand it.

A part of him and a part of her mixed together to form a child.

I imagine Sebastian going to pick the baby up and seeing Helena, then dropping the baby back to her.

They would always have that together, and I know that, Sebastian being Sebastian, he would dote on the child...and look after its mother. He wouldn't be able to help himself.

My stomach rolls. It makes me feel sick.

I think for a moment. Can a paternity test be taken while pregnant, or do you have to wait for the baby to be born?

Hmm. I grab my phone and type into Google:

Can a paternity test be taken while still pregnant?

DNA testing can be completed as early as 9 weeks along. Technological advancements mean there's little risk to mom or baby. If establishing paternity is something that you need to do, non-invasive prenatal paternity test (NIPP) is a blood test that analyses foetal DNA found in a pregnant woman's blood during the first trimester.

Shit, it's just a blood test. That should be easy enough.
I type into Google:

Can a pregnant woman be forced to take a paternity test for her unborn child?

Prenatal paternity testing is for 'peace of mind' purposes only

and is not admissible in a court of law. Most courts will require a
legally admissible paternity test to be performed after the
baby has been born to confirm paternity.

I wince as pain throbs in my forehead. I shut down Google in disgust.

Even just looking at this crap gives me a fucking headache.

I hear the front door to the apartment close, and I walk out into the hall. Sebastian isn't here. He must have left.

Hmm, typical.

I mean, I didn't want to speak to him, anyway, but I would have preferred him to grovel...or at least try.

I'm making myself a cup of coffee when I hear an echo going on outside, followed by loud voices and yelling. What's going on now?

I quietly open the front door, and I listen. I can hear Sebastian's voice bellowing from downstairs.

I frown. Who's he yelling at?

"What do you mean?" he yells.

I hear someone reply, but I can't make out what they're saying.

"I don't care how many people it takes."

Another reply from someone I can't hear fully.

"Find her!" he bellows. "I want charges pressed today."

Ah, he must be talking to Bart or the police or someone.

"Mr. Prime Minister?" someone calls.

He replies, and I can hear his voice getting closer. Shit. He must be coming back upstairs to our apartment. Damn this Prime Minister residence. I just want some privacy.

I quietly close the door and run up the hall to get into the shower and make it look like I wasn't listening.

I wash myself as my mind spins at a million miles per minute. Good, I'm glad he's angry. I want charges laid against the bitch today too.

I shower and dress in my work clothes, a black pencil skirt and a cream silk blouse. I apply my makeup. I may as well look decent, seeing as though the eyes of the entire United Kingdom are on me.

Ugh, I'm seriously over this. If only they knew what was going on behind closed doors.

I can hear the coffee machine running in the kitchen. Hmm, so he came back into the apartment and didn't come looking for me.

Typical.

I pull the top drawer out to put my watch on, and I stare down at the organized drawer compartments. One of the boxes has an empty space. Why does that space look weird?

Hmm. I put on my watch and go into the bathroom to straighten my hair.

I'm meeting Jeremy for breakfast. I need to vent.

Damn Sebastian has gotten me furious, and if there is anyone who I know won't judge, it's Jeremy.

I slip on my stilettos and open the top drawer again. What *is* missing from that drawer?

I try to remember how it normally looks, and then the penny drops. My passport.

He wouldn't dare.

Adrenaline begins to pump through my system, and, like a madwoman, I march down the hall. I find him in the kitchen, drinking coffee.

I put my hands on my hips. "Where's my passport, Sebastian?"

His eyes meet mine as he sips his coffee. He raises his eyebrow, unimpressed.

No longer scared, this man is angry.

Bring it on, because I'm ready to fucking rumble.

"I asked you a question. Where *is* my passport?"

"With mine."

"And *where* would that be?"

"In a safe place."

The last of my temper snaps in spectacular fashion, and I explode. "What?"

"You heard me."

"What I heard is that you're a controlling asshole."

He puts his coffee cup down, and it clangs on the counter. "Do not push me today, April. I am not in the mood for your dramatic fucking bullshit," he bellows.

My eyes bulge. "*You* are not in the mood for *my* bullshit?" I point to my chest.

"That's what I said. Use your ears and listen."

Oh my God. I see red.

"Listen here, you condescending prick. You don't get to take my passport. If I want to go anywhere, I *will* be going, with or without your permission."

He glares at me.

"Don't give me that look, Sebastian. I won't have it."

"And don't *you* lock me out of my own fucking bedroom." He slams his hand on the kitchen counter. "Do you fucking understand me?"

That's it.

I turn and storm to the bedroom to get my handbag.

That's it.

He remains in the kitchen, drinking his coffee, and, damn it, I have to have one last say.

I march back to him. "Don't you dare get angry at me for being upset that my new husband is a liar," I cry. "Do you have any idea how disappointing that is?"

"There's only one liar in this room, and we both know who that is," he growls.

I screw up my face. "When have I ever lied to you?"

"I believe the words were 'for better or worse'," he sneers sarcastically.

Our wedding vows. My heart drops.

He jumps from his chair, unable to hold his raging-bull temper. "If this isn't the worst, April, I don't fucking know what is," he yells. "The very first hurdle we face, you make me do it alone." He throws his hands up in defeat and then walks out the door, slamming it hard.

My eyes well with tears.

Fuck.

I sit in the café, waiting for Jeremy. I keep going over what Sebastian said to me before he left. *You make me do it alone.*

I hate that he sees it like that, and I wonder if this is what happened with him and Helena. He had an issue, and she locked him out and made him face the problem alone. Their sex life was both of their problem. But did she make him feel like it was only his? Then, being the stubborn bastard that he is, did he get so resentful that he locked her out in return?

Both of them not speaking, in separate beds. I wonder how long they lived like that.

Days, weeks, months?

I exhale heavily. Well, I'm too angry at this stage to even think about it anymore. I'm not letting him turn this around on me.

I haven't done anything wrong.

I never once said that I was blaming him for this, only that he should have told me the facts at the time in which they happened. And how dare he say that I'm making him face this alone when it was his choice not to tell me about it in the first place? He chose to do this alone, not the other way around.

Seriously, is open communication in a marriage really too much to ask for?

"Sorry I'm late." Jeremy smiles and falls into the chair.

I give him a weak smile.

His face falls. "Are you okay?"

"Been better."

"Why, what's happened?"

"You can't tell anyone."

He holds his hands up. "I wouldn't, you know that."

"Sebastian's ex-wife threw in a bombshell when I stopped the blackmailing situation."

He frowns, waiting for me to go on.

"She said she's fourteen weeks pregnant with Sebastian's baby."

"What?" he gasps. "They're still sleeping together?"

"Apparently, it was the night he and Bart were drugged in Bath. Helena says that he called her and asked her to come to him, but Sebastian says he remembers nothing."

His eyes widen in horror. "Can men even ejaculate when they're unconscious?"

"Apparently." I drag my hand down my face.

"Fucking hell." He takes my hand over the table. "Do you believe him?"

"Am I an idiot if I do?" I wince.

He shrugs.

"I honestly don't believe he would do this." I think for a moment. "And not just to me, but in general. I know he loves me, and I really can't see him calling her. Especially not for sex. They aren't even on speaking terms. But then, if he was drugged..."

Jeremy's eyes widen as another train of thought crosses his mind. "Hang on. So, did Helena drug them?"

"I don't know. I hadn't even thought of that."

He frowns. "Because if she drugged them, that means Bart's wife is telling the truth, and—" His eyes widen. "Bart *did* order the prostitutes himself like she is saying."

I hold my temples. "This is one big fucking nightmare."

"Hi," a voice interrupts us.

"Oh, hi." Jeremy fakes a smile. "Oliver, this is April."

"Hi, April."

"Hi."

Oliver pulls out a chair and sits down. "I've been meaning to call you."

Damn it, not now, Oliver, whoever you are. I'm in the middle of a serious crisis here.

Oliver chats on and on, and I really have to get to work.

Ugh...

"I have to go." I smile.

"I'll see you tonight, darling," Jeremy says.

"Tonight?"

"We have the welcome dinner."

I frown, confused.

"You know, the celebratory dinner. It's at Market Street in the ballroom. Black tie? You haven't forgotten, have you?"

Oh, crap, I completely had. "That's right," I lie.

Great, another dress I have to find today, for fuck's sake. I don't have time for this black-tie bullshit.

"I'll see you tonight?" I ask.

"Sure, baby." Jeremy stands and kisses my cheek. "Sorry," he whispers in my ear.

"Nice to meet you, Oliver." I smile and make a dash for the door. I text Sebastian.

What time is tonight?

A reply bounces in:

I don't expect you to come.

I narrow my eyes. Don't piss me off, fucker.

Don't be cute. What time?

I wait for his answer.

Seven.

Fuck, he's infuriating. Hotheaded twat.

I click out of my phone in disgust. Don't mess with me today, Sebastian, or I *will* end you.

"Are you ready?" Sebastian asks.

I hold my hands out. "Do I look ready?"

Sebastian glances over. His eyes skim down the length of me in my evening gown. "How would I know?"

I roll my eyes. I was going to try and make up with him tonight —apologize for not being empathetic enough to his circumstance —but it isn't even about the Helena secrets now. It's about him being a fucking pig. I'm not standing for it.

"Where's my charming husband who tells me that I look lovely?" I ask.

He shrugs. "I don't know. Perhaps he's sleeping on the couch."

I narrow my eyes.

And he's about to get smothered with said couch's cushions.

I fake a smile. "Witty."

We walk to the door, and he puts his arm out. "Are you ready to act excited to be on my arm tonight?"

I link my arm through his, and he opens the front door. "Not as excited as I am for a drink," I reply dryly.

He rolls his lips, unimpressed. "You're turning into a raging alcoholic."

"Any wonder why?"

We walk down the stairs to see the four guards waiting on the bottom floor. They all drop their heads in tandem, none of them daring to make eye contact with me.

Yellow-bellied chickens.

My temper gets an injection of fury.

Damn this man.

He has the entire house staff running scared of his temper, and now he has the hide not to talk to *me*. Well, he's too late, because I'm not talking to *him*.

"Good evening, Mr. and Mrs. Garcia," one guard says.

"Good evening," we both reply with a fake smile.

We walk out to the front of the house. "Hello, Mr. and Mrs. Garcia," Kevin says, holding the back door open. Sebastian takes my hand to help me in.

"Hello, Kevin." I smile as I get into the backseat, and Sebastian

482

gets in behind me. The door closes, and we sit in silence throughout the drive.

I get vivid recollections of how much Sebastian Garcia could infuriate me back in the day. Nobody could wind me up like him.

Nothing's changed.

Calm, calm, keep fucking calm.

The car pulls up at the ballroom. We get out, and Sebastian takes my hand. We fake more smiles and walk through the crowd as if we are the happiest couple of all.

"Where are our seats?" Sebastian whispers, passing me a champagne from a passing tray.

"What's wrong, darling?" I whisper, taking a sip. "Tired of holding my hand?"

His angry eyes flick over to me. "I am, actually."

I glare at him, our eyes locked. "Please, don't act happy on my behalf."

"Wouldn't be the first time I've acted happy, now, would it?"

Adrenaline begins to pump through my system. I lean over to him and put my mouth to his ear. "Keep being an asshole, Sebastian, and this drink is going over your head. I don't give a flying fuck where we are."

He narrows his eyes. "Try it and see what happens to you. I dare you."

I see red. *Game on.*

"Garcia!" someone calls, interrupting my impending explosion.

"Morton." Sebastian nods and they shake hands. "This is my wife, April."

I fake a smile. "Hello." I shake Morton's hand.

"Congratulations on your marriage. Sebastian talks so fondly of you." The man smiles.

My eyes flicker to Sebastian. "I'm sure he does."

Fury blazes in Sebastian's eyes, and I know for certain that we need to get away from each other before I lose my shit and really do tip my drink over the Prime Minister's head.

Fucker.

483

I step back and glance over to see Jeremy, who waves.

"I see someone I know. Will you excuse me, please?" I ask the two of them.

"Of course." Sebastian smiles sweetly. "Please, *do* take your time."

I grit my teeth. God help me. "Thank you...sweetheart. You're always *so* thoughtful."

He glares at me, and I glare right back.

I make my way over to Jeremy and kiss his cheek. "You look ravishing," he coos.

"Thank you. You too." I sip my champagne. "I'm about to punch Sebastian in the nose," I whisper.

"Excellent," he replies without missing a beat. He glances over to him. "I take it you still aren't talking."

"He's being a prick."

He shrugs. "Well, he *is* Sebastian Garcia. What do you expect?"

I roll my eyes. He has a reputation of being an asshole. Tonight, I see why.

Loud and clear.

Four hours later, I glance over at Sebastian sitting beside me in the back of the car. We are on our way home. Sebastian is staring out the window, a million miles away.

We haven't spoken all night, and the ridiculous part is that we aren't even fighting over the major issue at hand.

The baby.

I'm confused. I don't know what's happening, and I feel like things are unravelling between us at the speed of light.

Both of us are slipping into old habits. Him, silent and bitter. Me, expecting more,

itching to fight.

I hate this.

He drags his hand through his hair. He looks so sad, my heart bleeds. Unable to help it, I reach over and take his hand in his lap. He closes his fingers around it.

"You know that I love you," I whisper.

He nods softly, remaining silent. His gaze stays out the window to the scenery passing by, and my heart constricts. That was my olive branch.

Nothing in return.

The car pulls up to a halt, and the door opens. Sebastian climbs out and takes my hand to help me out. We walk up the steps and open the front door.

He drops my hand and walks straight up to the bedroom. I hear the shower turn on.

I exhale heavily. *God.*

I make myself a cup of tea and try to figure out a plan of attack. I don't want to get into a fight. We're already at each other's throat.

I hate this.

I hear the shower turn off. I wait ten minutes before I head into the bedroom. Sebastian is in bed and lying on his side with his back to me. I watch him for a moment before I head into the shower. I don't know what's going on in his head. I can only assume it's not good.

Twenty minutes later, I climb in behind him. His anger has gone, replaced with sadness. I can feel it oozing out of him like a river. I slide over and cuddle his back. He stays motionless.

"Seb, darling, are you all right?" I whisper.

"I can't do this."

I frown. Do what?

"She can't have my child, April."

My eyes well with tears.

"I... I... I can't hand my child over to her. I didn't give her this baby. She took it." His voice cracks, betraying his hurt.

I close my eyes.

Fuck.

What the hell is wrong with me, never once considering what

this means for him if it is true? All I've been worried about is my selfish self.

I roll him over and take him into my arms to hold him, his head nestled into my neck.

He's distraught, and rightfully so.

"It's okay, baby," I whisper as I hold him tight. "Whatever happens, we'll deal with it together." I kiss his temple. "I promise you. It will be okay."

He stares straight ahead with a cold detachment, and I kiss his neck. I slide my hand lower. We haven't made love for so long. Perhaps, if we did...

"Don't," he murmurs.

"Okay," I whisper.

He's too sad, even for sex.

I kiss his forehead as I hold him close. "Go to sleep, Seb. Tomorrow's a new day. It's going to be okay."

I wake with a strange sensation. It's dawn, and the other side of the bed is empty.

I sit up instantly, my senses on high alert.

I make my way downstairs, where I can hear a muffled voice coming from Sebastian's study. I creep down the hall to listen.

"Yes," he says. "That's right, the arrest warrant has been withdrawn."

Helena.

My heart begins to beat hard. Why did he have that removed?

Nobody is looking for her.

"You know what to do," he says calmly.

My eyes widen.

I push the door open in a rush, and he steps back, shocked to see me. He's fully dressed in his suit, ready for work.

"What are you doing?" he asks sharply.

I stare at him, confused. "What are *you* doing?"

He marches down the hall. His overnight bag is packed by the front door.

"W-where are you going?" I stammer as I run after him.

"I have to go away for work for a few days."

Panic surrounds me. "Where to?"

"Winchester."

Gone is the upset man of last night. This man is cold and calculating.

Determined.

This doesn't feel right. Something's going on here.

"I'll come," I tell him.

"No, I don't have time to wait for you to get ready. I have a breakfast meeting. I'll call you as soon as I get there." He kisses me softly and brushes the hair back from my face. "I love you."

I stare at him, fear infiltrating my system.

"Seb." I hold his hands in front of me. "Promise me you won't do anything stupid," I plead.

"I'm going." He tries to pull away from me.

I hold his hands tighter in mine. "Sebastian." My eyes search his. "What are going to do?"

"What needs to be done."

My heartbeat thumps hard in my chest.

Helena's in danger.

34

April

"W-what does that mean?" I stammer.

"Nothing. I'm going to work. You should too." He turns and heads out of the door.

"Seb."

He turns back.

I open my mouth to say something, but I stop myself. I don't want this to come out nastily. "Promise me that you won't do anything"—I search for the right words— "illegal."

He raises an eyebrow. "Are we going to fight again?"

"No." I shrug. "I'm just worried about you making a bad decision out of anger."

"Like what?"

I widen my eyes. I don't want to say it out loud.

He rolls his eyes. "If I did kill her, she had it coming." He turns and walks down the steps.

What does that mean?

"That means no, right?" I call.

He gives a subtle shake of his head, and I have no idea if he's disgusted in me for assuming that's the plan, or if he's impressed that I can foresee it.

"Promise me!" I call. "Seb, I mean it."

He exhales heavily and gets into the back of the waiting car. I watch it drive away while my mind goes into overdrive.

Right, the gig is up, bitch.

Today, I am busting your lying ass if it's the last thing I do.

That's if Sebastian doesn't have you killed beforehand. And I kind of have to agree with him. You really do have it coming.

I smile and wave as Sebastian's car pulls out and drives off, and then I run inside and call Jeremy.

"Hey, babe."

"Oh my fucking God, Jez. Everything is turning to shit. Can you meet me for breakfast? I need a crisis meeting."

"Okay, usual place in forty minutes?"

"Yep, see you there."

An hour later, Jeremy and I are eating breakfast, and I run my hands through my hair.

"This situation is spiralling out of control," I say quietly. "We can't find her. We have no confirmation if the baby is his or not, or if there even *is* a baby, and now he's retracted the blackmailing charges against her when I know for certain that he is going out of his head with worry."

"Why would he do that?" Jeremy asks. "I don't understand."

"I don't know. It's fucking strange."

"It is." He thinks for a moment. "What does your gut tell you about all this?"

I exhale heavily. "That the baby isn't his, and this is just another attempt from Helena to get more money and upset him."

"Okay, let's go back. What are the facts? What makes her story seem plausible?"

"Well, on that night Sebastian called her, there was an eight-minute call from his phone to hers on his register. Then, when he woke up, he didn't remember anything, but there was a bottle of

489

champagne as well as two wineglasses on the table. And the bedsheets..."

"What about the bedsheets?"

"Sebastian said that, at the time, he thought it was just the smell of strong laundry powder."

Jeremy rolls his eyes.

"Don't." I put my head into my hands. "I know how this sounds."

"It sounds like he called her for a booty call."

I think on that for a moment.

"But he wouldn't have." I frown with renewed determination. "They broke up because their sex life was shit. He wouldn't have called her for sex, I know that for certain. If he wanted sexual satisfaction, he would have ordered prostitutes. He has a thing for them."

Jeremy gives a subtle shake of his head, disgusted. He's still traumatized about the possibility that Bart slept with two.

My mind begins to race at a million miles per hour.

The more I think about it, the more this story just doesn't add up.

"I mean, she tried to blackmail him with video footage, but why would she go to all that trouble if she was already pregnant, you know?" I say.

"Yeah, you're right. A baby is the ultimate blackmail tool. It's not something you throw in when you don't get the cash handed over."

"True!" I cry. "That's so true. Why would you try and blackmail the father of the baby you were carrying?"

"So maybe she did set him up, which means Bart is an actual fucking scuzzbucket," Jeremy agrees.

I widen my eyes, and I want to say *I know that for sure*, but I won't. "How would she have set him up, though?"

He thinks for a moment. "She had the drinks spiked, got him to his room, had him open his phone, and she called her own number from his phone."

490

"Yes," I whisper. "She could have done that, couldn't she? I hadn't even thought of that."

"She could have left all the evidence to make him think that he did it."

"But surely..." My heart drops. "Surely she would know that we would find out who the father is as soon as the baby is born." My shoulders slump. "What if it is his baby? What if this is all some grand plan to tie Sebastian to her for life?"

"It could be." Jeremy sighs, and we stare at each other for a while. "If we just had the security footage of that night at the hotel. I know Bart asked the hotel for it, but they said there wasn't any."

I frown. "There has to be some. It's a five-star hotel. It's the law." An idea comes to mind, and my eyes rise to Jeremy. "Don't take this the wrong way, Jez, but what if Bart didn't want the footage to come out? What if he never even asked for it?"

Jeremy frowns. "You know, that's a strong possibility."

"You think?"

"Bart looks after Bart, and if he thought for a moment that there might be something on those tapes that would make me leave him for good, he wouldn't deliver it, no matter what the consequences. I know he wouldn't."

I drag my hands through my hair. "Shit, maybe I should call Penelope and ask her to look at the tapes. I haven't told her anything about the baby allegations, but maybe it's time I did." I look at my watch. "Damn it, I have to go to fucking work now."

Jeremy's eyes hold mine. "Are you thinking what I'm thinking?"

"That we both just got severe stomach viruses?" I wince.

"Exactly. I'm shitting through the eye of a needle right now. Aren't you?"

I burst out laughing. "You're what?"

He chuckles. "You get my drift."

"Not the needle drift, that's for sure." I laugh.

I take out my phone. "My God, I'm so getting fired. Since I've been with Sebastian, I have had so much time off."

"Who cares? You're going to have your own law firm one day, and they'll all be eating your dust."

I smile over the table at my dear friend. "Thank you."

"For what?"

"For always being here for me. It means a lot."

He gives me a beautiful, broad smile. "What are friends for if not to have fake sick days to bust cheating assholes and conniving ex-wives with?"

I laugh and raise my coffee cup to him. "Cheers to that."

I knock on Penelope's door, and she opens it in a rush.

"Hi." She leans in and hugs me.

"Penny, this is Jeremy. Jez for short," I introduce them.

"Hey." She smiles.

"Hello." He shrugs nervously.

"Come in." She gestures into her apartment. "Excuse the mess."

Much to our surprise, Penelope had the day off. When I called and gave her the dates and hotel details, she said to come straight over.

So here we are.

She pulls two extra chairs up to her computer.

"Here are the hotel details and date. We've been told that there is no footage." I shrug. "I'm not sure if there's even anything to look at." I hand her a piece of paper, and man, do I feel sick.

This could be the answer, but it could also be the confirmation I'm dreading.

Either way, we have to know.

Penelope begins to type furiously. Jeremy and I sit in silence as we watch on.

Ten minutes later, she hits enter. "Okay, let's see what we've got."

We hold our breath as we wait.

"Why didn't you call me before?" she asks me.

"Because this is illegal. Besides, we were told there was no footage."

"By whom?"

"My boyfriend, who incidentally woke up with two women," Jeremy answers.

"Hmm." She types at the speed of light.

My heart is hammering hard.

Please, *please, be innocent,* I silently pray.

Something comes up, and she hits enter. Something rolls on the screen. "We're in."

"What?" Jeremy and I sit up. "You got into the security system?"

"Yep." She types more things in. "Piece of cake." She picks up the piece of paper and reads the date. "Do we know the room and floor?"

I scratch my head. I look to Jeremy, and he shrugs. "I don't, sorry."

"That's okay." She brings up a second screen and logs into the reservations.

"Holy fuck," Jeremy whispers in awe. "This is the motherlode of fucking motherlodes of spying."

Penelope smirks proudly. "Right?" She scrolls down. "Here we go. Sebastian Garcia, room 313, level 3." She flicks back to the other screen. "What time are we thinking?"

I think for a moment. "He last called me at 8:20 p.m., so sometime after that."

"Okay." She scrolls down and hits play, then she narrows her eyes in concentration. "So, this here"—she points to a door on the right of the screen—"is his room."

We all lean in and watch.

A man walks down the hall and out of sight. Two women walk out of a room and get into the elevator.

The elevator opens, and we see a security guard struggling with someone. He puts his arm around a man to help him.

"Sebastian," I gasp.

He's so out of it, highly intoxicated and unable to walk alone.

The security guard walks into his room with him, and then he walks back out alone after another minute.

"So that part of the story is true," I whisper.

Jeremy smiles and taps my leg. "Told you."

Penelope speeds up the footage and we all sit and watch. She goes forward one hour...then two, and then three.

"This has to be, like, midnight by now." I frown.

Penelope points to faint numbers at the bottom of the screen. "That's the time there. It's 11:42 p.m., do you see?"

"Yes, okay."

A man walks down the corridor and looks left and right, eventually stopping in front of Sebastian's door. Penelope puts the footage onto real time.

We all sit up and lean into the screen.

He looks left and right again and brings a key out of his pocket. He swipes it through the lock and steps into Sebastian's room.

"Who's that?" I whisper, wide-eyed. My blood runs cold just knowing that someone was with Sebastian while he was unconscious.

"It's not Helena, that's for sure." Jeremy puts his arm around me and pulls me close.

We watch on and wait. Ten minutes. Twenty. Thirty.

"What's he doing in there? This is a long time," I say.

The door opens slightly, and the man peers out to see if the coast is clear. He walks out, and we get a full-frontal view of his face.

"Gerhard!" I gasp.

Jeremy's mouth falls open. "That fucking snake."

We watch on as he walks to another room before disappearing into it.

"He was staying on the same floor," I whisper. "What the fuck?"

"How else would he have gotten up to the floor? It's all secured."

Holy shit.

494

Penelope speeds up the footage again and we watch on while I hold my breath.

3:00 a.m.

4:00 a.m.

5:00 a.m.

I begin to hear my heartbeat in my ears. This seems promising.

7:30 a.m., and the door opens. Sebastian strides out, dressed in his suit. He marches down the hall and gets into the elevator.

"It was a setup." Jeremy claps his hands in glee.

I drop my head into my hands. "Oh, thank God."

Emotion overwhelms me, and tears of relief fill my eyes. "He was set up."

Penny laughs. "Stupid fucking bitch. We've got you."

Wait a minute. That means...?

My eyes meet Jeremy's, and he exhales heavily. "I know."

"Penny, can you look up someone else for us, please?" I ask.

"Sure."

"The name is Bart McIntyre."

Penelope flicks to the booking screen and looks up his room. We watch on in silence as she flicks through to his floor.

She puts the fast-forward on, and we wait. Bart walks out of the elevator on his phone.

"Do we have audio?"

Penelope frowns.

She plays with some dials, and then Bart's voice comes to life. He appears tipsy but nowhere near as bad as Sebastian was. He walks towards the camera and stops right in front of it.

"Goodnight, babe, I love you." He smiles as he listens to whoever is on his phone.

"Is he talking to you?" I whisper.

Jeremy shakes his head. "No."

My eyes flicker to his.

"We had a fight earlier that night. He wasn't talking to me."

Bart listens and then smiles. "When I get home, baby, you're going to get it good." He listens and laughs. "Yeah, yeah. I'll call

495

you when I get back to my room. I'm still with the boys. It won't be for a few hours."

His wife.

Jeremy drops his head in sadness.

My mouth falls open. Oh no.

Fuck.

Bart hangs up and then instantly dials another number. This is like watching a car crash happen. You know it's really bad, but you can't look away.

"Hello, Felicia, this is Bart," he says. "I'd like two girls to my room. 624, please."

He listens and then flashes a dirty smile. "No, I want the ones that were downstairs in the bar just now. Not the two I had last time I was here."

I put my hand over my mouth. Dear God, this is worse than I ever imagined.

Jeremy's jaw tics as he watches the screen.

"Yes, make it quick, please. I'm horny as fuck."

My eyes widen.

What?

This isn't happening.

Not only is there proof that Bart is still sleeping with his wife, but he also regularly sees female prostitutes too.

What the actual fuck?

Mind blown.

We all stare at the screen in silence, unsure what to say.

"And now I know why he would always cause a fight when we were in Bath," Jeremy whispers sadly.

Oh, my heart.

I put my arm around Jeremy and pull him close.

Penelope lets out an audible gasp. "What a fucking cockhead."

Bart walks into his room and closes the door behind him. Penelope goes to close the screen down.

"No," Jeremy says. "I want to see this with my own eyes."

She speeds it up and, forty minutes later, the lift opens, and

496

two gorgeous girls walk out. Penelope puts the footage into real time, and we sit in silence. The scantily clad girls knock on Bart's door, and he opens it with only a white towel around his waist, ready and waiting.

"About time," he says.

They walk past him into the room, and he slaps one of them on the behind as they pass him. He says something that we can't understand, and the girls both laugh out loud. The door shuts behind them.

Wow.

Penelope closes the screen down, and we all sit in silence, shocked to our core.

"And now I know," Jeremy whispers through his tears. He's staring into space, visibly devastated.

I hate that my joy came at the cost of his heart. I get a lump in my throat as I watch him. I always knew Bart was a scuzzbucket, but to see it like that is so raw and hurtful. He never deserved my beautiful friend's love.

Not even for a day.

"I'm sorry, baby," I whisper. "I'm so, so sorry."

The car pulls up at the press conference in Winchester, and I practically jump from the car. I came straight here. I wanted to tell Seb the good news myself.

I walk into the packed hall at the university and stand at the back of the crowd.

Sebastian is on stage, standing at a small podium and delivering a speech.

"As you can see—" He glances up and sees me standing at the back. A frown crosses his brow, and I smile as I go up on my toes with excitement.

He regains his focus and goes back to his speech. I tap my toes, waiting for him to finish.

Come on.

Hurry up.

I'm bursting at the seams to tell him the good news.

He didn't do it.

He never went there, he never... The happiness beams out of me.

Eventually, he says the words I've been waiting to hear. "Thank you all for coming today. I look forward to a long and prosperous relationship. Education is key for our future."

Everyone claps, and I smile proudly. With one last nod, he leaves the stage.

I stand on my tiptoes to look over the crowd. How do I get back there?

My phone rings:

April's Fool

"Hi," I answer.

"Mrs. Garcia, what are you doing here?" his deep voice purrs.

"I have news." I smile. "How do I get to you?"

"I'll send someone out to collect you. Go to the side door."

"Okay." I hang up and practically run to the door to wait.

Moments later, the door opens, and one of his guards appears. "Hello, Mrs. Garcia."

"Hi."

"This way, please." He stands back so that I can walk in, and then he closes and locks the door behind him. We walk down the corridor, and I see Sebastian waiting for me. I practically run to him and jump into his arms.

He frowns, surprised by my greeting.

"Where can we talk in private?"

"This way." He opens a door, and we go inside. He turns to me. "What's this mood swing?"

I smile broadly. "She lied."

He frowns.

"Helena was never in your room that night."

498

"How do you know?"

"Penelope hacked the hotel's security system. I watched the footage this morning. The only person who went in your room all night was Gerhard."

His face falls. "Gerhard?"

"They're in this together, Sebastian. We have proof."

"But there is no footage. Bart checked."

"Bart lied."

"What?"

"Bart didn't even look for footage because he was trying to cover his own sleazy ass."

Sebastian's face falls as he stares at me. "There's no baby?" he whispers.

"No." I smile. "We're free."

His nostrils flare, and he sucks in deep breaths as his emotions overwhelm him. I put my arms around his neck, and he drops his head onto my shoulder.

Tears fill my eyes as we hold each other, the relief between us palpable.

I've never felt such an overwhelming relief.

"I'm sorry you had to go through this." He squeezes me tighter.

"We made it," I whisper, and I squeeze him right back.

Our lips meet, and a door opens behind us. "We need to go," Bart's voice interrupts us. "Your schedule had us leaving ten minutes ago. You'll be late for your next appointment."

We both turn to look at him.

"Hi, April." He fakes a smile. "I didn't realize you were coming today."

Sebastian's jaw clenches as he glares at him.

Bart looks between us, sensing something is off. "What?"

Sebastian takes my hand in his. "Go home, Bart."

"Huh?" He frowns. "Why would I go home?"

"Because you're fired."

35

April

"I'M *WHAT*?"

Sebastian pulls me towards the door. "Fired."

"W-what are you talking about?" he stammers.

Sebastian turns abruptly. "The security footage from the hotel in Bath. Where is it?"

Bart's eyes widen, and he opens his mouth to say something.

"Don't you dare fucking lie," Sebastian growls as we walk out into the crowded backstage corridor.

Bart follows us out. "There isn't any!" he calls. "I told you that already."

"That was your last chance. Get out."

"W-what?" Bart stammers. "You've got to be joking."

"What I am is fucking furious," Sebastian bellows.

Everyone around us withers and scurries for cover.

Sebastian steps towards Bart. "I know for a fact that there's footage. April has seen it, and I also know that you've been lying to me to cover your own sleazy ass. Do you have any idea how stressful this last week has been for me and April?" he yells. "You didn't even ask the hotel for the footage, did you?"

Bart takes a deep breath as his eyes hold Sebastian's. He knows he's fucked.

"I didn't know back then that anyone else was involved," he says. "I knew I was drugged, and I had no idea what I had done. It was to protect Jeremy. I didn't want him to see me with those girls. I had no idea that, three months after, you were going to need that footage. By then, it was too late. I had already said I couldn't get it. I didn't think anyone was going to get hurt."

I close my eyes in disgust. *Except the apparent love of your life. Jeremy.*

I can't hold my tongue for one second longer. "Jeremy has seen the footage."

Bart's face falls.

"And it wasn't even the strippers that you ordered for yourself that was the worst part," I spit. "It was the conversation with your wife that brought him to his knees."

Bart's jaw clenches, knowing full well what this means.

Jeremy knows everything...finally.

"Why you think you can treat people the way you do is beyond me. When this story broke, you could have fessed up and saved Sebastian a world of pain. How could you be so selfish?" I ask.

Bart screws up his face in disgust. "And you are so quick to judge, April. Unlike you, I'm not sleeping with the Prime Minister. I don't get special treatment."

Sebastian's eyes narrow. "Leave. Now."

"You'll regret this," Bart spits.

Sebastian's cold eyes hold his. "I think we both know who'll regret this." Sebastian picks up my hand, and we walk down the corridor. He takes out his phone and dials a number.

"Melody, change of plans. I'm returning to London immediately. Reschedule the rest of my meetings."

He leads me out to the waiting car, and we get into the backseat.

Kevin turns to us. "Where to, sir?"

"Downing Street."

The car pulls out into the traffic. Sebastian makes another call. "Melody, have the police come to Downing Street. Yes." He listens. "I'm leaving Winchester now. Thank you." He hangs up.

I hold Sebastian's hand in my lap, but he's too angry to even notice. He's glaring out of the window as he silently fumes.

But that's okay. I notice.

I've got him in my hand, and I'm never letting go. As long as we're together, I don't care about the rest of the world or the lies that they tell.

We've got each other, and that's everything.

Sebastian

I'm sitting with the detectives, watching the footage of Gerhard leaving my room.

Furious doesn't cut it. I've never been so angry.

All this time, Helena was working with him. Were they going to split the money?

Or was he on her payroll? So many unanswered questions.

"That's it. That's the proof we needed," one of them says. He picks up his phone and makes a call. "Hi, Anne, this is Steven. Can you do a check on a Gerhard Klein for me, please?" He listens for a moment. "I need to know where he is right now. His home and office addresses. Call me back immediately with the details. Thank you." He hangs up, and his eyes come to mine. "Are we still pressing charges on your ex-wife?"

"Yes."

"But you took off the warrant of arrest."

"Only to bring her out of hiding. I want her charged." I think for a moment. "I want to speak with her when she's brought in."

"Okay."

Steven's phone rings, and he answers it. "Hi." He listens. "Who's he travelling with?" He narrows his eyes as he looks up at us. "Milania Henchworth." He scribbles the name down on a pad and then he writes the words:

"Get some officers to the airport's departure lounge immediately. I want them both brought in." He hangs up and turns to us. "Gerhard is booked on a flight to Germany this evening at 6:00. He's travelling with a Milania Henchworth."

"You think that's Helena?" I frown.

"I'll bet my life on it."

I roll my fingers on the table. It's 7:00 p.m., and we are in a restaurant.

"I'm sorry, babe." I pick up my phone and check it for the hundredth time. "I'm terrible company."

April smiles over at me. "They'll get them, Seb, don't worry."

"They should have called by now. Perhaps they didn't turn up for the flight." I sip my drink. "It probably wasn't even her."

"We'll soon find out."

I exhale heavily. "If they get to Germany, that's it. There's no chance of finding them."

"Seb..." April sighs.

My phone rings, and I scramble to answer it. "Yes."

"We got them."

"Both?"

"Yes. Helena was travelling under a fake passport. Another offence."

I close my eyes as relief floods me. "Where are they now?"

"London headquarters."

"I'm on my way."

The waitress arrives with our meals. "Here you go. Two steaks and salads." She places them down on the table.

"Thank you." The waitress walks off, and I stare down at the food in front of me. I can think of nothing worse than eating at the moment. I glance up at April, and as if reading my mind, she points to my plate with her knife.

"You're not going anywhere until you eat that. You haven't eaten all day."

"But—"

"But nothing, Sebastian. Eat."

I exhale heavily and begin to cut up my steak. "Hurry up," I demand. "We need to go."

"They're in jail, and I'm pretty sure they aren't going anywhere any time soon. Eat your dinner."

I bite my steak off my fork and smirk at her.

"What?" April raises an eyebrow.

"Why do you insist on telling me what to do?"

She smiles and goes back to eating. "Because I love you."

"And that gives you free rein to boss me around?"

"Yes." She chews. "It does, actually. You get to boss me around in the bedroom. The very least I get to do is to tell you to eat your dinner."

"Touché." I smile over at the beautiful woman in front of me. "Although you eating my cock and me eating dinner are two very different things."

April smiles. "Not really. Both are essential for good health."

I stare at her. There's so much love and acceptance surrounding this woman. There are no secrets, no lies. She loves me for everything that I am and, unfortunately for her, everything that I'm not. I'm grumpy, bossy, dominant, and damn it, I just wish I could be sweeter and more romantic—softer in the bedroom.

I cut into my steak with renewed determination. That's it. Tomorrow, I'm turning over a new leaf, and I'm going to try and be better. April deserves the best of me, and I'm going to make damn sure she gets it.

An hour later, I walk into the interview room in the police station. Helena's haunted eyes meet mine.

I glance up at the policeman standing by the door. "I'd like a moment, please."

He nods and closes the door behind him, leaving us alone. I take a seat at the opposite side of the table to her.

I bite my bottom lip as my eyes hold hers.

She drops her head in shame. "I'm sorry," she whispers.

I stare at her. She's so sad, and my stomach twists. "Helena..."

She keeps looking at the floor.

"Look at me."

She drags her eyes up to meet mine.

"Why?"

Her eyes fill with tears. "I'm scared, Sebastian."

"Of what?" I whisper.

"I'm pregnant with no money."

I frown. "There *is* a baby?"

She nods.

"Gerhard's?" I ask.

She nods again.

"This is good." I smile softly. "Congratulations. Life is as it should be."

Her eyes well with tears, and they break the dam and roll down her face. "How can life be as it should be when I have another man's baby inside of me and all I want is you?" She angrily wipes the tears away.

I get a lump in my throat as I watch her, and I take her hand over the table. "What we had is over—long over. You need to stop trying to punish me."

"I want you to hurt like I do," she whispers.

I frown. I don't even know what to say to that. "This ends here. This is the last time. I've protected you all along because I felt guilty for ending our marriage, but I won't tolerate it anymore. I'm remarried. April comes first now. She has to come first."

She looks at me through her tears. "Don't you miss me at all?"

"I did. For a long time, I did." I shrug. "But you've poisoned any good memory I had of the two of us."

"Gerhard slept with someone else."

I exhale heavily.

"A month ago. He says it was a mistake. We were going to Germany to try and start again and make it work."

"And you needed my money to do that?"

Her eyes hold mine, and I know that they did.

"Gerhard is an asshole." I sigh. "If a man is happy for his pregnant partner to blackmail another man for money, what does that say about him?"

She stares at me.

"About you?" I murmur. I can't believe she did this. My anger resurfaces, and I push my chair back. "Goodbye, Helena." I walk towards the door.

"Please, Sebastian. I don't want to be pregnant in prison."

I look back at her one last time. She's a sad shell of the woman I once married. "Not my problem."

I walk out of the office and see Steven waiting for me in the corridor. "Charge them both with everything. I'm done."

It's 7:00 p.m. when I drive into the garage. We are staying at home tonight. After the last week we have had, and then yesterday with Helena, I need the comfort of my own home.

I wait for the garage doors to go down. I turn the car off and open the car door. I retrieve the huge bunch of forty-eight red roses and the giant heart-shaped box of chocolates that I bought for April.

This is me, sticking to my promise of trying harder.

No holding me back. I'm going to be a sweeter, more romantic version of myself from now on.

I open the door and hear music. The tantric beat of "Sexual Healing" by Marvin Gaye is playing, and I frown.

Huh?

I walk around the corner to see April sitting back on an armchair, wearing a red leather corset and G-string, along with thigh-high black lace stockings. She's wearing a long black wig and sexy makeup.

My cock thumps with appreciation, and I stare at her.

"Cash or credit?" she purrs. She picks up a dildo and sucks the tip of it. "I'm so ready to suck your big cock right now."

I swallow the lump in my throat and hold up her roses. No words will pass my lips.

She stands and saunters over to me to the music. She licks my lips, and goose bumps scatter up my spine.

"Did you bring me a present, Mr. Garcia?" she whispers as she cups my cock through my pants.

Fuck.

Throb, throb, throb.

I nod. "Yes."

She licks my lips again.

"I—" Hell, I can't string two words together while she's like this. I hold the roses up. "I thought you wanted hearts and roses."

She takes them off me and inhales their scent. "Screw that," she whispers, and then throws the roses over her shoulder onto the floor. "I want you to fuck me like you hate me."

I smile.

Fuck, I love this woman.

I snap and grab a handful of her hair, dragging her down to her knees.

"Suck. My. Cock."

EPILOGUE

April

Fifteen Months Later.

SEBASTIAN TWIRLS me around the dance floor, and I lean against his shoulder.

"Time to get you home," he whispers against my temple.

"Hmm." I smile sleepily. "Okay."

We're in New York at a wedding of one of Sebastian's old boarding school friends. The function centre is out of this world: the top floor of a skyscraper with floor-to-ceiling windows, and the city lights twinkling way down below.

"One more dance," I whisper.

He chuckles as he holds me close. "You look tired, darling." He drops his hand to run it over my heavily pregnant stomach, and I place my hand over his as I stare up at him.

So much love between us.

In just three months, our dream is coming true.

We're having a baby.

Life doesn't always go to plan, but sometimes it's just to make room for what *is* planned for you.

Sebastian and I were always going to end up together, and this was always going to be our story. It's funny how things have a way of turning out. The song ends, and he tries to pull out of my arms.

"One more dance." I smile hopefully.

He smiles and kisses me softly. He knows what I'm doing. I do it a lot lately.

Stalling.

Cherishing the time that we have alone. Living completely in the moment.

Every single second is sacred.

Every look, every kiss, every touch...all of it. I'm dancing through life...*with him.*

I know the days of just the two us are numbered, and I can't help but feel a little remorseful. At the moment, I'm Sebastian's world, and I know that I will soon share his love with a little piece of us, and that's how it should be.

But just for now, he's all mine.

The song ends, and he smiles down at me. "Can we go home now, dancing queen?"

I chuckle. "I suppose."

He leads me from the dance floor, and we go back to our table. I grab my purse, and he slaps his friend Jameson on the back. "We're heading off, Miles."

Jameson turns and smiles. "Breakfast in the morning?"

"Yes, we'll be there," Sebastian replies as he shakes everyone's hand at the table.

Emily hugs me. Claire leans in and kisses my cheek. "See you in the morning."

Her husband Tristan does the same. "Goodnight, gorgeous." He rubs my stomach and winks in his best naughty boy manner.

I giggle. Sebastian sure does have some fun, hot friends. Not that I'm complaining.

My eyes rise to my very own hot friend.

My best friend.

Across the table, Sebastian gives me the best 'come fuck me' look I've ever seen, and my insides begin to thump. I know that look.

I live for that look.

He takes my hand, and with a last wave to everyone, we get into the elevator. His four security guards get in behind us. Sebastian loosens his tie and undoes his top button, and we all ride to the ground floor in silence.

Life with a Prime Minister is less than private, but somehow we make it work.

I kind of forget what it was like when there were no guards and no headlines.

Gerhard got off the charges; without any drug tests taken at the time, we had no proof, and because he had a key to the room, he said he was drunk and mistakenly thought it was his room.

Helena had her baby—a little girl. She's on a good behaviour bond, living in Germany with Gerhard. We haven't heard from her since the court case, and I think she's finally moved on. I'm happy...for her sake. No matter what she did, I always felt a little sorry for her.

Loving Sebastian Garcia is easy. Walking away from him is not.

I know that better than anyone.

The elevator doors open, and we walk out hand in hand before climbing into the back of the waiting car and being whisked into the night.

Sebastian turns the lights off and gets into bed beside me. We are in one of the Miles brothers' penthouses. The view over the city is spectacular. So spectacular that I won't let Sebastian close the drapes.

New York just has this electric buzz about it, like nowhere else on Earth, and I am utterly addicted.

Sebastian's lips take mine into a kiss, soft with suction, his tongue slowly exploring my mouth. His hand roams to my breasts and then down over my stomach. I smile against his lips. I can feel his rock-hard erection pressing up against my hip.

Our lovemaking has hit a new level.

No longer just taking my body, he now fucks my mind.

With my pregnancy, we've had to learn some restraint. We're unable to be as rough as we both usually like to be.

It's lifted us to a higher frequency and brought us even closer, if that's possible.

He rolls me over so that my back is to him, his body nestled up against mine, and he kisses me over my shoulder as he holds my face in his hand.

It's slow and unhurried.

Magnified.

His hand slides down to my top leg, and he pulls it over his body. His fingers drag up and down the inside of my thigh until finally he touches my lips. He brushes his fingertips softly back and forth over me, teasing my entrance.

We stare at each other as we fall still. No matter how many times we do this, the moment his body goes inside of mine is always something else.

He slides his thick finger in as his face scrunches up against mine. I thought he loved my body when I was smaller.

But now he's obsessed.

He adds another finger, and then another, his breath quivering on the intake as he slowly pumps me.

We stare at each other over my shoulder in the dimmed light.

There's nobody here but us, this feeling of intimacy so raw and real.

He lifts my leg and slides in deep. My body ripples around him, and he lets out a deep, guttural moan.

Fuck...there's never been a hotter sound.

He tenderly holds my stomach as he slowly pumps me, and I hold his face as we kiss.

The feeling between us is so strong.

"I fucking love you," he whispers.

I smile against him. "I know, baby. I know."

Sebastian

I hold April's hand, feeling perspiration dripping down my back.

She cries out.

I can't stand this.

I can't watch her go through this pain.

My heart is hammering with fear.

"One more push, April," the doctor says.

She shakes her head, petrified. "I can't." It's been a long labour, and she's exhausted.

"Come on, baby," I whisper. "You can do it." I kiss her temple. "Come on. Not long. One more." I kiss her again. "Last one."

She scrunches up her face and squeezes my hand so hard that I swear I feel my fingers break. She cries out, and the baby slides into the doctor's hands.

We pant as I hold her head to mine.

"It's a boy," the doctor announces.

A boy.

My eyes find April's, and she laughs. "A boy," she whispers, her eyes wild.

I hug her tightly.

They check the baby and lay him on April's chest, skin to skin.

He cries.

I lean down and look at his little face, all scrunched up and red. I touch his head that's covered in black hair. He has my colouring.

Oh.

Emotion overwhelms me, and my vision clouds with tears.

"Sebastian," April whispers. I look up at her, and she smiles softly. "Say hello to your son. Take him."

I stare at her.

"Hold him," she whispers.

I frown and pick him up. The nurse passes me a blanket, and I wrap him up and hold him in my arms. I'm so proud, the tears stream down my face.

My God, this is love.

"What's his name?" the doctor asks.

Unable to see, I wipe my eyes with the back of my forearm. "Arlo," I whisper as I stare down at the little bundle.

April smiles proudly. "Arlo Sebastian Garcia."

I lean in and kiss my beautiful wife. She's given me so much already, but this...

Magical.

Our new life starts today.

April

Six Years Later.

I'm lying on the deck chair, watching Sebastian playing at the water's edge with his children.

The sun is just setting. It's warm, and the sea breeze is comforting.

We have three sons: Arlo, Santiago, and Javier. We thought that was it and that our family was complete, but fate had other ideas. I'm now pregnant with a little girl.

Sebastian's so excited about getting a daughter. This little girl is already the apple of her daddy's eye, and she isn't even born yet.

We are in the Maldives on vacation with our best friends.

Bree, Charlotte, and Willow are all on the deck chairs beside me. They're drinking cocktails, while I'm drinking lemonade.

It seems like since we met, one of us has always been pregnant.

The boys, Sebastian, Julian, and Spence, are playing in the sea with the kids. We have quite a brood between us; with our baby girl coming, that will make thirteen. The kids are lining up, and the boys are taking turns throwing them up in the air. Laughter can be heard echoing all around us.

Life is very different at home. Sebastian is still serving as the

Prime Minister. It seems he is too good at his job, and they are happy to keep him. We have a nanny a few days a week to help us, and I've opened up a new law firm in partnership with Jeremy.

And get this: Jeremy is a third-year law student. I'm so proud of him. It turns out success is the best revenge. He's still single, but me and the girls are matchmaking like a pro for him. His grand love story is coming; I know it is.

I ran into Duke the other day. He's happily married to the most beautiful girl. They have three little girls and live in Kensington. He just retired from football and has started his own business. He seemed so happy, and it made my heart sing.

Sebastian gets out of the water and wraps a towel around his waist. I watch him as he walks up the beach towards us.

He's still the hottest man to walk the Earth.

He comes and sits on the side of my deck chair, taking my hand in his. "You okay, baby?"

I smile. "Uh-huh."

The waiter arrives with a large tray of cocktails. "Here you are." He places them down on the table. "Will that be cash or credit?"

Sebastian's eyes meet mine, and I smirk. Nothing's changed with us. We regularly play 'Escape Girl' in his naughty room.

It's still our favourite game.

"Cash," Sebastian replies. His eyes twinkle with a certain something, and he squeezes my hand in his. "Always cash."

The End.

Read on for an excerpt of Mr. Prescott...

MR. PRESCOTT EXCERPT

TO BE RELEASED IN 2025

Alora

I carefully set the letter to the side and open my computer.

I cannot believe that I'm even searching for this shit.

I promised that I would do every single last thing on this bucket list and I want to...but honestly?

This?

Nerves dance in my stomach.

I tip my head back to the ceiling. "Are you laughing up there, bitch?"

I type into Google.

Anonymous sex club for kinks

I read through the results.
First one.... No. Again...no...no.
I read on to the next page.

THE ESTABLISHMENT
The Establishment is a private facility five-star resort in Switzerland.

Explore your needs, wants, and kinks in a safe and anonymous environment.

How does it work?

We at the Establishment believe that everyone should live their life to its full potential and leave no stone unturned.

Many people have sexual desires or interests that are not cohesive with their lifestyle, current relationships, or religious beliefs.

We help you move past this without barriers in a clinical and safe environment.

One weekend.

Total confidentiality.

Names and personal information are never shared between clients.

How do I apply?

Submit your application and what experience you would like to explore.

If successful, we match you with a person or people of your desired sex with the same needs and wants as yours.

What can I expect?

Day One -*You will arrive at the resort and have one night in your private room alone.*

You will have access to a sexual psychologist if you would like a consult.

Day Two - *You will be introduced to your partner or partners as Jane or Jon Doe, under no circumstances are names ever exchanged.*

There are no names or data kept on the in-house database. A security breach or cyber attack is impossible.

You will then spend the next twenty-four hours in a private suite with them living out and enjoying your every fantasy.

All suites are equipped with a private swimming pool, jacuzzi, steam room, gymnasium, bondage and playroom, swings and the appropriate benches. All equipment such as toys and lubricant are supplied.

Day Three - *You part ways with your partner/partners and spend a night in your own private suite to recover.*

Day Four - *Satisfied...you return home to your life without the risk of anyone ever finding out.*
Your secret and health are 100% safe.

CONFIDENTIALITY IS WHAT SETS US APART.

The cost to visit THE ESTABLISHMENT is €70,000.

Don't live life wondering what if.
Apply for your dreams to come true today.

APPLY NOW.

"Seventy thousand euros...what the fuck?" I click out of it in disgust, that was sounding so perfect too.

Ughh...I knew it was too good to be true.

I flop back onto my couch, I guess at least at that price you know people are definitely going to be discreet.

I mean...I do have my house deposit money.

No.

My mind goes back to the hospital that day, it's so clear in my mind that it's like it was yesterday and I pick the letter back up and read Misty's bucket list for the ten thousandth time.

I promised I would do it for her, every last thing.

And I'm determined.

I'm living my life for the two of us now.

My eyes skim the letter, I have one thing left to do.

#9...... Peg a guy.

I smirk, Misty was a such a dirty bird. How the hell was an eighteen-year-old girl so deviant?

I don't want to do this one, *how can I do this one?*

It's so far from anything I have ever ventured into.

I click into Pornhub and type into the search bar.

Pegging

I peruse through the options and finally find one that I like.

I hit play and watch....

I begin to perspire.

It's weird and wrong and...*hot.*

Fuck.

What the hell am I getting myself into?

Edward

Paul looks over the top of his glasses across his desk at me. "Hello, Edward." He smiles.

I run my tongue over my teeth, this guy fucking pisses me off. "Hello."

"How are you today?"

I flick my hands up. "I'm here."

"And have you had a chance for any reflection on our last visit?"

"Yes." I glance at my watch. "I don't have long today."

He smiles calmly as he folds his hands on his lap. "Let's recap, shall we?"

I exhale heavily. "Do you have to say the same thing every visit? Don't you get fucking bored?"

Paul smiles and I imagine myself punching him out of his chair.

He reads his notes. "You are here because you have control issues."

"No."

Paul looks up at me, "Why are you here, Edward?"

"Because I promised my sister, Charlotte, that I would see a psychologist."

He runs his finger up his temple as he watches me. "Charlotte is important to you?"

I pinch the bridge of my nose. "This is a waste of time, this is my sixth visit and I'm not getting anywhere with you. Of course she's fucking important to me, why else would I be here?"

"You can't fix a problem until you admit it, Edward."

I sit forward in my chair. "I don't have a problem. I like control, I like to take it from people...I like to assert mine. That's not a problem...it's an asset."

His eyes hold mine. "How is that working out for you relationship wise?"

I run my hand through my hair.

He keeps reading my notes. "Take your time."

Fuck off.

I glance at my watch.

"On our second visit you told me that you have had a string of broken relationships. That you like strong women but they can only take your need to control for so long before they leave."

"I leave them," I reply, angered.

"Do you leave them because you want to, or do you leave them because you begin to feel out of control yourself?"

I roll my lips.

"You see, I think that you know that you have an issue, and that you hide behind Charlotte making you come here. That deep down you want to see me and you want to correct this."

I stay silent.

"Am I right?"

I feel adrenaline scream through my body. "Maybe."

"Tell me this, Edward, have you ever thought of tackling control head-on?"

"Isn't that what we're doing?" I roll my eyes, "Can you hear the things you say sometimes? How am I paying for this bullshit?"

"You are here because I'm left field and I get success. Regardless of how unorthodox my suggestions, there's no denying I do."

I exhale, it's true, he is supposed to be the best.

"You've told me that you're a highly sexed individual," he says.

"Yes."

"How often do you like to have sex?"

"Daily."

"And if you don't have sex?"

"I fuck my hand," I reply coldly. "Get to the point."

"What would you consider the ultimate handover of power to a sexual partner?"

"A woman?" I ask.

"Is that your sexual preference?"

"That's my only preference."

"Okay...let's run with that. How far would you let a woman dominate you in the bedroom?"

"I wouldn't."

He sits back in his chair and smiles. "Not at all? Not even in the moment?"

"Where are you going with this?"

"You came to me because I get results and we are getting nowhere in this office. Let's explore other possibilities."

He digs through his drawer and slides a card over the desk to me.

THE ESTABLISHMENT

"What's this?" I ask.

"It's a private facility in Switzerland, I think it would be very beneficial for you to visit."

"Why?"

He folds his hands in front of him. "I would like you to explore the possibility of handing your power over to a woman. Give yourself completely over to the experiment."

I frown as his words roll around in my head. "Meaning what?"

"Have you ever thought of visiting a Dominatrix?"

"Nobody is fucking me with a strap-on cock," I spit.

He smiles, clearly amused by my horror. "It doesn't have to come to that but I think it would be good for you to explore other ways to hand over your sexuality and vulnerability and to learn trust."

"No." I shake my head. "No fucking way in hell."

"You might like it." He smirks.

"Absolutely know I won't."

"It's one weekend. Confidentiality is assured and you will be anonymously matched with a woman who has the same needs as you."

"What woman would need this?"

He smiles. "I'd like you to find out."

"No."

"If you go and you can't go through with it...at least you'll know."

"Know what?"

"That there *is* a control issue and that way we have a good place to start moving forward."

"What in the hell is letting a woman dominate me in bed going to do?"

"It's going to free you from fear."

"I'm not scared."

"Prove it."

Alora

Six months later

"Is there anything else I can help you with, Miss Doe?" the bellboy asks.

Like what...?

Wait...do the bellboys give out sexual favors here too?

Oh dear god, I want to run far, far away.

What the hell am I doing here?

"No." I force a smile. "I'm good." I close the door of my suite and sit on the bed and look around. I'm at the Establishment, the kink hotel in Switzerland.

I flop back onto the bed and look up at the ceiling as I search for divine guidance. After going round and round for months I knew if I didn't do this now...that the wish list wouldn't be completed. I have no idea if my future boyfriend or husband is going to be into it and if he's isn't I can't do it with someone else.

It will be too late.

I'm using all my savings to do this, and I'm terrified and creeped out and I hate to admit it...a little excited.

I get up and turn on the taps as I run myself a big deep bath, I sit on the edge as I wait for it to fill.

Tomorrow I meet him, Misty's stranger.

I smile as I think how proud she would be of me.

I'm a little proud of me too.

I pace back and forth in my room.

This can't be happening. I can't go through with it.

I want to leave; I want to leave now.

He's due any minute and I don't think I can go through with this.

I'm wearing a black sexy date dress and heels; my dark hair and makeup is done.

I'm even wearing lingerie and suspenders.

All I know about my date for the weekend is that he's between twenty-five and thirty-seven, he's heterosexual and that he wants to be pegged by a heterosexual woman.

That's me....

No names or personal information are going to be exchanged and this is the only time we will ever see each other.

I swallow the nervous lump in my throat.

I glance over to the black box that was delivered an hour ago. The equipment we need for the assignment.

Fuck.... I can't even bring myself to open the box and look at it.

Bang, bang, bang...goes my heart.

"Shit, shit, shit." I hold my temples as I imagine how horrifically bad this could be.

Knock, knock.

He's here.

I glance to the window, wondering if I can jump out of it and escape.

Oh no, it's too late to leave. I've wasted all my money on paying for something that I'm unsure if I'll be able to go through with.

I open the door and am greeted by another bellboy wearing a white uniform.

"Good evening, Miss Doe."

"Hello."

He steps to the side to reveal the man standing behind him and the air leaves my lungs.

Tall, dark hair, and handsome with the biggest blue eyes I've ever seen.

Utterly gorgeous.

We stare at each other as electricity crackles in the air between us.

"May I present Mr Doe."

* Full story coming to your favorite bookstore in 2025.

AFTERWORD

Thank you so much for reading and
for your ongoing support.
I have the most beautiful readers in the whole world!

Keep up to date with all the latest news and online discussions
by joining the Swan Squad VIP Facebook group and
discuss your favourite books with other readers.
@tlswanauthor

Visit my website for updates and new release information.
www.tlswanauthor.com

ABOUT THE AUTHOR

T L Swan is a Wall Street Journal and #1 Amazon Best Selling author. With millions of books sold, her titles are currently translated in twenty languages and have hit #1 on Amazon in the USA, UK, Canada, Australia and Germany. Tee resides on the South Coast of NSW, Australia with her husband and their three children where she is living her own happy ever after with her first true love.